GENESIS ROAD

GENESIS ROAD

Susan O'Dell Underwood

Lake Dallas, Texas

FIRST EDITION

Requests for permission to reprint or reuse material
from this work should be sent to:

Permissions
Madville Publishing
PO Box 358
Lake Dallas, TX 75065

Cover Photo: David Underwood
Cover Design: Jacqueline Davis
Author Photo: David Underwood

ISBN: 978-1-948692-84-7 paper; 978-1-948692-85-4 ebook
Library of Congress Control Number: 2022931999

for Gavin

GRAVITY

My house was a grave for the baby I lost there. And when it burned to the ground a few weeks later, then it was Daddy's grave too. Any remains of him the firemen didn't find are tangled forever with the baby I will never have. My mind's eye threatens to wander again and again to the dying my daddy suffered. It takes all the energy I have to focus on the not-seeing, so I punish myself with the other losses. The gore that won't stop flickering. All the woodwork burned—even the oak banister and newel posts I refinished with a toothbrush. The beautiful gilt stencil work Kevin and I did together in the dining room. The tile I laid in the bathrooms, the chrome fixtures. The bed Kevin built for us, where I conceived and miscarried. Pictures of Mama holding me as a baby, the heirloom quilt handed down from Granny Pearl's mother, my wedding rings—all three of them. Nothing but a heap of black on the 6 p.m. Knoxville news. Black tumbling walls giving up ghosts of smoke, and firefighters in their yellow suits dragging hoses through my tulips. Twenty seconds of my life in ruins.

I want to ask the viewing audience slurping down their supper: Did you ever beg somebody to stay? Would you beg to stay someplace you love?

I wonder if they've really ever thought about Adam and Eve. The most famous exile ever. Poison ivy and kudzu choking over the path behind them. And the whole of civilization knows them for millennia as the first real, true fucker-uppers. I've never met even the most forgiving Christian who feels one bit sorry for the ancient grandparents we all supposedly come from. Of course, maybe that's because our family hardly ever went to church when Dunn and I were kids. Mama was too busy keeping us alive. Daddy was still too drunk every Sunday morning. And religion is not exactly rated PG in Newport. We're talking Pentecostals in hollers out toward the mountains. Holy rollers in the aisles drinking strychnine. I dated two boys who grew up handling snakes in church. They believed they could heal by laying on hands, who did plenty of "laying on of hands" with me.

Granny Pearl used to talk Bible to me, but I told her way back then that I was right fond of Eve. What did she do so wrong to get thrown out of paradise? In psych class my first semester of college, I perked right up to hear that we always blame the mother. It's exponential how much blame we heap on

1

the mother of us all. We forget, without her sex and sin and agony, none of us would even be here. Never mind that any second we might be headed into exile ourselves—bare feet blistered and sooty, nothing but sky and stars for shelter, the past a sunken garden of regret.

Time of death. The blood that morning at 5:23 wasn't the monthly failure I'd lived through for three years. By the time I woke up to the warm rush between my thighs, I was in the middle of my baby's actual dying, as if I could hear the wound in my life being made.

Blood soaked into the mattress by the time my feet hit the floor at a run. The baby I'd dreamed of seeped into fabric before I could catch him in my hands. Or her. It must have been too early to know. I hadn't even been to the doctor, a stupid sin to punish myself with for the rest of my days. All because I didn't want to share with anyone. I hadn't found a way even to tell Mama. I certainly hadn't told Kevin.

Our divorce papers glowed their spite on the dining room table every night when I got home from work. I would sit there in our empty, ticking house with my palm on my belly, starting to pudge a little—or maybe that was my imagination. I calculated the weeks before I'd probably start showing and the days before Kevin would ask again why I hadn't signed the deal I forced on him. I was so sure my baby would be a tourniquet to save us, a last-minute reprieve. I never even thought about miscarriage. I was arrogant. And vindictive.

If I could undo that sinning, would it make any difference? My baby, the dream I'd sacrificed for, through procedures and surgeries, hormonal juggernauts, injections, humiliation, insecurity. Every moment with that baby inside me was mine to feel. It wasn't simple biology. I had earned the right. Too early to sense movement or even a flutter, maybe even a pulse. But I knew inside me another human closer than any human will ever be to me, living because I lived, breathing with my breath, needing me as much as I needed.

So, I bargained after every at-home test on the market came back positive. *One more week*, I promised, and I'd call Kevin. I'd share the baby. I'd go to my doctor. *One more week*. I'd take Kevin back, and this baby would solve his betrayal. All the awful months he had lived a second life parallel to ours. But every day, yet again, I couldn't relinquish the thrill of my secret. Or my spite.

Kevin's signature was already on the line, a horizon I couldn't see past. Everything I'd ever asked him for came down to two final words: *Kevin Hamilton*. Should I sign Glenna Hamilton? Or rebel and stall for time to forgive? Should I sign Glenna Daniels? The lawyers would kick it back, but he'd get my message.

After I married Dawson and later Sam, I regretted not keeping my maiden name. But all my life I'd believed I could undergo a full makeover just by saying *I do*. Other women my age could be trendy and anti-traditional. Taking a husband's name equaled freedom from Daddy. Dawson and Sam labeled me, though, expected me to be a maternal chef one minute and a doll the next—static and mute and satisfactory, obedient. Made in the image of their imaginary wives. Boys have lifelong dreams too, I learned.

When Kevin proposed, he said, "Now you'll want your maiden name back."

I shrugged. "Mainly my name shows that Glenn Daniels didn't get the son he wanted on the first try. That's his stamp. That single 'a' at the end never gave me a lot of elbow room."

Kevin was the only person besides Carey I ever told about Daddy holding a gun to my head. I told him about the worst beating I ever took from Daddy, which I never told Dawson or Sam. There were no words except the most blunt and simple ones to explain the worst of all: that after all the abuse, I still loved my daddy, that he was one of the most charming men I knew, probably the most sensitive, vulnerable, boyish man I'd ever met. He was a magnet, and I'd been a little pile of iron filings my whole life.

"I want to be Glenna Hamilton." How easy it looked, finally having Kevin, aiming one more time for fidelity and love like nobody in my family ever had.

Wanting his name also came from my rightest right feeling about Kevin. I wanted a baby with him. Only him. Ever. Sure, over the years an impulse to hold a baby and smell its head had blurred my common sense. But then I would think about making Dawson a dad. Sam. A dad. And I recounted all the boys, guys, men. Before Kevin, I was a slave to birth control for twenty years, at least. Through half of high school and all of college I tried every latex, sheepskin, spongy, spermicidal trick to stay sure-fire *not* pregnant. Sometimes I doubled up with a condom and a diaphragm. And then I worked up my nerve in college to go on the pill. I rarely had sex without some kind of protection, not even with Dawson or Sam.

But Kevin. Kevin lit up whole rooms inside my future I hadn't imagined. When we were trying everything to conceive, gravity was my goddess, ally, doula. After we had sex, I would lie with my legs up in the air, hips crooked toward the ceiling. Nearly on my head, I worked my will and the forces of the moon and the earth's magma core and the polar axis, whatever it took. In those dreamlike states, images came into my head of Kevin holding a boy, a bright boy in sunlight, and they were laughing. I couldn't have known how much that dream would haunt me later.

Visualizing the baby I wanted was part of the hoohah a couple of women at work believed, along with talking to the baby before it's born, singing to it. They said while I was trying to get pregnant, I should try to avoid any negative thoughts, especially about Kevin. That I should let my hormones do all the talking and the screwing and let every cell feel how right my body and our

3

domestic situation were for welcoming a new soul. I should empty my mind of everything but a new space for a new life. And to envision as often as I could who that new life would be. I tried my best to picture the three of us, but what always came to me naturally was Kevin with a little boy who looked exactly like my daddy in pictures of him as a toddler. I never touched that beaming boy, blond and lingering. The two of them were always at a distance, a kind of stabbing blur, over-lit, like when the eye doctor dilates your pupils, and the sun threatens to burn your retinas.

That morning I miscarried, it was hours before I could get up off the bathroom floor. Daylight was high through the lead-glass window. When I could bear the cramps, after I'd cleaned myself up for the first time of many in the coming days, after I'd put on a pad and another and changed into another, I took my best kitchen shears and a butcher knife to the mattress. Did the neighbors hear me howling? The fire I built in the fireplace that dank March morning took an hour to burn my bloody gown and sheets, sputtering and sizzling with the ruby thickness I'd bundled up and carried downstairs, weeping and screaming. There wasn't a sad bone in my body. I was a fury. That rage pulled into my midsection like a tiny planet shriveled to cinder.

I couldn't look. Yet I couldn't bear *not* to look. That was the only time I would see my baby and parts of myself together. Clots like hunks of liver, something left over from a butcher shop, the warm smell that had been alive in me just hours before. Those were the remnants of a life I had already loved. That flesh all mine.

I found some kerosene in the kitchen and a half-empty bottle of bourbon covered in dust. Kevin and I had given up alcohol completely. Now I didn't bother with a glass. I swigged my first mouthful in years. Dousing the bloody clothing time and again with kerosene, I used nearly a whole box of matches. That private cremation smoke went ghastly blinding with the smell of burning blood. I built the flames up to a frenzy and threw in the hacked-up pieces of mattress, strand after strand of dark, clotted batting. At some point I dragged the hollowed-out shell of mattress to the street. I lay on the floor in front of the glowing fireplace and drank the last of the bourbon. I hoped that pain would never stop because it was the last sign I had of my sweet baby, my secret failure. I watched in drunken, spinning half-sleep until the dusty embers were barely warm. I woke up on the living room floor in cold, late dark, half-disappointed I hadn't bled to death.

I never dreamed that loss could happen to me. And that right there, that presumption is the worst sin of all. I thought I was immune, even though we have a word we toss around: miscarriage. As if it's a simple fluke, like a car backfiring. It happens all the time, but when it's you, you're dragged by an ancient horse-drawn runaway hearse of a thing, then sucked into a black parade of days.

A lull magnetized me, the numb letting go of the joy that had been promised to me for weeks. I tried to rearrange the future. Shouldn't I sign the divorce papers now? But maybe the few weeks I'd been pregnant were still enough to pull me back to Kevin. Maybe we could try again for a baby. I bargained, I groveled through a wish list, the regret of taking that tiny life for granted. But it wouldn't have done me a bit of good to know ahead of time. Even what we imagine of tragedy can't comfort us.

I must have imagined Daddy's death a zillion times. That he lived to be sixty was a miracle, really. I steeled myself for years for that phone call about a bar brawl, heart attack, truck wreck. His body was a walking trophy case of accidents, scarred torso, head and limbs. But to hear him tell it, he was a lucky man.

In the Army, stationed in Germany before I was born, Daddy fell twenty feet out of a sentry tower, discharged with nothing but bruised kidneys. Three Chevy trucks he totaled—'77, '84, and a '98 Silverado from just last year—are still on blocks in front of Mama's trailer, monuments to his survival. By the time I was eight or nine, I twice witnessed somebody threaten him with a shotgun and once with a knife. To a man, they all walked away laughing with him.

When Dunn and I were kids, Daddy would wave his mangled hand as proof he could've met with worse fates. "Only lost two knuckles to that knife. Cut clean through." The pink ends of his stubs were webbed with fine scars like fishing line. He tallied up the victories of damage. He broke his collarbone four times, cut open his forehead on two different shattered windshields. In his left arm alone: five fractures. Boyhood scars gave him an excuse to gloat about swimming the French Broad River, hopping the train from Newport to Knoxville, betting he could catch an open Buck knife or strangle a tomcat. His proudest life achievement? He'd never refused a dare.

Dunn never outgrew his adoration. Not once did he challenge Daddy, not that I saw. But even little, I couldn't stand not to dare him. Just like Daddy, I could never back down or call a truce. I was stupid-proud to match his mule-headedness, until I was thirteen, when he beat me the worst. Until then I had only proved his point that I lived up to my namesake, that I *was* more like him than anybody else on the planet. Obstinate. Willful. Always needing to be right.

But that beating taught me I had to outsmart him to survive. So, I learned to shut up and shut down. I held my tongue and bided my time, stoic and in-visible, flying below Daddy's radar. Just like him, I may walk around wounded, but unlike him I refuse to advertise or whine. Not Dawson or Sam or Kevin ever once saw me weak. Not once. Nobody can read me unless I want them

5

to. Carey loves me enough to leave that part of me be when I let him glimpse a fragile fracture. Even with Carey, I can hold fast to the hardest secret, vigilant to protect the most tender part of myself. That fortress is my best quality and my worst.

As much as he paraded his narrow escapes, Daddy was secretive about one thing—his worst injury. He snapped his right femur somehow when he was a kid. A dangerous break that required surgery and rewiring some veins and arteries. That leg grew stunted. He always walked with a tilt. But he loved the attention he got from complaining. After years of fawning, he finally got what he coveted—a monthly disability check. Government validation of his victimhood. But his lies about the way he broke that leg? Of course, I easily recognized the same shield he helped me master.

When I was little, I overheard Grandma Ruby tell Mama his secret, to butter her up to take Daddy back. In his mother's version, when Daddy was eleven, he wrecked a tractor his Granddaddy Sims forced him to drive. I never once heard Daddy breathe a word of what she swore was gospel truth. But get enough moonshine down his gullet, his story loosened up like a windstorm that never blew the same way twice. He broke his leg jumping out of a hay loft. A tree, struck by lightning, fell on him and he barely survived. He got tossed by the same angus bull he outran in all the other tellings.

Dunny would beg Daddy to tell the version about the chase. Daddy was his matador. Even his words had swagger.

"I tell you, Son, I lit out for home, that bull breathing down my neck the whole way. Even after I ripped through three, four fences. I could smell the fodder on his breath. Look behind me, I seen them eyes black as coals." He would lean into Dunn's face, nose to nose the way he never did to me, and *whuf, whuf, whuf.* Dunny's little mouth went slack, eyes wide.

"Barb wire and briars tore my clothes plumb off, I tell you, Son. But where the seat of my britches was ripped, that was pure bull. Come that close." He pinched his thumb and stub together.

"Yeah. Pure bull," I echoed.

He smacked me for my smart mouth. But it wasn't his story I disrespected. I was remembering years on the farm Dunny was too young to know, when we owned our own herd of angus cows and calves. As they snuffled into their water barrels, Daddy would scratch the tufts between their ears, like bad toupees. He cooed and patted their sides until dust rose around them, translucent in the sun.

Which version of my daddy was true? The power he had was amazing, to maul the past until it showed the face he wanted, whatever role he chose to play on any given day. Dictator, court jester, raconteur, good ole boy, whiny tyrant.

What my little brother has never seen is that Daddy rode his fine line at other people's peril. He didn't have to get behind the wheel on his revoked license to threaten damage. Without setting one foot out the door, his so-called luck hurt everybody.

A few years ago, he passed out on the commode and cracked his skull. His last Christmas he tumbled off the trailer's cinderblock stoop. He raised up a can of Bud to the doctor who warned he'd be dead in two years if he didn't stop drinking. He bashed his mouth and sprained both wrists breaking his fall. For three weeks Mama or Dunn had to unzip and zip him back up whenever he took a piss. Mama bathed him like a big, spoiled toddler. He sipped beer through a straw and blubbered to me about how lucky he was that *some*body in the family was willing to look after him.

After all the liver tests and kidney malfunctions, I gave up worrying about accidents. He was dying like any other old alcoholic, a mundane, self-pitying, slow suicide. How many times I've had a premonition of his last few helpless minutes.

In the dream I still dream sometimes, Mama and Dunn and I are the only still bodies in a sea of motion. The medevacs set the helicopter down right in front of the trailer. Men in white rush Daddy on a gurney through crowds. Traffic stops up and down the street. Everything washes pale. The sun glints off the helicopter, squatting like a huge insect. Then the liquid motion slows, the chopper blades twitch loud and ponderous, and Daddy is saying something to me I can't hear. Then I understand. He's afraid. I see he's a small boy in a nightmare. He has chosen me to comfort him, the one person he's allowed to take along into the air. His face shimmers like an overexposed portrait. His blue eyes are earnest and sorry.

Yes. Yes. A final goodness, a sweet, last-minute mercy pulls me up. But at the moment the helicopter lifts, my self separates, as if I'm watching a videotape of us. I'm bound stubbornly to solid terrain as the good daughter flies for the first time in her life, all for her dying daddy, afraid of nothing. But I'm afraid for her, risking everything for the deathbed good father. *And I'm jealous.*

The way he died, burned up, cinderized, cremated like my baby, my daddy didn't have a chance to mend one frayed edge of his volatile life. I punish myself trying to remember the things I said to him the last time I saw him. He was a hassle that morning on my doorstep. That shit-eating grin of his. As if rewiring my ceiling fan would straighten out whatever current feud we were having. I wanted to rip his whistle-while-you-work right out of his gullet. But I was too tired to argue. Against all better judgment, I let him in on an average Tuesday morning and went to work. And he burned my house down under a perfect April sky.

Only later would I remember the awful words I left hanging in the air around him. I still wrestle with him in my head. How can our feud ever stop, even though he's gone? There's no doubt that Daddy would argue I inherited his luck. He'd say I ought to be glad I hadn't been home. He'd take credit for suffering in my place. Shed a little self-centered tear. He'd say the fire just went to show me my life had been wrecked for a long time anyway.

"Three strikes, Sister," he said when Mama told him I was divorcing Kevin. "You might ought to stop blaming Dawson and Sam. And now poor ole Kevin."

Too late now to point out I didn't blame them. I blamed him. *It was always you,* I want to say, *stacking up my chances like cordwood, ready to burn.*

From day one, all he taught me was a botched, sigodlin family. No father-daughter dance for Glenn and Glenna. To everybody else, he was a rounder, the life of the party. To Mama he was an addiction. Even before Daddy died, my brother spun him into an ill-fated hero. For me? Daddy will always be my first memory, the first love of my life, my biggest disappointment, my warden, traitor, rival, the buzzard circling every sky above me. The smoke clouds Glenn Daniels stirred up way, way back always threatened any clear horizon I hoped for.

But he never took any blame, quick on the draw to point out Mama's flaws. He berated Dunn for being clumsy and ignorant. All the name calling and verbal abuse, the physical scars, all remain. The spirit flinches from slaps and punches and punishments. I always lacked the nerve to say to his face that he damaged me for good when he burned the foundation right out from under us. If he were here now, I swear I'd tell him, "Fire follows in fire's footsteps." That's the only way Daddy might have understood karma.

Nobody tells. Nobody talks. But when I was ten, Daddy burned down the first home I ever knew, the only real home I had until I married Kevin. I should have grown up in that beautiful farmhouse on Genesis Road. But as sure as he lived and died by fire, he torched it. What proof can I ever have? I was a kid. How could I accuse him? Half the grownups in Cocke County gossiped that he'd done it. Mama knew. His own mother knew. And they all let him get away with it.

Nobody died in the farmhouse fire when I was ten, but Daddy burned down the whole history of Mama's family, the work and labor. She inherited our farmhouse in Cosby from her mother, which Granny Pearl had inherited from her mama and papa as their settlement when the national park was formed. Eventually I would have inherited that house. He burned the life—past and future—right out from under all of us. All to punish Mama for leaving him. The first time she got away.

Those days right before she ran with Dunn and me, Mama thought she'd planned for every move Daddy might make. She took Granny Pearl and me into her confidence. My one job was to keep Dunny clueless. She'd stashed getaway cash in sacks of flour and cornmeal. The year daddy was in jail she'd started socking away every penny she could. She had put down six months' rent on a storefront in downtown Newport to open a beauty shop, instead of cutting hair out of Granny Pearl's kitchen. And she'd already rented a trailer in Newport where Daddy would have a hard time tracking us, for a few days at least.

"It's just temporary," she said. "He'll cool down. We'll go back to the house, and he can go live with his brother or your Grandma Ruby. Or he can move into this trailer by himself once the dust settles."

Then after Daddy wrecked everything to ashes, Mama took him back. Instead of pressing charges, she rewarded him. We all had to pretend from then on that the trailer was home. She went through with a divorce, and he signed the papers, too. But except for short stretches out from under his rule, she slept in the same bed with Daddy until the day he died. She's lived in that trailer nearly three times as long as we lived together on Genesis Road.

That first loss in my life, I grieved for a place, the fields and woods that rolled up to the foot of English Mountain, the snub-nosed outline of the ridge, the silver maples turning up their leaves before a storm, the birdsong. Morning after morning I woke up in the trailer's cramp, the dark, Formica-paneled hallway, with a kitchen that swamped the tiny living room. No front porch. No garden. If it's true we all blame our mothers, then I was right in line with statistics. I blamed Mama even more than Daddy, for every siren and motorcycle blasting down Main Street three blocks away. I blamed her for the glare of streetlights blocking out the stars. I was furious how easily she never looked back, as if the past were a pretty landscape in the rearview, folded shut around a curve in the road. She acted like we could never ask for anything better than that shitty trailer.

But I envied her amnesia. I couldn't forget the fresh-cut hay sweating in the sun, the sound of spring peepers and katydids. I tried and failed to forget liberty as natural as greening dogwoods, as easy as first frost on the fields. But there was no forgetting. The farm on Genesis Road *was* me, or who I knew I was at the time. That place was how I understood myself. And so, I was lost. I would never again see the trillium patch I loved in the back of the woods, the cool green ravine.

After those first months of selfish grieving—the way a ten-year-old grieves—I suddenly saw I'd mistaken Mama's silence. She hadn't made peace. She was seething. And spite like that is a black-hole rain puddle, a million secrets weighed down under a prism oil slick. All it takes is one backfire spark to set the whole thing off into an inferno. It's always just a matter of *when*.

Where do you go when you live under that kind of threat your whole life, when you can't go back? When you're ten and your mother is a traitor, an actress, a hostage right alongside you?

I kept my mouth shut at first. Then when I got over the stun, I said enough to be slapped plenty for sassing. By the time I was twelve, thirteen? I was old enough to take Mama's place as Daddy's full-on whipping girl. He pulled my hair instead of hers, left pinched bruises on my skin. He punched or slapped, or swung his fist, depending on how drunk he was.

It was my head and not hers he held a gun to the most awful night, a defining pass between us. And Mama never knew. I watched his eyes on either side of that pistol held to my forehead. And I never once begged.

Just as I planned in the years after that awful night, I left for college the minute I could. The campus was a half-hour's drive from Newport. I left the trailer exactly a half-hour before the dorms opened. I had a favorite sensation back when we'd lived on Genesis Road. I'd run as fast as my feet could carry me, over and over down a long hill between two maples, believing every time I might finally get airborne for just a second. Even then, I knew a place you love takes power to leave, a force so strong there is no way to stop the momentum.

I never did get liftoff, not really. I had to face the truth after Daddy died. I'm thirty-six years old with no place I love to hold me back. No husband. No family. No responsibility. I've lived mostly by default, one job after another, one man after the next. I've never lived more than fifty miles from where I was born. Even when I moved to Knoxville, I was only an hour's drive from Newport. Not counting trips to nearby North Carolina, I'd only crossed the Tennessee state line a handful of times. The farthest I'd ever been was a college spring break trip to Florida, but I might as well have told Daddy, Africa.

That whole summer before I left for college, the first in our family to even apply, Daddy wouldn't speak to me. The August afternoon I packed up, he stumbled out of the trailer when I started my car.

"How the hell you can afford this is what I want to know." He pulled Mama back and breathed beer into my car.

I wanted to feel he loved me, showing it with his anger. But I knew he wanted me under his thumb, ignorant as him, helpless, where he could use me against Mama. I wasn't about to tell him I was terrified. I'd exchanged a hundred-and-fourteen weekends in a row making biscuits at KFC for one semester's tuition and a Bondoed Datsun. How would I pay for seven more semesters? I had sixteen dollars cash in my pocket.

I idled in reverse. "Thing is, Daddy, even with that Republican shithead you love having in the White House, with my grades and scholarships—"

"You think you're something!" He flicked my nose so hard I smelled salt in the stung cartilage. "You got a hawk's nose same as me. But don't figure on getting off the ground, Sister. You ain't never going to get nowhere."

Words at parting are the surest kind of legacy. Against my will, until he died, part of me believed he spoke the gospel. Even when I wanted to run, I hung on like a grudge, pulled down by his words and my wounds. How many times my life threatened to cave in on top of me. All those years, being buried was easier than trying to fly.

That April morning my house burned, Sam played midwife, slapping my escape into motion. He showed up at my office to tell me my life had become a 9-1-1 emergency. I had learned the contours of his official cop-face way back working juvenile cases together.

Just as in my dream of Daddy's dying, I divided in two. One part of me sprang up in hopeful surprise. It was only Sam in that uniform. The rest of me hunkered down when I saw his dutiful eyes. My knees buckled. His hands were around my upper arms like blood pressure cuffs.

"It's Glenn," he said. My heart bolted like a rabbit in my chest. A synapse of relief scatter-shot through my dread. *It's not Mama.*

After his authorized terseness, riding in his squad car toward Newport, I wondered how he could need so many words. His voice was a cartoon bird, nightmare wings twitching in my periphery. He told me I shouldn't go to the site. *The site.* I marveled he could keep the patrol car between the lines on the interstate.

Wiring, he said. *Total loss. Autopsy. Smoke inhalation.* Little official phrases leached down into my core until there wasn't room to breathe.

"The whole structure was involved when I got there. Nothing the firemen could do. You need to know there were news crews there, Glenna. Be ready for phone calls."

I tried to take in my new celebrity with some kind of added dread, but I had hit the sub-basement, the crawlspace below the lowest cellar. Black shadows floated over my vision.

"A shame Glenn parked his truck so close," Sam rattled on. "Paint just bubbled up. They'll total it."

I pictured all I'd left undone. Dirty dishes in the sink. Cobwebs I'd been planning to sweep down when I could muster the energy. Dusty built-ins. Water spots on glasses. The unmade bed in the guest room where I'd been sleeping. Christmas wrapping paper still on the attic landing. The four-poster cherry bed Kevin built for us, without a mattress now, where I'd lost the baby.

Sam studied his rearview mirrors and cleared his throat into his fist. "You never answered me about Faye. Is she home or at the shop?" He touched my knee. "Any certain way you want to tell her?"

"Stop the car," I said.

"Okay, but we have to—"

"No. Stop the car!" I lunged toward the dashboard as he braked on the shoulder.

"Are you sick?" He unbuckled and leaned across to open my door.

I focused on the sound of the cruiser's dizzy blue lights clicking off seconds.

When he reached to touch me, I grappled and broke free, holding to the car for balance as I walked back down the interstate, willing time to go with me. *Go back. Turn around.*

"Glenna! Where are you going?"

Sam's touch on my shoulder brought me to my hands and knees. On the gravel shoulder I hung onto the spinning day. The percussion of eighteen-wheelers lashed my hair against my face. I watched his boots pace upside down on asphalt. I could feel it. He would touch me again, pet my head or rub my back.

"I can have an ambulance here—"

"No. I'll be—Just don't touch me."

He squeezed my shoulder like a doctor who can't change the awful diagnosis. I heaved up nothing much besides my morning coffee. He bent to wipe my mouth with his handkerchief.

"I'm begging you. Don't touch me, Sam." I wrenched the cloth out of his hand. "Please. Just, please. I'll get up. See?" I motioned him back. "I'll be a model prisoner, okay? We'll go tell Mama that Daddy's dead." I pulled at my skirt and brushed little gravels out of my pocked palms and knees. And there it was. A run in my hose. The only pair I had to my name now. How ridiculous.

"Goddammit." I stalked down the embankment toward woods and fields and the blue of English Mountain where our old farm had burned and sunk away. I could walk that far. It might take me days. By then the telling and crying and the burying would be over. The fire would be out. I could go home.

I could not go home.

Sam stumbled to balance in front of me on the hillside, palms like a wall. "Calm down, Glenna. You need to calm down." He steadied his weight, put one hand on his holster.

"You're going to shoot me?"

"Stop screeching. I want you to calm down."

"I am calm. I'm perfectly fucking calm. Could you maybe just stop talking and touching me for one goddamn minute?"

"Glenna." He pushed his hands through his blond hair. "Why can't you just be normal? Just be upset like a normal person? A normal person would cry."

"A normal person like you?" I turned around and started climbing back up the hill. "Like you're upset about my daddy's truck? My daddy is dead. My whole fucking house up in flames, and you're worried about his *truck*?"

I scrambled on all fours away from his reach. We stepped onto the shoulder and I pulled away from him again beside the car. "And you're asking me how to break this to my mother? You didn't seem to have any trouble telling me. So, go on and tell her Daddy is dead. You tell her that part, and when you get to the part about how, you just tell her there was an accident."

"So, see? You do want to tell me what to say. Like always. You always pretend you don't need it to go your way." He reached to open my door.

I pivoted to face him. "Okay," I said. "If you want my advice so bad, maybe you ought to go with something like: 'The good news, Faye, is that Glenna's house burned down.'" I leaned close and stared into his sunglasses. "Or is that the bad news?"

He flinched back a step. His cruiser ticked like a worried clock. I opened the door for myself. Sam got behind the wheel and didn't check to make sure I was buckled in. He didn't pat my knee or say a word the rest of the way to Mama's shop. He ran the siren and passed every car. I peeled off my ruined hose and held my face out the window, flying blind into a ninety-mile-an-hour wind.

From the parking space in front of Mama's shop, I watched through her plate glass window. Sam led her into the back room and shut the door. He came back alone and cleared out her customers. He sat in her barber chair like a boy waiting for a haircut. I slipped in barefooted and sat in a bonnet dryer chair. The big sooty fan whirred over the transom, and Main Street traffic shimmered past. And inside those noises, the sound of Mama's footsteps scuffing the linoleum in the back room. Back and forth between the rusted utility cabinet and the washing machine. She kicked the hollow metal with her leather Keds.

When she started crying, I pulled the dryer hood over my head and turned it on full blast. But I couldn't stand the smell of scorched hair and chemicals. The night our farmhouse had burned, nothing was as ugly as the oily stink of burned plastic, all the Formica and melted Naugahyde, Mama's lime-green melamine dishes, my poor Barbies and baby dolls. Nobody questioned how Daddy saved all his fishing gear and guns, garbage bags of clothes for us all, the photo album of us smiling on the rescued pages.

Mama came out, pressing her forehead with a towel. Her hazel eyes fastened on mine with a fevered sheen. She bent double in a sob. Only Daddy cried in our family. I'd only seen my mother cry twice her whole life, once when Dunn was nearly hit by a car, and the time Daddy beat me the worst. Relief and outrage. I couldn't tell, truly, what kind of crying she was doing now.

Sam looked at me and gestured, but I couldn't go to her. He went to her where she leaned against the sink.

"Did you tell her how?" I asked. Mama hid her face in her tumbling blonde hair. Even with Sam's arm across her shoulders, her body moved in little circles, the way water pools down a drain. All I wanted was for her to stop crying, but I'd made it worse. Nothing else mattered except she had to stop.

"Mama," I said sharply. "You remember how we managed when the farmhouse burned. This is lightning striking twice, is all. We'll get through."

13

"What farmhouse?" Sam said.

"A long time ago. Daddy burned down our house in Cosby."

"What in the world are you saying now?" Mama stepped away from Sam and hooked a stare on me. "What's the matter with you to say a thing like that?" She looked as if I'd slapped her.

Nearly thirty years of silence and shame, broken. The code broken. But Mama had stopped crying. I'd managed that. She put her hands over her ears and shook her head. "What good is that going to do, Sister? The minute your daddy's not here to defend hisself. What good's it do?"

In a bluster, she picked up her purse and hit the main switch to turn off the fans. But her face was pale and dry, smooth as if I'd washed it with a soft cloth. She flicked off the fluorescents over the sink with a sharp lash of her wrist. She stood straighter.

"Your brother. Lord, he'll be pulling in at the trailer any minute now—" She broke off, but she did not cry again.

Dunn begged Sam to say it was a lie. He begged Mama. How did we know it was Daddy in the fire? He wailed before his body went still with weeping, as if the shock paralyzed everything but his face. He worked his mouth around words that weren't words while snot ran to his lip. Sam sat beside him on the couch, looking across the countertop into the kitchen, from me to Mama and back again. I reached across to hand Sam the handkerchief he'd pushed on me earlier.

Mama started a pot of coffee and we cleaned out the fridge to make room for the food people would bring. Without a word she handed me moldy, rotten, dissolved leftovers to throw in the trash. We loaded the dishwasher and stashed clutter in the cabinets, opening and slamming doors.

Sam slurped down a cup of coffee and said his good-byes. Dunn sank into the couch. Mama lit another cigarette and stared out the window above the kitchen sink, the altar where she always goes to wait and worry. I sat near her on a stool behind the kitchen counter. We had already sunk into that new time without Daddy. I rubbed my finger into the nicotine burns. There wouldn't be any new smudges. Daddy was the sloppy one. Mama smoked slowly, tapping her ashes into the sink. Her hands were steady as she picked up the telephone.

Even before sun-up, people pulled in and out of Mama's gravel driveway on their way to work. All morning they dropped off casseroles and cakes, pots of green beans and heaping bowls of potato salad, pies and fried chicken and canned hams stabbed silly with cherries and pineapple. Mama and I sipped coffee and waited in her too-bright kitchen for all she'd cooked for Newport's sick and dead to return to her in kind.

Along with food, Grandma Ruby's church friends must have scrounged every size twelve black dress they could find from closets all over Cocke County. That's how I knew everybody had magically found out that my house and all my things were gone. I was a charity case. When Mama and I got back from the longest day of my life making funeral plans, seventeen dresses choked my old room, layered on doorknobs and hooks, a dark gallery of goodwill in shades from charcoal to ash. Sleeveless, empire-waisted, suit-coated, A-line-skirted, rayon, polyester, cotton, worsted wool, dry clean only, tumble dry low, delicate cycle.

They hung like people waiting for comfort. I turned on the bedside lamp Mama bought for my twelfth birthday, a ballerina en pointe. She had balanced that bulb and shade for twenty-four years. I wanted to throw the lamp across the room and save her any further effort.

In the light I could see smudges of makeup on the collars of the dresses, little stains, chalky deodorant smears. Rips needed mending; loose hems needed to be stitched. The dresses were alive with the smell of stale perfume and fried food, cigarettes and sweat. I finally fell asleep on the couch, away from the cocktail party of empty shrouds.

I would have been bound to wear one of those awful dresses, not to mention boxes full of faded hand-me-downs, if Grandma Ruby's fainting fits hadn't forced us to postpone the service. And if Carey wasn't the best "girlfriend" I've ever had. My second morning at the trailer, while Mama was showering, he knocked at the door. No casserole, no flowers.

His first words were the only true condolence I'd heard. He put his whole body around me and said into my messy hair, "You know? That saying, 'Shit happens,' just isn't funny anymore."

The smell of him came out of years gone by, an innocent peace that buckled my knees. The sameness of him, the continuity and safe space he always was. I hadn't seen him in nearly three years, but time accordioned. I held to his warm jean jacket, the first man I'd touched since Kevin. He didn't let go until I did, only when I was sure that not even this comfort, not even Carey, could make me cry.

He set a shopping bag from Saks on the kitchen table and poured us both a cup of coffee.

"You didn't have to come." We sat across from one another.

"But you're glad I *did*." He reached into the bag. "Here. Try *this* on. Oooh. Remember your first time in Saks with me, in Buckhead?" He handed me a butter pale rain coat, slight and cool as silk, but sturdy.

"Carey, this had to be way too expensive." I folded it back into the bag.

He stood up and pulled out the coat again and laid it on my lap. "You don't *really* think you have the luxury of turning me down. It calls for rain the rest of the week. And, I mean, Glenna, it's just a jacket. I'm all set to take you on a by-God shopping *bender*, and you throw the very first thing I give you in my face? I mean, are you planning to just nasty away in Faye's lovely *ensemble*?" He fingered the worn shawl collar of Mama's green chenille housecoat and eyed my filthy hair.

"So?" I smacked his hand away.

"*So*? We're going to buy you some actual clothes. Today."

I laid my forehead on the table with a groan. "Carey, I hardly have the strength to sit in a chair."

"You need everything," he said. I knew he meant, *you need me.* "Let me do this for you." His voice was narcotic. I had a rush of surrender, like the moment Valium seeps in before a medical procedure.

I showered in ten minutes and wrapped in a towel to borrow clothes from Mama. We could hear Carey greeting people and putting more food in the fridge.

"What are you going all the way to Knoxville for?"

"Mama, I don't just need a three-pack of panties from Walmart. And my car's still in the parking garage at work. Uncle Johnny's offered to ride with us and drive my car back here."

She sank down on the edge of her unmade bed, on sheets that still held Daddy's smell. "Your daddy's laying up there at Foxe's and you're going to the mall?"

"You didn't seem to mind shopping yesterday for a suit for Dunn. Like he ever put on a suit his whole life. Has he even tried it on yet?" I pulled open her dresser drawers one after another with my free hand and held the towel closed with the other. "And that casket. Nearly four thousand dollars' damage. We could bury him cheaper in a damn used car."

Mama shoved me aside and bent to open the bottom drawer. "I ain't in a mood to be sassed," she said. She dumped my arms full of clothes. "You don't like the clothes people have give you, or mine, just go on ahead and spend another four thousand."

I fit in a pair of her Wranglers, a little loose in the ass; and I hid a Dolly-wood T-shirt under one of Dunn's sweatshirts. With double socks, a pair of her sneakers fit me. Carey sat on the edge of my bed while I finished.

"Look at these things." I shook my gray pumps toward him, dangling from my fingers like open-mouthed fish. "Can you believe I wore these to work Tuesday? Nice luck. The most miserable shoes I own."

"So, if they hurt, throw them out."

"Throw away the only pair of shoes I've got?" I fingered the arch that never fit. Kevin hated them.

Carey looked at me, daring. "I mean, they're just shoes. We're getting

16

you lots and lots of new ones." He raised his eyebrows high and shrugged and mouthed, "*Lots.*"

On the way out, we stopped at the kitchen trash can. I dangled the shoes as frivolously as empty beer cans.

"Do it!" Carey. The face of my childhood conspirator. The shoes thudded and I swallowed a giddy choke. We peered into the trash to see them smeared with coffee grounds and crumbs and chunks of eggs.

I clapped my hand across my mouth. Carey's brown eyes went wide with triumph. "Now that," he said, "is what I call a fashion statement."

Hysterical plunder through the mall sank like grit in my chest as we loaded our bags into Carey's Jeep. No more avoiding. Time to get back to Newport and dress for the visitation.

"Mama will be on her ear." In less than three hours, Carey had bought me a dressy black suit, with pants and a skirt, and black dress peep-toes, blouses, jeans, two cashmere sweaters, sport sandals, dress sandals, sneakers, T-shirts, pajamas, a silk robe, and a ridiculously expensive pair of waterproof hiking boots. I'd bought my own bras, enough underwear for two weeks, a couple of plaid flannel shirts and corduroys that Carey refused to pay for out of principle. Who had we been just minutes before? Teasing each other. Flirting with clerks and jostling through the mall crowd. Slamming down lattes.

Hardly anything had been on sale. Carey wheedled me. "I mean, we don't have time to dig through sale racks." At the last store, I balked with a sudden jolt of pride. "Stop freaking out, Glenna. Let me do this," Carey said. "I married rich." He laid his hand on his heart and said only half-joking, "Do this in memory of Stan."

Hearing Stan's name tweaked an old wound between us, and guilt. What had Carey gone through in that long illness and death, through Stan's funeral? I hadn't gone to Atlanta. I couldn't work up my nerve to call for a month. I sent flowers and a sympathy card. I'd watched Carey lay his credit card in half a dozen upturned palms, his inheritance. I'd never liked Stan. And now I couldn't take any of my hatefulness back.

I looked at the shopping bags stuffed into Carey's Jeep, grateful and ashamed. He slammed the hatch. "I'll have insurance money soon, Carey. To pay you back."

He rolled his eyes and opened my door for me. I climbed in. I thought of telling Carey about the baby. I wanted to tell him right then we should have been shopping for maternity clothes. I wanted the day through the windshield to stop spiraling. My ribs squeezed. How could I go back to that trailer I despised, for how long? How many days could I eat breakfast, lunch, and supper from the sympathy buffet?

To get back to Newport, we had to pass UT again, where Kevin and I had met. Past the exit for our house. I wondered if Kevin had gone to see the ruin of it. Two-and-a-half days later, I still hadn't heard from him. Sam told me that Kevin knew about the house. So, what if Kevin came to the funeral home? What if he and Dawson and Sam had their first face-to-face right there in the middle of all that death?

"Let's just keep heading west," I said when Carey buckled his seatbelt. "What's the limit on that card? We could be Thelma and Louise." Carey wrinkled his brows. "Okay. Ted and Louise." I tried a weak laugh.

"You know they die at the end, right?"

"Okay, whatever. But I've never even been to Nashville. Farthest west I've been is Chattanooga."

"Chattanooga is *not* west, silly wabbit." He looked at me over the top of his sunglasses. "And just for the sake of argument, I get to be Louise."

Carey and I have always known that when we can't make each other laugh things are truly bad. Our sophomore year, I was absent for nearly two weeks after Daddy beat me. First thing when he saw me in the hallway at school, Carey tucked my hair behind my ears and squinted at my puffy dark eyes. He pushed up my sleeves and looked at the bruises on my arms. He fingered the raw patches on my scalp where Daddy had pulled out my hair. But he knew not to say any of it out loud. He passed along the story I told him to tell, that I'd had mono. He'd survived his own battles, physical and worse. He suffered bullying outside his home, but heart-breaking isolation from his family. He knows the art of deflection. He doesn't ask about my secrets because he has carried so many himself. He knows exactly how to be my friend.

I should have settled in with him on that ride back to Mama's. I should have trusted our history together. But maybe because every nerve ending I had was on alert, I could feel a chasm, the years, the unsaid, unshared years. I wondered if Carey was aware of the little blips between us too. The half-beats and stumbles in our conversations. I didn't have room yet to face the reunion Carey and I had ahead of us, the weeks to come when we would have nothing but time and space for healing. Or not. There was remorse over Stan, some hard feelings that would come out sooner than I could have known. The grudge and envy I'd hung onto for years.

Carey left for college and never came back to Tennessee. I always marveled how easily he'd escaped and left me, as if he had a birthright to Atlanta's urban wild-scape. His mother didn't name him after Cary Grant for nothing. With those brown eyes and a dancer's grace, even glasses and a PhD in history couldn't dent his boyish sophistication, that assurance that always said, *You know you'd follow me anywhere.* But he hadn't asked me to follow.

Our high school class voted us "Most Likely to Marry Each Other," a category they invented just for Carey and me. Surely some of them thought it was a cruel joke. Or maybe some people voted as an apology for abusing Carey for twelve years. *Gay boy. Sissy. Faggot.*

But even the nerdy yearbook gang was buffaloed when we actually showed up to have our portrait taken. I wore Carey's church suit, which fit everywhere except my boobs. The coat gaped open, so I wore a wide 1970s tie, paisley turquoise. Carey wore a feminine blouse nearly the same shade, and tight jeans. It was the eighties. Mama helped us both make our hair really big. We wore eyeliner. We'd had our ears pierced the year before and split a pair of cubic zirconia earrings between us. He wore his in the right ear because he'd heard that was a symbol for being gay.

"Left is right. Right is wrong," he used to repeat.

He loved that we *provoked their anxiety.* He talked that way even when we were kids. And then I was left behind. Some of our old classmates still ask me, when I run into them downtown or at Mama's shop, "What do you hear from Fairy Carey?"

He always forgave even the worst bullies, the vicious ones who brutalized him, as if he knew he'd never have a choice not to be the bigger person. I never mustered his mercy, not for nobody, nohow. I was stuck in a self-tormenting duel with Daddy, hell, with all the men I ever knew, whoever punished me, mired down in the mud we made together.

"I just can't believe my daddy is dead," I blurted out.

Carey pulled off the interstate, punched on his flashers, undid his seatbelt, and reached under my seat. He pulled out a Rand McNally map of the U.S. And then he pulled back into traffic. The sky was smeared with dull clouds. Redbuds bloomed where nothing else had greened, a pink mist haunting the gray thickets. The world was vapor, with nothing solid to hold me. Carey kept sneaking looks as I turned the pages on my lap. *Kansas. Wyoming. California.* We hardly said a word until we got to Mama's driveway. Uncle Johnny had washed my car, shining like a gun without anyone to fire it. If Carey didn't say yes, I knew I would never have the nerve to strike out on my own.

"I mean, let's do it." He turned off the ignition, but then put both hands back on the steering wheel. The garish sunset glowed against the trailer's mildewed siding.

Mama opened the door and peered out, one hand shading her eyes. I was afraid she'd break the spell Carey was under.

"I mean, ever since Stan died I've been *locked* in Atlanta. Locked in myself. No one else to blame. Two years. I just couldn't stand traveling alone. I mean, every place reminds me of him."

My heart was an animal trying to find its way out of my chest. "You're not shitting me, are you, Carey? Seriously, I have big insurance money coming."

19

"Now, just so you know, my classes aren't over until early May." He glanced at me. "Graduation is like the eighth or something." All I could do was nod.

I watched the decision come over his face and then flicker away as we sat in Mama's driveway. He looked excited, as if we had already gassed up his Jeep, packed and ready to go. Then he looked skeptical.

"But your job," he said.

"I'll take a leave. Hell, I'll quit if I have to."

For a woman like me, a hillbilly who has never even been on a plane, the tip end of the continent shimmers in mind as a pure and blue place, pacified but lightning bold. All the ugliness of your former life, all the damage and the trauma. Where does it go when you stand on a cliff edge hanging over the waves? If you get there in the nick of time, my age—thirty-six, barely mid-life—you might set the second half of your life right. You might have time to even out your raggedy ways. Wasn't the West made for a woman like me, with nothing left to lose?

What came out of Carey's mouth was almost a dare. "I mean, how many times, Glenna, did we swear when we got out of high school we'd strike out for the Rockies? Or the Pacific, where nobody knew us? Where we could be anything?"

For him, it was the easiest step in the world to take. Just two old friends deciding to set out on a May morning in five weeks' time. Just a drive across America to see what we might find. Pitching our tent under new skies every night. So, it was only right I ought to run with him, like we were cutting class again.

Carey laughed and gripped the steering wheel as if he could see the road ahead. It was that easy for him to get free. "Where—"

"Wherever! Everywhere." I was aware that Mama looked out again, but with the sunset in her eyes, I had to be nearly invisible. "Anywhere."

I held my hands together so they'd stop shaking, so hard my arms trembled. She slammed the trailer door. In the last light, the new square of red clay she had dug the week before glowed. She was still trying, after all the years in exile, to raise a garden on her little scab of yard.

Maybe the worst thing about a death in the family is the family.

"Keep focused," Carey advised as we walked into the funeral home. "Breathe. Have your script ready: 'Thanks for coming. Daddy would appreciate it.'" He squeezed my hand. "If all that fails, think about our trip."

I thought I was prepared, but right off, Sam was an obstacle, stationed in front of Daddy's metal-gray casket as if he were still married to the next-of-kin. He had his arm around Grandma Ruby, leaning beside Dunn and Mama, who wore one of the black dresses I'd rejected. She was still a beauty, natural blonde with that olive skin. She was the grieving widow.

20

I had only seen the casket empty with its benign satin lining. Now it held the scooped up charred, greasy remains of Glenn Daniels. It held the spirit soot of my baby. My feet went impotent like a dreamer's. I swear, Carey felt me falter before I did, tucking his body against mine, his arm on my elbow like a rudder. His ballast kept me on course until we were somehow standing between Mama and Dunn. Then as if he were admiring a piece of furniture he touched the casket, bent to look at the framed snapshot of Daddy with his bird dog.

Carey was standing where my husband would have stood if I'd had one.

"This won't work," I blurted. Footsteps jarred outside the closed double doors. Early arrivals were signing the guestbook.

Carey stepped toward me. "You okay?" He nodded until I nodded back. "You'll be okay, Glenna."

"Yeah, but don't—Don't be hurt, okay? But I think I have to do this by myself." A question furrowed his face. "Honestly you've been so good to me. It's just, I don't have the energy to introduce you to everybody."

He laughed. "I grew up here, Glenna."

"Hell, Carey, half these people won't know *me*. But the thing is, explaining. They're going to think you're with me."

"I am with you." He studied my face and pulled close to kiss me on the cheek. "I *am* with you." He smiled and wandered through the mingling crowd coming in the door.

Sam followed him, so Grandma Ruby reached for me as she plopped heavily into the wheelchair someone had brought for her just in case. Her cheeks were flushed with whatever "nerve" pills her doctors had given her. Her pupils were pin pricks, and her hand on my arm was cold. What could I say to her about Daddy? We were a wordless quartet. I concentrated on holding one expression, a mask. I rooted into the field-green carpet, air rising dewy cool in a forest of ferns and bitter lilies and sprays of roses and carnation wreaths dyed electric colors.

I concentrated on the hands that clasped mine, hands like Daddy's, thick and damaged, grease-stained hands with bruised fingernails and callused palms. Cold hands with flashing bright nails and sharp jewelry, pudgy hands like dough, hands with fingertips like butterflies, hard-grasping hands that had milked a thousand thousand cows, chopped wood through dozens of winters, hands that had fired shotguns and gutted fish and spanked children and slapped wives. Hands that had touched my daddy.

One hand at a time, and then Dawson's voice before I spotted him. "I apologize, the way I'm dressed," he was saying as he pumped Dunn's arm. Dunn started to cry again, there in front of his favorite ex-brother-in-law. Dawson leaned over to pat Grandma Ruby's arm. "Your boy," he called Daddy, loud as if she were deaf, "was sure blessed. Everybody loved him. I said to Dunn, sorry for having to come on my way to the graveyard shift." He ducked his head and flushed for saying *graveyard*. He said he was sorry over and over.

Sounds like old times, I wanted to say. "It doesn't matter. It's fine," I said. "Thanks for coming." I stepped back to let him pass, but he closed the space between us. And just like old times, I flinched.

He rambled without noticing. "Mama wanted me to be sure and say she's sorry she can't make it. She ain't doing too good since Rayanne's moved to Pensacola. I reckon you heard she got married?" He breathed in quick. "And that I got married again?" He turned pink again and flashed the wedding band on his thick freckled hand. Fine wrinkles spread under his green eyes. Twelve years since our divorce, his jawline had thickened and his waist.

"Yeah. Mama keeps me up to date. I'm happy for you."

"Maybe nobody's told her—nobody much knows yet." The news I saw coming pressed me back, nearly against the casket. "We're having a baby."

"I'm happy for you," I repeated. "Okay. That's great! Congratulations. There's really a lot of people crowding in here." I stepped away to give him room to pass, but he grabbed me and crushed me into his thick chest and biceps and thighs. I looked for Carey, then, for my escape.

Dawson stepped back with wet eyes. "I just wanted to pay my respects, is all. Your daddy was a hell of a man, Glenna. And what's past—" He wiped his eyes. His regret was the nostalgia of an ignorant bully, admiring the man who had taught me to take a good beating.

The line dwindled. Mama drifted further to the side, talking to an old high school friend. Then she was gone. Even after all the years, she wasn't immune to Grandma Ruby's snubs and histrionics. I reached to shake one of the last few hands and recognized the face of the funeral home attendant. He gestured like Vanna White. "Your mama had me come fetch you."

Coming out the chapel door, head down, she nearly ran me over. "Be nice." She gripped my forearm. "I'm taking your brother home. He's a wreck. Come on directly."

I walked into the darkened chapel and knew. "Glenna?" In the low light, Kevin's outline stepped into the aisle. His features came clear in the next couple of heartbeats.

"I didn't think you'd come." I lied. I walked under the chapel beams and thought about the arbor Kevin had built for our wedding. We sat across the aisle from each other, and I thought that question ushers ask, *Bride's side or groom's?* "You didn't have to."

"Yeah. I did. It took a Herculean effort not to come see you before now."

He leaned forward, elbows balanced on his knees. It's always amazed me, the length of his lean taut angles folding up like a sleeper sofa.

After forever we looked each other in the face. "You okay?"

"What's my other option, you think?" I hugged my arms around myself. "It's cold as shit in here."

He stood up and started to shrug out of his coat sleeves, the kind of gesture I'd been dreading, the one that might break me. How to bear the smell and warmth of him that close?

"No." I half-stood. "No, I'm fine."

"Really, take my coat." He held it by the shoulders and moved toward me.

"No." I panicked. "Really, don't!" He stopped, his eyes blue as glass, those eyes that had watched over me in every possible circumstance two people can share. *For better or worse.* He sat down hard with the coat in a wad on his lap. One more thing on the list of all I had refused from him, even when I wanted everything he could offer.

"They must have to keep it cold." I looked forward at the stained-glass Jesus. "You know, the bodies." I flinched. "Body heat, I mean. From all these people. You heard from Sam, right?"

"Yeah, Sam." He coughed an awkward laugh, rubbed his hands together as if he were washing them. "Bizarre, right? I kept thinking you'd call, or at least have Faye call if you couldn't handle it."

"I handled it. I could handle it," I said. "Not that this really concerns you."

"My God, Glenna." He leaned toward me. "You're punishing me even now? Our house? Your dad is dead, and still? You're the most stubborn woman I ever met."

"No. You've met my mother," I said. "What did you two talk about?"

"She says you've got some cockamamy idea you're quitting your job and leaving."

"Whatever happens, you don't need to worry." I stood up.

He stood and stepped toward me as if he might ask me for a dance or smack me. "You think none of this has any effect on me at all? It was our house, together."

"Not anymore it wasn't. Isn't."

"It was still a place I loved. And I was willing to sacrifice so you could keep it."

"I never asked you to sacrifice one damn thing on my behalf," I said. "I never asked you to give up *anything* that was naturally yours. *All* yours."

He scanned my face to be sure I'd intended to jab the wound between us. I pushed my fists behind my folded arms and did not cry.

Kevin. Those gestures I love. Those hands and that toss of dark hair. Of course, he'd done the worst harm to me—out of anyone ever—because I loved him the most, because I would have given him anything. But he wasn't capable of that sort of sacrifice. He ran his palm over his mustache and beard.

I swallowed to keep from saying his name. "What happened isn't your problem. There's nothing malicious in saying that. I've talked to my lawyer, and he says it's fair to split the insurance money, since I owe payments to you."

"How can you think I care about money? I'm asking what you need, what I can do for you." He pulled on his coat. "Look, maybe when you get over being so bitter, or pissed, if that ever happens, maybe you'll decide you want some photos or some of the things I have. Someday you might actually want to remember."

Remember. Remember. I turned the word over and over in my mind, like an eleventh commandment, the one we can't break even if we try. I was so tired of remembering that I thought I would sink through the green carpet at his feet.

When Kevin quit working at Children's Services and went back to get his teaching certificate, he read botany and biology books in bed. We made love among all those fertile names—*petal, pistil, stamen, pollen*—desperate for a baby. He would read to me while I lay with my heels against the wall, feet in the air, his sperm sinking into me. Once he told me about a theoretical substance in space so heavy, a teaspoon of it laid on the ground would push right through the earth's surface, from one side to the next. Now our memories were like that, heavy wreckage. My heart pounding a hole through my gut.

"I need to get back to Mama," I said. "I know it meant a lot to her you came."

"You know I didn't come for your mother," he said. His face was resigned, but his eyes burned. With anger. Maybe with love. He turned and walked up the aisle, wearing the same suit and shoes he wore the day we got married.

Dunn ambushed me when I walked into the trailer. "You're bound not to give Daddy a minute's peace, ain't you?" He paced smoking in front of the mute TV, rattling dishes in the cabinet. Mama lit a cigarette in the dark kitchen.

"What is it I did now?"

"You'uns leave me out of this," she said.

"What you told about Daddy, blaming him for burning down your house." Dunn lumbered.

"I never said that." Then I realized he'd misunderstood. "If you mean the house when we were little. Who told you anyway, what I said? Mama?"

"You made your bed, Sister," she said.

"You lie," Dunn stormed. "If you say Daddy burned the house in Cosby when we was little! You lied to everbody tonight. Like you give a shit he's dead."

I sank down on the dingy love seat. "What you think I said about my house, you got that wrong. But about our house in Cosby, that's not a lie. Just because you were too little to remember doesn't mean it's not true."

"Just admit you're glad he's dead!" he said. "He come all the way to your house to help you, and you go and bad mouth him. He died helping you out—"

"So, you're going to blame this all on me?" I lurched up and across the room at him. He swung his hands as if he could erase me. "Sure. I masterminded the whole catastrophe. I begged Daddy to come to my house when I'm already late for work and bully his way in, so he could burn it to the ground! Just what I always wanted. Because I needed one more thing to be mad at him for."

Dunn turned away and went to the back door, hands braced against the frame. Mama opened the window over the sink. Her cigarette smoke pulled out the screen.

"It ain't right you was the last one to see him alive," he cried.

"You're right," I said. "There's nothing fair in that." That morning Daddy wouldn't stop bringing tools into my house, even though he knew I was mad, frantic and late, my arms full of coffee thermos and file folders and my purse.

It came to me: *I don't have time for your shit*, I told him. I didn't want him snooping around. I worried he would wander upstairs and find the bedroom in shambles, my bed with no mattress, the fireplace still a mess from the fabric I'd burned there, the smell of charred blood.

No one had been in the house since I'd lost the baby. A sacred ground. And Daddy the most vulgar trespasser possible. But he wouldn't leave, no matter what. He sat at my kitchen table. I told him I'd call the cops. He laughed at me. I remembered asking, *Do you think a little handy-work can make up for years of your fucking abuse.*

And I remembered then: *We would always, always have been better off without you.* Those will always be the last words I said to my daddy.

Mama's TV ran on, mute and blinking. She ground her cigarette into the sink without breaking her gaze out the kitchen window. I realized she and Dunn were both looking at the rusted shed and doghouse where Daddy's old bloodhound was tied up in April mud, wondering where he was.

"Did anybody feed Dolly?" I asked.

"People has fed her all day," Mama said. "Joe Stiller's going to take her."

The weight of memory pulled my legs like an undertow. I was ten. The night after Daddy burned our farmhouse in Cosby, he got up from the supper table and said he had to go feed Lucy, his old bird dog chained up beside the barn. Her house was the top half of a sawed-off outhouse big enough to hold her and Dunn and me. Whenever we climbed in beside her, we always coughed from the dusty burlap sacks she slept on, the old dog smell of her.

I'd forgotten Lucy, out in the lonesome dark field at our burned down house. Food stuck in my throat, and I carried my still-full plate to the sink.

"What say, Sister?" Daddy came behind me and pressed his hands on my shoulders. "Come go with me."

"I ain't setting foot back there." As terrified as I was to see our ruined house, I could not bear to see Lucy. And more. I couldn't bear to let Daddy see my sorrow and defeat. He had won.

He spun me around and bent to my face. "Don't pull that lazy-ass shit on me. Get your shoes on and get in the truck."

He lurched us hard around familiar curves on the way. At the foot of the farmhouse driveway, I strained in the dark to see what I couldn't stand to see. *I couldn't bear not to look.* The truck headlights swung across the charred walls and caved-in roof, like a doll's house on a rubbish fire.

I climbed out of the truck to follow Daddy, dreading Lucy's open, speckled face. I had long ago betrayed her after years of afternoons together. We had been young together on the farm, and then she'd gotten old.

When I was eight, she had a litter of pups, some tan, some barely marked with burgundy speckles like her, one nearly black. "Mutts," Daddy called them. Weeks before they were born, he would roll Lucy over on her back and tap her sides. The flesh of her swollen belly wriggled, and Dunny and I would hold our hands on the knuckling mass. But it was Daddy she looked up at with her amber eyes, her thick tail slapping.

Every day Dunn and I ran straight to Lucy from the school bus, without stopping at the house. She met us with her teats slinging side to side, tail curled with pride, sniffing as if she were counting the pups we chose two at a time from the tangled, churning knot of bodies.

One day the pups tumbled on their own out into new clover around the barn, rolling to meet us as we ran laughing up the path. The next day we ran expecting those faces, but there was no sound, no pups. Lucy lay curled on the hard-packed dirt in her house. The tip-end of her tail moved as her eyes searched our faces. Her tongue tested the air, searching for flesh to lick. The burlap sack of her bed was gone. I pictured it wriggling like her belly, full of pups, Daddy hauling the weight into the woods, to the creek, or to the county dump.

That night past the black hull of the house and the smell of rancid burn, I trudged up the hill behind Daddy, carrying a coffee can of supper scraps. I hoped Lucy wouldn't look me in the face as I fed her. Daddy shined his flashlight behind us once more, across the walls of bubbled black paint. He swung the light up the path, and the house sank beneath the dark trees like a ship going down. In the middle of a warm summer evening, there wasn't a sound from the field or the black walnut trees or cedars, not a single cricket or jar fly or bird calling.

Then Lucy heard us. She barked and went into a desperate whimpering. Her chain raked across the boards. In the flashlight glare she barked and wriggled.

Rearing like a horse, she choked against the pull of her chain and pawed toward us. Daddy patted her hide. He laughed and called her "old girl."

While I held the light, Daddy stooped to feed her. Starved as she was, she broke away from gobbling whenever he talked sweet to her in a calming falsetto. I dumped her old water and poured new from the milk jug he handed me. While she ate, he rubbed her graying head, squatting beside her bowl. Whenever he stood from touching her, she slunk back from the big-shadowed height of him, crouched ready for the lash of his voice. But she curled her body toward him again and again, patting her tail across his boots, fearful but begging for his affection. Her flesh remembered the sting of his palm, his brute power. But she couldn't help her whining, submissive yearning for him to stay. *Stay.*

GRACELAND

At Daddy's funeral, Dunn opened his mouth to sing, but it was Daddy's raw baritone that shot through me. The sound of Daddy I had loved. When I was little, he sang while he carried me on his shoulders, and I felt the rumbling of his song in my calves as he gripped them pressed against his chest. I watched the farm from high above and moved like a queen.

Our first day on the road to Memphis, Carey said, "You have to move forward."

I pointed at the windshield. "Good thing that's exactly where we're headed." But moving through space is only physics. It's got nothing to do with the brain's hot little terrarium of regret. Outside there's the hum of tires, cars and trucks flashing, blurry trees and buildings and lives. Inside I buried Daddy over and over. Inside I relived the miscarriage. I did the math of how many weeks pregnant I would have been right then, how many inches long the baby would have been. What weight. The seatbelt mocked me all day, across my empty abdomen.

I'd never ridden in a car for more than seven hours straight, and that had been years before, college spring break. Just west of Knoxville, I already dreaded the road, hours, days, weeks, trapped while the miles went by. Crossing a continent is way too much thinking room. Carey's Jeep was a trap of reconstituted bad choices. I had lost so much sleep the past few weeks, but I couldn't nap for the images in my head, flickering and random and dark. My arms and legs felt full of sand.

Carey said, "You can't dwell on the past." He laughed without conviction. "I mean, I know that's ridiculous coming from a historian."

We were both traveling with ghosts. If I had Daddy on my back, Stan had to be there among the luggage and our packs. It hung with me, that same sensation I'd had at the funeral—that if I turned, I'd see Daddy like a smug cat on the back pew.

When Dunn had started to sing a second funeral hymn, a wave of crying went through the church like a contagious yawn. He'd been in tears all morning after Grandma Ruby said we'd never hear the Daniels boys harmonize again. My poor brother. He ducked his head while the pianist played the refrain again.

He stiffened and swallowed, rubbing one hand and then the other over the buttons of his new suit. He gripped the pulpit with Daddy's beefy hands and gathered himself the way Daddy had taught, lifting his face with closed eyes.

"*I've reached the land of corn and wine,*" he began the verse again. All I could see, plain as day, was Daddy standing in green corn, tugging back the shucks to see the kernels, plotting whiskey. Eternal acreage to distill into an alcoholic's paradise.

Dunn belted out the buoyant refrain after every verse:
"*Oh, Beulah Land, Sweet Beulah Land, as on thy highest mount I stand,*
I look away across the sea, where mansions are prepared for me,
And view the shining glory shore. My heaven, my home forevermore."

Of course, this hope in eternal joy is what a church funeral is all about. It's a beautiful hymn. It's a beautiful Kool-Aid everyone drinks in with those verses. But just as I felt the waves start to take me over, I thought about Daddy's mistrust of an open horizon. How much he despised the ocean. They ought to give the grieving daughter a shot at the pulpit. I can't sing, but I could tell them the truth. In the unlikely event Daddy really was invited across Jordan, he'd be too stubborn to leave Cocke County.

No saving grace for me. My saving rage held back any crying I might have done. I hung on to it like a life raft. If I weren't angry at Daddy, what would happen to me?

"Done been across the pond back in the Army." Daddy would shake his head. "I'll be damned if I cross it again." He always swore, *Well, I'll be damned.*

If anyone could sing him into heaven, Daddy's friends were bound to try. After Dunn's solos, they gathered for a rarefied old-time send-off, opening up guitar and banjo cases, tuning and retuning while people coughed and got up to say hey to people they knew. At last, even old Carson Somers limped up on stage to help them sing "I'll Fly Away." Then they stepped back from the old man like waves parting. He hummed a note or two and bowed his palsied head. Then he raised his hands, and his quavering voice tore open the air with an old mountain dirge, a shock after the rousing standards. His plaintive voice lifted up primal a cappella in a minor key.

"*And am I born to die? To lay this body down?*
And must my trembling spirit fly into a world unknown?
A land of deepest shade, unpierced by human thought,
The dreary regions of the dead, where all things are forgot?"

The old man stabbed into me, trying to sing Daddy to a place of eternal amnesia. That's all there was to it, then, a handshake to forget the whole damn mess? A raging peace came over me for just a second. I could, couldn't I, forget? Even if I never forgave. Why do the dead get all the clemency?

29

I thought I could shut up a lifetime of conflict in Daddy's casket. I didn't know there was a lesson to learn before I could bury all our years of battling. There's no easy handshake to say it's over. The worm of blame niggles its way in. There's an endless resurrection of *what-could-have-beens*. The loose ends left between Daddy and me tangled and knotted like an impassable laurel hell.

But the preacher gave Daddy the farewell Grandma Ruby had assigned him. Never mind what Mama wanted. I'd seen his revered mother hand over the yellow legal pages at the funeral home. Inside the whitewashed Freewill Baptist Church of Cosby, her preacher gave Daddy the overblown eulogy reserved for prodigal brethren. He remade Daddy into a victim of his own undoing, to be pitied and forgiven, loved as large in memory as he was misunderstood in life.

Then it was bald, full-on preaching. He used Daddy as a reminder that salvation is intended for those in the flock who stray farthest. He punctuated his sentences with dramatic gasps. Sweat rolled down his face. Suddenly he slammed his palms on the pulpit and spun and pointed at Dunn, sitting in the cushioned elder's chair, head down, with his guitar between his knees like a cello.

"I say *Amen* to you! What a revelation!" He strode across and latched his palm onto Dunn's head. "Look at this a-here boy, his daddy killed in such a tragedy. He's got the faith to get up in front of you. Because he knows! He knows his daddy has gone on, waiting for him at Heaven's gate!"

With that, my brother became a paragon of mercy. On his behalf the preacher bestowed grace on Daddy, even though Daddy never accepted one iota of blame. He might have claimed to be sorry, but he led a broken-record life. He could rise up resurrected every day and apologize all over again, but it would never solve the years of wreckage.

In memory he had become eternally impotent to convince me of that old lie Mama always fell for: *I promise, I won't never do it again*. No. He couldn't just die his way out of this turmoil. The whole congregation stood to sing a last hymn about mercy and grace. Grace in unbelievable amounts for us all, for Glenn Daniels. Especially for Glenn Daniels. I pictured snow falling in bolts of pristine white to cover every sin equally. And Daddy pissing his name into it.

At the gravesite, I was the only one cruel enough to myself to be dry-eyed. Grown men stood just outside the tent swabbing at their faces. Some of them Daddy had cheated or threatened drunk. Dunn swiped his nose with the sleeve of his suit coat. Hadn't Daddy whipped him with the same belt he used to whip me? Dunn had gotten the same fists I got, the same brute words. Down the row, Mama gripped a mascara-stained tissue, and even her own mother, Granny Pearl, our refuge from Daddy, was weeping.

The sun stung my eyes, but I didn't want a soul to dare think I was shedding a tear. What would I have chosen to cry over, anyway? My house? Kevin? I had cried a lifetime quota for my baby. I could have told them all, crying is useless for any undoing.

The mechanism lowering Daddy's casket into the ground clicked and the spray of roses shuddered. Grandma Ruby had sprung for that. She seemed jubilant with grief, the mother of the dead. On the way to the church, she'd hummed "Blessed Assurance." She was steady again after a couple of days of fainting spells. She championed everybody to remember *her* version of Daddy, reminding visitors that her boy had been washed in the Blood of the Lamb in the French Broad River when he was ten. Maybe it was his only act of contrition. But what altered him later? I never could reconcile the grownup bully he became with his Sunday-school picture. It couldn't have been a lie, that little tow-headed creature with a cherub's round face.

Whatever she believed made Grandma Ruby sturdy. She would never consider the part she played in making Daddy negligent and selfish. Whenever Mama and Daddy were on the outs, Grandma would come to the trailer and paint a fiction of Daddy laid up at her house heartbroken.

"They're his children. You're his wife." She would plead his case to Mama. "It ain't right treating him this a-way." She pawned off his fury and binges on everybody else's shortcomings. Nobody was immune to her blame, but the central culprit was always his Granddaddy Sims, Grandma Ruby's "Papa." To hear her tell it, Papa was a monster. But it always sounded to me as if she was describing *my* daddy, not hers.

"You ought to get on your knees and thank the good Lord for a daddy like Glenn Daniels. Law, now you take my papa." Her recollections were sermons.

"Now there was a man to reckon with. I ain't saying your daddy is perfect, Glenna. Nobody is. But it don't take the sense God give a turkey to see it's no wonder your daddy wouldn't inherit some of Papa's bad habits. He taught your daddy to cuss up a storm, for one.

"And you want to see drunk? You want to see black and blue? My daddy beat Glenn with the grip of a horse whip one time. Glenn had to learn early to defend hisself. You can't fault him for having to get tough. Papa had fists the size of hams."

My great-granddaddy Sims died when I was four years old. I have just one recollection of him, a shrunken man sucking on a thin, hand-rolled cigarette. He poured coffee out to cool in a saucer which he lifted with trembling hands to a mouthful of gums. Not a tooth in his head. I've never been able to match that timid mummy with Grandma Ruby's monster. I had enough monster of my own to deal with.

But Ev Sims haunted our life as Daddy's scapegoat. Grandma would wipe my face when I cried, until I stopped crying entirely when I hit thirteen. She would wash my legs if the switch or belt Daddy whipped me with had brought blood. She couldn't stand to see the tiniest mark he made, so she put bandages over the bruises.

"You'll live," she'd say. "You bring this on yourself, but be glad it ain't nothing but scratches. 'Spoil the rod and spare the child,' Papa used to say. He beat my poor Glenn within inches of his life many a day, whether he deserved it or not."

I never understood that logic, that any kid *deserves* to be terrorized by somebody big enough to wipe him off the planet. It's because of her stories I wanted to rescue kids from abusive homes. I owe Grandma Ruby my MSW and my profession. I knew she was wrong and yet entirely spot-on to blame her dead daddy for the whippings I got. Even when I got to be taller than she was, she would egg me on to fury. She hated that I had learned to keep from crying, no matter what. She would clutch my hands in hers, as if she could wring tears out of me, trying to break me.

"I swan, you got to see how much your daddy loves you, Glenna. Elsewise he wouldn't get so het up. It's just his nature."

"How can you take up for him?" I would slap at her hands, like claws trying to dig out my sympathy.

"You go on with your stubborn, selfish self," she'd say and shove me away finally. She would cry big sobbing episodes on Daddy's behalf. "If you just knew. You ought to of seen the way my papa done him. You'd cry then. It'd break your heart. But you ain't got a heart."

Carey had made enough mixtapes to get us to California and back five times. Around Nashville it was Dolly and Emmy Lou, Loretta and Tammy. Carey called them "I've-had-it-with-your-crap" songs. We belted it out with Jeannie C. Riley's "Harper Valley P.T.A." Songs Mama used to sing when Daddy was nowhere around. Carey saved the best for last, knowing how I love "These Boots Are Made for Walkin'." Mama always shimmered when she sang that song. But I knew even when I was little that a woman needed more than boots to get out. She needed more than sass.

I didn't have to ask for a replay. Carey played it three times, and we sang at the top of our lungs, hysterical.

"I should have bought you go-go boots!" Carey said.

"I dare you! I would never take them off! That song made me want a pair of white go-go boots my whole life."

Going to Memphis meant a pilgrimage to Graceland, so after Nashville it was Viva Elvis full on. One minute it was the fat self-parody Elvis singing "In the Ghetto," and then it was back to "Blue Suede Shoes."

32

"This is some kind of manic-depressive magical mystery tour here, Carey."

When I tried to see his bag of tricks, he swatted at my hand and swerved out of our lane. "Stop! You'll hear it all in good time."

"So, you're the self-designated Grandmaster Flash. And I don't even get a veto?"

"Let's say you get one veto in every state. But no do-overs. So, you'd better choose well. You want to veto The King?"

"Don't you be talking crazy," I said. "Daddy built up my Elvis tolerance way early on. Lullabies were Elvis all the way. I bet you remember. He and Dunn sang 'Love Me Tender' when I married Dawson. Hell, my daddy taught himself to play 'All Shook Up' on the freaking banjo."

In Daddy's high school yearbook photo, taken just before he dropped out his sophomore year, his hair is in a sleek pompadour. *Enough grease to run a car,* he used to brag. In some of my earliest memories, he is swiveling around the farmhouse kitchen on knee-wrenching, hilarious tiptoe. He'd sing "Little Sister" and try to kiss me with his snurling upper lip. He'd grab Dunn out of his highchair. I'd hang on to his legs like somebody overboard hangs on to a life preserver, my arms and legs weak from spinning and laughing.

"Daddy sang 'Little Sister' to me a hundred times. A thousand, maybe." I turned sideways to look at Carey. "Did I tell you about when we sort of saw Elvis?"

"How can you sort of see Elvis?"

"How did I never tell you this? One summer. I must have been ten or eleven, we followed Elvis."

"You mean, in an Airstream? Like Dead Heads?"

"No." I laughed. "More like stalking. He played a concert at the Johnson City auditorium. So, we went to see if we could find where he was staying."

Even if we'd had money for tickets, the show was sold out. But Daddy found out Elvis was staying in Bristol. We drove round and round, criss-crossed State Street a dozen times, where the town straddles the Virginia-Tennessee line.

"Look for a tour bus," Daddy coached. He swerved as he looked. "Or a limousine. They'll be some kind of a sign."

We all knew better than to try and talk Daddy down. And nobody wanted to. He was in one of those rare moods, so golden we went to an A&W for burgers and the first root beer floats Dunn and I ever had. Mama fed Daddy french fries while he drove and fanned him with a church bulletin. Finally, amazingly, the clue Daddy wanted, at a little hole-in-the-wall motel. Every window on the top floor plastered with aluminum foil.

Daddy's mouth hung open. "Well, I'll be damned," he said.

We sat idling in the parking lot of that two-story motel, built cockeyed under an embankment of kudzu. The midday heat seemed to come from those silver squares glaring down on us.

"What's it mean?" Dunn asked.

"Means he's got more money than God," Mama said. "He can rent ever room so they ain't nobody stomping around to keep him up. And can't nobody figure what room he's in."

Daddy cut the motor and got out of the car. He took off his cap and held it to his chest, as if he were at a military funeral.

I pictured Elvis sprawled on a bed the size of a tank, the slab of him snoring in a huge deep freeze. Nobody believed his fetishes then, just a few years before he died, rooms as dark as the grave, peaceful as death, no noise, no light, no memory in the narcotic dark. But we saw firsthand.

"That was maybe the best time we ever had," I told Carey. "Chasing down an American fantasy."

Memphis looked big, but once we got through downtown, the Mississippi River dwarfed the city. Carey drove straight to it. I hadn't understood until I saw. A demarcation, he called it, between the pioneers and the rest of America. A world class river, like the Amazon or the Nile, a rolling boundary, daunting to cross, dividing East from West, before from after. The line between now and the rest of my life.

Mustiness and fish-smell filled up the car. Carey pointed to the huge pyramid built on Mud Island, which I'd seen in that lawyer movie with Tom Cruise. Clouds reflected in the tilt of its black glass.

"I mean, it's perverse," Carey said, "putting up all these pyramids. The Luxor in Vegas and the one at the Louvre. At least in Memphis it makes sense." He seemed gratified when I had no clue what he meant. "Memphis? The capital of ancient Egypt? Pyramids? Architects love to throw up a pyramid like a damn carnival tent. People forget, a pyramid is a grave."

He droned on about burials and mummies while I rubbernecked to see the tops of buildings, glass and steel and concrete. The city was nothing to Carey. But outside my one trip to Atlanta, this was the most extravagant organized chaos I'd ever seen, traffic and neon and sidewalks and sirens and people crossing like the unstoppable current of the river.

Beale Street, on the other hand, stretched in the late afternoon sun like a comatose hound. We parked the car in a gravel lot and walked past open doorways to the tune of clinking barware being set up for a big night ahead. Down the way somebody swept the sidewalk. Carey checked his watch again while I peered into a pawnshop, spangly drum sets in the window. Like shining fish electric guitars suspended from the ceiling on nylon wire.

"We should have made our Graceland reservation for earlier," Carey said. "Then get a hotel and see Beale Street when things wind up after dark."

"You're the one who said we should reserve late tickets because it would take us till five o'clock to get here. And we already decided to camp our first night."

"No," he said. "I told you we'd gain an hour. And that it would be too hot to camp. We could've done Graceland, then go see the ducks at the Peabody. I'll spring for hotels, I told you."

"Why are you obsessed with ducks at a motel?"

"Hotel," he corrected me. "It's primo Americana. Best of all the kitsch and weirdness Stan wrote about in his dissertation. Ducks parading out of this marble fountain, and down the red carpet. Tourists snapping pictures like paparazzi."

"We can see ducks at every pond across the country."

He stopped and took my hand, blinking foolishly. "Aw. Is this our first fight?"

We came to the edge of a little park and squinted up at the stout bronze man holding a trumpet. A jet glinted high in the sky like a needle on blue felt.

"W. C. Handy," I said.

Carey read the plaque. He raised his eyebrows. "So you don't know Memphis was in Egypt, but you know who this guy is?"

"Look at you, freaked because I know something you don't! You forget. Kevin ate, slept, breathed music." We looked up again. "Eats. Sleeps. Still."

At a dive near Schwab's dry goods store—a relic full of relics—we drank a couple of happy hour drafts. We were the only customers besides two white kids. Their guitar cases might have been full of air. White faces served us. White hands dried highball glasses. Black faces stared down from frames on shelves between old liquor bottles.

Through a staticky speaker, snare drums and a saxophone played against a trickle of piano notes. "You know these?" Carey nodded at the photos.

"Some." I craned my head. "That's John Lee Hooker. I think that's Howlin' Wolf. Muddy Waters. Big Mama Thornton. She's the one who really wrote 'Hound Dog.'"

I pointed. "You have to know Robert Johnson. Surely." Out of the photo his ebony eyes looked straight into mine, a cigarette hanging off the blister of his lower lip. He bent over his guitar as if protecting a child. "Kevin called him 'Oblivious Divinity.' Said there wouldn't be rock and roll without him. All these people got ripped off by white musicians."

"Right. The one who sold his soul to Satan so he could play." Carey looked at his watch. "Shit. Time to get to Graceland." He stood up and drained his beer. Billie Holiday's wracked voice followed us out. Every bar we passed was hollow as a mausoleum with piped-in music. Somebody dead singing everywhere.

When I was first with Kevin, understanding his music was like working a math problem. He said, okay, hit rewind, and started me on some gateway songwriters he said were kin to Loretta and Tammy Wynette. He played me Nina Simone and Big Mama Thornton. He'd have me drive all over creation while he played cassette tapes he had lined up. I knew where I stood right away. He told me about an old girlfriend who gave him an ultimatum. "Her or my sax." He grinned that grin. "Now. What's a poor boy to do?"

The saving grace was that he loved old-time and bluegrass as much as jazz. I could understand his fiddle just fine. And so could Daddy. Maybe the biggest surprise about Kevin was that Daddy liked him. Even though Kevin is a Teva-wearing agnostic, urban liberal, and Daddy was a backslid Free Will Baptist, disenfranchised-agrarian Republican, hillbilly music gave them a common ground. The two of them and my brother Dunn formed an easy trio. Another surprise: Dunn wasn't jealous of the two of them when Kevin would join in. But I was.

Daddy tried me out on the banjo when I was eight, way before he started teaching Dunn to play. He would lift me to stand on an old milking stool he dragged into the farmhouse kitchen and lay the banjo like a baby in my arms. He stood behind, forearms around me, his hands on top of mine. There was no written music. I mimicked his fingers on the strings.

One day he let me go, like a kid on a bike. My hands remembered the way. I could feel the echo of his touch for a few phrases, when to tug the strings, where to press against the frets. Daddy clapped and clogged around the kitchen, hollering and laughing.

For a while after I made such a splash, I couldn't stop practicing and pleasing my daddy. I played every day after school until my fingers were callused. I worked up a few simple songs pretty handily. I loved how the tones vibrated into my ribcage. When I held that banjo against me, it warmed up like Daddy had, proud of me, happy. I could make wood and metal and strings happy. So, there was no telling where my very first power might carry me.

By summer I was sitting comfortably with the banjo on my lap. I could keep up while Daddy's sang without missing any notes. Then one Saturday morning as we sat in facing chairs in the farmhouse kitchen, Daddy laid his hands on the frets and stopped me. He pulled the banjo out of my arms.

"Now, you go on, sing while I pick awhile." He grinned and nodded. "I know you know 'Little Liza Jane.'"

There flared up a hot realization, how mute I'd sat all those weeks. I had never sung along before. My throat seized up with nerves. The words were easy to say from memory, but I was a rusty pipe squeaking.

"You ain't singing, Sister. You can't just talk out the verses. Sing, girl!" Daddy started over on the banjo and I cleared my throat. I was used to singing hymns in church with adult voices layered over mine. To sing alone was terrifying, but I tried to let the notes rise up simple as breath out of my chest. There was only Daddy, after all, smiling over his banjo.

"Whoa! Whoa, Sister. Back up and try again." He laughed and started over a second time. I pushed the song up out of me. He stopped playing again, doubled over laughing. He set the banjo on the kitchen table and hopped around laughing until tears beaded up on his cheeks.

"Lord, God, Faye, come listen here at this young 'un."

I refused to sing for her. He told Mama I couldn't carry a tune in a bucket. He laughed at me, and she started giggling, too, with a nervous question on her face. He laid the banjo and guitar in their cases. My lesson was over.

The next night after supper, Daddy seemed to think we'd pick right up where we left off. I surprised him right back by not even opening up the banjo case. He played a few licks on his guitar. I could tell he was getting mad, but I didn't budge. He finally forced the banjo into my hands. I set it down.

"What do you think I want to play the damn banjo for, anyway?"

He slapped me for sassing. And then he smacked me again for cussing him. I know what I said. The same thing I said the morning before he died, that I didn't have to take his shit. He yanked a hank of hair out of my scalp that night, the first time. When I wouldn't budge, he made me sit on the milking stool holding the banjo until my arms were shaking. I nearly fell off in my sleep after he made Mama come to bed and leave me. But I never plucked one more string. Who finally carried me to bed? I never asked or remembered. When I got up the next morning, the banjo was in its case, leaning in the corner like a punished child.

How loose and easy Dunny held that same family banjo. And had a deep, beautiful singing voice. Daddy always told people that someday Dunn would sing at his funeral.

Their voices changed people, made them stand up in church and cry as everybody sang along, made people sway in the dark or jump up and buck dance. From the time Dunn was ten or eleven, he and Daddy played on porches, in church fellowship halls and honky tonks, standing on industrial pallets for a stage. Mama and I could only watch and listen and wonder how these were the same dark and silent men we lived with every day. Their voices purled and blended, and when the time was right, they shifted to cause—I swear—a chemical reaction in the crowd, bubbling up like self-rising flour and buttermilk. They closed their blue eyes at the same tone or word. I could hardly stand sometimes to feel the warm spark pass between them and zing around the room into every other person within earshot.

Kevin fit in with my daddy and brother the way other musicians did—who-ever happened along who could keep up. Plenty of summer nights the three of them pulled out lawn chairs behind the trailer, and before it was over, a group of men and kids gathered to listen or join the picking. Mama and I would wash up supper dishes and watch through the kitchen window until all we could see were the orange tips of the cigars they smoked to keep away mosquitoes. Their silhouettes dissolved until they were nothing but sound.

I tried to hide that I was jealous of what they knew in common.

"It's okay you don't play. Not everybody from Appalachia plays music," Kevin said. "That's a stereotype."

"Doesn't matter. Daddy holds it against me, just like the fact I don't like poke salad, and won't own a gun. Oh, and I don't know how to quilt."

"Well, I won't judge you for not being Super Hillbilly." Kevin laughed. I hadn't told him at that time about the few months I tried to learn or began to learn. Why mention such a shame, and that sore contention that had started my rebellion against Daddy? I didn't know where to start the truth about Daddy's musical hands, his open hands, how they turned against me into fists.

Kevin couldn't hide his surprise whenever he knew something about Appalachia that I didn't. One Saturday evening he had his heyday, showing our whole family one of the proudest places in the region. You can have Christmas and all the stressed-out, drunken holidays. All that expectation led to trauma in our family. No. The best times with my daddy were spontaneous. It really threw Kevin when I didn't know about the Carter Fold. He badgered me to remember family outings there that never happened.

"Surely Glenn took you when you were little, and you just don't remember. It's not two hours from Newport." He rubbed his beard and showed me the brochure. A photo of Mama Maybelle and A.P. and Sara. "They play every Saturday night. Not these three, of course."

"Well, that would really be something to see, wouldn't it? Ghost pickers."

"Close as we can ever get, some Carter descendant still plays. Every Saturday since 1974. No way you've never been."

"Call Daddy and ask him," I said. "Maybe he took Dunn. But not me." I dialed the number and handed him the phone. "It's your party."

When Daddy said he'd never heard of the place either, Kevin went into hyperdrive. In less than an hour we were in Newport. Mama and I packed some cold fried chicken and Little Debbies, and Cokes and a six-pack of Bud in the cooler, and Kevin showed Daddy the map. I got squeezed into the backseat of my own car between Mama and Dunny after Kevin offered Daddy shotgun. By the time we hit I-81, they had gone through the entire history of the Carter family, starting before the famous 1927 recording sessions in Bristol.

"Is there a quiz?" I jabbed Dunn, but his head lolled against the window. He was drooling in his sleep. Mama snapped her gum, craving a cigarette, I knew. Her eyes followed fields of grasshopper yellow tobacco, cut and staked like tilted teepees.

Daddy and Kevin talked in the front seat, flipping from one radio station to the next, working to find just the right country stations, so they could quiz each other and lord over the rest of us. When we turned onto winding roads off the interstate, and the close mountains blocked our reception, Kevin put in a tape of John Coltrane. Daddy couldn't have understood one note, but instead of his usual gripe about "ear pollution," he kept saying, "Well, I'll be damned. Now, where'd you hear this?"

The sign we had arrived was a slew of cars parked up and down the narrow back road. Kevin passed a full gravel lot and parked on the grassy shoulder. Mama scrambled out of the backseat. She lit up and leaned against the car. Daddy went for the cooler and opened a beer. Kevin had already told them: no drinking or smoking inside.

Kevin said he and I would go buy tickets for everybody, that we'd meet them at the door, and he pointed at one of the biggest barns I've ever seen. Dunn made a beeline for who knows what. Kevin and I pushed through crowds milling around cars parked in the shade. "So, seriously. Saturday night in a barn?"

"You wait, Miss Skeptic," Kevin said.

He nodded to three guys tuning up around the back end of a pickup and then he slowed and took my hand. He made sure I saw the band's banjo player.

She was sitting on the tailgate where she changed her baby's diaper. She tuned the banjo laid across her lap whenever she had a free hand, a queen on a Chevrolet throne. The baby curled his fists and squealed and pumped his legs every time she gave the banjo a twang. Kevin squeezed my hand hard, but I didn't dare look to see the want and hope on his face. I couldn't have been more jealous of anybody in the world than that banjo picker with her baby. In that crowd, loud and pressing us, Kevin and I were suddenly alone. Not even married yet, but we understood the desperate sense that what came so easy to other people—family, peace, kids—might not come to us. We might never know the wholeness of putting the best of ourselves into a little genetic combination of us.

I looked for Mama. She was beside Daddy several people behind us, standing discombobulated with her hands folded across her chest. Those were my genetics. Those were my nurturers. Why did I even want to continue that cosmic thread? Cosmic threat, more like it. What kind of mother could I possibly be with them as my makers? Stunted. Would I lash out at a child with no way to stop myself? Wronged and damaged. Could Daddy have stopped himself? Dunn and I were the best they could do. That thought made me sink somewhere inside.

I could see as we bought our tickets that the place truly was just a huge silvered-oak barn. The line pressed behind us. "We better get some seats," Kevin said.

We found Dunn and told him to wait at the door with tickets for Mama and Daddy. Kevin led me up the sloping dirt floor, along bleachers made from school bus seats set on old railroad ties tacked over with carpet. We settled onto a rump-sprung bench seat in an open row. The wall behind the stage was covered with carpet samples, an acoustic crazy quilt. A group checked microphones, and people were already eating popcorn and passing fountain drinks back and forth. Above, there wasn't an actual ceiling, just the galvanized underside of barn roof. Speakers hung from the oak rafters near big, slow-spinning fans.

Just as people stood whooping and clapping, Mama and Daddy and Dunn squeezed along our row. The old Carter brother and sister, Janette and Joe, came onto the stage and after applause made introductions like folks trying to hide their pride at a Thanksgiving feast. She was broad from her head of iron gray to the hem of her long dress and launched us right into revival territory. Old time religion. They opened with "Shall We Gather at the River." Then they dug deep with "The Old Rugged Cross."

"You think we're all about to get baptized?" I whispered to Kevin.

"It's a conversion experience. That's for sure," he said, pointing at Daddy whose face hung open and expectant like a kid's.

Janette asked who was there for the first time, and like reluctant church visitors, we raised our hands, along with half the audience. When she asked who had come the furthest, people shouted out, South Dakota, Hawaii, Mexico. There was a whole family from Luxembourg.

I poked Kevin in the ribs. "Now how'd those people get here, and my daddy never heard of this place?"

"That's what I want to know." He had to shout a little above the clapping and the ballad Janette started up.

I think everybody faded a little through the repetitive verses, but Janette breathed heavily into the mic and welcomed us again, glancing off stage over and over, stalling. Two guys adjusted the microphones and brought out two, then three guitars.

"We got a real special treat for y'all tonight." She breathed roughly again and beamed.

"Something's up," Kevin said. "Look at the stage hands hustling."

"A real special guest who's been awful kind to come on out and sing a spell for us. He's been real good to us and our whole family over the years, and well, he's been a part of our family for years, and we're just proud as we can be to have him."

Kevin put his mouth up to my ear and whispered, "Johnny Cash is here." His eyes flashed as he leaned back, but his face was serious. A buzz went through the audience, and I could hear people repeating Johnny Cash's name.

"Don't even shit me," I said. "That would never happen."

"Why not? He's married to June Carter. You know that, right? They have a house here on her family land."

I looked across Kevin at Daddy, leaning so far forward he nearly had his nose in the big hair of the woman in front of him.

"Please welcome to our stage," Janette pulled at the mic and interrupted her introduction again. "And like I said, we're just pleased and real honored, and you folks should be too, to have him back with us here at the Carter Fold."

Kevin squeezed my hand and stood up.

"Give a big welcome to Mr. Johnny Cash!"

Daddy reared up and out of his seat and fell back so hard I worried for a split second about his heart. The whole audience went wild, whistling and hooting. Dunn and Daddy pulled each other up by elbow and shirt sleeve and collar as an ovation blocked their view of the Man in Black, black from boots to hair, striding to the center of the stage. He was a surprisingly big man, broad-chested, and his wide, wrinkled face and neck were ruddy tan, as if he were choking in his tight, high black collar.

He rolled his fist around the microphone, bent forward and in a happy growl said, "Hello. I'm Johnny Cash."

Mama looked at Kevin and me as if we had resurrected Jesus himself, her mouth open in a slack grin, one hand in her blonde hair.

The buzz and talk never stopped as Johnny Cash went through humble thanks, people careening against one another to run down front and snap photos as he broke into "Folsom Prison Blues." I could hardly take my eyes off Daddy's rapt face as he mouthed the words like a prayer. I guess he had sung that song as many times as Johnny Cash himself. He made that song his anthem after the year he spent in prison.

The clotted, strangled voice grew more solid through a couple more old favorites, but the notes in the last number disappeared in a palsied shiver. Johnny Cash was a man nearing the end of his career, the last years of his life. His wide guitar was barely audible as he closed with the old hymn "Wayfaring Stranger," which I thought Daddy didn't like. It was one song he always, always refused to sing. Whenever anyone requested it, he was likely to get downright pissy.

But that night, people in front of us turned around at the sound of Daddy's harmony to the mournful, hopeful chorus:

"I'm going there to see my mother. I'm going there no more to roam.
I am just going over Jordan. I am just going over home."

On the last verse, Daddy stopped singing and pulled a bandanna out of the back pocket of his overalls. He sat and pawed at his eyes, suddenly small in the crowd around him. He leaned up as the song ended and pulled Mama to him, across Dunn. He kissed her quickly, a mark of affection I hadn't seen between them in years. Big oily tears ran down his cheeks.

I was so caught up watching Daddy that Johnny Cash left the stage before

I was aware, and the audience roared for more. But he didn't reappear. I leaned into Mama as we clapped. I pointed at Daddy with my elbow. I had to yell into her ear over the noise. "What's with the waterworks? All for Johnny Cash."

She shook her head at me. When things got quieter, she leaned close. "Your daddy ain't crying over Johnny Cash. That's the hymn he sung at his Granddaddy Sims's funeral." The man who had left Daddy for dead in an August hay field. Broken leg that never healed. She could see my confusion and leaned back to look at me again with meaning. Her words found me out, a reckoning with my own antagonizer.

She said, "He may have been a son of a bitch, but he was your daddy's son of a bitch."

"Do they have an ambulance waiting outside?" I asked Kevin as the Konnarock Critters lit into another rousing round. The young mother we'd seen was wailing on her banjo. The fiddle rang around her intense licks. I thought her hair might catch fire if it touched the strings.

"You mean for that guy?" He pointed at a huge man who was dancing like somebody might shoot him if he stopped. Below the stage a slab of concrete was worn to a sheen, a mosh pit for old mountain cloggers. They jigged around each other like clothes in a washing machine, flannel shirts and dungarees and more overalls than I'd seen in one place in years.

"Those two have to be in their nineties." I pointed to a couple so stooped they couldn't look one another in the face.

Daddy danced, like lots of the other buck dancers, by himself. He was red-faced and sweaty. He had made Mama go out for one good two-step, but she had been on her feet all morning at the shop. As if he'd had a miracle cure, his bum leg worked fine.

He was suddenly a face in the crowd I barely remembered, dancing the old way, evolved from ancient Scots-Irish reels, his upper body tucked loosely into itself. Head and neck and torso and arms held still while he worked his feet. He lifted his knees at the high notes, and his thick legs jolted in their disjointed jerk. His hands hung limp and harmless at his sides.

At the end of each song, the dancers dispersed. Most of them barely retook their seats before another song tempted them back. We clapped as Daddy came heaving back up the sloping aisle.

He reached for me just as the next song started and pulled me up by the arm before I could resist. We did a tug of war in the aisle until he had me laughing.

"Listen, Sister, let's us go around just once. They're tuning up for 'Little Liza Jane.' Remember when you used to play that one on that old banjo we had?"

That sobered me, and I pulled back and sat down. "You know I never could play."

He sat with a thud beside me, breathing hard. His face was a question. "Why I know good and well you did." He laughed at Kevin across me. "She said a banjo wasn't good for nothing but making a hillbilly racket. But she sure made it sing!"

"I never said that."

He laughed. "You should of stuck with it, Sister. Never stuck with nothing. Throwed off the banjo and then it was on to baton and then it was wanting to be in the damn Girl Scouts all the way to Morristown and back. But you played basketball in high school for a good while, didn't you?"

"I knew about the basketball," Kevin said to me. "But you never told me you picked a banjo."

"I never was a bit of good at it," I said. "That's why."

"The hell you wasn't," Daddy said. He leaned toward Kevin again. "I swear, I never seen such a girl, Kevin. She was playing songs on that banjo it took me three years to figure out. Don't you remember, Sister?" He slapped my thigh and squeezed my knee. Kevin's look went back and forth. He beamed at Daddy and looked at me like somebody might an animal they'd never spotted before.

"Don't believe a word out of his mouth," I said to Kevin. "I'm not just being humble. He knows it was all his doing. He'd stand behind me and play the notes with my fingers. How hard could that be?"

"I never done it!" Daddy looked truly hurt.

"Now who doesn't remember?" I tried a weak laugh. To keep the peace, to keep from wading into my own history too deep.

He shrugged at Kevin. "Stubborn as a mule. Bull-headed. But that's why you was good at it, Sister. Why, hell, you could have—Kevin, she could have been as good as that girl up there. She was that good, I reckon."

Kevin smiled at me proudly, but he rearranged his face when he saw my expression. Daddy didn't remember his hands helping me get music out of those burning strings, pressing my fingers until they hurt. He didn't remember teaching me to breathe when he breathed, to steady my back against his chest. That was the closest we ever held one another, hours and hours with his arms around me. Maybe he didn't remember making fun of my brave, awful voice.

Daddy stood up. "You forget how to dance, too?" He held out his big empty palm to me. The same palm that slapped me, that curled into a fist and hit Mama, hit Dunn. Hit me. Had he made more havoc than music? The two always twined together with Glenn Daniels, the volatile abuse and the volatile high times.

I looked to his face, which made even less sense than his hand reaching for me. He wanted to force me, but his eyes flickered with his narrowing choices. He felt around inside for his switch, careful in that dark where I knew him so well. He gleamed with ruddy joy, joy as bossy and hard as his rage. He pulled his hand back and rubbed it down the gallus on his overalls and smiled at Kevin.

"Suit yourself, Sister." He turned and buck danced like a court jester down the aisle, smiling at strangers. I'd fixed it so he would never dare ask me again. But I paid for my win with a moment of the old tremor. There would be hell to pay. Always he would remember my refusal. One more refusal to punish. How did I sit there and sit there? He could live it up all over again, knowing I wasn't hurting anybody but myself.

Graceland is hard to find.

Carey swore we left Beale Street in plenty of time to make our tour. He said he was sure he would have remembered the backstreets he and Stan had taken to get there. Past railroad tracks he crossed and re-crossed, industrial parks we turned round and round in, through slums and projects and shopping centers that he found unfamiliar, finally on the highway we were looking for, we hit a snarl in traffic.

"It's a wreck. I can see." He tapped his fingers on the steering wheel and checked his watch again.

"It's fifteen 'til." I held our tickets in my hand like playing cards.

"We'll make it. I promise."

Past the clotted crossroads, faded clapboard houses gave way to pastures and trailer parks, and revived to half-boarded-up strip malls. We passed flat-busted, rusted-out gas stations. Laundromats and Chinese restaurants, liquor stores and pawn shops and check-cashing rental centers. At red-light intersections, black people waited for evening buses on cracked sidewalks crawling with weeds.

Everything that had grown up along Elvis Presley Boulevard was the red-headed stepchild of Graceland. The tacky hugged up to the decadent, just like Elvis. Poverty surrounded the kingdom. Finally, down the highway, we spotted the entrance to Graceland, but we hit every light red behind delivery trucks and grandma drivers. Carey's Elvis tape was on its third go-round for the day. The dashboard clock gave us two minutes to make our tour, the last tour of the day.

Somehow, ten minutes later, Carey still believed we'd make it, some miracle would happen and we'd slip through the gates. He bottomed out on a speed bump in the parking lot, did a half-doughnut into a parking space.

"Where do we go?" I caught a little of his faith. We got out and slammed our car doors, running as we looked. I could see the visitor center and Elvis's jets.

"Yeah, this way. Come on, Glenna!"

The girl at the counter told us the last tour bus had just left. Carey argued with her about our tickets. He asked for the manager, asked for a refund, a rain check for the next day. All sold out. I looked out the windows, trying to see Graceland, but there were just cars and pavement and walls.

Outside the visitor center, he pointed across the highway. At the crest of a long hill, obscure in the shade of tall trees, Graceland sat like a movie set fa-cade. I squinted to try and make it fit what I'd imagined: some opulent, gloried spectacle. Instead, it was just a subdivision house on steroids. White columns and a bland, overblown confection of mortar and brick. It tried too hard. We walked through the lot and when traffic stopped for the light, we crossed the highway to the foot of the sloping driveway.

Elvis may have built the first gated community, all to himself. The double, gilded gate was enormous, the two sides shaped like elaborate harps. The tour bus was parked at the top of the hill and visitors were piling out.

"We just missed it," I said.

"I'm sorry, Glenna," Carey said for the dozenth time. "I'm so, so sorry! This is all my fault."

"Will you for God's sake give it a rest, Carey?"

"But it's all my fault."

"It's not your fault! What is it, anyway, that people come to see?" We kept watching the gate as if it might swing open for us. "Nothing but a gaudy house nobody lives in with a kitchen nobody uses. Pianos and guitars nobody plays. A swimming pool nobody swims in."

"Well, people come to see where he's buried. With his parents."

"What kind of people pay to see some stranger's grave? People who probably never even go to their own family's graves."

"I know you're just trying to make me feel better," Carey said. "But you have to be disappointed."

"Name me one thing that's *not* disappointing." I turned my back on the whole place and pushed the button for the crossing light. "The city on a hill. Is that what Elvis wanted? Some kind of paradise for himself to show off? I've been remembering, when I was a kid, all those descriptions of heaven, all the stuff about streets paved in gold? That freaked me out. And all the crowds. Like this place, with bajillions of people?"

"I don't think that many people get in," Carey said.

"You mean here or actual heaven?" The light changed and we headed back toward the car. "So, do you believe in it?"

"Heaven?" His voice squeaked.

"I guess that's too personal?"

"Well, I mean, no. We've been personal from way back, but I mean—"

"We've never talked about it before, have we? With Stan, about him, I never asked. And I wasn't there."

"I think—I mean, I think it doesn't matter what anybody believes," he said. "I mean, is there an omnipotent being so needy that he—she, it, whatev-er—requires you *have* to believe, like Tinkerbell or Santa Claus, and then you get to come to the party?"

We came to the parking lot, and he stopped to look back at Graceland. I kept walking and he caught up. At the car I grabbed the car door handle and willed myself not to look back.

"I really try not to think about it," he said. "I mean, when I think about Stan being somewhere, anywhere, without me, it could drive me a little loony." He laughed softly. "Or watching me, I mean, eat oatmeal or drive to work? It's just not something I can dwell on. I know you and Glenn weren't—well, it was rough. But when somebody dies—Give it time."

We got into the car. I could have told Carey about the baby then, that I imagined that lost child somewhere, okay and whole. But why did it have to be a kid? Maybe that soul, or whatever, was ancient. Maybe an old spirit just trying to get back to another start. What were the words that could do any of it justice? I had never sensed a body or the slightest flutter, but there was an essence, something separate from me. But with me. People around the globe argue about when it's a baby. I had learned the hard way, it's a baby when you believe it is. I just hadn't believed hard enough, maybe.

As if he could read my brain, Carey said, "Maybe heaven's nothing more than what we want to believe. A wish." He started the car and closed his door. The A/C washed across me.

"So, you think we get a do-over?" I said.

"Remember? Tickets for tomorrow morning are sold-out," he said.

At first, I didn't follow him. "No, a cosmic redo, to go back and fix our mistakes."

"Oh, that's way too hopeful." He pulled onto the highway, heading west again. "I mean, that could be a hell of a lot of work. Like AA? Making amends?"

"Just little things. But maybe we get to pick what the do-over is," I said. "My daddy had a beautiful voice. It was the best thing about him."

I couldn't say out loud what I wished. A person's death is not like candles on a birthday cake. I told Carey I really needed to leave the music off for the drive to the campground. If I couldn't hear Daddy singing "Little Sister" ever again, the way he used to sing it—just to me—then I didn't want to hear anybody sing it.

The Sun and the Moon
and the Stars

Flat on my back in the dark tent on the outskirts of Memphis, I gave myself up to the Mississippi. That river might just smell like the inside of a uterus, promising and ripe with muscular mystery. Way past midnight a baby cried in the campground, a phantom sound, heartless and wounding. My secret burrowed into me, the way the root wad underneath the tent was grinding into my pelvis. I shifted crazy restless from the stifling heat and wished Carey were awake. My whole torso smothered, a caul of sweat on my face and neck. My pulse beat in my gut like the throb of umbilical sap, the humid mop of my hair, my crotch, every inch of me on the verge.

For the first time in my thirty-six years, Mama was in a different time zone. Not a waking soul within four hundred miles knew me. The sizzle of a mosquito sent me flailing up, like a fish against the pull of lake water. I slapped at the noise, but Carey didn't budge. Even when I crawled around to check the tent zippers, he shifted unfazed. His boxers glowed pale, both arms flung over his head. Victorious. Back on the high school dive team, he would stand above the crowds, stretch his arms and plunge through the air, a falling star. What wish did I make on him?

Across the Mississippi River the next morning, Arkansas opened like the big old muddy palm of God. On the bridge I held my breath for what was next. More road. And then more road, riding a narrow ridge between soggy cultivated miles. Levees rose up from time to time between shoals and bottomland and whorled rice fields. Lifelines of dark trees pointed to the horizon. Sitting still at seventy miles an hour was a whole new kind of bored anxiety. I took off my watch and put it in the glove box. I'd tell time by the sun, which finally broke through the humid overcast behind us.

In rows perpendicular to the interstate, a sporadic burnish of green lit up, new growth tender and fine as hair. The furrows flashed by in a mesmerizing flicker, a sort of visual noise, like the song a comb makes when you zip along the teeth. When I was little, I drove Mama crazy at her beauty shop, zinging every comb I could lay my hands on. As I got older, she gave me an allowance to pitch-in after school and during summer. My favorite task was cleaning combs in tall beakers of blue disinfectant. Before laying them out on towels to dry, she flung off the excess. But my method was to run my thumbnail across the tines. Metal or plastic, long, broad, or thin, every comb had its own tone, the smallest stringed instruments in the world.

Mama's shop was the most solid place I knew after Daddy burned the farmhouse. As much as I hated the cramped trailer, I loved the downtown storefront she still rents to this day. Daddy never came there. No men allowed was the unspoken rule, not even Dunn. In that rowdy safe house of gossipy, giggling women, I could depend on hairspray, apple-scented shampoo, peanut butter crackers, and the hum of the Coke machine. I could depend on Mama. "Faye's Clip 'n' Curl" kept us all clothed and fed while Daddy was perpetually between jobs. My mother never went to cosmetology school or studied business. She apprenticed a little in high school, but she figured out all on her own how to perm and dye and balance her books. Our future was secure on her native talents.

Security wasn't the only comfort, though. Working, we inhabited a vacuum. We lived one minute to the next, without worrying what went before or what came next. Mama kept the shop open twelve, thirteen hours a day because when a woman's hands are busy, she doesn't have to think. I didn't have time for self-pity or anger, not even homesickness for the farm. There was only laundering towels, sweeping up hair between customers, and keeping us on schedule. That routine numbed my questioning. So much that I didn't realize Mama held control over more than just making a living.

I never asked, never thought to, what became of our farm. And if my own house in Knoxville hadn't burned Mama would still have her secrets, just like I have my own. I didn't know the burdens she held all those years behind her boundaries. But she spilled them all into my life. And then they would be my burdens.

It is hard to fathom that for a quarter of a century, Faye Daniels has coifed and maneuvered the unruliest heads in Newport. She curls straight hair and straightens curly hair. Half-bald old women can't tell where their own hair stops, and their weaves start. Women still come in who want Tammy Wynette hair. Nobody in town does teased, bleached hair like Mama, piled high as meringue on custard pies. And it's not a job she likes, but she has dolled-up plenty of customers to look better than ever in their open caskets.

As talented as she is with special effects, Mama is a genius with a simple haircut. "The secret," she says, "is what any man knows: You got to have the right tool for the job."

Every month, little by little as her business grew, she invested in expensive combs and an arsenal of scissors she still sharpens herself on one of her granddaddy's old whetstones. Nobody but Mama ever once cut my hair. She tended my long curls like a fine vineyard, with expensive German-made scissors. When I was young with bangs and layers, she used three or four different comb and scissor combinations. My hair has been one long length for half my life. She might spend ten minutes beveling the ends for a fuller spill down my back.

In a world of perms and big hair, Mama and I have stood our ground with what nature gave us. Of course, rumors still run amok that she peroxides her hair, but that wash-and-wear, loose blonde bob is the god-given highlight of her, the sophisticated sweep of waves completely mismatched with her flannel shirts and Wrangler jeans.

Granny Pearl cut off Mama's pigtails when she was just nine and never let her grow her hair long again. I used to beg her to let it grow. Mama only said her hair was too fine and fly-away.

"Your hair is strong enough that it's healthy long," she explained. "It says somewhere in the Bible that long hair on a woman is her glory. Your Grandma Ruby'd preach you chapter and verse. But what they don't tell you is that long hair is a hell of a lot of work."

She laughed. "Not everybody's got a mama who gives them hundred dollar hair cuts for free. Way I see it, your hair is *my* glory." I envied her blonde, but Mama made me feel radiant even with my plain brown. I outshined everybody, her brightest star.

Mama was proudest of my hair loose in natural air-dried coils. But for weddings or funerals she'd tame it on big rollers into broad swoops. Or she'd up-do it in a formal heavy twist. For really special events she'd work two hours to finish a single French braid. Even that thick, condensed plait hung long.

She worried about damage to my hair, but when I was a teenager, once in a while she'd iron it, lank as a horse's tail. Without the curl it hung like velvet drapery. With hair as heavy on my head as a jeweled veil, I knew the prowess of a queen. I started high school at thirteen, learning my body among boys who were clumsy and shy. With them, my hair was a source of safe flirtation. I learned the command I could wield through trial and error, shapeshifting to suit my needs. Days I wore a ponytail, I couldn't count on arousing much of a fan club. But when my hair spilled like a perfumed waterfall, nobody with a penis could pay attention in class. I left Daddy and his trashy kingdom behind to walk high school hallways as if through parted walls of water. Mama bestowed on me the power to beguile.

The twist was, the tool of my seduction was also the source of my weakness. I learned in the world of real, adult relationships, my dominion had limits.

49

Attracting a man led to pleasing him, and pleasing him meant accepting that eventually he would tell me how to dress, when to be where, and worst of all, he'd tell me how to wear my hair. Every boyfriend, then Dawson, Sam, and even Kevin, all had in common that they saw my hair as evidence of ownership, as if they had staked a mining claim or sunk a flag into new territory. There was never a treaty signed, but I understood I had new boundaries. I wasn't a wild thing anymore.

After all his talk that he loved me for being my own person, even Kevin made me promise, just like I promised Dawson and Sam, that no matter how wrinkled I got, no matter how much gray showed, I'd keep my hair long for him.

"Whatever you do," he said, "no matter what, just because you're past thirty doesn't mean you have to get that boring soccer mom cut."

I felt the threat rise up in me like a bargain with God or the devil. "You ought to know by now," I said, "I would shave my head bald every day for the rest of my life for just the outside chance to be somebody's soccer mom."

After I lost the baby and then my house, all those weeks I lived with Mama in the trailer, I could hardly put my feet on the ground in the mornings, much less wash and manage that lifelong weight. My hair was exhausting. Whenever Mama coaxed me to the shop to wash it, I showed her magazine photos of short bobs and even shorter boyish pixie cuts. She got so pissed. But for me just the thought of cutting my hair was like a doorway into a new life, exhilarating to imagine. Why not sacrifice the last precious thing I had, the feature that defined who I had been? I wasn't her any longer.

And for once, my hair had nothing to do with a man. Chopping it off? That big of a gesture was the surest way to break Mama's control. She wanted to settle me down again in Newport. Cutting my hair was the only way to convince her that I had to leave with Carey to save my own life, like severing an umbilical cord, the flesh between that gives life, but can strangle.

Every single day at Mama's trailer, I kept reminders front and center that I was going out West with Carey as soon as his semester was over. Mama came back with ten thousand reasons I needed to stay put. Even after I'd used up my sick leave and made her read my letter of resignation to Knox County Child and Family Services, she was still surprised I bought hiking pants and a down coat instead of blouses and pantyhose.

"What if a great job opens up?" she asked. I reminded her I'd just left the best job of my life.

"What if your Granny dies or Grandma Ruby? Or me?" How could she reach me if she got sick? Or if I got sick? Didn't I know there were evil people out in the world? Didn't I know Carey couldn't protect me? She dreamed up reasons to call me from the shop three or four times a day. Could I set out the roast to thaw? Had Dunn taken the lunch she packed for him? Did I need anything from the Rite-Aid?

In the evenings, right in front of her, I mail-ordered camp supplies. I made sure she overheard me making plans with Carey on the phone. I left national park bulletins open on her kitchen table. Every morning at breakfast our silence grew into a smaller and smaller battleground.

Then, two weeks before Carey and I were set to leave, she pulled out her big gun. Before she left for work, I handed her a check for rent and groceries. She refused to take it, so I laid it in front of her coffee cup.

"Just stay put," she said, as I got up to set my cereal bowl in the sink. I stepped around the counter into the living room. "Glenna, I said sit back down here." She wadded up my check and pointed me back into my chair with her cigarette.

"You think you can pay me money like I'm some goddamn bed and breakfast and just traipse off into the sunset?"

I sank back onto the chair. "Mama, look, I'm trying—"

"What you're trying is to run away from your problems like you're scot-free and not obliged to nobody. Well everybody's obliged to their mama. You can't just pull up stakes and run."

"I'd like you to show me the stakes. What the hell's holding me here? You did notice that my house burned down?"

"Oh, poor pitiful you! You act like somebody kicked your dog." She pushed her hair away from her face. "You think you're the only one in bad shape? Let me tell you. I ain't saying life with Glenn Daniels was a cake walk but living without him—" She swallowed hard. "All I can say is, living with you ain't a hell of a lot easier."

"Bingo. You've made my case for me. Even *you* don't want me to stay."

"What I want is for you to wake up and get real, Sister. You figure you got no husband, you got rid of a job you spent thousands of dollars and years of studying to get, you got no address, so all that gives you some special license? No. Nobody as old as you can just up and run off." After a long drag and exhale, she squinted at me through a cloud of smoke, waiting for me to talk. But I was done.

She stubbed out her cigarette like she was killing an insect in the cracked, amber ashtray. She reached for her big purse slumped on the counter, dug into it, and slapped a manila folder on the table in front of me. I didn't say a word.

Her face flushed red. She stood and took a last slurp of coffee, slung her purse cleanly over her shoulder as she put her cup in the sink.

"You want to tell me what this is?" I said.

At the door she turned. "That's your life," she said, pointing at the folder. "You want to run away? Well, there's a little reminder of when I tried to do the same thing. You go off half-cocked and your whole life can blow up in your face."

51

"I can't make heads or tails what in the world you're talking about, Mama."

"That's your inheritance. From me." She looked out the door and fumbled with her keys. I felt light by comparison. I only had my car key and a borrowed key to her trailer. I could carry them in my jeans pocket and hardly feel them. Pretty soon, I wouldn't need a single key. Carey would do the driving.

I looked at the folder. I dreaded it. Inside I knew there was nothing but a hurt. I stood and pushed my chair to the table. I followed Mama's gaze through the screen door into the fog. Everything was muted, even the birds singing on the telephone lines.

"I've been living in this trailer going on twenty-six years," she said. "You see how far running away got me."

"I don't see how you can blame that on yourself, Mama. You and Dunn and I might have moved back to Cosby if Daddy hadn't—"

"Glenna, smart as you are, I swear. You think it's that simple?" She turned to look at me again, her hand on the door handle. "I'm giving you the deed to the farm. All of it. Everything I left behind when I was just about your age. Stupid enough to think I could ever get shed of your daddy."

For a moment that felt like an hour, my mind went dark in waves. When I could focus on the folder again, I thought it might burst into flames. Mama came back and sat in her chair. She looked at the folder between us.

My legs went vague and I sat too. "Mama, you always said—"

"What'd I ever say?" She gave me an obstinate look and lit another cigarette. Her fingers were trembling. "What do you ever remember anybody said? You wasn't but a kid."

I couldn't stand the dark circles under her eyes. I argued at the tabletop and the folder. "We bought stuff with a lot of money. That land's been sold for years."

"I never said pea turkey about selling my land. What money we got was the same as the insurance you're about to get. Covered the house. My twelve acres didn't go nowhere. I wasn't about to sell land my granddaddy give your Granny Pearl, and her to me. I got divorced to be sure that land was all mine. Your daddy couldn't touch it. Never. Now it's yours. Let's see what it can teach you. Because you sure as hell won't listen to me." She pushed the folder toward me. I stood up and away from it.

"I can't even fucking believe—"

"Watch your mouth! After you scream at your brother for using that word to me." She hefted her purse and pulled the strap high on her shoulder as she stood.

"Hell, Mama. What kind of words fit a stunt like this? The land was always right there? It's not ten miles away! And we just never went back? We could have—"

"Never set foot on it again. I never laid eyes on the place since." Her voice faded, but I swear it was triumphant. "What would the point be?"

"The *point?* The point was that it's your *home.* It was *my home!*"

She put her hand on the screen door latch, opened it a crack and then closed it to face me again. "You want me to say it? You're so smart. Okay. Your daddy burned the house. Down to the ground, just to spite me because I took you and Dunny and left him. I never would have dreamed he had it in him to do a thing like he did. But the big surprise was having to take him back. Because then he was the only home I had left.

"You leave." She paused. "You leave and you can't always be sure of getting back home, is what I'm saying. What you leave behind might not even be there when you get back."

Before she dumped our whole burned up history in my lap, I had stopped hassling Mama to give me a haircut. When I clipped my fingers like a clothespin on a hank of hair above my ear, she smacked my hand away. She knew I wouldn't dare let anybody else cut it. That morning, with the folder singeing a hole in the kitchen table, even before her car pulled away in the fog, I tore the kitchen junk drawer apart looking for scissors. It was crammed full with dead batteries, corroded pennies, wads of twine and masking tape, dried up ballpoint pens, plastic fishing worms, lead sinkers, hooks in a clear plastic box.

I ran to her bedroom to find her excuse for a sewing kit, one of Daddy's old tackle boxes, cluttered with dusty spools of thread, Band-Aids, pink and blue sweetener packs and antiseptic wipes, an ancient bottle of dried up calamine lotion, and I swear, somebody's goddamn baby teeth in a pill bottle. At the very bottom of the heap, rusted pinking shears and tiny scissors too dull to clip nose hairs.

Next, I disemboweled the bathroom drawer, dumped the contents onto the linoleum. Nail clippers, dental floss, an old toothbrush for cleaning grout. I nicked my finger on a rusty razor and sat on the commode lid, fussing at myself out loud. "A grown woman should only get this frantic looking for a condom."

Think, I thought. How could a beautician not have scissors? I had rummaged through the debris in the trailer's black holes until my fingernails were grimy, my pulse and rage slowing and my nerve nearly gone. Then, on my next tear through the house, hanging right in the open on a nail by the phone in Mama's bedroom, a long pair of black-handled scissors, sharp as a scalpel.

"Cut that cord." I rushed down the hall.

I whacked the first long, thick snake of hair below my left ear before I got to the bathroom mirror. In the fluorescent glare I met my lopsided image. A wild woman clawed at my head in brutal swipes. After each scissor bite the coils of hair slipped down my body in whispers quiet as snow falling. My head was light.

In the mirror, nobody special stared at me. A woman with a dark sun halo of ragged curls. A woman without armor or magic. At my feet a felled forest. My bare legs rising out of a silk pool the color of burn.

Early evening, from the bedroom where I stuffed my new duffel with new underwear, new socks, new T-shirts, jeans, and sandals—all the spoils Carey bought me—I heard Mama home from work hit the door at a dead run. When she's upset she always has what she calls her "cooking therapy." Three trips to the car, each louder than the one before. I knew she'd seen the folder with the deed still on the table. She slammed cabinet doors and opened and closed the fridge a dozen times. Pots and pans clanged rapid fire. I didn't obey her passive-aggressive momentum even when the food processor chewed in intermittent groans.

I listened to her fix dinner for an hour, knowing I hadn't gotten anywhere. So what? I'd performed a stunt, acted out like a toddler. My heart pounded and my head rushed, the way they had when I was eight and she caught me smoking Daddy's Winstons, or when I took the keys to her Pinto before I had my license. She still had hold of my conscience, hair or no hair.

I opened my bedroom door and took a deep breath. The perfume of chicken broth, comfort food. Down the short hall past the back door in the living room. She was lifting the steaming pot from the stove, pouring chicken and dumplings into one of her grandmother's big china bowls. Just at the moment she saw me, she was leaping back from the boiling splatter hitting the floor, the bowl flying in shards, the pot bounding its metal gong behind the counter between us.

She stared at me flushed, with her hands in her hair. I covered my ears from the noise. We faced each other like mirror images.

"Sissy," she breathed. Her hazel eyes were wide. And then in one gesture, she quelled every sign of her disappointment. She shifted her attention to the floor, her hands to her hips. "Well," was all she said.

"Mama."

"Just stay there," she said as I leaned over the counter. She held up one palm to me and reached for the broom beside the fridge with the other hand.

"But did you burn yourself?"

She shifted the broom from one hand to the other as she scanned her pivoting legs and bare arms. She didn't look anywhere but down.

"Some of it got on your jeans." I pointed, but she just started sweeping. "It's lucky you didn't have on shorts."

"Yeah. Lucky me." She swept the goop of chicken into an even broader swath and then bent to pick up the china fragments and the pot.

"I didn't mean—" I was shot through with clanging when she threw the pot into the sink.

"Your hair just got that way by itself, I reckon." She swept uselessly and streaked the floor with gobs of dumplings.

"No, I didn't mean—"

She laughed as she dug at the floor with the broom. "You spent half your life trying not to be like Glenn Daniels. But just like him what comes out of your mouth is pure horse shit. You mean to do exactly what you done, just like he meant what all he done. And you neither one wouldn't ever own up to it."

"What the hell?" We both startled at Dunn's voice coming through the screen door. He held it half open as he looked across my shoulder at our ruined dinner. Then he looked at me and jumped back. "Shit, Glenna! What the fuck did somebody do to your hair?" His look split horror and triumph right down the middle. For once in my life, I wished he would laugh at me.

"Here." Mama leaned the broom against the fridge and tiptoed over the opaque swirl smeared onto the kitchen floor. She grabbed her purse off the counter and tossed it to Dunn. "Get a twenty out of my wallet and go get us a pizza. And spend your own money for beer this time."

He fumbled with the bills and dumped her wallet and purse on the chair by the door. He looked at us again. "Ain't neither of you going to tell me what the hell?"

"Well, son," her voice lilted as she swept. "What happened is that your sister is fixing to run away from home and there ain't a thing I can do to stop her."

He was halfway down the steps when she yelled at him. "Budweiser. In bottles. None of that cheap crap! And no onions, you hear me?"

She looked fiercely at me and reached for the mop. "Good for nothing but heartburn."

I bided my time through two days of silence. I didn't have to ask why when Mama called me to come to her shop after closing time. Without a word I reclined with my head in the deep sink.

"No. Sit up." She motioned with a towel in her hand. "Keep your britches on." She put her hands to my hair and tugged at it roughly. Then she scraped a sharp, metal comb hard through it, pulling the uneven ends down below my earlobes to gauge the length.

"Lord, Sister, you couldn't've haggled it worse if you'd took a dull butcher knife to it. It'll need a full two inches more took off the front just to even it up with the back." She tied a plastic smock tight as a noose around my neck. I leaned back and closed my eyes against the punishment of scalding water.

When she was done washing, we moved to the front of the shop, and she pumped the hydraulic chair down instead of up for the first time in my life. In the mirror her mouth was drawn and tired at the corners.

"We don't have to do this now." I shifted.

She raked through short tangles I wasn't used to. "This ain't no favor. I just got to thinking if my customers was to see you, I'd be out of business."

"They're liable to run you out of town." I tried a weak joke.

"Good thing I don't budge easy as some do," she said.

"There you go!" I turned to look in her face, but she pinched my temples between her palms and jerked me forward.

"I said to sit still."

"That's all you ever wanted was for me to 'sit still.'" I pulled my head away and slumped. She wouldn't meet my eyes in the mirror. "Where has sitting still ever gotten me? I still live forty-five minutes from where I was born."

"No. Right now you live five minutes from where you was born. Just like me. You think you're the only one that ought to get to leave? When's my chance to run off?" She lifted her scissors as if they were part of her hand and spun the chair around.

How many hours had she stood here working? How many days did she open up her shop alone and lock it alone? She could have run. From more than her burned up inheritance. A bruised pang bloomed in my chest to think she could have left Dunn and me with Daddy, left us all and never looked back. There were two or three times she tried to get away. She had finalized the divorce, so she was free. She could have had a life with Ben Miller. Not once had I ever doubted her, not even in retrospect. She could have abandoned us all. I'd been sure of her, though, the most certain thing in my life.

She ran the comb over and over through each section of hair between slight snipping. Little flat, dark circles of hair fell wetly onto the floor.

After a time, I said, "I didn't know that's what you wanted. To run away."

"*Wanted*? When did what I *wanted* ever matter a hill of beans?" She put down the comb and scissors and chose some styling gel from the shelf. "Shit." She wiped half the goop from her hand onto a towel. "I forget you ain't got much to work with now." She massaged the sweet smell into my hair and lifted the ends with her fingertips.

"It'll grow," I offered. "It's summer. Hair grows fast when it's hot, you always say. By the time I get back it'll be down my neck."

She pivoted the chair. In the mirror I looked older but stylish. My face seemed trimmer beneath the new tousle. Ready and open. More than that. Expectant.

"You sure you're coming back?" Mama asked. "I reckon I always figured anybody that leaves might decide to not ever come home." She handed me a hand mirror to look at the layered curls in the back.

I didn't know how to lie. But how could I admit her suspicion was right? Maybe I wouldn't come home. A feeble plan to land somewhere else was in my mind. Maybe the way she'd never gone back to Genesis Road was the best way. Leave your birthright behind. Spend the insurance money. Keep your crazy, burned up life in a folder until you can pawn off the whole sorry mess onto somebody else.

My fury against her purled up again. I was tempted to use her own words to spite her. *Never set foot. Never laid eyes.* How could she not have confided in me? She stayed, sure, but she hadn't kept me entirely with her. We locked eyes in the mirror.

"You still look pretty," she admitted, and took the hand mirror from me. "You'd look pretty baldheaded, I guess." She shook the smock out as I stood up. And then she brushed her hands down my back, touching the ghost of my hair.

Past Little Rock the yawning farmland eased up into woods and ridge lines, hazy blue in the late morning. For a while I-40 skirted a pine-covered bluff and I could see the tailbone of the Ozarks, the only mountains I'd ever seen besides home.

Green hills rumpled to the Oklahoma state line. We nearly missed the welcome sign, hidden beside an overpass. Our dull mood careened into manic energy, just to be in another state. That easily. Half-a-day of driving, one state farther. Carey knows I'm not much for musicals, so he threatened to play the *Oklahoma* soundtrack from border to border, all three hundred and twenty miles. But what he put in was a mixtape with "Okie from Muskogee" and more Merle Haggard. As I drove, he kept randomly belting out *"Oklahoma,"* until I thought we'd wreck from laughing.

He answered with an exaggerated "OK" when I suggested a picnic at the info center near Sallisaw. He made the okay sign, and winked and said again with a grin, "OK," before I got it. We ate crackers and cheese and apples standing up at triangular concrete picnic tables under tall tripods of poles. I recognized before he did that they were teepee shapes. We stretched and looked for routes away from the interstate. I scanned the names of rivers and towns on the Oklahoma map: *Checotah, Keota, Hitchita, Okmulgee, Chickasha.* I played them out in my mind against names from home: *Cherokee, Oconaluftee, Nantahala, Santeetlah, Appalachia. Tennessee.*

There was a pay phone beside the restrooms. I thought of Mama. She'd given Carey instructions to remind me to call her. She'd bought me an AT&T debit card but said to call collect if I had to. But how would our first conversation go? Nothing could explain to her the lifetime you can live in just one day of traveling, years like miles. Flashbacks and grudges. The misery of regrets. I'd known the landscape would alter, but far from home, home itself began to change. What kind of names would I call my new life now, any new place I settled down?

About fifteen minutes past our lunch stop, Carey saw signs for the historic western Cherokee capital.

"Talequah's the official capital," he said. "But that's way north."

"We just took a break," I said.

"We'll just stay ten minutes in honor of Mr. Leslie. You remember Mr. Leslie's history class, sophomore year? The Trail of Tears. I mean, the man cried."

"I remember you had a crush."

"No! He inspired me to teach. I mean." He grinned. "It doesn't hurt a smart guy to be pretty."

Learning about the horrors the Cherokee went through really had hit me hard. Exiled, nearly extinguished. I'd been to Cherokee, North Carolina, just over the mountain on the other side of the Smokies. No one had ever told me about the Removal, though. Maybe those four thousand deaths along the way didn't hang in the minds of my classmates. I took their trauma personally because I'd been ousted against my will. A drop beside a raging waterfall of anguish. The Cherokee who survived walked the distance it took Carey and me two days to drive. Lost in a bewildering new place.

The doors to the log buildings and exhibits were open, but we were the only people on the place. No tour guide, just a yellow cat tormenting a toad on the gravel path. Inside we glanced over newspaper articles, historic documents, glass cases of artifacts and photos of the western band's tribal elders. In the old courthouse, a loop tape played hymns in their language. "Amazing Grace" followed us out in clipped Cherokee syllables.

"Weird little place," Carey said. "If people would just go stand in a place and see that history isn't in a book. And, I mean, that's a history professor saying that."

"It's not history, though," I said. "They'll always be separated into two groups. These Cherokee in Oklahoma don't know their family in North Carolina. They've never even seen where they're from, never set foot—"

I hadn't told Carey about the land I'd just found out was still in my family. Land that was mine. That for the first time in twenty-five years I had gone to see it. Nothing recognizable in the green of that place.

"No one can ever put together again how their lives should have gone," I said.

By the time we hit I-40 again, he was into full-on lecture mode about the Trail of Tears, and I was back to begrudging Mama and her secrets and lies. She'd diverted the whole course of the life I might have lived.

Carey said, "At least the landscape here looks a lot like where the Cherokee came from. Especially it reminds me of North Georgia."

I opened the map again. From North Carolina to Oklahoma. From there to there. A vast gap.

"Nope," I said. "It's a piss poor consolation that Oklahoma looks a little bit like home."

The first time I ever spent a night in a motel was in Cherokee, North Carolina. I must have been about nine. We still lived at the farmhouse, on Mama's land. I don't ever recall not understanding that Mama had grown up in that house, that Granny Pearl had grown up in that house. That Granny's family had moved to Genesis Road after they were ousted from land the government took by eminent domain for the Great Smoky Mountains. The story they stuck to was that Mama's great-granddaddy refused to cash the government's check. He believed until the day he died that if he didn't take the money, he might have a shot at going back home.

That trip was probably a last ditch effort for my parents' marriage, just a couple of months before Mama left Daddy. But Daddy was giddy. His parole must have been up. Otherwise, he wouldn't have been legally able to cross the North Carolina line. We had been on lots of camping trips, but this was a real vacation, with a suitcase and a brown paper bag for our toothbrushes and toothpaste and shaving lotion. It was winter. I watched snow fall into the half-frozen swimming pool. There was a tiled shower stall, a color television on the dresser, two double beds, which Daddy laughed at Mama for making up before we checked out the next morning.

He sang to Mama as we drove, and she laughed. Dunn and I didn't fight in the backseat. For the first time in my life, we went to a restaurant where a hostess ushered us to the table. Daddy walked, I remember clearly, with his good hand pressed lightly into the small of Mama's back. He pulled out her chair for her and made a silly little bow before doing the same for me.

We might have been the model TV family. Anyone looking at us might see that we were simple but good people. We lived in a house on a farm at the foot of English Mountain. Anyone would have thought we were lucky to live in such a perfect place.

All our flaws diminished from a distance. At home it was too obvious that Daddy drank way too much, worked way too little. Weeds had grown up around the tractor, which had been broken down for over a year in the middle of the field. The barn roof was rusted through in patches.

But traveling, even just over the mountain, I could be anyone. We could be any family if we kept traveling, I thought. I couldn't sleep, too excited to be in a new place, strangers between rooms where other strangers lay sleeping, all of us on the road. What an overwhelming thing to have in common. We were carrying new selves to new places. What our names and lives were, no one knew, so there was a chance we might go far enough to forget ourselves.

When Mama and I went back to Cherokee together years later, after the casino opened, the town of Cherokee had cleaned up for company. I wanted to find the tacky, cheap magic the place had when I was a kid. But the town sank in claustrophobic hollers where ridges jutted up. Like a lot of deep mountain places, Cherokee seems dim all day long. The through highway sluices through narrows beside the river. Businesses and motels hug the road at their fronts and steep hillsides at their backs.

Plenty of old tourist traps were still there, hybrid road fronts renting out second-story motel rooms and selling ground-floor trinkets. As a girl I loved the dancers with feather headdresses from scalp to knees. Mama still has a Polaroid of Dunn and me with the "chief" in his costume. He stood on the side of the road with his stern, pouting face while his son snapped two-dollar shots for tourists. We're wearing new moccasins made in China or Taiwan, and Dunn is holding his plastic tomahawk. I'm vamping my long hair so the camera shows the prize souvenir Mama bought me, a handmade yellow glass-beaded barrette.

I loved it, my one truly beautiful possession, the only jewelry I ever owned as a kid. Its minuscule marigold-colored glass beads glimmered, woven into a broad sunburst arch.

When we made our trip back to Cherokee, Mama hadn't been past the Newport city limits in more than two years. Our bargain was that I would gamble with her as long as she went with me to the Museum of the Cherokee. Exhibits and artifacts ranged along a hallway, winding and curving to represent the Trail of Tears. Out of the dioramas and tribal relics, Mama's favorite was so simple I nearly overlooked it, a display of stories the Cherokee tell about the constellations.

Summers on the farm, Mama and I would sit in the yard at dusk and watch the stars come out one by one. The moon got smaller and whiter as it lifted off the horizon. Then, as it did when the moon was new or pale, the starlight grew more distinct. She showed me the major groups of stars just as her grandmother had shown her from the same porch.

When I was five, the summer Daddy came home from prison, I understood that a great thing was happening. A man was walking on the moon. Mama stood in the yard looking up half the day. She explained he was farther from home than anybody had ever gone, so far he could see all of us at once, the whole world, even in daylight. She laughed because I didn't know why we couldn't see him.

When we moved to Newport, into the trailer, Mama still took a few minutes most evenings to check the night sky. But competition from streetlight glare dimmed the constellations. Her favorite was the Pleiades, which she called the Seven Sisters, even though only six stars are visible to the naked eye.

"There's one star hiding," she told me. "The shy sister. We just have to trust she's there."

At the museum, Mama read every word of that Cherokee story about the Pleiades. She retold it to me in the car later, more like a warning than a myth. They call the constellation "The Boys," for disobedient sons who ran away from their mothers and transformed into stars. The seventh boy, the Cherokee believe, was punished the worst for going astray. He turned into a pine tree, always reaching up, trying to follow his brothers. He's stuck forever between one life and another, in between, pointing toward a place he can never reach.

Of all the places Mama might have run away to, I doubted Oklahoma City would have made her happy. There in the epicenter of the U.S., a thousand miles from home, distance was no longer just a concept. But the biggest city we'd been through put us in slow motion. Through rush hour traffic, we puttered for nearly an hour, past the backsides of strip malls and office buildings, creeping past the city skyline. Carey said it was nothing worse than Atlanta, but I gagged on the fumes and had the urge to get out and walk.

The locals had gotten used to terrorism through the past four years, but being so close to the site of the Murrah Federal Building was sobering. We were silent while radio DJs and helicopter crews bantered about wrecks to avoid. Tractor trailers belched in a steady line. Asshole drivers snaked their cars into tiny, prime slots in the slow-moving parking lot. The day was normal for everybody but us.

How exhausting to think of the balance of the state ahead, and then another state and another, the miles of road. My eyes hurt. My legs were stiff. Besides our picnic lunch and the Cherokee historic site, the only other stop had been for gas and a hot fudge sundae at the McDonald's in Henryetta, home of Troy Aikman. We'd seen signs all along I-40 advertising famous sons and daughters of little Oklahoma towns: Will Rogers, Woody Guthrie, country star Roger Miller, astronaut Thomas P. Stafford. But nothing compared to the hero worship in Henryetta. We had pushed through the doors of that McDonald's into a reverent hush and, I swear, a scent like the flesh of a new football. The whole place was a shrine to Troy Aikman, walls covered with memorabilia. The man who became a Dallas Cowboy was still Henryetta's golden boy.

"Football. The religion of the late twentieth century." Carey turned to me as he handed me my sundae.

"The First Troy Aikman Church of Grease and Hot Apple Pies," I said. We were catty about it all—signed press photos and posters, old high school jerseys under glass, framed clippings from the early holy wars. Those pitiful, stuck people eating Big Macs and chowing down on fries, frozen at the altar of hero worship.

A couple of hours past Oklahoma City, we deserved a real meal, we decided.

And a break. Little towns and wheat fields had given way to wide open. The woods vanished to endless pastures with sharper angles. Thickets of vetch ranged along fence lines for miles between houses. On the radio, traffic reports had evolved into farm reports, the price of hogs, the benefits of fertilizer, predictions about late May rain. We wanted to stop, but there was nowhere, nothing but exits that led to two-lanes that led to distant small towns.

Just as we were about to give up on a hot meal, there was a sign for the Cherokee Trading Post. It stood alone at the exit, surrounded by farmland. On the hillside across the gravel parking lot, a bison hulked inside a steel rail fence, Oklahoma's state animal, Carey told me. I tried to hide my disappointment that the first bison I would ever see was captive, a herd animal in solitary confinement.

And, of course, at the Cherokee Trading Post, there wasn't a Cherokee in sight. In the diner farmers in dungarees and overalls talked across rickety tables or hunched over plates while their wives twisted in their narrow chairs to talk to wives at the next table or scold their kids. The smell of cigarette smoke pushed me over the edge to homesickness. I missed Mama against my will.

In the store, after we ate greasy chicken casserole and green beans, Carey and I looked over tacky souvenirs, the kind I'd loved when I was a kid—tom-tom drums, keychains and whistles decorated with fluorescent feathers. In plywood bins, dozens of hollow, plastic Indian baby dolls dressed in fake suede with little fake suede moccasins and headdresses. Big Caucasian smiles to match their big Caucasian eyes. For the high-end tourist there were ceramic sculptures of eagles and wolves, split oak baskets, wall hangings crafted from wood and leather. All of it made in China.

But there was one display cabinet of authentic Cherokee jewelry, colorful glass beads woven into bracelets and necklaces. On the lowest shelf I was stunned to find a hair clip of translucent yellow beads. In a fan shape. I could not have told the difference between it and the one Mama had bought for me when I was a girl. I had the clerk open the locked display.

"Why do you need a hair clip?" Carey asked when the clerk handed it to me. He tugged the short hair at the nape of my neck.

"Oh. Right." I looked at the intricate beadwork. Someone in North Carolina or Oklahoma had made it by hand. Where had I lost its twin? In the first fire?

"The symbol for constancy," the clerk said as I handed it back to her.

"What?"

"The sunburst, that design. It's an Indian symbol for constancy, like loyalty, you know? Like the sun never fails to come up every day." She traced the arch with her fingertip and handed it back toward me, knowing full well she'd made her sale.

I bought it and some postcards Carey picked out, of Oklahoma wildflowers, and penny candies that were a nickel apiece. The cashier tucked the beaded clip into a fake suede pouch small enough to carry anywhere I would travel.

We raced the sunset across western Oklahoma. The state park we were aiming for, Foss Lake, was still miles away, and we dreaded setting up camp after dark, or worse, not finding a campsite. For a while we squinted into the ball of orange sun, and then the light kissed the horizon line, burnishing everything. Hills of red clay reared up, sculpted by the same constant wind gusting against the Jeep. On the tops of beveled bluffs, deep emerald grass wavered, crests of hills like ocean waves.

The light was electric. Color saturated without distortion of mist or cloud, the sky a deep cobalt behind us, the sunset a crimson and petal pink. The sides of tractor trailers shivered their silver, like giant flashing trout, and streetlights lining I-40 flickered on at the tops of their glowing poles.

By the time we reached our exit, the broken hills fell twilight dark. Along the two-lane to Foss Lake, over a rise, sudden lights lifted up on the strangely elegant scaffolding of a grain elevator. Like a high rise, it was the only pure light we could see besides the first stars and the Jeep's high beams.

I was tempted to ask Carey to stop at the pay phone when we got to the park kiosk, so I could let Mama know where we were. But I was afraid she'd answer. So far, I'd left one quick message on her machine when I knew she was at work.

At that point, there'd be hell to pay whenever I did finally talk to her. I could sense her expecting a call any minute all day long. And every minute I didn't call, she was more and more certain that instead of hearing from me, she'd get news *about* me, wrecked, lost, raped, robbed. Or at the very least scared and ashamed. Apologetic.

Carey and I worked against a nearly constant wind to set up camp by the Jeep's headlights. Protected by two large trees, between a fence line and the picnic table, our blue dome tent shivered. Home for the night.

Carey was asleep in minutes. I pulled on my sweatshirt and jeans and slipped back outside the tent. The moon, a slim shard, hooked its sidewise horns into the limbs above. And then for an instant, my breath was gone. For the first time in my life, looking into an atmosphere so dark and clear, I could see the pale pinwheel arm of the Milky Way. A trail of stars like faint smoke divided the flecked black.

The way Mama showed me, I finally found the constellation Orion in all that misty starlight. I followed his belt until I spotted the Pleiades, the Seven Sisters. The Cherokee brothers who ran away. The brother who stayed behind, rooted into the ground, transformed into a pine tree. Was I him? Or was I daring the road to make me into someone new?

We'd been wrong to make fun of the Troy Aikman McDonald's. Henryetta's hometown boy is his people's satellite. His finest moments beam above the heads of families who might never venture past their county lines. He's poised in a way they understand, always ready to throw that long pass in the middle of America.

Like people in Newport, like Mama, Oklahoma people mostly stay put. Maybe most people most places stay put. I had been those people. For the first time, for only two days, I was learning what it meant to escape a place that had that kind of hold.

That Oklahoma boy who grew up to be an astronaut saw the whole globe spinning. He could watch his past and finally understand the broken, beautiful hills of home. People in his hometown anoint him their witness. Common people who never stepped foot outside Oklahoma but went to church with, taught math to, cut the hair of the boy who saw the Earth from space.

I sat at our campsite picnic table in the dark, thinking I might get the lantern and write a postcard to Mama. I had never, ever written to anybody in my family. I hadn't been far enough away to need to. What would it change to write her? For weeks I had wanted to tell her, *I was pregnant, but I lost the baby*. But how could I have made my mouth say those awful words out loud? How could I write that burden on a postcard?

I don't come from people who use the words they really mean. Mama and I, close as we are, don't say things directly. We don't admit, *I'm sorry*. Hell, we heard Daddy repeat his apologies enough to know they might mean nothing, anyway. We stubbornly hold back *I forgive you*. We sure enough don't say *I love you* out loud.

The barrette I'd bought made an uncomfortable wad in my jeans pocket. I pulled it out of the pouch and touched the beads like braille in the dark. Instead of keeping it for myself, I'd mail it to Mama the next morning, a message in code. No words. Just that symbol for our connection, doggedly there. Constancy. Past the tent, in the Oklahoma dark, the field of blonde grass glowed, so far away from home it may as well have been moon dust.

SOMETHING OLD, SOMETHING NEW

By the time my eyes adjusted to morning light on the Oklahoma hayfields, we passed a big sign: *Welcome to Texas—Drive Friendly, the Texas Way!* A Texas-sized lie. Rude traffic and big rigs blasted past us, wheels whining on hot blacktop. The sky widened above the barren Panhandle. Wild, dry grass ran to the horizon without so much as a rise or ridge. Every now and then with no warning, the plain dropped away to deep ravines. Carey said these were the first coulees I'd ever seen. Huge yuccas and gnarled mesquite trees clung along dry creek beds.

"Arroyos," he said. Texas needed a whole new vocabulary. I thought, *So, this is where the West begins.* I should have known that we'd entered a land of illusions.

I'd never been anywhere so flat. In relation to the domineering sky, the land seemed to be an afterthought. Faraway trailers, water tanks, galvanized silos, barns, whole farms slid in tandem beside us for miles, then the horizon swallowed all of them.

Like every other thing on the dry pampas east of Amarillo, the biggest cross in the U.S. created optical tricks. Carey had it highlighted on his list of Americana sites. He said we were obliged to stop for anything that bizarre. We watched the blinding white cross for a long time as it enlarged in contrast to fence lines and utility poles. From the parking lot it truly was gargantuan, even in relation to the girth and appetite of Texas.

"What's it fur, ya reckon?" I put on my exaggerated hick accent.

"Duh," Carey answered. "Great big state. Great big sinners. And don't forget, great big pocketbooks."

"Ha. If there's an admission fee, you're going it alone."

He laughed. "Who the hell would pay to see this?"

"My Grandma Ruby would. Seriously," I answered. "Lots of people."

"No! I mean, you can see the damn thing for, what, thirty miles?" He cut the engine and leaned against the steering wheel, squinting up through the windshield. We got out and walked across the blazing pavement, craning our necks and shading our eyes. The cross stood probably two hundred feet, an indomitable rocket of aluminum siding, so white the cloudless noon sky looked dark.

"Christ!" Carey stepped ahead of me into the shadow of its monstrous wingspan.

"Well, yeah." I pointed. "What'd you expect?" Around the circular brick wall, he hadn't noticed, the Stations of the Cross in near life-size bronze sculptures. A Roman soldier nailed an anguished Jesus to the cross. Pilate washed his hands before a Jesus crowned with thorns. Counterclockwise back to Judas's kiss.

"God. It's worse and so much better than I ever imagined." Carey lifted his camera to his face to pan the scene. "A New Testament Disney World."

I centered myself in the shade of the cross, while Carey in rapture snapped each figure of Christ from a different angle. Other folks who'd gotten there after us spread out a map on the hood of their car while the kids fought over sandwiches in the backseat.

A big gravestone across the way cast its own meager shade. I walked over and squatted. I had to take off my sunglasses to read its "dedication to victims of abortion." The pious surprise of it stood me back up straight. The whole place was a protest, like those thousands of small white crosses staked on hillsides back home.

Near the base of the granite stone, the Savior's bronze hands thrust out as if reaching through a solid fog, stigmata on the wrists. His palms cradled a premature fetus, naked bronze body burnished where tourists had touched him. People had prayed here, wanting, sorrowful, wounded. The baby lay on his back, dead eyelids closed, anus and scrotum exposed, arms and legs tucked into a curl. Propaganda so perfect he seemed ready to take a breath.

I suffocated. It was simple to calculate: Right at that moment, if everything had gone right, a baby that same perfect size would still have been protected inside me. The bronze baby glistened in the sun, without a heartbeat, just like my baby. The unfairness nearly buckled my knees, rebuking me. How could there possibly be so much to grieve?

Carey's hand on my shoulder was a shock. He saw my hurt before I could recompose my face behind my sunglasses.

"What's happened? What's the matter?" He looked at the gravestone, which took a second to register. "Oh," he said. "Pretty grim."

"Men make this kind of place," I said. "With money from offering plates. But they can't possibly have any idea. It's like a bad riddle: What kind of choice isn't really a choice?" I had to walk away.

Carey followed after a few steps, silent. I knew he wanted to ask. He wanted to know if I had, ever. People wonder if a woman my age without kids has had an abortion. The first generation after legalized abortion. Even Mama asked me once if I would have, if I could have. Right there with Carey, my legs had gone to Jell-O from the temptation to tell all, just start talking and not stop until California.

For years, my life depended on the durability of latex and sponges and spermicide, or that daily pill out of twenty-eight, a circumference of free will. Three or four times in college my period was so late I pumped myself full of courage. It was nothing worse than having terrible cramps, friends had told me. I had a couple of scares with Dawson. Married that young, with a bad marriage from day one, I would have crossed the picket line at the Knoxville clinic. I made the calls. I read all the brochures. I'd been ready.

While Kevin and I tried and failed again and again to conceive, I couldn't believe I had ever thought of making that desperate choice. How weird to reverse that fear and worry. To try deliberately to get pregnant. Kevin and I stopped using birth control months and months before we even talked about getting married. I was barely thirty. I had time to enjoy the pure want. I was finally going to have the family I had never let myself believe was possible. That I hadn't thought I deserved.

A friend once told me about watching in a mirror as her baby was born, that it was like watching her family line become immortal. Part of her genetics would live on and on. I never cared about anything so cosmic. In fact, I tried *not* to think about DNA, considering a percentage of Daddy was in the mix.

What I held onto was the idea of a new life. Those two tiny cells—one of mine and one of Kevin's—coming together marked the genesis of a whole new person who had never existed before. And I would get a chance to start all over, as somebody's mother. There would be a new me, too.

Would have been.

After shooting three rolls of film at the cross, Carey was hellbent to see more of what he called "landscape kitsch." He confessed he had an ulterior motive. He'd kept to himself that he was taking advantage of the trip to research American oddities. Three days in, he was a man with a purpose. And there I was bereft of a meandering partner. At every mile post, I had less of a plan than the mile before.

All the way to Cadillac Ranch, he kept the race-track pace, with Lyle Lovett blasting, eight lanes careening, tailgating, braking, swerving. I held my breath in tractor trailer canyons, locked in formation with chicken trucks, long stacks of flattened wrecks, trailers of fat pink hogs. We smothered in weaving odors of horse sweat and cow shit and diesel. Animal flanks and shoulders and rumps swayed past, all of it consumed west, west, west.

"Sheesh. Can't you back off a little, Carey?"

"Just holding my own," he said. "Same tattooed trucker buzzards we have in Atlanta. They think they own the road."

"They do," I said.

We spotted Cadillac Ranch from I-40. Carey called it "a cockeyed automotive Stonehenge." We parked on an access road, and he scribbled that into a little notepad. He was in research heaven as we wandered among the ten Cadillacs, buried single file up to their dashboards, as if someone had driven them at a forty-five-degree tilt out of the sky. They faced dead west, surprisingly tall, fins and taillights overhead like rockets.

"How American. Cadillac shade." Carey leaned on graffiti. Tourists had painted and repainted every surface. Some had printed slogans, even poems. Hundreds of signatures. Everyone wanted to leave a mark: *I was here.*

One pace away from the shade was hell in Texas, no trees, no bushes, no relief from the blazing sun. I pushed up my sleeves, but then my skin was just closer to the fire. I tugged at the seat of my jeans, plastered to me. "Give me the keys."

"Where you going?" Carey asked.

"Take your time. But I've got to get on some shorts. And sandals."

He grinned across my head at the interstate. "Truckers will see you."

"I've got nothing they haven't spent good money on." I caught the keys he tossed and set out across the cracked soil, crushing starved shoots of corn in random patches. Traffic wavered through transparent lines searing the air.

I pulled out my summer clothes and changed barely hidden by the Jeep, which Carey had snugged up to a ditch. I'd been in more compromising positions in the great outdoors, but usually in the dark, and not without a tree to hide behind. In the back seat I pulled off my boots and socks within view of tourists. I blocked myself as well as I could and shucked off my jeans. I was tugging on my shorts when a truck barreled up the access road. Whether he saw panties or not, he hit a few blasts on his horn. All I could do was wave. The little flap over his exhaust pipe waved back.

I wrestled out of my shirt and into a T-shirt, and stepped up on the bumper and then onto the hood of the Jeep. A mountain woman will always try for the highest possible view. I scanned the dead level with shaded eyes, turning to see 360 degrees of bald wide open under sky like an endless blue flame. South, Cadillac Ranch angled up out of the ground like a monstrous fin. West, interstate and grass flowed over the horizon. North, a few trees and fence lines, longhorn cattle. Random oil wells plunged their heads like black insects devouring a carcass. And east, Amarillo's strip malls and chain restaurants shimmered at the corner of nowhere and dust.

The Road—with a capital R—a roaring wide river of commerce, powered every motion forward to somewhere else. For the first time, I saw that the Road wasn't built for going to the mall or the store for a gallon of milk. The Road isn't there for a Sunday drive. It's for the faithful. I might as well have stood there naked, taking my first footsteps as a nomad bride on the frontier-of-hauling-ass. I was marrying the unknown future, forever devoted to nothing except what comes next.

This is where the real West starts, I thought again.

We left the interstate and wound through Amarillo's outskirts to Highway 87, a diagonal stretch to New Mexico's high plains. Gulches and, once in a while, a dirt driveway snaked right along the road's edge. The only other sign of people were ranch gates of wrought iron like neon. As I drove, Carey hit the scan button on the radio. Nothing but ghost static for long stretches.

And when it did hit a station, it was nothing but ads for silo rat deterrents, fertilizer, irrigation equipment. Farms scattered like monopoly pieces under storm clouds. Three splattering raindrops fell in a dotted line on the windshield. They looked huge against the distance. In Dalhart, we jostled across railroad tracks during what looked to be the farm rush. Between sentinel grain elevators, I felt the momentary throttling of enclosure. I was getting used to miles of elbow room between cramped towns. And every transition began the true West all over again.

Through empty graze lands, Highway 87 was suddenly blacktop with a freshly painted yellow line. Carey looked up from the map at the sound of our tires on new pavement.

"We're in New Mexico," he said. "Mountain time."

I was trying to wrap my head around being in a second new time zone when two far green hills swelled up out of the plain like rising dough. He pointed. I couldn't keep from laughing. After driving across the flat ranch lands all day, those hills were like grail. I knew the road would run to them.

When we hit the scrawny cow-town of Clayton, New Mexico, people were rattling home from work in old trucks or on motorcycles. It was just four-thirty local time, but we were two hours more tired than that. Carey said we ought to stop for the night. The town actually had a visitor center, fronted with bright plaster dinosaurs advertising local fossil digs. The guide said camping was our only option.

"Hotel in town is full up, they say, for a big wedding." He drew a line on the free map. "Campsites get gone early at the lake this time of year. I'd head on out. Thirteen miles past the mountain."

"*Mountain*," Carey mouthed at me, rolling his eyes.

We bought Cokes out of the vending machine and set out toward the two peaks getting larger and larger as Carey glanced at tourist brochures.

"I guess they are sort of baby mountains," he said. Down a craggy ravine, a ridge of broken red rock rose around us. Yellow brush swept up the slope of the two big hills, completely naked of trees. I'd never seen mountains without foothills of some kind.

"Yeah, yeah, yeah!" Carey bounced up and down like a kid. "I thought so," he said. "It says right here, Glenna Daniels is seeing her very first volcano. Extinct. But a volcano!" He grabbed the steering wheel and we both screamed as he gave us a few little swerves back and forth on the empty road.

"Stop! Stop it!"

"But aren't you excited? It's Rabbit Ear Mountain. Named after a Cheyenne Indian Chief, Orejas de Conejo. Chief Rabbit Ears." He wiggled his fingers above his ears.

"Like Bugs Bunny?"

"No," Carey said. "It says. Let's see. His ears were raggedy from frostbite. Like—see that jagged ridge line? All this red rock is ancient lava flow. Listen, this is amazing, too. Nearby, the Santa Fe Trail ruts are still visible, gouged that deep."

"Stop reading, Carey! You're missing what we came for."

"No, listen. You know the road from Amarillo, Highway 87? It intersects with 64 in Clayton, and the two roads run together for about a hundred miles to Raton.

"But what I'm getting to. It says, 64 is the only highway that still runs un-broken from coast to coast—not interstate, I mean. And 87 runs from Mexico to Saskatchewan. That means dinky little Clayton, New Mexico—" He looked at me to see if I understood.

I shrugged.

"We're at the by-God crossroadest crossroads," he shouted. "Trans-fuck-ing-continental, baby! We found the middle of America."

We topped a rise on the road, and nothing I'd ever seen was so out of place as the blue of Clayton Lake in that red-rock landscape. After we set up camp on the bare high bluff above, we stretched our legs along a quarter-mile trail through what Carey said were pinyon and juniper trees. Everything smelled like Christmas times ten. At the end of the trail a tract of fossils had been excavated, three-toed dinosaur tracks and worms. Prehistoric everything had bored its mark into the earth. Along with the world's biggest cross, half-bur-ied Cadillacs, fence lines, oil wells, ancient volcanoes, the Santa Fe Trail, and cross-continental black-snake highways. Every being that ever lived and died had staked a claim.

Me? I was bound and promised to keep moving.

After state-park bathhouse showers—our first in two days—we debated about supper. I voted to go back into Clayton to see what was shaking. I begged for real food.

"It'll be twenty-five miles going and coming," Carey warned. But I wouldn't take no. Miles were starting to show their true colors as a luxury.

Seven o'clock local time, the sun was setting, and there were no parking spaces near the Eklund Hotel and Saloon. Besides that one place to eat, only the Luna was open, an old movie house across the street. Above the marquis a yellow moon face alternately winked and smiled into the dusk. The saloon's sign ringed yellow bulbs around *EAT and DRINK*, as if it advertised a carnival. Music and talk erupted as people came in and out. As the Plains went dark, we'd found the pumping heart.

My whole body relaxed into a beer and the leather booth. Shania Twain and chatter drowned out the television over the bar. After two days it felt great to be clean and part of small town life, even for an hour. We were halfway through our hamburgers when a big group of what looked to be rodeo stars pushed with a blast through the swinging doors, the men all wearing denim shirts and white jeans, leather chaps. Even the women wore cowboy hats and boots, the whole group of them in pale chambray shirts and white denim skirts.

Then I remembered the wedding the visitor center guide had told us about. In a bit the bride and groom came in to cheers. They were both in white—white Stetsons, white boots with silver stitching. On the brim of the bride's white cowboy hat, the veil piled up like snow on a ledge.

Like everybody in the place, Carey and I couldn't keep from leaning out of our booth to watch down the long bar, where the whole wedding party took up residence. One of the groomsmen shoved quarters into the jukebox, and they surrounded the bride and shouted into their longnecks with Tammy Wynette, "Stand By Your Man." The bride plugged her fingers in her ears and doubled over in a fit of laughter.

At the first notes of a Linda Ronstadt song—"Different Drum," a tall man, the bride's dad, pushed through and handed off his empty beer bottle. As Carey and I made our way to the door, I turned back once to watch him lead her in an easy two-step, holding her loose but close. No one needed to hear what they said to prove they were happy.

"Toast! Toast!" The call went up as the door closed behind us. I looked through the window, and except for the father's smile, he could have stepped straight out of a Marlboro ad. A dad of mythic proportions. He made Glenn Daniels seem like a silly cartoon villain.

Dancing and alcohol at a Baptist wedding would be like bringing cupcakes and balloons to a funeral. And I married Dawson at Grandma Ruby's church, at her insistence, before I ever grew half-a-nerve. I was only twenty years old. It was a dry wedding, except for Daddy. He's lost more flasks than most people own in a lifetime.

Like always he managed to be the center of attention. His takeover was the reason I had private ceremonies the second and third times around. Mama advised me to elope with Dawson. "Your daddy'll horn in 'til it's all about him," she warned.

We all knew Daddy could be like a spoiled kid ripping into everybody else's Christmas presents. But at first it flattered me to see him so proud. And he seemed changed. He bought us a set of nesting cast-iron skillets. Inexpensive, but the only gift he ever bought me himself. He fumed when Mama and I went to the florist and bakery without him. He ended up in the backseat of my car three sheets to the wind the day I drove my cousins Stacy and Mindy to be fitted for their bridesmaids' gowns. He made me stop at every hole in the road he knew, gas stations and country stores, the feed-and-seed, to show me off to anybody he'd ever met. He rolled down his car window and howled, happy as a truck dog.

But I soon figured out my wedding was just an excuse for him to take a springtime bender. He came drunk to the rehearsal dinner. He walked me down the aisle hungover and nervous as a cat to say four little words like the preacher instructed: "Her mother and I."

Until ten minutes before the ceremony started—when he was already a half hour late—Mama and I fended off questions about where he was. She said he was stalling to get attention. But I thought it would be just like him to be wrecked in a ditch. In the room off the sanctuary, Mama touched up my braid and straightened my veil a dozen times. Dawson's mother sat and fidgeted in her pastel dress, like she was about to be called in for a pap smear. Dawson's sister Rayanne and my cousins preened, in bubblegum-pink taffeta I was sorry I'd let them choose. They called it fuchsia.

Once Daddy came in, the peace—forced as it had been—was done for. His form in the room unleashed frustrations. Mindy set in to bickering with Mama that I should have had a flower girl. Dawson's mother blamed Stacy that the dress didn't fit Rayanne right. Mama fussed with Daddy to put on his tie. He refused. I stood at the window, fading into the curtain sheers. Dawson's mother finally exclaimed how nice Daddy looked, that she could barely believe her eyes.

"Damn monkey suit," he replied sourly. I pulled him aside before she got a whiff of him.

"He does clean up real good," I said. And he was handsome. The charcoal gray suit showed off the solid black of his hair. He looked ten years younger, but he needed some Visine.

"Faye?" He whirled around looking for Mama and staggered toward her. "These goddamn shoes're killing me." His voice was as loud as his breath. He leaned forward and back, the leather creaking. "Cost half-a-damn fortune. Like to pinch my feet off."

"Glenna, make him hush," Mama whispered. "Hush up, Glenn. You got nothing to complain about. I paid the bill for them clothes. All anybody is asking you to do is wear them for one hour."

"You did not." I forgot to whisper.

"You think he's going to spend his money on a blessed thing?"

"I get paid Monday," I said. "I'll pay you back."

"You'll do no such a thing. If anybody pays me back, it'll be you, Glenn, you hear?" She poked his shoulder and he jerked away. "He gets his check next week."

"Why should I pay for some goddamn get-up I ain't wearing but once? Shoes like a vise." He looked at his feet, his hands swinging loose. He pouted.

"Maybe we could just take everything back," Mama said.

"That would be so wrong, Mama."

"Well, that way it won't be a total waste," she said.

He was alert enough to hear that. "What? Now, what're you saying? How about that white dress your girl has on? Ain't that a waste? It's a damn-sure lie."

"Glenn, hush up." Mama stepped between us. "The whole church can hear you."

He spoke louder and stepped around her toward me. "Who're you trying to fool, Sister? Anybody here knows you and Dawson's been shacking up." He coughed a laugh. "The bloom's done off that rose."

I usually would have raised a stink to match, but after he'd had his say, I let him walk me down the aisle. I felt vindicated that everybody had heard the harassment and abuse I was marrying out of. In ten minutes, I would have a new last name. A new family. I'd be a clean slate.

Not that I was ashamed for anybody to know, but Dawson and I had been living together, during my last semester of college. It was a religious school, so I could have been kicked out for "fornication," which egged me on even more happily. For a small town in the South, cohabiting in the '80s was scandalous. Mama had to tell me about a customer's snide comment. And her friend's offerings of prayer. They thought Dawson and I were renegades. But I was only impatient for a dull and predictable life.

That last semester I commuted from Newport, where Dawson worked at the Firestone plant. We lived just a few streets over from Mama's trailer, but I had my own kitchen and a new box springs and mattress, and a man bigger and stronger than Daddy. Who cared if it was just a refinished apartment? Including our porch, we had more floor space than Mama's trailer. We set up a whole new life in the biggest house at the top of the highest hill in Newport's downtown, on the nicest street.

Daddy said I was getting above my raising. At first, he wouldn't set foot past our porch. But as soon as we started planning the wedding, he smelled a party. He showed up for Saturday breakfast three weeks straight. Then he started dropping by during the week with a six pack. Before long he made it into our bedroom—where Dawson had his prized possession, a big color TV—laughing it up over re-runs of *The Beverly Hillbillies* and *Gomer Pyle*. I took my time cleaning the kitchen until he was drunk enough to leave.

Daddy wriggled his way into the planning. Instead of his steady diet of Bob Seger and Lynyrd Skynyrd, Dawson started listening to tapes Daddy brought in, of Doc Watson and the Stanley Brothers and Bill Monroe. Daddy carried his guitar, a steady sidekick. Pretty soon he was playing along for Dawson nearly every night.

I told him, "There's no way my daddy is picking and grinning at my wedding."

"Our wedding," Dawson said. "Ours."

"Not if you're going to make stupid decisions." The little warning voice in the back of my head zinged. The more I avoided standing up directly to Daddy the more I took out my anger on Dawson.

"Look." I leveled out my voice. "I just can't say it plainer. I'm not about to walk down the aisle to Daddy's goddamn hillbilly music."

But one night after too many beers, when it looked like Daddy was never going home without some kind of win, I compromised. He and Dawson could have free rein over the reception. But Daddy wasn't happy singing a few numbers in the fellowship hall. Before I knew it, Dawson had promised half our budget for a rented tent and picnic tables and beer on ice for half of Cocke County. Dozens of Daddy's cronies showed up that evening. Like bloodhounds they found his Uncle Ed's farm on the French Broad. By the time the barbecue was served, it looked like the Fourth of July, not a wedding reception. And I was too drunk to care.

Nearly everyone changed into T-shirts and jeans and sundresses and shorts. Like a groupie, Dawson put on overalls to match Daddy and Dunn and their band. Mama kept trying to get me to change out of my wedding dress.

"They's already grass stains all over the train, where you've traipsed around, Sister. You'll ruin it."

"What am I going to need this dress again for, Mama?"

She shot me a snarky look.

"Really? That's what you think? Well, I've paid three hundred dollars to wear it for one day, and I'm bound to wear it out." That dress announced, with every hand I shook and every smile I forced that I was finally clean, beyond the quarrel. For weeks I hadn't said an intentionally unkind word to Daddy. In tying myself to Dawson for the future, I felt sure I had undone the past.

I walked alone down the cow path to the edge of the river. Dusk turned the deep June world into a jungle. The river spun under a rising fog, its rush nearly blotting out the banjo and fiddle. I knew the folds of white stood out against the poison ivy and kudzu and creeping vines. But I felt invisible and immune. Out of Daddy's reach, I would make a new refuge and never look back.

Twenty years old. What did I know? Before twenty-four hours passed, the idyll I envisioned was wrecked. Dawson and I had lived in the same house for a few months, but we'd never been together without the buffer zone of study or work or wedding plans. Away from routines, we were awkward. We left for the honeymoon the morning after the wedding, hungover and arguing before the first cup of coffee.

"Highway 70 to Asheville is way prettier than I-40." Dawson lolled in bed flipping channels while I packed.

"But that's nearly a three-hour trip." I sat on the bed to lace up new sneakers. "Interstate will put us at Biltmore in just over an hour. Anyway, you're liable to get carsick on 70, even without all the drinking you've done. Especially on those curves past Hot Springs."

He sprung up. "There you go throwing Hot Springs in my face again! Just because I didn't want to spend my honeymoon in a damn jacuzzi."

"Did I say that? No. All I did was mention a town on 70, the road *you* want to take. And it's not a jacuzzi. It's a historic natural spring. And I'm over the fact you never want to take me there." I hadn't meant to rile him, but he was a sucker for even unintentional bait.

"It ain't ever enough for you, is it? You got to gripe, even though we're doing what you want for two whole days." He slammed his dresser drawers, tossing faded T-shirts onto the bed.

"Well, your idea for a honeymoon was fishing on Douglas Lake, which you do nearly every weekend." I shut off the blaring videos on MTV. "And the Asheville Day's Inn isn't exactly romantic, but it's all we can afford after that reception."

"Now you drag up more I done wrong! You want everything to go your way."

"I just want to get to Biltmore sometime today. We're already behind because you wouldn't get out of bed. And you're not even packed yet."

"Goddamn, Glenna! You want me to punch a fucking time clock?" He pulled out his duffel and crammed in socks and boxers. He tugged a pair of jeans out of the dirty clothes, jerked them on, and tucked in the Charlie Daniels T-shirt he'd slept in.

"That's what you're wearing?" I asked. That was one step too far for him to let me win the battle. It took three hours to drive Highway 70 to Asheville.

After a quick tour of Biltmore and the gardens, we stood on the stone terrace overlooking layers of blue mountains. A river ran between freshly mowed hills, and the scent of hay sparked a sensation from days on the farm.

"I don't get it," Dawson interrupted my remembering.

"You said the same thing inside." I held back a sigh. "Go ahead and say what you mean."

He shrugged and turned his back on the view, leaning against the low stone wall. He'd been sullen all afternoon, unimpressed by the table to seat fifty, the library with thousands of leather-bound books, bored with the bowling alley and swimming pool in the basement. He sat on a bench while I wandered acres of roses. I pictured being married there. Thousands of golden pink and ruby roses and overwhelming sweetness.

Now Dawson was unimpressed even with the view, as if God himself had presented distasteful colors. He slumped with his hands shoved into his pockets, the last moments of a yawn stretching his lips across his wide teeth, hair unwashed under his baseball cap. *Who doesn't bathe on their honeymoon?* I wanted to scream at him.

"I don't get any of this." He gestured as if he could make it all disappear. "It's stupid. Just because somebody—I don't care how rich—put up some Frenchy building where he wasn't even kin to nobody. Entertaining a bunch of his Yankee friends. He just shows up poor people all around here. And now a bunch more people from everywhere else and up North have an excuse to look down their noses at us. Like we don't know what to do with our own land. You ask me, the guy was a dumb fuck. Spending all the money he had just to show off his money."

"You don't get why he wanted to make his family and friends happy? Why people want to visit an American castle? Just look at the view, Dawson."

"Well, hell, anybody would want the view. But what right did he have to claim how many square miles? All for hisself?"

"He had the money to do it."

"That don't make it right," he said.

I turned and started down the stone steps, wishing he had gone fishing, gone to his mama's for supper.

"You're just jealous. And a pain in the ass," I said over my shoulder. Dawson was beside me in a split second. He jerked me by the elbow to his side, eyes furious. I didn't mean to cry out, more surprised than hurt, though the pinch left a bruise. He stopped, aware of people watching us.

We were silent all the way back to the motel. After a nap, Dawson insisted we order a pizza and get the most out of our HBO. He laughed at *Beverly Hills Cop* while I kept an eye out the window. Over misty rooftops and parking lots, the lights of cars headed to dimly lit restaurants and downtown shops. He pulled my last twenty out of my wallet to pay the delivery guy.

I could only eat one piece of pizza, but I helped him down two beers out of a six-pack. Dawson lay back on the bed beside me and reached under my shirt trying to unhook my bra.

I was up in one swift move as I peeled off my shirt. "You want to fuck me while you're watching Eddie Murphy?"

He stood up and seemed ready to protest or defend himself. But then he reached for my hair. I pulled away and unzipped my jeans, stumbled out of my sneakers, naked in seconds.

"Okay. Let's see what else we can do to make sure Dawson is happy. You need another beer, Sweet Pie?" I bent to reach for the cooler. "God forbid we might have sex while you're sober. Do it to me like last night. Best two-and-a-half minutes I ever spent in bed."

"Stop it, Glenna." I looked for the first time directly into his face, red and aroused. He grabbed the can out of my hand.

"That's right. Wreck my other arm, too. Matching bruises to take home from my honeymoon." I couldn't stop, though the part of me watching from inside my head was sending up warnings right and left. I've never known how to back down from a dare, from a warning.

"I said to shut it, now." He pushed me down on the bed and held my hands over my head. He kissed me hard, but he could tell I didn't want him yet, struggling against every touch to my breasts, thighs, his fingers in me, but by the time he came, I was bucking underneath him. I got up and took a shower for twenty, thirty minutes, until I could hide my outrage. He had goaded me. But I had broken my promise to myself to be a good girl, for better or worse.

During the nearly two years we stayed married, I never asked Dawson to take me anywhere else. And he never offered. The one rule for peace was to keep the living minimal. Nothing exciting equaled nothing to negotiate. The routine was safe once I learned the boundaries of his temper. And I was a quick study after years of on-the-job training with Glenn Daniels.

When Dawson said he wanted to move, I resisted. But no use. He bought a trailer without telling me and set it up on land he bought without telling me, in Del Rio, forty minutes outside Newport.

A trailer. When he drove us out to show me what I'd be helping pay for, he thought I was crying for happiness. He didn't even know me enough to see it would kill me to live there, backed up against the ninety-degree pitch of a mountain, a red clay clawed-open yard, where not even a garden could grow. We rode every morning into Newport for work together and rode home together. I was free during the forty hours a week I worked at Child and Family Services.

The sheer logistics of having an affair with Sam—in an exchange program for a few months training young recruit cops—looked impossible until he transferred to the Knoxville police force. Dawson believed my excuse about a huge raise—which I did get. But Sam was the reason I took on a new job and a three-hour commute every day to Knoxville and back. Sam and I had flirted for weeks. Way too much foreplay in my book.

The geography and schedule that had shut me in a trap for nearly a year meant there wasn't a snowball's chance Dawson would catch us, and I never paused for guilt. I rationalized that my infidelity paled beside Dawson's accumulating betrayals—words that stabbed, slaps and shoves and punches that pushed me toward a new possibility, or at least a good time for a change.

I was sure no one in Knoxville knew Dawson, so there was no danger he'd find out. But Sam and I swam in a small pond, where every colleague knew my paperwork had a box checked "married." Sam and I knew it would take just one nosy person from human services or legal aid or juvenile justice, one storytelling fool, to get us fired. Co-workers dated and married, but adultery was grounds for dismissal.

Keeping secret wasn't just exhilarating, it was exhausting. For a while it was great to be together in secret. But privacy eventually wrecked us. That and Sam's over-protectiveness; those two things went hand-in-hand. After the wedding we subsisted on little else besides one another, the most peaceful life I've ever had. But also the most smothered. Sam thought he could fill my every need. He was offended when he couldn't. He learned that I was perennially dissatisfied with one thing: being coddled. Which was a lesson I had to learn too.

But at the start, it was festive. "If we did go on a honeymoon, where do you want to go," he asked me.

"I don't want a honeymoon. I told you. I want to get married the day my divorce is final, and that's Friday. Then I want to move in with you and stay put."

"But if you did want a honeymoon, where?" He was so earnest.

I gave him the same answer I'd given Dawson two years earlier, my simplest unfulfilled wish. "I want to go on a horseback ride. There's a ranch on the French Broad just near Del Rio. I want to ride a horse and then go to Hot Springs in North Carolina."

Sam laughed and his wide brown eyes were gleeful. "Hot Springs is just a step. We can go there any old time. We'll go. We will." He ran a hand through his blond curls and grinned. "You know where Sheri wanted to go for our honeymoon? Shopping in Atlanta and then stop by the mall in Chattanooga on the way home."

Early on I enjoyed the litany of contrasts he made between his first wife and me. Sheri was, as Sam put it, "a high maintenance girl." But after awhile a second wife who hated perfume and nail polish and strappy heels got dull. In Sam's memory, Sheri became an exotic difficulty. I was frumpy in my boots and turtlenecks. I should dress sexier, join a gym, not eat so many sweets.

"Sheri always watched her weight," Sam would tell me. Sheri was petite and weighed a hundred pounds. Sheri wore a thong bikini. Sheri gave good back rubs. Sheri could tie a knot in a cherry stem with her tongue.

But that was as close as Sam ever came to comparing sex with me and sex with Sheri. Even without her as a gauge, and right up until the end, we both agreed that neither of us had ever been so physically addicted. That's not to say the sex was satisfying. We were always a blur. Nothing tender or intimate, just a frantic urge, like flesh explosives. Cheaters are probably at risk for a high-intensity diet of one another. Long after our marriage should have been over, the crazy rush of sex held us to each other. A honeymoon would have been wasted.

And maybe the truth of it is that no one should take a honeymoon. A trip for the tenth anniversary as a reward makes sense. But there shouldn't be a reward for making it through a wedding. And maybe everybody should have a civil ceremony. The simple gesture of it stays untainted for me. At the end of an average work week, Sam and I stopped in at the justice of the peace at the courthouse. No family, no fanfare. The notary public and Sam's partner Kyle were our witnesses, sworn to silence. But Andy Frank from central booking surprised us at the office door to make our picture. We'd forgotten we were in the building that registers marriage licenses.

A couple of Sam's buddies on the force blocked our way at the threshold to the main hallway and told us we had to wait. Secretaries rushed into the conference room with plates and cups, cans of nuts and butter mints. Somebody had run out and bought a stale cake that read, *Happy Wedding Day, Glenn and Sam.* The misspelling caused a ruckus of laughing around the room. It was easy to see where the word "birthday" had been scraped off and revised. Red roses had replaced blue ones. After a couple of slices were cut, the whole cake blurred to purple. I made sure Andy took pictures of it.

Sam mentioned popping some champagne, and we all joked that Judge Taylor would smell it from his chambers and put us under house arrest. I fed Sam a piece of cake and he kissed me in front of everybody who threw strands of shredded documents like confetti. We plowed out into the fall wind and ran for Sam's cruiser. When he started it, the siren went off, and the lights; the radio was on full blast. We jolted out of our skin into full-blown hilarity, circling around the parking lot as a couple of Sam's deputy friends chased us on foot waving their regulation side arms.

When I married Kevin, I was five years and an MSW smarter. Wary. Less desperate to please anybody besides myself. Tired of pretending to be pleased. I was earning more money than ever before. Maybe because we were in our thirties, the rituals and the wedding—as well as the sex—were more satisfying, comforting. With Kevin, I learned to inhabit the meaning, not the party. His attention was deliberate. He was alert to vivid tenderness, and he invested in the details. Our wedding was his gift to me. He planned the whole gig.

His mentor in the graduate program, an ordained minister, married us on his sloping lawn overlooking the Tennessee River. A friend played hammer dulcimer as we stood under a bower Kevin had built, which we later put in our garden, to train climbing roses. Those two were our only witnesses. Kevin's every choice was a communication, especially the music ringing out across the green afternoon. And he gave me a bouquet of Siberian irises to match my lilac linen sheath. The whole day his face burned with shy intensity, and pride, I think, over the wedding he created, more corny and beautiful than I had ever imagined a wedding could be.

He quoted a poem by Elizabeth Barrett Browning that seemed prim and unlike him. And he seemed surprised I read the passage from Corinthians about love. The minister asked if we would vow to be loyal and generous to one another, to give and accept unconditional love. In tandem we said, "I will," and it was done. Kevin had helped write Dr. Lyle's blessing, a final surprise for me, I could tell.

Kevin was there in every word: "You can't love audaciously until you've truly learned to put away selfishness and judgment. Put away fear and reproach. Put away the grudges and guilt of your life before. To love truly audaciously means to have mercy, honesty, a zealous peace with one another, a rare and powerful fidelity. You must be brave. Because the opposite of love is not hate. The opposite of love is fear. Live and love as if each moment is your last. Yet also as if it's the first moment to start anew."

Kevin and I held each other's eyes. His smile made fine wrinkles around his eyes, but he looked young. In the flicker of light through the leaves, I noticed gray in his beard, the vulnerable and the strong intertwined. We slipped gold bands onto each other's fingers, engraved with his favorite John Coltrane song, "A Love Supreme."

The day after our wedding hangs in my mind like golden dander. Kevin took me on that horse ride for our honeymoon, my first time on horseback since I was a girl on the farm. The morning was fair and warm as we rode through early September dew. Kevin in front of me lifted his lean, taut arms to point out the leaves starting to change color, the late summer wildflowers and river bamboo growing in sycamore shade where the trail wove through rustling trees. The whole world smelled the way it had when I was new, when I was a girl.

On horseback in the sweltering morning, I felt solid and sure for the first time in ages, maybe ever. Memories built as if they had worked into my skin and flesh by the movement of the horse, flighty images that seemed situated in my body more than in my head. It occurred to me that they were all good memories. And the days ahead looked good because of that shift.

Out in the wide-open field, the smell of the horse like dark mint, its neck sleek and strong. I loved the jolting vibration through the core of me, the lurch and sway, the creak of leather, the coarse brush of the horse's mane against my palm. Kevin looked like a boy. I watched the curve of his spine through his T-shirt, the tender stain of sweat, the height of him in the saddle.

In our B&B in Hot Springs, we fell into bed before we showered, smothering in the saturated air as if we made our own atmosphere. Our lovemaking had never been more than quiet, warm coupling before the wedding, but that evening we made so much ruckus, the owners couldn't look us in the eye when we came down for dinner.

We'd made an appointment for a soak at Hot Springs after dark, but in Indian summer, the water and air seemed the same temperature. Our jetted tub—filled with the water of the natural, historic springs—was on the edge of the French Broad, so we watched the river rolling past. Ivy-covered lattice and a wooden roof sheltered us from everybody else, and even from the dusty starless sky. For a while we were halfway submerged, subdued by wine and exertion, but one touch between us was electric. I was surprised when Kevin pulled the crotch of my bathing suit aside and slid into me. We made our own tide in the water. Our hearts pounded against each other, and I thought of the horses we had ridden, young and sleek headed into the wide open.

Morning brought a sudden clearing chill, as if someone had taken a broom to sweep the air clean. Overnight the last humidity of the season vanished. The sky was high and empty blue, and we laughed at each other's goosebumps, our breath like smoke in the early air. We pulled on all the clothes we'd brought, joking about how many layers we would have to peel off to get at one another later.

After a huge breakfast and Sumatran coffee at the local Appalachian Trail outfitter, we browsed maps and trail guides on old wooden shelves, fingering wool socks and capilene underwear and freeze-dried meals. Kevin told me about his seven months hiking the AT. Between stories about the time he shared his shelter with a skunk and the lone woman he met on the trail who baked him an honest-to-God blueberry pie on her camp stove, he mentioned Max Patch.

"I've heard of that," I said.

"Heard of it? You've never been?" His face looked honestly sorry for me.

He said it was his favorite spot on the whole 2700-mile trek. I'd heard lots of hikers say that, but I had no idea a natural bald could be so beautiful. Twenty miles of hairpin road and an hour later, we climbed the naked steep meadow to the crest of Max Patch, on the line between Tennessee and North Carolina. Halfway up we looked back, and down, the panorama of hills rising outward to the undulating mountains. The highest far peaks burnished with russet. We laughed and chased each other to the top, and we turned round and round until I was dizzy, taking in the 360 degrees.

In the stiff wind, Kevin braced himself against my back, with one arm around my waist. We turned as one pivoting point in the universe. I saw for the very first time how the place I lived my whole life had formed and eroded. The oldest mountains in the world, but still changing.

The circumference we stood on lay like a convex bowl with a blue mountain brim, held together in a curve of gravity and time. Standing against me, Kevin lifted my hand in his and pointed with our outstretched arms, as if together we made a human compass that would always find the right direction.

Metallic jackhammering jolted Carey and me upright out of a deep sleep. In the adrenaline panic, I had the tent unzipped before I could think, to see a little woodpecker make another go at the metal roof above our picnic table. He looked down on me and cocked his head. A few more deafening bursts and he flitted away. I had to laugh when he set off an alarm at another campsite, which rang off the ridge around Clayton Lake. Fishermen were already in boats on the dark blue. The sun was just pushing its fire above the horizon. The last three or four stars pinpricked the cobalt western sky.

Carey squeezed into the tent threshold beside me, with his hand on his heart. "How does one bird make that much noise? Jeez, it's only, what—" He looked at his watch. "It's 5:45."

"But it's nearly eight at home, then."

Just over the mountain timeline, the sun had set early. But we forgot it would rise early too.

"I was dreaming. I can't remember what. Stan was there." He crawled back inside and lay back down. "He loved New Mexico."

I dressed in the little vestibule of the tent and left him to his dream. In the dry chill I pulled on my new fleece jacket and tried as quietly as I could to make coffee on the camp stove. Faint music and the smell of bacon drifted from campsites down the steep bluff below. There was the echo of somebody already washing out dishes, clattering pans.

Carey and I already had a good rhythm for breaking down our site every morning, but we moved slower than everybody else, it seemed. While I waited for him to brush his teeth and pack his things, I collapsed the tent and stuffed it into its sack. The ring of moisture where the tent had been evaporated in less than a minute. Red rocks and soil and the lake were lit like no sunrise I'd ever seen at home. I knew that even if I lived in the desert the rest of my life, I would wake up every morning surprised at the absence of trees and vines and leafy shadows.

My curls had gone lank from the lack of humidity. And that was only a visible sign. Everything about me had shifted in that landscape. I was starved just minutes after breakfast, thirsty even though I started drinking water the minute Carey started the car. I felt poured like willing sand into the blue New Mexico landscape. Through the morning I rode with my window down, thinking about the newlyweds at the Eklund Hotel, just waking up to their first married morning.

I wondered if Carey thought of them, after his dream of Stan. They had bought a house together in Atlanta and drew up their wills even before Stan's lymphoma. They'd had some kind of ceremony in California. I'd seen photographs of them on a beach, barefoot in white tuxedos, holding each other around the waist, everything bathed in a gold light. Carey and I had argued once when he tried to hide those photos from me. It hurt that he hadn't trusted me to be happy for him. He didn't understand that I could mistrust Stan yet believe they had every right to marry. Truly, not just pretend marry. Who imagines we can legislate love? Who imagines they have the right to stop anyone from making a family in their own image? From that sanctity.

In photos from all of my weddings, everybody looks happy, too. Nice, heterosexual matches. But after each divorce, pictures were just bad reminders of my mistakes. The fire had taken my copies of those photos. But I could easily recall them. They showed how I looked when I stood on the cusp of a new start. Dawson and I were posed like kids going to the prom. Sam and I looked like Bonnie and Clyde. Kevin and I squinted against the sun.

Farther west, the plains gave way to layers of geometrics, trapezoidal mesas and lopsided, sunken, defunct volcanoes. The sun bloomed straight out of those long hills. Mid-morning, we caught sight of Carey's first planned destination for the day. Capulin Volcano, a nearly perfect upside-down cone, sheared off at the top, clinker black. Closer, I could see junipers and pinyons on the slope. A thin ruddy line exposed the red earth in a curve around the cinder cone. I gasped to see it was a road.

"Well, surely they don't let you drive up the thing," I said. "I don't see any cars."

Carey laughed at my doubt. Past the visitor center, we wound up the narrow dirt road, coiled like a loose spring. We passed a couple of cars on their way down, and I held my breath as Carey edged the Jeep over, no guard rail between us and gnarled, sun bleached limbs embedded into the crumbling black of ancient lava. There was a parking lot at the top, one thousand feet above the plains.

We looked right into the mouth of that volcano. The dark rock radiated the sun, furnace hot even when a cloud passed, shadows lumbering like undersea animals. On the very top of Capulin, there was no protection for flashing lizards and flickering birds, every surface exposed.

Of course, Carey read to me from the brochure. "Rabbit Ear—you know, in Clayton—that's extinct, but Capulin is dormant. Only 10,000 years since its last blast." He grabbed my arm. "Oh, no! It could blow any second."

He could joke, but hiking the narrow trail around the circumference, I sensed the sleeping force beneath my feet. Far down and around us, every gouge was evidence of the ancient past, visible from horizon to horizon, 360 degrees. We could see four states. Carey pointed. To the east Black Mesa, the highest point in Oklahoma. South to Texas. To the north, Colorado. And New Mexico spreading west, in dark green swaths, pools of water in indentations like giant footprints, blue mesas capped with jags of lava, and hollowed volcanic hills rolling to paler and paler blue stretches until the peaks at the horizon met almost imperceptibly with the sky.

Four days I'd stayed vigilant to see just where the West begins. On dirt roads and the highway ahead, criss-crossing the plain, I could see into the future. I had thought traveling meant I could shut the past, make it extinct. But all that old history is only dormant.

But the future is dormant too. Miles of blue rolled out like possibility. I thought, *this is where the West begins.* Because I could see the West isn't a place. The West is a promise, less a matter of geography and more a state of mind. The West is a risk, a sacrament with the unknown, like a woman facing a man, for better or for worse, a woman facing the landscape like a blank page and writing her name there, a brand-new name.

UP THE RIVER

Carey said *Raton* is Spanish for mouse, but he didn't know why they call Raton, New Mexico, *Raton*. He turned to watch the next-to-last family in front of us get seated at a turquoise naugahyde booth.

"Wait." I grabbed him by the elbow. "Something you don't know? Let's check the temperature in hell." He grimaced at me. "I mean, to see if it's frozen over."

"I know what you mean," he said. "And I mean, I'm going to punch somebody if we don't eat pretty soon. Do you smell that?" Sizzling plates of meat and onions wavered all over the room. "Can you say barbacoa, Miss Smarty Pants?"

The El Matador lunch crowd had waitresses on the move in Spanish, and just like that we were straddling two Americas. The only other whites in the place were highway workers at a big round table, devouring mangled enchiladas. Weather-worn ranch workers leaned back from empty plates, resting their hands on belt buckles, boots cocked heel on toe.

I pointed them out to Carey. "I wouldn't have believed people did that, except in movies."

And then I thought Carey was watching me for my reaction as I watched a mother push tidbits into her baby's mouth while she rattled off commands to four other kids. All of them eating off each other's plates, reaching with tiny dark hands, looking at her with big dark eyes, as if she were the actual Madonna.

For just a few bucks we stuffed ourselves with pork and smoky thick beans, fresh salsa and my first sopapilla. Carey said the Navajos call it fry bread. Whatever it's called wherever, I was a little worried that I liked it more than Mama's biscuits. What was left, we dredged in honey, and couldn't resist refills of oily, black coffee.

Up hilly back streets, looking for a grocery, we got lost in a neighborhood of clapboard houses with rotting shutters and rusted roofs, scraggly yards separated by crooked fences and riots of hollyhocks. In front of one trailer, babies and kids splashed half-naked in a plastic swimming pool. Except for the location, it looked like home.

We browsed in a couple of antique stores. One advertised a museum of barbed wire, which turned out to be a few dozen different strands nailed on a board. I was surprised I'd never realized that somebody actually invented barbed wire. Fences back home always seemed to grow like shrubs or vines, a natural boundary to the next field. Photos and historical accounts boasted that barbed wire had tamed the West. The guy who owned the place heard Carey grouse that it also ruined native ecology, and they had a quick spar on our way out.

Next door was a place filled with ranch tools and kitchen implements and dishes—estate dregs. Carey and I leaned over dusty boxes filled with black and white photos of settlers, panoramas of high school graduations and ribbon cuttings. I didn't see a single Hispanic face like those in the restaurant, only white people. Carey liked the posed studio portraits of obviously wealthy, handsome men with big mustaches. The ones that drew me in were like old pictures from Granny Pearl's family, women looking destitute in dirty aprons. The difference was the background: sod houses, prairie sloughs, rock outcroppings.

Most curious to me were the women my age and younger. And that there weren't many photos of old people.

"I mean, the average lifespan was probably late forties," Carey said. Lots of women were posed in formal clothes, holding tightly wrapped babies or toddlers.

"Why do they look so sad? And really dressed up?" I shuffled through the photos to show him the women with babies. "You think they were scared of the camera? Or homesick?"

"I mean, well, yeah, some of these people, they're serious because they had to hold really still, and they'd never had their picture made before. And it was expensive." Carey took the photos out of my hand. "Oh. These—haven't you seen pictures like this? It was a custom to take pictures to remember dead relatives. These babies have died."

The nonchalant way he said it and the recognition, all of it hit me in the sternum. I squinted at the swaddled bodies and tiny faces.

"They just look asleep," I finally said. I laid out several photos like cards in a game of solitaire while Carey went to look at some books. There in six photographs, the same woman, older in each picture, holding a different baby at a different age. All her infant and toddler corpses.

Six children she buried. I wondered if she ever had a child that lived. I bought all six photographs for five dollars, no name or mark or date on the back of any of them. When Carey asked why I wanted them, I said I couldn't understand who would sell off family pictures, especially now that all mine had burned up.

"But some of these people didn't leave any descendants at all," he said.

I thought I might be sick as he started up the Jeep, to think it. That woman had left her home and all she'd known, maybe, to come west to settle her future. And she ended up without one, except what was lost and anonymous at the bottom of a cardboard box.

Mid-afternoon, just as we'd given up and were about to ask directions, we found ourselves back on Highway 64, and right there was a grocery to restock our milk and melted ice. The luxury of air conditioning swirled like invisible snow. Pale high school girls and pimply-faced bag boys manned the place, but the customers were mostly small, dark people with flat faces and compact bodies. They moved around us as if we weren't there. One old leathery man nodded soberly at us.

I was used to an obligatory shelf or two of Tex-Mex foods, with a few real Mexican labels for the influx of migrant workers in Newport and the area. But in Raton, "Made in Mexico" was the staple down half the aisles. Most customers congregated in produce, where avocados piled in black-emerald cairns. And then there were bins of foods I barely knew or had never heard of: papery tomatillos and jicama and cilantro. The fumes of so many strange hot peppers and chilies gave me a coughing fit. I found Carey picking out apples.

At the checkout, Carey's choices looked trifling and pompous: a little tub of hummus, a four-dollar box of cereal, gourmet cheddar. That little mouse of a town made me feel tall and white. Even at my fairly average five-six, I hovered, the way I'd hovered over the migrant Mexican families I'd worked with early in my career.

It had made me squirm to be the most powerful person in the room, the one who held all the rules, making home visits and judging them. Those immigrants didn't know my family had lost our farm. Those first-generation kids didn't know I was the first one in my family to go to college. They didn't know I was one generation removed from their paycheck-to-paycheck lives, that my brother drew unemployment. My dad had been on disability. That my mother lived in a single-wide trailer. They only knew I had a car. I had a desk and a briefcase. I had the home-team advantage.

The small dark woman in line in front of Carey set bell peppers and lettuce on the worn conveyor belt. I leaned up and whispered to Carey. "Doesn't it seem ironic whenever you see migrant workers buying produce? Like they're hired to pick all day."

He looked back at me confused and then smiled. "These people aren't migrant workers. I mean, I guess there's maybe a migrant ranch hand here or there, but these people have lived here forever. I mean, their ancestors survived the Conquistadors and the damn Catholic missions. Back when this was part of Spain." He watched my face and waited for it to sink in. "I mean, Glenna, they're locals, not like in Newport or Knoxville. They're Native. Americans. We're in New *Mexico*."

"Don't look at the postcards," Carey warned me at a hole-in-the-wall gas station in a place called Cimarron. "You'll spoil what's coming up." Behind his back, while he paid and peed, I spun the rack of postcards and looked. But he was wrong. I was still amazed as we came into Cimarron Canyon a few miles later.

You have to be in a place, stand there, to really get it. To see the people to really get them. And even then, it might not sink in. You might end up a stranger in your own skin.

After the high, open desert, entering the dark canopy of the canyon was an abrupt embrace of cavernous green. The sky was pinched between narrow walls, the Palisades Sill I'd seen on the postcards, tight molten pillars and ruddy lava cliffs, angled up hundreds of feet above the river. The sun reached only the high crowns of green pines, a living green fire.

"Stop. Let's stop." I pointed Carey to a pullover. Two or three cars were parked in a wider space across the road. Families were wading in the river. A father called in Spanish to his son and held a fish on a line. Like Daddy, never happier than when he showed off his catch of the day.

"Trees!" I opened my door the minute Carey braked in the gravel. I stepped into the thickest perfume of resin I'd ever smelled. Carey got out and stretched. "I had no idea all that sky was so exhausting. It's weird. I've never been any place like this, but it's a little like home. You know, those hollers where you don't see the sun till noon?"

Carey laughed. "Same reason I feel at home in a big city," he said. "All those skyscrapers like mountains."

Even though it was just a little past four, we decided to camp there, so early we had our pick of sites at a place called Blackjack. No RVs, no parking lot, even. We parked just off the road and hauled our first load of gear a few hundred yards through a stand of huge pines. Carey said they were Ponderosas, and he kept humming the theme to *Bonanza* while we set up the tent at a bend in the river.

"You saw the bear warnings, right?" Carey asked.

"Ain't scared," I said. "I've seen my share of bears at home."

"Well, I haven't. I mean, I just want to follow the rules. The sign said put our garbage in the bear-proof cans and clean up and store all food in our car. You promise you never had any food in that tent?"

"I'm the one who taught you that rule! No food. Not even soap. I try to remember not to even take a tube of lip balm or gum or mints. You want to look for a Holiday Inn?"

"Tomorrow night, for sure. My ass is broken."

I laughed, but I dreaded a motel. Under the high branches beside the river was a perfect spot. I don't remember a time before I knew how to take care of myself outdoors. Maybe that was Daddy's twisted inheritance to me, the comfort zone of the place I knew I could thrive in. I built a fire in the iron grate first thing. Carey and I both had to put on sweatshirts to knock off the chill, that close to the Cimarron, running so high and loud, we had to holler to hear one another. Mostly we were quiet. When the shadow of the canyon walls stretched across us, I set in to cook the biggest picnic of the trip so far, centered around a pan of fried potatoes, translucent slices curling into gold. Carey complained the smell would attract bears for sure, but he ate more than half the can of salmon I heated, broken into warm, pink chunks. I teased him that bears wouldn't find anything more tempting than his breath. For dessert I fried a pan of apples to go with a leftover hunk of sopapilla.

We stacked the dishes and lay back on the picnic table, too full to move. Too full to fend off a bear. We watched the last pink of sunset between the Ponderosa pines, their bark a crackled terracotta. The river grew darker until we could only make out the white rapids. The sky turned deep blue, and the first stars showed. We groaned to think of the dishwashing still ahead.

"It's only fair we both do it," Carey said. We took the flashlight and carried the pans and dishes up the trail along the river. Past neighboring tents and campfires we washed things at the communal spigot near a compost toilet, an opportunity I took.

Through the fiberglass walls, I heard Carey talking to somebody.

The guy nodded to me as I stepped out. Carey put his arm around me as if we were a couple. "He says last night there was some bear activity."

"Oooooh. Activity." After being inside the dark toilet, the night seemed vividly bright. A wide slice of moon had risen above the craggy outline of canyon rim.

"A mama and two cubs." The guy re-tied a do-rag around his head. "Some asshole left his cooler out, full of fresh-caught fish. And baloney."

I bent to pick up our clean dishes from the cement around the spigot. "Probably not too much to worry about if the guy left," I said to Carey.

But Mr. Do-Rag wouldn't let it go. "That cooler was just the appetizer, and then they went around scratching for the main course. We laid there awake for like two hours, man, hoping we weren't next," he said. "The dickhead was in your site. And bears learn fast. They might be back. They'll rip into cars to get to a cooler."

"Rip into cars?" Carey's face was full of earnest anxiety.

"Oh, sure. Like a can opener." The guy was proud to be freaking Carey out.

"Shit." I heard some hillbilly remnants in Carey's awed voice, and I could barely keep from laughing. I took the dishtowel from him and wrung it out again.

"Thanks for the warning," I said. I showed Carey how to clank the dishes to ward off any bears as we walked back up the trail. "Just make noise. The only thing is not to surprise a bear. They won't come around if they know it's too much trouble."

We fit all the food and even some of the dishes into the cooler, to seal off odors. Carey carried it to the car through the woods, looking right and left at every sound. I followed, aiming the flashlight beam at his feet and the trail, hooting every few seconds to signal our presence. The sound of our car doors slamming echoed alone and human off the canyon walls. I covered the cooler with a blanket, and we made sure the hatch and all the doors were locked, as if a bear thinks like a common thief.

Then after all that, it was me who had the nightmare, the kind where you dream you're still awake right after you fall asleep. I dreamed I was lying beside Carey, paralyzed with terror because a bear was scratching outside the tent just beside my head. My mouth wouldn't work to warn Carey. Those plate-sized paws were digging for me, and her snout made a pass around the perimeter of the tent, stopping near my head to snort. Her fur brushed the nylon like heavy wind. I couldn't breathe, as if I were drowning.

And then I dreamed inside the dream that I woke up from that nightmare. In the new dream, I was relieved, but the tent was gone, peeled away. Carey had vanished, and a huge bearish figure stood near me, watching. The silhouette moved closer. Then it laughed, Daddy's laugh, and in the dark lifted a paw to its head. The orange ember of a cigarette glowed in the dark.

I bolted upright then, as the wind pushed at the tent with a loud shush, the river roaring like a growl. Breathing through my heart pounding, I knew I'd been holding my breath in my sleep. I would have sworn I smelled cigarette smoke.

I turned to make sure Carey was there. The tent was close as a coffin, and I could not stop hearing Daddy's ghost-laugh. I was desperate to breathe, no matter what animals were outside. Some things are way scarier than a bear.

Carey snored as I unzipped the tent and re-zipped it, sneaking out. I sat on the picnic table wrapped in my sleeping bag, shivering from the dream or the cold. My breath shuddered into the air. But I got used to the chill off the water as I breathed. Breathed and breathed and breathed.

Underneath the strange dry smell of New Mexico there was a scent like the rivers at home, the dank smell of death turning back into life, the sweet mineral rot of stone dissolving. Carey told me we would cross the Continental Divide the next day. But right there, the water I was smelling would be joined with rivers flowing west out of the mountains of home, the Pigeon and the Holston and the French Broad.

The moon was long gone, the canyon black. I could barely even see the whitewater of the Cimarron. But the river roared. The noise and dark shut out everything except the cold, and the nightmare which kept creeping back, the sensation of someone watching me. Inside the sound of the rushing water, I couldn't have heard a bear approaching, or a man, or a ghost.

When I was five, I knew something very bad had happened. Daddy held me in his lap on the porch swing and explained he had to go away. Why never occurred to me. "Where?" I remember asking.

He laughed when I asked if I could come with him.

The year Daddy was in jail was a fifth of my life at the time. A huge portion. The wreck between us started then, I think, when he went missing in action. It registered as abandonment, grounds for a lifelong grudge. Worse than having a record, when he came back, we had turned into strangers. We had learned to live fine without him. What other sanction did he need to never completely come back to us?

I learned quicker than Dunn that we had to make do with less. We lived without more than just Daddy. We lived without a tobacco crop that was usually a major part of his income. Mama sold off the cows and calves I had loved to feed with Daddy. And Dunn and I had to survive without Mama, too, when she opened the beauty shop in town. During the days we stayed with Granny Pearl in her house down the road from our farmhouse.

For that year, Dunn and I were inseparable. Mama took down his crib, and he started sleeping in the bed with me. During the day we watched Granny's soap operas with her, while she peeled apples or folded laundry. I taught Dunn to play dress-up or Tarzan in her empty back bedroom. Warm weather we roamed outside, played toss or chase in the field between her house and ours, or in the orchard until the fallen apples attracted hornets and wasps. We played in the dirt road sometimes. In the creek.

Mama insulated us from every other soul. We stayed home even in July and August, like we did during long winter months. Mama stopped taking us to church then, and we never went into town on crowded Saturdays. When we did go with her, for new shoes or groceries, she told us not to talk to anybody. If a man stopped her on the street to ask about Daddy, we never heard her answer. The women looked at Dunn and me with sad faces. I knew the heated flush on Mama's face was part of Daddy's absence, too. Even at home we never talked about him. Mama and Granny would only wonder out loud about "him" when we were supposed to be out of earshot. They put his clothes and shoes away.

It was years later before I understood that Mama wasn't embarrassed. She was protecting Dunn and me in case Daddy really didn't ever come home. The vacuum he left became a space for her to cushion her kids. But Daddy was still lit up for me, grand and limitless. His absence grew from the size of a blind cinder until it consumed every corner of the house. Even outside, in the woods, Daddy's space followed me around, a potent fiery vacancy.

One day in late July, after a year of that kind of life, Daddy reappeared. Mama was getting supper ready with Granny Pearl. Dunn and I sat coloring at the kitchen table. A man stood in our kitchen. We jumped. Then we froze. The early afternoon jammer of insects surrounded the house. The pots boiled, letting off their steam while Daddy stood there like an apparition. Sweat drenched the brown coveralls he wore. The iron-rust scent of him filled the room. For a few seconds more we were sealed off, as if we'd been canned in a jar. Then he laughed and the lid popped off.

"Didn't scare y'all, did I? Look like you seen a haint." He looked from face to face. He pushed his hands into his pockets. "Ain't you going to say nothing? Faye?"

I'd forgotten his voice, how he moved. I'd forgotten what he looked like in his body and not just in my imagination. Mama had hidden every picture of him. It had gotten so I couldn't remember his eyes. When I tried to remember, I would squint my eyes and hold my breath.

Before he left, it had been our ritual for me to sit beside him in his big chair while he watched TV. I'd hold his wide-knuckled hands in mine. I rubbed the calluses and turned his wedding band round and round his finger. His right hand was my favorite. One knuckle was missing from each of his three middle fingers, and the tip was gone from his little finger. I would tap the ends. I had hung onto that memory.

I looked for that tell-tale damage, but he kept his hands in his pockets. Dunn started to wail. I couldn't make myself move. I wasn't sure I believed it, even when Mama pressed me. "Go on. Give your daddy a hug."

For a year I had pictured running across the yard to meet him, carrying a handful of buttercups. I was ashamed I couldn't stop myself from crying, and I leaned on the table with my face in the crook of my arm. The coloring book blurred. Daddy squatted down beside me, and his damaged hand reached toward me. Those fingers were so familiar, wrapped around my hand, but I didn't know who they belonged to.

So young, the hard details of Daddy's crime were lost on me. At five I knew the word "moonshine." I knew Daddy was important, that he had a lot of friends. When he came back, Daddy referred to his time "up river" in broad, fairy tale strokes, so that I came to picture it as a camp where men sat and watched the water roll by, fishing and playing guitar, maybe. And there were no wives or children to tell them to get a job or take a bath or stop drinking.

Years later, when I was nearly thirty, in a criminal justice seminar, I finally understood the legalities of Daddy's felony offense. He had thought he was safe as long as he didn't own the still. He was just the delivery man. But he was ignorant about how far he could go. He probably could have gotten away with selling moonshine locally, but he pushed into North Carolina, and the feds got him crossing state lines. He lost his rights the minute he was convicted of a federal crime. I hadn't known until then that all the election days he threatened to vote the Democrat bastards out of office, he was blowing steam. He wasn't ever allowed to vote again.

But the worst punishment wasn't the lost year or losing rights. It hardly fazed Daddy that he couldn't carry a weapon legally. He could say all the guns in the house were Mama's. And he definitely didn't care that he had a hard time finding a job. What killed him was that he couldn't enter the state of North Carolina, on penalty of having his probation revoked for the full ten-year sentence. He'd been born in North Carolina, just across the line in Haywood County. He'd been used to going wherever he damn-well pleased. The ultimate insult and biggest dare of his life was that exile.

That fall after he came home, I got a firsthand lesson about the year Daddy spent in jail. My first day of school, penned up in that classroom full of little hot bodies, all I wanted was to be home, but we were quarantined away from our families and freedom. There was a time for everything—pledging the flag, reading practice, for playing and for eating. I hated time, watching the clock, slow as a slug. By the time the hands met at the top, my stomach was seized in on itself with hunger. The lunchroom smelled rank as cabbage, and purple mimeographed pages smelled like rotten flowers. Mama betrayed me to Mrs. Watkins, who smacked me with her thin paddle just because I stood up without asking, because I talked.

School put me in a jealous frenzy. At home, I pictured Dunn and everyone I loved together without me. I wanted to help Mama fold clothes and feed the chickens and roll out pie dough. I wanted to play with my baby dolls. I wanted to pee without asking and have a cookie for a snack. All day I pictured Mama and Daddy and Dunn and Granny Pearl drawing and playing ball and reading story books and laughing out loud, without me.

But somehow all the fun I imagined was over by the time I got off the bus. Dunn was usually taking a nap. Granny would meet me at the door and stay with us most days past dark. Mama was working, of course, which I had a hard time getting straight in my mind's eye. Daddy usually wasn't around. And if they were home at the same time, Mama and Daddy yelled at each other or sat silent in separate rooms. I could see she was right, that Daddy never did any work. Sometimes by the time I left for school, he wasn't awake yet or hadn't even come home. He was gone for days, or he sat in his chair and watched TV while he drank beer. He rarely changed out of the coveralls the prison had issued him when he left. The more Mama complained, the less he took a bath and shaved.

In October, one weekend while Daddy was out hunting, Mama hired a local man to mow the fields and mend the fence. Daddy hadn't bought new cows to replace the ones she'd sold. The little square of late garden he'd set out was grown over with weeds. The man mowed that over, too. When Daddy came home to find everything bush-hogged and paid for, I saw him hit Mama for the very first time.

But I wasn't just afraid of Daddy. Mama was raggedy looking, like a hag. On her days off, her hair was a mess, and she wore the same clothes all the time. She had puffy eyes and dark circles, bruises on her arms and legs. She screamed at Dunn when he cried. She forgot money for my lunch. Most days I dressed myself and combed my own hair.

School started to seem like a playground. I made friends. I could climb highest on the monkey bars. I wasn't afraid of the seesaw. The teacher smiled at my drawings of cows and horses and barns. I loved to add and subtract. But best, in the evenings I could read books to Dunn. I rubbed my finger under each word, sounding out the ones I hadn't known before that moment.

I had given up one imagined freedom for a real one. I was good at school. Reward after reward happened right there in my mind, which I somehow knew I could depend on for the rest of my life. Learning made me feel secure and powerful, a refuge.

One morning I came downstairs while Mama was dressing Dunn. Daddy was slumped over the kitchen table, his arms straight across the top, as if he were reaching for the stove. The kitchen filled with the smell of cow manure. When I woke him up, he started whining like a baby. And then he started crying. His face was streaked with dirt, and there were leaves in his hair. The one boot he still had on was caked with mud. Home felt backward for him from what it should have been. That's the first time I felt sorry for him, realizing that we were his new prison.

If Mama was his warden, then I was Daddy's conscience. I felt the burden of his vices—the drinking Mama begged him to quit, the betting, the cockfighting. He made me his complicit companion. I knew the elaborate lies he told her. But I also knew it wouldn't get any of us anything but trouble to rat him out. During my first few years in school, I kept the peace by keeping his secrets. And for all my moral struggle and guilt, my reward was to go with him, riding back roads in his old Chevy truck. I didn't know that the dares and chances he took might hurt me. Or maybe I ignored his obvious instruction label: Trust at your own risk. Either way, I learned too young that a girl might have to save her own life.

The last trip I took alone with Daddy I was about to turn nine. When we turned down old Highway 70, I crossed my fingers that we were headed to his favorite place to fish along the French Broad. He had pointed it out to me once with the promise I'd swear never to tell a soul, not even Mama.

I swayed in the truck as we swung around tight curves, proud and special on that the humid summer morning, full of promise. Nothing could go wrong, I hoped, nothing to splinter the clean streak Daddy had going with Mama at the time. Just a day of fishing, just the two of us.

We stopped at McWalter's ramshackle store for supplies, and the promise deepened. New line and lead sinkers. Daddy grabbed a couple of bags of peanuts and told me to reach into the tub of ice for two RCs. Several miles on, he turned down a pitted road nearly hidden in kudzu. The cool of the river sifted through the window. He braked on a grassy bank near a trickle of waterfall. Fog was lifting off the river under a blanket of birdcall.

We climbed out of the truck, and I ran to the edge of the water, where grasses wavered under the current, so clear. But deep pockets were dark and roiling. I knew those places where the river might seem still ran at a terrific force. I had slipped and fallen before. I knew to be careful to wade out only so far on the slick rocks. There were whirlpools, places where a person could get a foot hung and never get loose alive. And the water was cold. I wedged the two bottles of cola between rocks in the icy water, and my hands went numb in the freezing tug.

Daddy and I unloaded some of the gear and checked the bait bucket. We had dug for nightcrawlers the night before, and a couple of them writhed on the surface of dark loam. I lugged the bucket up the path and set it down in the shade of river bamboo. By the time I looked again, Daddy lay on his back under low branches, his barn coat tucked under his head, cap over his eyes. My stomach complained a little. I'd already eaten my whole bag of peanuts. I wished I'd asked him to buy some Little Debbies or a fried pie. I sat there wishing until the sun slanted through the still trees. We needed to get a fire built and fish caught and cleaned and potatoes scrubbed for the cast iron skillet.

I went back to the truck and lifted out more gear, then walked along the riverbank, looking for a good place to cast, making as much noise as I could, tromping through tall reeds and slamming the tailgate.

"Daddy." I stooped over him. "Daddy," I lowered my voice a little, trying to sound like Mama when she woke him sometimes. "Ain't we going to fish?" I waited for any movement besides the rise and fall of his chest. "Say? Daddy?"

"Now what do you think, Sister?" Nothing moved but his lips. I hated when he answered questions with questions. But I couldn't keep from answering him back.

"Well, I reckon I thought since we dug up them nightcrawlers and drove all the way to the best spot—"

"Glenna." His voice was a threat. He raised his cap just above his right eye. "If I'd known you was going to whine and bitch, I might as well of brung your mama." I hated, then, to be compared to her, even though I felt wrong.

By the time he was snoring again, I had set up the fishing poles as well as I could. I was good at baiting the worms onto the hooks, but I splashed the lines feebly and couldn't reach the water's deep spots, a failure at casting. I'd reeled in plenty of fish, but Daddy always cast my line for me.

Hot and sweaty rage boiled up. I was impotent to make Daddy do anything against his will. And in that moment, I saw it all clear. I understood why Mama nagged him, as he called it. He would lie there under that tree even longer, I knew, simply because I had asked him to get up. I got the church key out of the truck and opened one of the RCs and drank it as I wandered. I walked a ways under some sycamores and peeled off pieces of papery bark and threw them in the air like confetti. I could hear a car every now and then on the highway through the trees.

I gathered up the flattest rocks I could find and one by one skimmed them on the surface of the water. One rock skipped seven times, my farthest ever, but no one saw it. Once I'd seen Daddy skip a rock fourteen times. That had been on lake water, an even surface. I determined I would out-skip his record right there. I spied calmer water, but it looked deep and dangerous. Trash racing by told the water's speed. While I stood there, a couple of plastic bottles and a rusted can swirled past.

One time at the river I'd seen somebody's baby doll floating by, without any arms. It looked like a real baby for a split second, and a scream rose in my throat right before I saw that it wasn't. I'd just begun to hear in school about awful things people did to their kids, beating them with belts way worse than Daddy whipped me, breaking their arms and ribs. I knew a boy who had been burnt with cigarettes. I'd seen the circles up and down his arms.

The sun was straight above, the sky hazed over. Sweat rolled down my spine as I walked. High in the trees, insects buzzed. And then the quiet was broken by a plane I couldn't see, its engine boring down like a giant, annoying fly. Minutes hung. As I swayed, widening silent circles in the river pulsed. I gave up and sat in the damp grass, held myself upright with my arms around my bent knees. The inside of my head was like cotton batting centered in the droning landscape.

Boisterous voices of men broke the air, and I was surprised to find myself out of my own bed. The tops of my knees and forearms were red where my sleeping head had been. I sprung up to look through dense saplings. Daddy was standing up, slapping at his pants legs with his cap. I recognized one of the two men reaching to shake hands. Sully. I'd heard Daddy argue with Mama about him. But I'd never seen the old man. I couldn't tell if he was stooped from age or laughing. His filthy overalls slack on his bent frame. No sounds came out of his toothless mouth. I stared into that hollow until he snapped his jaw shut and looked straight at me. As if I'd willed him. I had the impulse to run.

He spat out a stream of tobacco juice and pointed at me. "That your girl yonder?" All three men stopped laughing and turned to look at me.

"That's Glenna." I thought Daddy sounded proud, but then he said, "She's come along so's her mama wouldn't pitch a fit." He squinted and raised his voice, "Ain't that right, Sister?" They laughed. He didn't even mind saying I was nothing but his decoy.

The three of them stood around Sully's ancient rusted-out Ford like buzzards guarding a carcass. The old man leaned on the rounded hood. Daddy smoked cigarettes with his foot propped on the running board, his elbow stuck into the dark interior. Their vague voices raised and lowered between bursts of laughing. I sat back in the whorl of damp grass that still held the impression of my rump. Birds called in sycamore limbs. Across the river, a cow bawled and bawled.

I wanted Daddy to notice that I had turned my back on him, not like a mute stone, but actively stubborn. But my attention didn't hold. The water mesmerized me. I had to close my eyes against the hard light and heat. I'd focus for a little while on despising Daddy, but then my willfulness lapsed into episodes of boredom.

I woke up nearly at the same moment I was on my feet when a siren careened on the highway above the embankment. My pulse jumped in my throat. Everything was silent in the aftermath of that wailing, no cows, no birds, no voices.

I had a sick hunger in the pit of me, drenched in a panicked sweat. The light had shifted so much that where I'd been sitting was in full shade. Beyond the trees, Daddy's truck was gone. Sully's truck was still parked on the wide, packed dirt, but I didn't see anyone. I was breathing hard before I started running, up the path along the river. There was nobody. I stopped to look behind me. I'd heard about kids getting lost in the mountains. I thought I could trust Daddy to find me if I stayed put where he'd left me.

Near Sully's truck, I was relieved to see our fishing gear where I'd set it. At the river's edge the little bucket of worms I'd set in long morning shadows now rested in the hot glare. A few nightcrawlers had surfaced. They were dead as shoelaces.

A claw gripped my shoulder, and I knocked over the pail as I whirled around.

When I rared away from the old man, I stepped into the river, wet to my ankles.

"Whoa. Whoa!" He laughed. "You ain't afraid of a little pile of worms, are you?" He bent with a grunt to set the bucket upright and pushed his face toward me, as if he couldn't see well. But his eyes held mine. "Say?"

"You snuck up on me."

"Aw. A girl like you? You ain't a-scared of nothing."

He had watched me run like a fool. He'd spied on me while I talked to calm myself down. And before that, he'd watched me sleeping in the sun.

"Where's my daddy?" I stepped out of the water and around him. My sneakers squished.

"He done went with Sully. Said you could come go home with me. You know how to make a man some gravy and biscuits, don't you?"

My tongue was a warm stone in my mouth. My legs like pillars welded into the thick soggy grass. His words might be teasing, but his eyes told a different story. He leaned up and fingered his tobacco wad, tucking it against his gums.

For lack of any other way to defend myself, I turned my back to him.

"I believe you're about too big for your britches. A man's liable to take a switch to a young 'un like that." He reached out and yanked the hair on the back of my head. I cried out only because it surprised me. He fluttered his grimy fingers and several strands of my hair floated away.

"Your mama ain't much for your daddy's friends, now, is she?"

I pictured Mama at home with Dunn. She'd looked so tired when I left, but hopeful. She told me to catch a fish and have fun. Even in the early light the kitchen was a mess. I felt guilty to leave her. But Daddy was waiting for me in the truck.

"Naw, she don't allow your daddy much fun a tall. A woman, now, she ought to give a man a inch or two ever now and then. Look a here. You listen to me. You go tattling and there ain't no telling what kind of a bind you'll land in."

We both looked up at the sound of Daddy's truck pulling in. I felt the claw on the top of my head, just as I was about to run. He drew me to his sour breath. "You better keep your damn mouth shut."

He left me soldered to the bank as he joined the other two men. Daddy looked like a stranger while I tried to figure out what the old man wanted me not to say. Something ugly had happened, but even if I'd wanted to tell, I didn't know the words to explain.

Daddy and Sully carried two quart jars apiece by their rims. Moonshine, I knew. In the long sunlight it glowed like liquid fire. Sully pulled lawn chairs out of his truck bed. The three men started to drink before they sat down around the fire-ring I'd gathered rocks to build earlier in the day.

I sat in our truck, waiting to see how long it would take Daddy to notice me, to remember I hadn't had a bite to eat but peanuts all day. He hadn't said a word to me all afternoon. But worse, he didn't seem to mind that I returned the favor. I held out hope he'd come find me and we'd try our luck at fishing. I was starved. I was stubborn. I tried casting a line again while there was daylight left. Waiting for a fish to nibble, I remembered the second RC cooling in the river. The carbonation filled me up for maybe fifteen minutes, but by dark I was seriously hungry.

Digging around Daddy's truck floorboard I found the sack of potatoes slid way back under the driver's seat, all shriveled. I washed off one and peeled it with a knife he let me carry. I gnawed the raw pith, tasteless, but not much worse than an old apple, except for a little grit. The men slapped each other and laughed at old lies. The wind across the water was chilly. I climbed onto the hood of the Chevy, still warm from the day's heat. But pretty soon my soggy feet hung heavy and cold.

Daddy opened a second quart of moonshine. The old man sipped his portion out of a cup. Daddy and Sully sloshed the jar back and forth like part of the conversation. Their voices rose and fell around the fire, promising warmth. But I had my pride.

Sully whooped and jumped up when a bullbat dove at the insects around their heads, drawn by the firelight. He clapped his hands and hopped a dance over to his truck and dug around the seats. I thought for a sinking moment that he had another jar of moonshine, but the jar when he held it up in the firelight seethed with green.

"See this here, Glenn?" His voice went sing-songy with whiskey. "I plumb forgot I caught these here for bait, hooked them in with my headlights last night."

"What the hell's got into you?" Daddy swigged deeply.

"Let's me and you wager is what I'm saying. You're bragging about all them bets and dares. I'll bet you twenty dollars you can't swallow one of these here bugs alive." He twisted the jar lid loose.

I'd seen Daddy take harder dares for no money at all. He was serious now, absorbing the challenge. He stood up and wiped his hands off on the seat of his pants.

"Tell you what. You keep your damn money. If I swallow one of them bugs, you got to do the same thing." He stuck out his big open palm.

Sully hesitated but shook Daddy's hand, then shoved the jar in front of him. Daddy dangled his fingers deep inside and hooked a huge katydid. Sully sat back down, and the old man's jaw went slack. The angled legs and green wings fluttered in Daddy's loose fist. I slid down the hood of the truck to get a closer look as he lifted the awkward insect over his upturned face. He opened his mouth and plunged it in. He turned up his half-empty jar of moonshine, and with a couple of huge gulps, swallowed the whole bug.

Should I have laughed or cried or gagged? That stunt. That was the real man my father was.

Sully shoved up out of his chair. Strangled sounds came from his throat as we all watched Daddy hand the jar toward him.

"Eat up," he said. I thought Sully might be angry, but he looked defeated. "About stuck in my craw, Sully. Believe I can still feel him crawling around in my gullet." Daddy took another swig of moonshine and belched. The old man's laugh rang out like a crow caw. He writhed in hysterics, manically standing up and sitting back down.

Sully held a lifeless moth so close to his nose that he was nearly cross-eyed.

The bug was soft and small. I thought even I could swallow it. He closed his eyes and grimaced. He lifted the jar of moonshine with his other hand, ready to wash down the bug. He stuck the moth into his mouth and took a swallow but choked and reeled, pushing his face up toward the sky. He took another drink then coughed and thrust his head away from his body, gagging. Strands of slobber trailed to the ground.

Daddy jumped up and pointed his finger into Sully's face. "Don't puke. If you puke, that's it. You owe me twenty dollars."

Sully stood bent and heaving as if he'd been running. He slung his hands in protest. He strangled through a few words nobody could make out. "That wasn't no part of the bargain. Alls you said I had to do was swallow it. And I done it. Hell, I'm liable to puke bug or no bug."

"Well, you best hold your liquor *and* your bug," Daddy said. He grappled into the jar and plucked the legs off a stout grasshopper. He popped the limbless bug into his mouth like he was throwing back a baby aspirin. Trickles of liquor ran down his chin, glowing in the firelight like streaks of molten gold.

Daddy never set up the tent, so when I got sleepy, I climbed into the truck cab. I thought he had packed our sleeping bags, but I was too stubborn to ask. I could hardly sleep for being cold and cramped. I finally scrunched into a halfway comfortable position, wedged with my knees against the steering wheel. I pulled a burlap sack around me and left on my damp socks and sneakers to stay as warm as I could. I dreamed on the surface of sleep about fried catfish and bugs squirming in mashed potatoes.

It seemed I'd only slept a few minutes when the truck door creaked open. Huge hands fumbled at my legs. I sat up and yelled into the dark. Then Daddy's face came clear.

"We're going to take us a little boat ride, Sister," he said. I could hear somebody else stumbling around and cussing. Sully was stamping out the fire. "Come on now, we got to get a move on. It'll be light before you know it."

I didn't know how the dark would ever stop, like a cloth I strained to see through. Above the river, the sky was lighter than the woods. The barest wisps of fog swirled like ghosts. I followed Daddy to the water's edge. He seemed to be following other heavy steps and splashing. Sully's silhouette climbed into the wide back of a john boat.

"Where'd the boat come from?" I asked. "Where's that old man?"

"He's our getaway man." Sully said. Behind us his truck started up and headlights cut like daggers through the trees.

"Shut up, Sully," said Daddy. "Glenna, quit asking so many blame questions and get your ass in the boat." Under the fog the night seemed brighter, but there was no moon, no depth in the solid dark the outboard motor pushed us through, plowing up the French Broad River.

No one said a word, and Daddy leaned from side to side in the narrow front of the boat, so we made sickening, lazy curves. I thought maybe that was what it felt like to be drunk. Daddy hugged the front of the boat, kneeling with his head forward above the water, as if he were praying. In the time it took him to look toward me, the sky lightened to charcoal gray. The river and its shadowy banks were gloomy and dripping. Even the flitting shapes of birds and their chatter were inside the liquid.

"We're in North Carolina now." Daddy's voice came through layers of gauze. "This is the place, Sully," he called over his shoulder. "Slow her down."

He turned to me. "I can smell it." In half-light I could see the obstinate set of his jaw. Even sidewise he looked at me hard. "You can smell it. Can't you." It wasn't a question. He dared me to defy him.

We came up hard on a rock in the water, then. It seemed impossible that it could matter. I hadn't thought to be afraid of anything. Lazily, the front of the boat crunched across the rock, and the current pushed us up at a tilt. Sully stood stupidly at the back of the boat, which made us pivot. He fell toward us, sliding, and when Daddy stood to help him, the boat tipped upside down. The motor drowned out.

I was lost in the wet, black deep. My whole body turned to burning ice. In the freezing black I sank and sank, blind. I left the night above and entered another night. My lungs urged me to breathe, my heart a white-hot urge. My chest spasmed, craving air, but I plunged heavier and heavier down. And then I couldn't tell the pull of the river from gravity. I kicked with my sneakers, like lead on my feet, and fought to drag myself in the direction I thought was up.

Then there were rocks, slick and cold, just under me. Pushing off them I could get my head above water, just barely. One searing gulp of air, and I fought and pounded the water with my fists, and then with my palms. I struggled toward the faint gray above, but slipped back under again. The noise of my thrashing was the only thing that kept me alive. I fought for a foothold on the slimy rocks. My hair smothered and blinded me as I dug my fingernails into mud and thick, short grasses. I pulled up with one last claw-hold and crawled out of the river. Crouched on the bank I breathed in throatful after throatful of painful air. I stood up but couldn't make my shivering legs take steps at first. The pale sky was red to my right, and I walked in that direction. In the water there was no sign of the john boat, nobody.

I looked up toward voices, up a steep embankment. Daddy's back was to me where he and Sully climbed, scrambling up and falling and laughing. At a level spot Daddy stood upright and shook his hair like a wet dog. He fell again in a drunken spin. His laughing flickered through the trees. He got up again and pulled himself up on tangled vines and little trees. All I could do was follow him.

Halfway up I grabbed at roots and slipped backward with a frantic wrangle and grunt. Daddy turned around. He remembered, finally, to look for me.

"Well, Sister, can you make it? We ain't got all day." He lunged ahead again. I was close enough to hear him breathing hard and shaky.

I slipped on rocks and roots, but I didn't fall. I stepped across felled limbs into dark holes, but I kept going. In my drenched clothes I was so cold I might as well have been naked, but by the time I got to the top I was warm from the effort. My legs were trembling. Through a line of trees there was pavement, and Sully's truck lights blinked red in the hazy dawn.

Sully pulled his tailgate open and threw himself into the back of his truck where he lay on his back laughing, one foot dangling into the gravel. Daddy bent double hooting and laughing and pushed Sully the rest of the way in before slamming the tailgate. I tugged onto the dashboard and heaved myself into the truck cab where the old man sat grinning gape-mouthed at me. An old coat was bunched beneath me, and when I lifted it up, it gave off odors of old piss and shit and oil and smoke, but I pulled it around me. The lining was warm.

Daddy pushed in beside me, breathing like a bull. In a few miles he was snoring into the warm heat that filled the rattling truck. We passed a little sign: *Tennessee State Line.* Daddy looked like a stranger with his head resting against the window. I wanted to lean against him and sleep. But I had learned to keep my eyes wide open. I pulled the dirty jacket tighter around me and looked into the brightening western sky, paying close attention to the rearranged world I was still alive in.

Ahead, there was the silhouette of the hills behind the trees, black shadows in a shifting mist. There, a far light in a valley house. There, the last star was disappearing. Ahead the sky was bleary but lifting clear. Behind us, I didn't have to look to know, the sun like a cigarette was burning a quick hole in the sky.

Dream Baby

In my earliest memory, I'm light and soft as a bird in a nest, safe in my daddy's arms. He's carrying me in lunges up dark stairs that creak and groan, but he's talking in a low voice. He asks if I want to go see the baby boy. All I care about is that he's taking me to see Mama. I know she's beyond that golden rectangle at the top of the stairs, waiting for me. If Daddy carries me up to the light and into it, the world will be right. Time and love will start again.

For years I tried to convince Mama that I remember coming to see her after she gave birth to Dunn. I describe the interior of the old stone hospital to her, which not long after they boarded up and built the new one. How could I know what it looked like unless I'd been inside? I describe the October morning, trees outside blazing. I describe Dunn and his little tow head. But she never believed me.

"You just pieced it all together in your head, Sissy, from pictures and stories we told," she said. "Why you can't any more remember when I had Dunn than when I had you. You wasn't but fifteen months old. And not there five minutes before the nurses got mad. It wasn't allowed to bring kids in the maternity rooms."

"Which was a ridiculous rule," I said. "They don't exclude family like that now. I've got a friend who gave birth right in front of her other kids."

"Well, that's about overboard. I bet them children's scarred for life. I didn't even want your daddy to see me ripped open that a-way. They's some things better left a mystery."

"Aw. You didn't wish Daddy was there?" I teased. "He'd have been a big help."

"He went and slept in the back seat the night you come into this world. And with Dunn he was working. For a change. Now, do you remember that? Granny Pearl and Ed come over in the middle of the night to drive me and take care of you."

"No. That's not what I remember."

"You come into the bedroom where Mama was helping me to get ready, and you wanted me to read to you, and it two in the morning. Ed thought you hung the moon, so he found you a storybook, and I just had to wait. He carried you out to the car, and there I went, lugging my own suitcase. Your granny just wrung her hands. I was a mind to leave the lot of you and drive my damn self to town."

How could I explain that what I remember is missing her, and knowing that she missed me too? And needed me. I listened to her story, looked at old black-and-white photos of her holding Dunny, but none of it was ever as real as my vision of floating up the stairs in Daddy's arms, a gift he's bringing to her.

After I miscarried the baby, I took three days off work. On the third day, I got myself into the shower and drove to Mama's shop. I should have gone to the gynecologist, but I was sick of doctors, especially fertility doctors, who had probed and gouged and just about wrecked me. All I needed was to see Mama. I didn't intend to tell her about the miscarriage. I just knew she would somehow help me see straight. And keep me from making the huge mistake of calling Kevin.

I walked in and told her I needed a trim. My hair was still wet from my shower. She didn't quiz me or ask why I wasn't at work. She didn't ask if I'd signed the divorce papers yet. She just sneaked me in between customers and brushed the tangles out of my hair, out of my head.

After, I bought her the Waffle House works—pork chops and hash browns—scattered, smothered, covered, and chunked. I nibbled on raisin toast and drank caffeinated coffee for the first time in weeks. When I popped a couple of ibuprofen, Mama asked what was wrong. I didn't really lie. I told her I was having my period.

"You remember when you first started?" she asked.

"Well, hell, who forgets something that traumatic?"

She laughed. "You used to get so mad. When I'd tell you it was just natural. And that you'd be glad someday when all that trouble got you a baby."

I stared into my cup. "I remember," I managed. It was impossible to fix a new version of myself in my mind. Just a few days before, I'd been pregnant. I needed a question to deflect her gaze and my grief. "What were you thinking about when you were in the hospital with me?"

"When they handed you to me, I thought they was crazy. Giving me some other woman's baby. They had me so doped up, I didn't even know I'd had you. But now, when I had Dunn, I was wide awake. I remember laying back looking out at the sky just getting light, wondering if your granny ever got you back to sleep."

"You were thinking about me when you were having Dunn?"

"Well, Lord, Glenna, I was used to being with you ever waking minute. I hadn't never left you alone hardly at all, much less in the middle of the night. I was in a hurry to get on with it."

"You never believe me," I said, "but I remember Daddy carrying me up to see you in the hospital. You were in the room at the top of the stairs, just to the left. After those dark stairs, it was blinding, the sun shining on your hair, all piled up on top of your head. I remember Daddy lifted me across those cold metal bars on the bed, and my legs sort of caught on them because I was afraid."

"You like to cried. Your little lower lip all squared up." She smiled into her grits. Always the last thing she eats.

"You smelled good, and you were smiling. You had on this pale green—like a mint green—house coat that had a bow, that felt sort of satiny when I scooched next to you. And I remember you said, 'Good morning, Mary Sunshine,' like you always used to do when you woke me up."

Mama had stopped stirring at her grits. When I looked up at her face, she glanced down and made a quick rummage into her purse to put her cigarettes away.

"I reckon you do remember," she said. She pushed her hair around her forehead and looked at me over the rim of her coffee cup, nothing to read but her eyes, looking into mine as if she were seeing somebody new.

The narrows of Cimarron Canyon, where Carey and I had slept and dreamed, widened as he drove. Steep mountain pastures steepened higher, and past a long curve, my first sight of the real, true Rocky Mountains shivered through me. Carey said to be on the lookout for Wheeler Peak, as if I could have missed it, the highest point in New Mexico, a powerhouse above the blue-black hide of piney foothills. Its slopes still held hollows of snow. Like the sharp edge of an old bone, it scraped the underside of rain clouds.

The sky changed instant to instant, blue bright to sudden dark, shifting shadows across high fields of wildflowers. Ski resorts and condos tucked into coves around Eagle Nest Lake, its surface the faded silver of an old mirror. Past a ski area, shining aspens were spinning their green-gold leaves. Road signs told us we climbed seven thousand, eight, nine, nearly ten thousand feet, nearly twice as high as I'd ever been on the planet.

I was dizzy to be at that altitude with my ears popping around every curve. The colors and the long white arms of the aspens made me think of fairy tales Mama used to tell when we lived on the farm. We would walk up through the cool woods after a hot morning in the garden. She knew Rumpelstiltskin was my favorite, the little man from the woods who spun straw into gold to save the miller's daughter. The queen-to-be promised without hesitation the only thing she would have to give someday, her first-born baby. But years later, once she had a baby and the time came for payback, maternal instinct kicked her into a rage. Of course, she's the heroine. But I've always felt sorry for Rumpelstiltskin. All he wanted was somebody to love. Here he had the power of alchemy, to spin straw into gold, but he knew only a baby would change him. Is he the evil one? He's not the one who welshes on a bet. He's not the one willing to traffic in his own flesh and blood. What kind of person promises to give away her baby to save her own skin? It's hard to tell who's the bad guy and who's the worse guy. In the end, when the queen reneges and keeps her baby, Rumpelstiltskin is so anguished he rips himself in half.

For most of my life, it was a mystery to me that anybody bases their happiness on a baby. I thought surrogacy was idiocy—women carrying their own grandkids, having their sister's husband's offspring. Sperm banks. Egg donors. In vitro. People willing to spend tens of thousands of dollars to adopt an infant when there are thousands of kids in foster care.

But when I lived that want myself, I regretted my judgments and understood the desperation. I'd worked with kids in foster care, the ones whose own parents couldn't put up with them. But even they started to look like a potential family to me. I knew then that I was ready to sign my name on any list, pay any sum, sacrifice my health, and not just for the chance to look in the face of a person who mingled Kevin and me together. But then I found the boundaries of what I was willing to go through, and what I could accept.

From my first period at thirteen, I was scared a baby was something I could catch as easy as poison ivy. Using birth control was like buckling a seatbelt. But one night not long after we'd had that talk about previous partners and blood tests, Kevin opened up his stash of condoms and saw that we were out. It was late. We were already in the middle of things. There was mutual exhilaration, like tandem trapeze artists, so secure in each other's rhythms they fly without a net.

We barely congratulated each other on the freestyle sex, but we talked ourselves to sleep that very night about our baby, as if one already existed. I teased him that he might have to walk a pregnant woman down the aisle. He touched my belly and said that was okay. We could invite the one extra guest. We never dreamed a moment's trouble. But by our first anniversary, getting my period was more nerve-wracking than any late period had ever ever been. We had no idea the grueling stress ahead of us. And I had my first inkling that Kevin had a renegade sense of himself still as a loner. Selfish.

Nearly three years in, getting pregnant turned into a competition with our bodies. The articles we read gave us statistics and clinical protocols. The sexual peak I'd looked forward to became a daily chore in a maze of confusing information. I went to three gynecologists. One doctor said morning sex had a greater success rate, to do it every single day. Another doctor said the male should withhold arousal and ejaculation as many days of the month as possible, to store up sperm for ovulation. She showed me how to chart my cycle. I took my temperature to indicate days Kevin and I started calling the "egg drop." And we scheduled those must-have-sex days on the calendar. Those circled dates stared at me.

For a long time, we took the daily approach. Sex every single morning of our lives for nearly a year, workdays, rainy days, busy days. I had never imagined life's greatest rapture could be as routine as taking a shower or brushing your teeth. Every morning I would turn to Kevin and wake him before the alarm clock. I felt it was up to me to start the engine, so I would stroke his back, sliding my fingers down to the tip of his tailbone, his one fail-proof erogenous zone. After we were done, it was his job to make a big pot of decaf while I lay on my back with my legs in the air, resting my heels high on the cool plaster wall.

Twenty minutes, some days thirty minutes, I held my pose, visualizing the internal drama, the warm temptress egg, the seductively aggressive sperm. There had to be some excitement somewhere, intrigue and lust on a cellular level. I held my hands across my abdomen and imagined cells fusing and splitting into a cosmic seedling, the thick lining of my uterus like rich delta soil.

But I never knew such a sweet time with any other person in my life. Romance was gone, but every obstacle and hope aroused solidarity between Kevin and me. We went to every doctor appointment together. Like runners in a relay race, we passed the baton of strength or weakness, hope or worry, fear and humor back and forth. One of us was always strong.

Kevin read everything he could about preparing my body, but he wanted to sacrifice with me. No alcohol. No caffeine. As athletic as he was, he'd never been a health prude. But now he brought home the first organic vegetables I'd ever heard of. No junk. He took vitamins recommended for fathers-trying-to-be. Instead of solo bike rides, he took me on long hikes in the mountains. We slept eight hours a night. We stayed away from microwaves. We read food labels to avoid MSG, sodium, aspartame. We were study partners, getting ready for the exam of our life.

Then Kevin broke the rhythm and stepped outside our circle. I came home one Friday evening to a celebration dinner. He'd bought flowers, a bottle of sparkling apple juice, which he poured into champagne flutes. He brought me into the dining room, ready with a homemade lasagna dinner and sat me down to the news that he had taken a fertility test. The results showed normal sperm activity.

"Great motility. And quantity, the doctor said." He smiled. I pictured his little tadpole swimmers out for the championship trophy. But his sperm full of speed and vigor raced toward black-hole defeat. Wasted on me.

"You're not happy." He was baffled by my silence. I tried a smile. "You should be hopeful. Knowledge is power. We've got another piece of the puzzle."

"I know. I do. And doctors recommended it. But. Just. For you not to tell me."

"But why worry you? And now we know."

"Yeah. Now we know. We know *we're* not infertile," I answered. "*I'm* infertile."

If coping with that verdict was hard, the dread of my own diagnosis paralyzed me. Kevin made the call for our first appointment with a gyno guy who specialized in infertility in women, the only one in the whole East Tennessee region. Six weeks we waited to see Dr. Jackson, who required that husbands be present at consultations.

"He makes sure there's a husband?" I pushed. "Like it's a prerequisite. What if a single woman has had it with men and wants to go it alone? What if two women come to him to have a baby?"

"Well, two women together would pretty much be infertile." Kevin tried a laugh.

"No. They wouldn't. You know what I mean." I resented going to a doctor who judged lifestyles along with women's insides. But since my body was the flawed one, my cooperation was critical. I tried to fight the sense that I was damaged, which reduced Kevin to a cellular contributor. While my whole body needed fine-tuning to house another human being, he only had to spend a few seconds of ecstasy and aim one hardy sperm into my vast Mojave.

Half the time I had to pretend to appreciate his moral support. I was sick of his little reminders on the refrigerator that I should take my vitamins, avoid stress, remember he loved me. Too many shoulds.

At Dr. Jackson's office, fear made me even more rebellious. I had a surge of strange, wounded power. Before I sat down, the receptionist took a Polaroid of me for my file, so that the doctor could remember my face.

"Why didn't he want a picture of both of us," I whispered to Kevin. "For proof I have a *husband*." I pictured us in one of those photo booth strips, the required husband rolling his eyes and pointing at his infertile wife.

"It's good," Kevin said. "It shows he wants to know you as more than just your problem."

And there it was. *My problem*. "*My* problem," I repeated.

"You know what I mean," he answered, his face red. "We're here for the doctor to fix you."

"*Fix* me," I repeated. "Like all the other walking vacuums in here."

Kevin hesitated with his mouth open, and then closed it. I'll give this to him: better than any other man I ever met, Kevin knows when to shut the hell up when I'm riled. He knows terror makes me mean. He thumbed through issues of *Working Mother*, all the pretty shining women on the covers with their babies. The decor on the walls was even more cruel: gilt-framed Mary Cassatt paintings, mothers in soft pastels holding chubby hands, helping pink, round children. Everybody smiling.

Kevin thought he spotted a silver lining after Dr. Jackson gave us his initial reality check. The female orgasm can play a part in fertilizing the egg, the muscular contractions pulling in the semen. They had a chuckle. But I saw my one fringe benefit turn into another obligation. I responded with a tight smile. I couldn't remember half my symptoms. Kevin pulled out a list he'd typed. He asked all the questions. When I thought of concerns, he interrupted me. The doctor never looked me in the face unless I moved or gestured. Mostly he talked to Kevin.

Based on a diary Kevin had kept of my temperature fluctuations, the doctor said he suspected endometriosis. "May be hard to diagnose in her case," he said. "She's fairly asymptomatic, no abdominal pain, no erratic bleeding." By the time the meeting was over, he and Kevin had agreed on a treatment plan. He suggested we could start with a six-month regimen of drugs to inhibit possible rogue endometrial tissue. If the medication didn't work, I'd undergo tests, sonograms, x-rays, more blood work. Or since we'd failed for so many months to get pregnant, we could go ahead and schedule exploratory surgery.

I came to my senses as Kevin paid the attendant in the parking garage. "What just happened in there?" I asked. The barricade arm swung up to let us through.

"What do you mean?" He checked traffic and pulled onto the street.

"I mean what the hell? I go in for blood work, to check my hormone levels, and he decides to cut me open?"

"Glenna, you heard him. The laparoscopy is probably a last resort if we want. We have choices to think about. So that might not even happen. Plus, it's minimally invasive. They make two little incisions. One above your pubic bone, one—"

"I saw the pictures! You act like I wasn't there, but I was."

"Glenna, don't get upset. He knows what he's doing. Did you hear how great his statistics are? He's the top man from here to Nashville."

"He's a weaselly little bald-headed fucker from somewhere up North."

"Wow. That's kind of personal. You really care where he's from? Because we can go to Atlanta or Charlotte or wherever. But you know that a specialist anywhere else is probably going to say the same thing."

"Will they talk about me in third person? And say stupid things? Did you hear him say at my physical in a few weeks we'll 'check thoroughly down there.'

He actually said, 'down there,' Kevin! Either he's got some hangup or he thinks a hillbilly doesn't know her hoo-hoo from a hole in the ground?"

Kevin let out a little laugh but knew better when I looked him in the eye at a red light. "This is the guy you want cutting on me?"

"Depends on how long you want to wait. How long did it take us to get in with him? And this was just a consultation to see if he'd agree to take us on, Glenna. Do we have a choice?"

"*We?*" There was only the sound of the blinker in the car. "Let him cut *you* open."

Pharmaceuticals showed me every woman's future. And it ain't pretty. For six months I took drugs that threw my body into pseudo-menopause to halt endometriosis. I was prepared for hot flashes and night sweats. But my skin and body revolted. And my mind wasn't far behind. I forgot whole days of my life. I'd be driving, and then couldn't remember where I was headed. I had bouts of ping-ponging anxiety and depression. And a vagina as dry as cured lumber. Every month I gained more weight. Every month Mussolini would have been proud of my period, right on schedule.

Along with the slow torture, Dr. Jackson ordered what he called "procedures," to rule out one problem at a time. Or keep his colleagues in business. Every procedure made me more aware how alone I was in my uncooperative body. It was my feet in the stirrups, my veins punctured and tapped, my breath held for the sonogram, my pulse writing its jagged line, my undone blouse, my naked self wearing those paper gowns. I was a specimen, inspected by beeping machines and hoses and x-rays in cold little rooms. My organs were shadows on one screen after another.

The procedures did not seem minimal to me. First a barium enema the doctor said might prove whether endometrial tissue had formed adhesions in my abdomen. I was sleepwalking into another dark room after a long night in the bathroom, thanks to self-induced diarrhea. I was emptied out, laid-out like a corpse on a bare metal table with a tube up my ass. At least they told me what to expect: ten minutes of humiliation and cramping bowels.

Then they signed me up for a hysterosalpingogram with no heads up whatsoever about how awful it would be. They didn't even warn me to bring a driver, though luckily Kevin was there.

It sounded simple. The radiologist was a voice in shadow, explaining that he would simply force a dye into my uterus, and that x-rays of the radioactive dye would reveal any abnormalities in the uterus or cervix which might prevent conception. No one, not the nurse, not Dr. Jackson, no one so much as hinted that I would suffer.

I always assumed that the worst a woman faces in labor is the pain. But the worst thing about pain is not knowing when it's going to end. From normalcy to agony in seconds, I waited for the pain to diminish. But it grew, solid and consuming. I tried my best to keep from moaning, then to keep from writhing. The technician's helper asked me politely to stay as still as I could. For a while I was alert enough to be embarrassed. But pretty soon I was worn out from pretending. There was nothing else in the universe but the solid block of muscle inside my pelvis seizing up. The other two people in the room were oblivious ghostly planets. I clenched my fists and focused on breathing, trying to keep my teeth clenched around the groaning so I wouldn't scream.

And while I tried to stay on the table, the radiologist talked about his kids' soccer games with the technician. She stood by my head telling about her husband's birthday party. I focused at the end on hating them, their apathetic leisure while he slowly studied my insides on that blue glowing screen. My uterus wadded up in a vise-grip convulsion.

He pondered. He shifted position. Just as he was releasing his instrument, a small part of me, way in the back of my brain, wondered if the pain I was feeling was anything like labor. And then, for just a second of clarity, I was heartbroken to think this awfulness might be the closest I would ever come to knowing what childbirth feels like.

All for nothing. The tests were inconclusive. Dr. Jackson ordered the laparoscopic surgery. We had wasted six months of my body's life, and time, money, hope. Kevin took me for the outpatient surgery predawn. I was the first one whisked through electronic doors into the eerily empty waiting room. I signed the insurance forms. I held out my wrist for the hospital bracelet, gave over my hand for an intravenous line.

The idea of anesthesia terrified me, artificially unconscious in front of strangers without any will. Their hands would lift my body from the gurney to the operating table. They would touch my most sensitive, intimate parts.

The forms I had to sign blurred. The attendant was required to read each one aloud to me and watch me sign. The generic "I" designated in legal jargon meant me, only me. Yes. I understood the intubation tube might knock out my teeth or damage vocal cords. Yes. I agreed not to hold anyone else responsible in the event I suffered an allergic reaction or became brain-damaged or died from the anesthesia.

I signed that if the doctor discovered a problem while I was under, Kevin as my proxy could decide.

I thought then, if I was ever able to get pregnant, if I had a kid, would I ever admit that I hesitated? Because I did hesitate. Were there limits to what I was willing to risk physically? That's what those forms meant that morning.

And the answer I hadn't known until that morning, that very moment, was my signature, my name alone on that line. No. There were no limits.

Drifting in and out of anesthesia, my torso was locked inside a dull torture. I detached myself from the pain and kept drifting, even though a woman's voice nagged me to wake up. In gray dark, I heard myself saying over and over, *it hurts.* But my lips weren't moving. The pain was in someone else's body. A hand on my hip, a huge presence, meant to soothe, but the slightest touch woke up the pain more vividly.

The woman's voice said, "I'm going to give you something." After the needle pricked my hip, the first thing I saw when I could open my eyes was a child in the bed next to mine. She was about eight, struggling with two nurses, fishing her way back into the world.

Immediately then the room went white, and softness suffused through me. I was more awake, but the pain diminished. I fought to lie straight like the woman's voice told me. But my body kept seizing in half. My muscles tightened out of my control, and I made noises. Maybe I asked a question. I was a hard center in cotton fog.

"It's normal, a little spasming," the nurse said. "You're just coming around. Don't fight it." Her face came into focus. The little girl in the next bed thrashed. There were other bodies in other beds. "Can you tell me where you are?"

"Knoxville." My voice came back to me.

"But where?"

"The hospital."

"Good. You're in recovery. You can see your husband as soon as you wake up a little more. And then as soon as you pee, you can go home."

"What did they find wrong with me?"

"The doctor is going over all that with your husband," she said. "You just focus on waking up now."

By mid-afternoon, Kevin was driving us home, filling me in on the details of my own surgery. I never saw Dr. Jackson for one second. He came in after I was knocked out and sliced little holes in me to insert cameras and lights and lasers. He discussed my body with Kevin while I was still in recovery, then on to another surgery.

"That's standard," the nurse said, as I groused from the wheelchair. Halfway home, I woke up in a slurred fury.

"That's the way they do it." Kevin shrugged. "The patient is asleep, so they tell the family. They gave us the videotape to watch."

"I don't want a damn tape. How will I know what I'm looking at? I don't want to see my insides. I want my doctor—*my* doctor, you know—to—"

"Glenna." Kevin's voice was maddeningly patient. "Like I told you, and the nurse, he found endometriosis. And it's treatable. He lasered away what he could. He described it like sort of scraping the abdominal cavity. He said it had probably been worse before the meds. I wrote down some more technical stuff."

"Great. I'm a grocery list."

"Glenna, come on."

"What? The guy specializes in women and talks to men all day."

"No. He specializes in *couples* facing infertility. Together."

"No. I get to say how this feels." I lay my head against the cool window while the woozy world spun past. "How can I be out of the loop? I *am* the goddamn loop."

Recuperating gave me time to try to feel lucky. I'd read and heard so many horror stories. Women whose endometrial tissue invaded their lungs, brains, spines. My case was typical and simple, binding the membranes of abdominal organs, clogging my uterus, occluding fallopian tubes, disrupting ovarian function. I pictured my insides like the hull of a sunken ship, barnacled over, a passageway where nothing would grow, just the flow of would-be life pouring out of me, month after month.

Before the tissue could regrow, during the window just after the surgery, the doctor prescribed fertility treatments. I agreed to play tricks on my body one more time. Twice a day, fourteen days a month, I gave myself an injection at sixty dollars a vial to activate hyper-ovulation. Dr. Jackson said the optimum was to stimulate five or six follicles a month, upping the number of actual eggs and our chances for an embryo. The risk was multiple embryos.

"You want to be those people with a litter?" I asked Kevin. "Quadruplets, quints? You want to be those people on TV begging for a minivan and diaper service?"

"It's a risk I'm willing to take." His answer should have been a relief.

After the needles and years of disappointments, at the next visit, Kevin asked Dr. Jackson about egg donors and in vitro fertilization, which he'd barely mentioned to me. I felt ambushed.

"We talked about this before," Kevin argued on the way home.

"But we didn't talk about *talking* about it with Dr. Jackson. We're already out ten thousand dollars or more. We've got a few hundred left in savings. On my salary and your grad school fellowship, how can we afford some other woman's egg?"

"Well, I didn't want to waste the seventy dollars we're paying for his advice today."

"Okay. Here's some for free. Have you stopped to imagine—just imagine— the shoe on the other foot. How you'd feel to watch me pregnant with some anonymous man's child? Not to mention when the real baby comes along. You look at it, and you're not in the equation. Now imagine how I'd feel. My body carrying some other woman's baby. Your baby with somebody else. In my body?"

He didn't answer, but his face was dark with something I didn't understand yet, not at that point. I never dreamed we were gestating the conflict that would end us.

"Sorry. I'm not that strong," I told him. "I'm too jealous or whatever to raise a kid that's half yours and half from some Vanderbilt cutey cashing in her eggs so she can finish her MBA."

"That's the ultimatum, then? We found the line?" He finally broke his silence as we pulled into the drive. He shut off the car. "That you can't love—or don't want—a child that's mine? Unless it's also yours?"

I wondered later whether that day was the turning point, all those limits we rattled off, the words we said without even knowing what power they held.

One winter evening Kevin came home from studying at the library earlier than I expected. I'm not sure how long he watched me from the bedroom doorway, watching myself in the full-length mirror. I had stuffed a rounded pillow under my tunic sweater. Sideways or front ways, I looked perfectly pregnant. I rubbed my hands over the mound in circles, as if I were rubbing a magic lamp. His shadow caught my peripheral vision. I turned and threw the pillow behind me and sat on the bed.

"Glenna." Tears shimmered on the rims of his eyes.

"Stop it," I said. "Stop."

He knelt in front of me and pushed his face into my lap like a broken-hearted boy. But every touch left me empty. How could I comfort him when there wasn't any comfort for my desperation or my shame.

He pushed me onto the bed and lay on top of me, pressing me into the mattress. I rubbed my hands in a vague rhythm up and down his back but panicked when his position changed. The subtle current from his beard and lips on my neck were smothering. I resisted, rigid. When he didn't stop, I pulled myself from beneath him.

"We can't, Kevin." I knew the words were absurd, but he raised up on one elbow to lean beside me. "I won't ovulate for a couple of weeks yet. There's no point."

He leaned back to study my look. "No point?"

"Kevin, look, I'm sorry, but—"

"No, no." He stood up and fumbled with the bedside lamp. The glare was awful. "Don't be sorry. I'm the one who's sorry. I'm sorry I want to make love to my wife, not just, whatever—copulate—for the first time in months." He held his hand up when I started to protest. "I'm sorry everything you want I can't give you. I'm sorry I'm so inadequate."

Kevin was rarely angry. The sense of his withheld rage careened through me.

"But see," I said. "That's what's wrong, thinking you can fix this, that you're the one who's inadequate. Like my body or what I want is within your control." I stood up and dumped clean clothes on the mattress and started folding them, sweet fragrance washing the air between us.

He watched blankly. "There's something wrong with me wishing it was me and not you? Wrong to want to make you happy?"

"Yes, it's wrong to wish this were your fault. Because that just reinforces that it's my fault. Or that you can make me happy. Like you could just create a baby for me."

"For you? What about for us?" He shook his head, breathed in deeply. "No. You're right. I do try to make you happy. Try to love you. And all you do is reject me."

"See? You. It always comes back to *you*. This is not about you. That's what I'm trying to say. Stop wrapping your ego up in whether I get pregnant or whether I'm happy. Get the hell over yourself and try to imagine what I feel like for a change. This is not your insecurity and your failure. It's mine. This is about *me*."

"No, that's where you're wrong." He grabbed a blanket and a pillow, like a scene from a bad Hallmark drama. "This is about *us*. Us. You're the one who forgets that." He turned back to face me. "What's going to happen to us? If we don't have a baby? Or if we do have a baby? When will you need me again?"

"I need you," I lied.

"No. You're convinced you don't need me at all. You just need some semen."

He had no idea how close he skirted to my true feelings, and I was even more ashamed and defensive. I looked at the clothes I had folded. For a second my vision blurred. I pictured stacks of onesies and bibs and receiving blankets and tiny little socks.

"Where do you go, Glenna?" He came close and reached toward me, but then let his hand drop when I didn't move to him. "You don't exist anymore. You've sacrificed us. You've sacrificed yourself for a dream."

I screamed then, trying to push away my fury, trying to push my way back to him. To push myself back into even that awful evening, into our bedroom, our lives, our house, which didn't have a baby living in it anywhere.

Carey drove us through Taos. "Here you have your artsy as well as your fartsy," he said. "I mean, it's touristy."

"Well, we're tourists," I said absently. I had no idea he'd reached his limit with my "mood," as he called it. He pulled over in the town square and complained that I'd been a lousy companion all morning.

"Why are you such a sour puss? We might as well skip the plans I've made for Taos Pueblo," he said.

I tried to think of a quick fib to cover the pity-party-for-one I'd been throwing. I sat there and just absorbed his silence for a minute while sidewalk crowds rushed like Christmas Eve shoppers with armloads of bags, pulling kids window to window, in and out of western wear and leather and T-shirt shops.

"You're right, Carey. Especially that this is touristy. I don't think I even need to get out of the car. It's like the Gatlinburg of New Mexico. You want to move on? I forget what you said about the pueblo."

"Okay? So maybe just grab a coffee, and go straight there?"

As we sipped and drove, I thought I could distract him back into professor mode by pointing out the mountain ahead of us, though I'd already looked at the name on the map.

"The Sangre de Cristo Range. Which means 'Blood of Christ.'" He went on about the early priests and the infusion of Catholicism. For all their powerful namesake, the peaks cowered under purple clouds scudding above the adobe tiers of Taos Pueblo. Up close the ruddy structure seemed to dwarf the mountains in the distance. Carey said it was an ancient apartment building.

"You have to love this," he said. "The adobe is always layered on by the women—not the men—generation after generation. I mean, the buildings are maintained by the matriarchal line. The great-great-great grandmother's labor is there beneath the newer layers."

Every corner was rounded soft, so I was surprised to find the walls were brick hard, a softer, brown color than terracotta. Under my palm the walls were warm, laced with strands of straw that shimmered, riddled with tiny fissures.

The closed doors facing the plaza were painted, no two colors alike, bright green, yellow, deep rose and red, sky blue and aqua. Wooden ladders, hand-made from thin branches, leaned against the walls from the first floor to the second, from second to third, the only way to ascend, from rooftop to rooftop and through narrow portals, in and out of the communal areas.

Carey led across the open square, where vendors sat in front of open doors and windows or inside lean-tos and market stands. Lattice roofs made shadows whenever the sun spread from behind the quick clouds. A few women selling fry bread sat outside a row of low adobe houses, broken and leaning. Their roofs were covered in a short layer of growing grass. Adobe ovens swelled out of the ground, each mound stoppered by a chimney plug, like pregnant bellies, navels protruding toward the clouds.

The women didn't try to sell us anything, but they did stand up when we walked closer. They stopped talking in their slow, clipped language to look at us. And the men studied us, too, as we passed a wide-open shop of musical instruments, thick wooden flutes and drums made from hollowed logs, covered with leather.

Faint swirls of dust whisked along the plaza as if an invisible broom aimed to blast us with the fine, dry grit. We ducked under a low door frame into one of the shops. With its low ceiling, the room was dark and cool, like a cave. I blinked the dust out of my eyes and looked back through the doorway to see the plaza framed like a hazy dream. A group of children ran by the door on the heels of two or three skinny dogs. The storm of feet and laughter disappeared in a split second, all covered with a still, sudden shadow, as if I'd just woken up. The dust and the wind and voices gone.

Carey moved over to a tall, rough table covered with circular decorations. I hadn't noticed until then that a man stood behind the table in a square of dim light from a small window. A dingy curtain curled in and out like a person's breath. The same circular designs were hanging there, turning in the wind.

"Might get some rain," he said, his gaze following mine. Then he leaned forward on his elbows with hands clasped. He bent his head forward to push up his glasses with the knuckles of both thumbs. "But, then again, maybe not. Hard to say, even with the clouds." He looked at me through thick lenses and smiled. "Some people say we got a bad drought coming on. Maybe for years ahead."

"See, he's making dreamcatchers, Glenna." Carey motioned for me. "Can you tell her about these? She's never been out West before."

"You've never seen Indians, heh?" He grunted as he grinned.

"Oh, no, yeah. I've seen Indians, sure."

"Cherokee." His nod made me nod back in agreement. "But you never been to a pueblo." He lifted up one of the circles and held it out to me. Filaments crossed the open diameter, like a spider's web.

"It maybe looks like a spider web to you," he said. He'd probably heard tourists make the comparison a hundred times, but I had a strange sensation when he repeated what I was thinking. I took the circle and remembered Daddy's warning that once a peddler gets something into your hand, it's as good as sold.

"But it will catch better things than flies." He shrugged at his weak joke. "Maybe you don't want to risk catching a dream. Some people? Scared of dreams. Hang this above your bed at night. And your nightmares. See? They pass on through." He took the dreamcatcher back and pointed through the open spaces. "But good dreams, they get caught, see?" He dangled it between us.

"How come they're all so different?" I touched the others, lying flat.

"Oh, I got to make it a challenge," he said. "I don't want to get too satisfied with my work. See? Here's one for beginners. Four points of connection. Easy. The strands can mean many things, though. The four directions, maybe? North. South. East. West?" In turn he pointed at the four walls of his room. His index finger was taped with a dirty bandage.

"Maybe the four seasons? The four elements? Fire, water, earth, air. Lots of fours in the universe. But the ones with six strands. Two other elements." He held up a more complicated dream catcher. "Deluxe model." He smiled with a missing tooth.

"There are only four elements," Carey said.

"You're thinking Greek, man." Carey couldn't hide his surprise at the guy's comeback. "You got to think science. You got to think Indian, maybe." He laughed, then looked at me again. "Lots of people got dreamcatchers. You think maybe they're ticky-tacky. Yeah? New age Indian gadget to sell white people. It's true. Maybe. Or maybe mine are special. Only natural fibers and materials."

He lightly ran his finger around the dreamcatcher I had first picked up. "There's bent wood under the leather wrapping. Goat leather. I do all that myself. Tan the hide. Little beads are just for decoration. The filament is cat gut." He laughed again. "I got to buy that. It'll last forever. I try to make something unique. One of a kind."

I couldn't tell if he was a bullshit artist or a really good, sincere salesman, or whether there was a difference. He stuck out his hand. "My name is Thomas."

"I'm Glenna." We shook hands. "And this is Carey."

"Think science?" Carey repeated, getting back to Thomas's quiz.

"Albert Einstein." Thomas laughed. "There's a hint."

"Relativity? E equals MC squared?" Carey laughed but frowned. "Light?"

"You're close. Give up? Earth. Air. Water. Fire." He paused and looked at Carey. "Space. Time."

"Time, Carey." I bumped his shoulder with mine. "He's a history professor. You think he'd know about time."

"Oh, I think history is not really about time, yeah?" Thomas said. "But then I'm Indian. Pueblo people, you know? We've been handing down stories for centuries, the same stories still getting told. Yeah? That way history isn't past. History is alive, man. History is a living choice. Yeah? Every day."

He reached for a dreamcatcher down the counter. "See this one? Seven strands. Odd number. Very difficult to make. It catches the most complicated dreams." He took the one I held and handed me the larger. "Seven. Lucky, yeah? A sacred number. You guess, now, Glenna. The seventh element?"

He looked right at me. My face went hot because I knew immediately. Carey turned to me. I could tell he didn't have a clue.

"Us." I pointed to Carey, pointed my finger at my heart, then at Thomas. "People. Human beings."

"What?" Carey said.

Thomas nodded and leaned back as his whole body laughed. Maybe he was truly delighted. But I had a doubt that maybe he was talking in riddles to bait foolish tourists out of their money. Or maybe my answer made a true connection. Or maybe whatever answer I gave was right for me in that moment.

"She's right. Flesh and blood, man." He smiled again at Carey.

Whatever the case, he knew he'd sold me.

In Santa Fe, I hung the seven-stranded dreamcatcher on the bedpost in the first hotel of our trip, a sprawling hacienda on the four-lane highway, with courtyards, balconies, flowers in footpath lights. The only room still available for two nights in a row was bigger than we needed, with a kitchenette, two beds, a sleeper sofa. Still, we'd only been there a few minutes before I felt confined, shut out of the glowing, sunset desert.

Carey turned on the television and looked at his watch. "I forgot the time change. It's the ten o'clock lineup at eight." He stood restlessly in the middle of the room and clicked channels with the remote. "What do we do now? Dinner? We had that late, heavy lunch. But it's only about a five-minute drive to the Plaza."

"Are you kidding? I ain't getting back in that car," I said. "I'm happy to just eat out of the cooler."

"Or there's a couple of fast-food places we could walk to."

"I'm too grimy even for that." I unzipped my suitcase. "Didn't you see that pool?" I waved my swimsuit at him and grabbed a towel off the nightstand. He fell back onto the bed, still flipping channels when I came out of the bathroom.

The swimming pool was liquid sapphire in the dusk, enclosed by adobe walls covered in flowering vines. I sank into the sun-warm water and moved just enough to float out to the middle. An acrid aroma lifted from gigantic red geraniums. Insects made shadows, flying above the underwater lights. A noisy Korean family patted each other dry and left, and an old couple soon followed.

I was alone. Maybe the lights were on a timer, or a motion sensor. But the whole courtyard went dark. The stars went bright in the deep blue above. I closed my eyes. Under the weight of water, I couldn't hear voices or car doors or highway noise. I tucked my knees up to my chest and floated and sank in the dark, buoyed by elements outside myself, warm and cradled.

To sleep late, shower, eat a warm breakfast somebody else made, to leave our stuff in one place for a whole day and night was luxurious, especially since I'd gone queasy and weak in the knees. I thought maybe I'd gotten a touch of food poisoning. Wandering in and out of shops on Canyon Road seemed to worsen my churning stomach. Lopsided archways and timber doors opened to tile floors and log beam ceilings, adobe corner fireplaces, wrought iron balconies and hinges and railings. Every bare space was stuffed dizzy with silver jewelry and scarves, candles, wines, soaps, paintings, cowhide pillows, long horn skulls, Indian blankets, pottery. Even outdoors, away from so many decadent things for sale, I was lightheaded. The high desert intoxicates everybody, Carey said, and that Santa Fe was a favorite for Stan, the wooden gates and rugged timber doors and sheltering cottonwoods skimming across tile roofs. Clay pots and sawed-off barrels and squares of dark earth spilled with every color and shape and odor of leaf and blossom. The air held a thousand blurred fragrances of leather, sage, smoke, juniper, ripe fruit, jasmine.

My head floated. For a split-second foolish rush of adrenaline, out of habit, I wondered if my wooziness meant I was pregnant. *Stupid.* Even in the city of Holy Faith, there wouldn't be any immaculate conceptions. It'd been months since I'd had sex, something I hadn't been able to swear to since I was fifteen.

But in a public restroom just off the Plaza, seeing that first faint pink tinge on the toilet paper set off a sinking in my chest. Blood never loses its shock. The headache, nausea, insomnia. How foolish I hadn't recognized my symptoms. The old monthly let-down. Blood was proof of a precious wasted chance, failure sloughed off into the toilet, flushed away.

Carey was waiting for me against a pillar on the shadowy cool terrace outside the Palace of the Governors. Down the long, wide portico, one whole length of Santa Fe's old town square, Indians leaned against the wall selling sterling jewelry and crafts. When I complained that everything in New Mexico seemed to be up for sale, Carey explained that the market dates back nearly four hundred years, as long as the center of town has existed, the oldest government building in the U.S.

I could barely focus on him among the tourists haggling with the Indians, who mostly squatted or sat with legs folded. Only a few sat in cheap lawn chairs. I thought suddenly how marvelous that the white tourists had to bow down, bent and stooped, as if they were worshiping the makers of earrings, inlaid knives, necklaces and bracelets of hammered silver.

Several women had kids with them, scolding while they vaguely talked to customers. Two Indian women near the very end of the portico sat with their hands folded across swollen bellies. I tried not to stare, but I marveled as I always do at pregnant women. It's as if they're oblivious to the amazing, imminent baby. One of the women was very young, but her companion looked a little older than me. Their faces were so similar. I thought for a moment they might be sisters. But it occurred to me they were probably mother and daughter. Both of them pregnant. It was staggering, and silly, too, to imagine Mama and me pregnant at the same time.

I stooped down to look at their jewelry. Carey urged me to buy something, but I just wanted to be near their big promising bodies.

"It's all too pricey for me," I whispered to him.

"Pick something."

The older woman stood, and I could tell then that she wasn't pregnant, just one of those women—especially petite women—who are permanently reshaped by all the children they've carried. Mama's little pot belly always seemed so unsightly when I was a teenager. But mid-life, I was jealous I might never have the luxury of that maternal pudge, a physical, permanent feature to prove I had made a life. To prove I'd *had* a life. Among their work I spotted a simple pure silver bracelet to look at more closely, and Carey reached for it before I could stop him. He handed the younger woman the money, and the old woman wrapped it up in a square of bright yellow paper. But I slipped it on my wrist before we were out of sight, a circle made of two twined silver strands.

Around the periphery of Santa Fe's plaza, deep in cottonwood shade, how many lifestyles swirled together, the makings of how many couples and couplings. Everybody started out as somebody's newborn. Lost skateboard boys with tattooed, sweaty torsos and funky piercings. They yelled to each other in some contemporary primitive tongue. A group of college kids in tie-dye and Birkenstocks lazed in the grass near an empty bench. A trio of African men bent together over djembe drums. Young couples with kids and groups of retirees swarming around a tour bus. Hispanic men selling roasted corn.

Before we found a place for dinner, Carey wanted to show me the St. Francis Cathedral, just off the plaza. I'd never been inside a Catholic church before. I'm used to churches that are locked all week long except for the preacher and secretary and organist. The dark chapel was full of parishioners, not just tourists. A children's choir practiced invisibly in the balcony, sweet high voices. Several old dark women knelt or sat counting their rosaries.

Stained glass colors dappled the dark indoors, but the riveting image was the body of Christ, lean and pale above the pulpit, draped on the cross, bloody and torn. I had seen those sorts of images in books, but that large, it was horrifying. I was used to people wearing little plain crosses on necklaces. But now those crucifixes seemed to lie with their emptiness. They ignored suffering.

In the dim vestibule a black wrought-iron stand held tiered rows of votives flickering. I was surprised to see Carey drop a quarter into the coin box and light a candle. He stood for a moment with his hands folded. At first it seemed sacrilegious to break the boundaries of religion. But he was sincere, I could see. He was moved. And when he saw me, I could see the agony and strength in his face.

I wanted, suddenly, the kind of prayer that depends on a living flame, burning after the words are said, the thinking has been thought. The potential of those little sputtering wicks drew me. I stepped beside Carey, but I couldn't find a quarter in my pack or in my pocket. He reached across me, and I heard the clink of a coin.

"I'll wait out in the sun." He smiled.

To send up a prayer, a simple enough transaction in the ultimate tourist town, where everything for sale was displayed front and center. A box full of quarters at the end of every day. I felt duped for a moment to think of my trinkets—the dreamcatcher, the bracelet, the beaded hairclip. I'd fallen for each item because of sentimental superstition. What did it mean to buy a prayer? To buy a dream?

I picked up a long thin reed and touched it to a flame. I thought of all the people I could pray for—Mama, Granny Pearl, Grandma Ruby. Daddy. I knew Carey must have lit his candle for Stan. I pushed away Kevin. I doubted a sack of quarters could buy me all the wick-time I needed with him.

I dipped the flame on the end of my reed to a new pure white votive. It flared and snapped and went dark. I tried again, three times before the wick caught and the flame wavered. I thought of my failures, the smallest, largest want in my life.

Before that moment I had never spoken a word, not a single breath of prayer for the baby I lost. That loss had no existence outside myself. I was the only being my baby's bare life ever touched. I stood staring at that tiny, hesitant flame. For just that moment I felt grief for that little life without grieving for myself.

A being who would never be. That one unspoken prayer might be the only motherly, selfless act I ever achieve. I remembered then to breathe. I stepped through the doorway into blinding sun like the light from a billion candles.

Next morning, I deliberately left behind the dreamcatcher, hanging on the bed post. It had given me everything in its power, and I would never need it again. The second night in our room, after my prayer, I slept under its web, my uterus knotted with menstrual cramps. In the morning there was blood on the sheets. Blood stained the inside of my thighs. Like the morning I'd miscarried.

In the dream that I'd been given that night, I push and push until my pelvis aches. Through what seems like hours of pain, there's no one to help me deliver the baby I need to pull out of my body. The hardness of a human head presses me open. The round, solid skull swells when I bend double. I can see dark hair beneath a thin membrane, and streaks of blood. The pain is a wad of fire.

Then every sensation is of the baby struggling, as if my body and its body are the same. Its tiny fists push the hammock of my pelvis open. Feet grip and thrust against my diaphragm so hard I can't get a breath. I fold myself in two, to the breaking point, and make myself a wide hinge, pulling my ankles against the sides of my hips. I hold myself steady until I can reach my palms to cradle the baby's head. And then its whole body slips out of me, a thick joy of flesh.

We balance there on the axis of my hips in a dim light, and I pull the baby onto my chest and lie back. My heart is pounding and there is the baby's breathing like a whisper, its heart pounding with mine, but separate now, and whole. And perfectly safe. I look into the face of my baby. I wipe away the web of myself from its mouth and forehead. The eyes that come clear are ancient, like stars across an unreachable distance, the first eyes that have ever known me completely, but forgive me all the same.

Out of Eden

The desert northwest of Santa Fe was a paradise of color. Silver-aqua sage mingled in eternal fields with blooms of lemony yellow. A ceiling of pure blue was gated at the horizon with cumulus columns. Cactus with peony-pink spindles and everything spiky rolled toward purplish bluffs of juniper and pinyon. Illuminated cliffs of gold, bronze, and coral eroded at the top layer into gray grottoes holding a mirage of wizened faces.

My astonishment wrestled with a big old bout of homesickness. I wanted woods. Dripping and foggy. Green underbrush for miles that you can't get a foothold in. New Mexico was pristine as a painting. A girl can't live in a painting.

"Find Abiqui on the map." Carey shifted in the driver's seat. He planned our first stop at Georgia O'Keefe's stomping grounds. In Santa Fe we'd seen her work: flowers, skulls, doorways. But the Ghost Ranch we found, which Carey said was connected with her, turned out to be a ramshackle orphanage for damaged animals. Broken birds on dead limbs peered out of cages. A coyote trotted back and forth in a pen, panting frantically. In separate confinements a bobcat, blond mountain lion, red and gray foxes curled in slim shadows. In the last cage a black bear paced without any shade at all in the outrageous morning sun. A sign explained his mother had been killed on the highway years before. Years of that pent-up life. His snout ranged along the dust.

When I was little, the first bear I ever saw was trapped like that, in Pigeon Forge, where to this day businesses use live bears to bait tourists. The bear I saw when I was a kid was probably an orphan too. The cheap motel owners banished her to a chain-link cage beside the main highway. For more than twenty years, when I drove past, she was pacing the same circles on concrete, within cruel sight of mountains in blue.

We rode into higher and drier desert and stopped for gas at a place called Dulce—which the map showed on the Jicarilla Apache Reservation. A bunch of kids were riding bicycles way too small for their long bodies round and round the gas pumps. Men loitered near a wall of firewood. The clerk was beautiful, her braid a rope of dark water down her back when she turned. The whole time she was speaking a language of sharp-edged words to a young guy leaning against the counter with his back to her. A raven-black ponytail hung across his collarbone. He stared straight ahead, but he would answer her every now and then. His flannel shirt was open to bronzed, broad cleavage. The ridges of his thighs showed through tight denim. He looked at Carey and the two of them gave each other a nod and smiled.

"Friend of yours?" I quizzed as I got behind the wheel.

Carey laughed. "You never saw me flirt before?"

"If that was flirting, you need some lessons. But was he gay? You can tell?"

"I mean, if he said the secret password, it was in Apache."

"Be serious." I pulled onto the highway. "You must get some vibe. What makes you *think* he's gay?"

"I just want him to be. Didn't you think he was pretty? Queer or not."

"Carey! I hate that word."

"Oh, give me a break. Who decided 'gay' is any better, anyway? 'Bugger, fruit, fairy.' I mean, 'Fairy Carey?' Please. I'll take 'queer' any day," he leaned back. "'Faggot' is my people's 'n' word, though. Just so you know.

"Anyway, every group disagrees on terms for themselves," he said. "You call yourself a 'hillbilly.' Don't you know people who hate that? Native Americans call themselves Indians. I mean, they prefer tribal names. Some of them are just coming up with words for homosexual. Historically they don't even designate sexual preference. Although—some Indians out here use a term the Jesuits got from Arabic."

I groaned at another lecture.

"No. Listen." He waved his hands. "It's a word from the Spanish, who got it from the Moors: *berdache*. To refer to native men the priests observed taking on female roles. I mean, cross-dressing and cooking. The Indians accepted behavior like that. Not all cultures ostracize gays."

"You're not ostracized," I said.

"Hello!" He turned in the passenger seat to face me.

"You live how you want in Atlanta. You had some kind of ceremony with Stan. Bought a house with him."

"*There*, yeah. But why do you think I left home?" He looked at me with a crooked smile. "You really don't think I wanted to leave, do you? I mean, if that Apache guy had grown up gay in Newport, one of *my* tribe, you think he'd be hanging out at the local filling station? Nuh-uh." He faced the road again. "I didn't have a choice. Atlanta is *my* reservation, honey."

I'll give this to them, the Apache in north New Mexico settled themselves in a place with trees. Close stands of timber blocked our view of everything but the steepest wooded hills. Not a sign of a village, no houses, no trailers, no human mark at all except for no hunting signs and odd shelters of rough hewn branches. Residents had cloistered themselves down dirt roads that once in a while wound between hills covered in evergreen, a cloak of invisibility.

But it was somebody else's sanctuary. I had nothing but a borrowed space in Carey's car. An unnerving lost sensation crept into me crossing the reservation, into more barren miles. Sandstone boulders heaped from roadside to hill, as if some giant had collected them. I was weary. A week, and the car turned into a mobile prison.

By the time we reached Aztec Ruins National Monument, Carey was famished, but I was sick from the road and my period. I just wanted to be still. Or click my heels three times. If there's no place like home, where was mine? I lay on a picnic table under cottonwood trees. Carey ate and chattered on. If I'd walked away, I swear he wouldn't have noticed.

He poked my arm and pointed. "You know this place wasn't built by the Aztecs?" His mouth was full of chicken salad. "White settlers were stupid enough to think the Aztec empire spread this far north. But the Anasazi—which just means 'ancient ones'—" He set down his sandwich to make quotation marks in the air.

I groaned and put my forearm across my eyes. "No. I mean, look and you can see," he said, poking my ribs this time.

"Carey, stop!" I sat up and scooted away from his reach.

"Really, it's cool." He pointed. "The building design proves the Anasazi are the ancestors of all the Pueblo people. See, like an ancient version of Taos Pueblo?"

He was right. I could see it clearly. No adobe skin, but the same bones. Same shape, rock on rock held by only gravity, all those centuries. The roof was gone, though.

"This says hundreds of people lived in that building." He shoved the brochure into my hands and wadded his trash. He took my hand and pulled me toward the ruins.

"Can you believe it's still standing like this? Powerful masonry," Carey said. "Even though the early settlers nearly demolished it, stealing rocks to build houses." We walked in and out of rooms, ragged conjoined boxes.

"It's like a big Holiday Inn," I offered.

"Well, sort of. Community property. These were some of the first indigenous people on this continent who figured out agriculture."

"So that's a big silo?" I pointed to a huge round structure, with a restored roof.

He laughed. "Kiva. A church, sort of, for ceremonies." Inside was cool, the curved walls and dirt floor centered around an opening Carey said was a fire pit. A hole in the roof to release smoke let in a ray of dusty light.

Back outside, the heat moved like an invisible animal. I followed Carey through T-shaped entries under the jagged ends of broken beams. Houses. Abandoned. Up close the hand-chiseled stones really were remarkable. Wavy layers of chink-stones reinforced larger rocks, golden and pale green and rose-pink and gray. All the colors in the cliffs we'd passed that morning.

Carey wandered, reading the brochure. "The kiva here is one of the biggest. But the ones at Chaco—I mean, Stan and I went there. A thousand years ago, Chaco was the biggest city outside Mexico or Europe. Thousands of people and then *poof!*"

He stopped and turned. "What happened, you ask?" I rolled my eyes. "Seriously, Glenna, you're not interested?"

"It's hot, Carey. It's a lot to take in. I'm tired. I'm thirsty. Is there a quiz?"

"Yes. If you learn anything, remember that the Anasazi disappeared. A mass exodus. They abandoned places they'd lived for centuries. And some of them came here. Probably from Mesa Verde, too—where we're headed. Something, drought or war, forced their exile. I mean, the Israelites got nothing on the Anasazi."

Exile. The word rolled around in my head. It sounded more right than *homeless* somehow. Was I in *exile?* How long had I been exiled? Who to blame? *Poof.*

Outside the maze of rooms, the outline of fallen walls reminded me of playhouses I used to map under the farm's apple trees. I'd arrange rocks and sticks end to end for make-believe rooms. Tree roots made my pretend staircase. I was safe, housekeeping among the birds and sheltering arms of trees, a world I never dreamed would collapse.

After Mama deeded me the farm, I knew before Carey and I left I had to get brave and go see the place. I didn't want to give her the satisfaction of asking directions. I knew enough to drive toward Cosby and look for English Mountain Road, but beyond that I had just my mental map, the memory of ten-year-old me.

The address on the deed is generic. Rural Route 2. But when I was a kid Mama and Granny called it Genesis Road, a lost name now, not on any signs.

On either side of English Mountain Road, pastures spread around brick ranchers and neat frame houses. Fields separated by fence lines are laid out with spectacular gardens—corn and bean rows and squash and all sorts of plants I wished I could recognize. But that agrarian life was yanked out from under me. Even after the pavement turns to gravel, the smaller, poorer farms are tended with dignity handed down for generations, laundry on the clotheslines, cats on porches, gleaming horses, a bare-chested boy on a tractor.

The unpaved road narrowed to a single lane. I eased down wooded hollows, though I hadn't passed a single car. The hills were so close I lost sight of the

Smokies, but when the route dead-ended at a T, I knew to turn right toward English Mountain. After that I guessed left at a fork in the road and stopped to let the car idle when I recognized the old dairy. A quarter of a century since I'd been there. Around every curve there was something familiar, but I felt like a trespasser. At ten miles an hour I looked for Granny Pearl's yellow house, which had been just down the road from us. She lived there until she married Ed, just before Daddy burned our house.

At a field where Angus cows grazed, somebody had bulldozed a mess of dingy cedar carcasses. One spark and they'd resurrect in a bonfire. I crept forward, losing my sense of direction for a second. Then I braked. Beyond the dead wood, a discarded slow-dying house. Granny Pearl's house, weather-worn down to raw clapboard the color of driftwood. The front porch collapsed into what was left of the yard, which held a mangled heap of rusted farm equipment. The mossy peak of the roof was sunken in on the starved bones of the house. Half the boarded-up windows were bashed out like blind sockets.

The sick-hearted part of me wanted to turn around. My hands shook on the wheel as I kept easing along. I'd driven back and forth twice when I saw a gap in the ground cover. I parked on the roadside and stepped through tangles at the edge of the woods. The undergrowth and saplings were sparse enough that I could trace the driveway sunken like a long grave beneath the trees.

Just the thought of copperheads kept me watching the ground, so coming up on the burned foundation of the house shocked me. A single charred half-wall was covered by kudzu and wild grapevines and poison ivy. Three windows in that wall opened onto a wild paradise beyond. The hulk of ruin barely imposed its human failure in the green. Sumac and oak seedlings bordered the outline of the foundation; a colony of mayapples hung their leaves, ashamed they'd been abandoned.

What had I expected? Open, docile land, just waiting? All around me twelve acres of wild woods rang with birdsong and insect burr. My playhouse orchard was lost, eaten alive by everything tangled and overgrown where cultivated fields used to promise harvest. Green had taken over, swallowed up the lost garden.

When Carey drove across the Colorado border, a nervous numbness hit me. Steep green hills sparkled with aspens in late-day sun, but I could only worry we were traveling too late to claim a camp spot at Mesa Verde. I voted for a motel in Durango, but Carey wanted to push on, thirty-five miles more. How could I explain? My bones were rattling in my skin?

"It'll be so worth it," he promised. "So green and cool. Not at all like the desert we've been in. One of Stan's favorite places."

No arguing with that reasoning. But when we got there, I felt sorrier for

Carey than myself. In the years since he'd traveled with Stan, the foothills of the mesa had burned in a couple of major fires. As we drove up and up, there was no break in the devastation. He kept swearing to me, to himself, that it would get better, it would, but from the mesa top we looked across miles of gnarled charcoal. The park campground, which he'd described as oaky and lush, was scorched and dry as tinder.

No surprise, the camp host said he had plenty of vacant sites. Signs listed the fire danger in the park as extreme. No campfires. Bruised clouds pushed the odor of ozone on us, threatening lightning strikes. As we set up the tent it hit me, we were trapped in a forest of kindling, high on a vast mesa, with one road out. We ate a quick sandwich and drove to an overlook. The sunset glow caught the debarked branches, oddly orange under an orange sky. I imagined the sound that fire had made, raging for square miles.

By nine-thirty we were in the tent with the camp light out. As usual Carey slept and I was fitful. Fire-eaten trees lurched and creaked as the wind pushed down into the valley that held us. Dry lightning flashed. But it was the odor that wouldn't give me peace. All night I smothered in the smell of dead ash, the singe I could have sworn I still smelled on Genesis Road.

The next morning, from overlooks outside the burn perimeter, Mesa Verde finally lived up to its name: *green table*. From a windy vantage point, Carey showed me that the forest plateau is formed in finger-like mesas separated by canyons. Even in the threatening weather we could see long blue mountains and other mesas way beyond.

We stood in a long line first thing, for tickets to ranger-guided tours into two Anasazi cliff dwellings. A brisk wind whipped our jackets, but no rain. The ranger said any thunder or the first sign of dry lightning would cancel our tour. But the low clouds held quiet as we hiked down to Cliff Palace with a group of tourists. It was hard to understand how people lived there until we stood under the massive overhang, looking out of the dwellings. Square towers backed into a deep crevice in the canyon wall, like ancient condos. A safe perch from enemies and animals. Tourists meandered as the ranger talked, whispering to each other as if they were discussing the mortgage rate, utilities, the commute.

The ruins called Balcony House were smaller and more humble but more challenging to get to. Before he led us through the gate at the trail head, the ranger warned that the tour involved climbing high ladders, and then later some crawling through tight passages. We'd be getting dirty. He gave us a last chance to ditch the tour. If Carey's fear of heights made him waver, I couldn't tell. When we got to the base of the canyon wall, I was relieved that the first wide ladder was lashed tight against the golden rock. But its worn timber rose thirty or forty feet up, suspended over the heights of the canyon. Carey hung back with me to watch people climb.

"Just don't look down, like he said." I motioned Carey forward.

"Are you telling me, or yourself?" He squinted up. "I've been here before, but it looks higher, I swear." Two little kids clambered up fearlessly ahead of their parents. I stepped onto the bottom rung while Carey tightened his sandal's Velcro straps. Under my arch the wood was slick. I focused on gripping the round rungs, one after another, but I couldn't help looking down at the floor of the canyon far below.

I stepped carefully over the last rung and turned to look down at Carey, the last in our group. When he finally stood beside me, he was breathing hard from adrenaline. We looked out of the cleft, across to the far canyon rim. The guide was explaining what the Indians would have seen in that expansive view of the mesa top, the layers of earth providing the soil for their corn and squash and beans, the trees that fed their kiva fires.

"Without a written language," he said, "the Anasazi didn't leave a history. Their descendants, scattered now among the nineteen pueblos, have oral knowledge of the time their ancestors lived here and at other places like Chaco. They're very secretive of that oral history. Their private ceremonies are probably similar to the rituals practiced here hundreds of years ago at Mesa Verde."

Carey stood close to the guide, with his arms folded, as if he were evaluating a student's oral report. He nodded at certain phrases. Our group milled around; kids shifted from one sneaker to the other.

"Imagine whole families living here. And at Cliff Palace, hundreds of people," the guide said. "Archaeologists used to think the Anasazi vanished, extinct. But their pueblo descendants are living evidence they moved on to other places. The mystery is why. We don't know why they abandoned these cliff dwellings so suddenly. Early pioneers took pottery the Anasazi abandoned. And baskets. They hadn't rotted even after centuries in the arid climate. Therefore, a great deal of what we might have been able to discover about their exodus was destroyed or stolen."

Small swifts caught my attention, flickering in and out of slits in the overhang. They didn't slow a wingbeat, as if they were vacuumed into the cracks.

The ranger pointed out the next group, waiting at the foot of the ladder for us to move on. "Before we go, if you look on the stone behind you, there's a petroglyph." We all turned to look at the drawing on the stone. "See? A coil. Which some people think represents a snake. Or maybe an interpretation of canyon birds riding thermals.

"But I like to think of the spiral as a way of considering the Mesa Verde people. They unwound from this central location." He moved his hand over his hat in a slow circle, as if he were tracing the path of a hawk. "They spiraled out in different directions and started over. A spiral of survival."

He'd been serious about the crawling. To leave Balcony House was like being born through a channel into the light. I wasn't sure my shoulders would fit, as I crawled and scrunched on my elbows and knees. We all managed to shrug our way out. The ranger had described the genesis stories of the Anasazi, that they had climbed out of holes in the desert. The contrasts were drastic, exposure to the high plateau and then the claustrophobic, birth-tight passage. It would take every inch of me, every touchstone to convince myself to let go of one rung before I grabbed the next, starting over, squirming out of strange ground and aiming for a home I'd never seen before.

We headed south the next morning, into the northwestern edge of New Mexico. For square inches of map, there were no green patches, no trees, just Navajo Reservation. We passed a sign at the border that read, *Welcome to Navajoland.* Like Dollywood or Disney World. But the map said we were on "Defiance Plateau" on Route 666. Carey said that number is the stupidest Christian superstition. But we had no idea then we were entering wicked strange territory. Indian territory.

Signs were in English and in Diné, the Navajo language, which Carey told me just about single-handedly won World War II as a code language. But clerks at a gas station spoke perfect English.

Carey asked directions to Shiprock, and when the guy finally understood he meant the peak and not the town, he withheld Carey's change in his hand and said, "You don't want to go there."

"We're going sort of out of our way to see it," Carey insisted. "I thought maybe there's a reservation road that cuts through to Canyon de Chelly?"

"You want to stay on the paved highway." The guy handed Carey his change and wiped his hands on a rag. "Rain coming. People drown every monsoon season. Even in a four-wheel drive, you get stuck in that mud, you never get loose."

"It can't be that far off the highway, to get a closer look," Carey argued.

The guy shook his head. "Nothing there but snakes. And scorpions. Mud and snakes and scorpions."

Even from the highway, the peak was a monstrous wing of rock thrust into glowering clouds. The hard innards of an old volcano. I talked Carey out of turning down three or four dirt roads that might or might not have led to Shiprock.

"They don't want us there, Carey. You're the one who said it's a sacred place.

You know that guy warns every whitey who comes through about snakes and scorpions. Why take the chance and offend somebody? And he's right about the rain."

We rode for maybe two miles more between a wall of dark to the west and clear sky east as far as we could see. The number of cars dwindled, distant headlights in brown dark. By the time I was begging Carey to pull over, high waves of sandy wind and debris hit the Jeep. There was no more clear sky. Harder and harder gusts, and no people, no buildings, nothing but dust and us inside it.

Carey turned on the headlights and gripped the steering wheel to steady the rocking car. In an instant, sheets of rain came out of the sandstorm and hammered the dust into mud on the windshield. The black sky swallowed the horizon's light. We couldn't see past the flood of water coursing down the glass, a deafening roar. Even on the fastest speed the wipers couldn't keep up with the rain. We crawled. Fifteen miles an hour, ten, then five. One-thirty in the afternoon and the desert was eclipsed by torrents so loud, Carey and I had to shout to hear each other. Phantom-mad wind shoved us around. Lightning broke open the dark at the exact instant thunder shattered through the car. I yelped.

"You have to stop!"

"Where?" Carey squinted side to side. "I can't even see the shoulder!"

"I have to pee!"

"Funny!" He yelled, but then he looked at my face. "Where are you going to go in all this? You have to hold it!"

By the dashboard clock ten excruciating minutes went by and we still drove through pounding rain. I grabbed my raincoat when a slight break showed a small building ahead. I motioned and jerked on my coat, and before he stopped completely, I opened the door and dashed.

I shook like a wet dog when the door shut behind me, water sluicing off my coat. But in the restroom the storm was still happening. Dirty water ran through the sagging ceiling and down the sheet rock and swirled down the grimy drain in the floor. I pulled my raincoat hood back over my head and hoped the roof would hold. The lights cut out before I finished. I felt around for soggy toilet paper in the dark.

When I came out, Carey stood there holding his coat. "You might as well put that thing back on," I said, opening the door to show him the flood pouring in. "And you might want a flashlight."

He fished a tiny light out of his pocket and grinned at me. "Boy Scout rule."

We waited in the dark store the next twenty minutes at a rickety table between shelves randomly stocked with dusty boxes of Q-tips beside boxes of crackers, diapers between canned meats and hemorrhoid cream, toilet paper beside potato chips. Carey said we ought to buy something, so he picked a warm bottle of apple juice to share.

"You ever felt so far from home?" I asked.

"Welcome to Navajoland," he said.

An hour down the road, the sun came out. By the time we crossed into Arizona, everything was gold and dry. Treeless again. But we were still on the Navajo Reservation, the biggest in the country, Carey said. The most prominent objects were small block houses, trailers like boxes huddled together at intervals way out on the open desert. Scrubby trees reached toward dilapidated roofs, and pots of flowers cluttered among rusted cars and trucks in dirt yards. Lines of laundry snapped in the wind, and plastic bags struggled on fences like trapped ghosts. Some places reminded me of Mama's trailer.

Carey slowed for animals grazing by the roadside. As far as we could see out into the long fields, no animals. Except for a few corralled ponies, the livestock grazed in the narrow ribbon of grass between the fence and the highway. At a convenience store in Chinle, the largest town near the national monument, cows nibbled at a plot of grass between gas pumps.

As we started to set up our tent at Canyon de Chelly beneath the reprieve of cottonwoods, a pack of scruffy dogs came out of nowhere. Carey and I whipped the nylon forward to protect ourselves, but they sniffed harmlessly along the ground as if we weren't there. We were getting comfortable with them consorting around when a warm wind kicked up, another haze of dirt and dander. In seconds we were both spitting out grit and blinking dust out of our eyes. I tied a bandanna around my nose and mouth. While the tent straps worried around us and kept us from staking things, two other campers literally pulled up stakes and drove away.

"Are you spooked?" Carey said. We were both breathing hard from the work.

"I would swear something wants us off this reservation. Damn flash flood in a—what did the guy call it?—a monsoon? When are the locusts and frogs getting here?"

We cinched the tent down, heaped extra rocks on the flyline. It flapped in the wind like a dying bird. Finally, the wrestling paid off and we stood back to make sure nothing would blow away. Just then the wind suddenly died. A stout black dog strode past us growling, its hackles raised. It stood at the base of the slope just beyond us and ranged back and forth barking furiously and snapping at the vacant crest of the hill. Carey and I squinted up into the hanging dust and sun, stepping closer, but neither one of us could see a thing. The dog cowered under the invisible spell.

Carey laughed when I gripped his arm and stood close. "We aren't supposed to be here." I was only half-joking. "Something wants us gone."

Driving along the south rim of the canyon, I couldn't shake the sense that we were being watched. The beauty of the evening sun on red rock held a strangeness. No one we saw spoke English. The tourists were French or German or Asian, passing binoculars back and forth to see the cliff dwelling called White House. Down below us, Navajo still lived in the canyon. Round houses sent up smoke signals from chimney pipes, and an old woman in a dress and apron corralled a little herd of sheep.

At the farthest overlook, called Spider Woman Rock, dual spires of red stone rose more than a thousand feet from the canyon floor. Carey said it's where the Navajo believe the divine world meets the physical plane. Long pines grew on the sloping canyon walls, tiny in contrast to the sheer heights. It stunned me to think that people lived within walking distance of that sort of church, towering above them, and how they could ever, ever bear to leave. Though many of them had.

The sun glowed just above the long mesas on the horizon. We sat on a ledge at the westernmost overlook and watched the sunset and ate a sandwich. Carey sliced off pieces of hard red apple to share as the walls went luminous orange. Far below a hunched woman in a long colorful skirt and white blouse stepped out of her house, a hogan, Carey said. Her brilliant green garden pointed its rows toward the red cliffs.

"She doesn't have electricity," I said.

"Neither do most of these people." Carey motioned with his Swiss Army knife to trailers and houses scattered beyond darkening rocky flats. Only a few of them were lit, below a sky streaked in deep purple and yellows. "Plenty of them are lucky to have real houses. I've heard that some banks will only make loans to people on reservations for *mobile* homes. Easier to repossess and move."

"I never thought of that." I pictured Mama's trailer, parked in the same spot for nearly a quarter of a century. She hadn't planned on staying when she ran away from Daddy with Dunn and me. But the trailer was cheaper than any car she ever bought.

"These people are poor. And you feel sorry for them." Carey looked at me. "But this is as good as it gets for plenty of First Peoples in America. The heart of the Navajo nation. Diné, they call themselves. Biggest reservation and the largest group of Native Americans, a quarter of a million."

"I'm not feeling sorry for them. That's not it," I said. "I feel like I get it. How hard they have it."

"Well, not as hard as other tribes. They were allowed to at least come back here. I mean, look out there and try to imagine," he said, "when Kit Carson rounded up all the Diné, this canyon was their last refuge. The last of them hid here. You think the Trail of Tears was bad for the Cherokee. Thousands of Navajo died, too.

"And I mean, we didn't just force them off their homeland. Carson and his men killed all their livestock and burned their homes. But worst of all, he destroyed the pride and joy here in this canyon. Which you'd never guess." He paused. "Peach trees. Thousands of peach trees. They just hacked them to pieces."

I couldn't keep from gasping. I looked again, and the canyon floor looked newly robbed. Millions of peaches should have been glowing like stars in that twilight.

"But at least they released the people who were still alive. And let the Navajo come back. They had nothing but government rations and sheep, then, but they started over. You know? I'm not sure, but they may be the only tribe that really got to go back home."

"But there aren't any peach trees," I said. "They *didn't* come back home. It's not the same place. Not at all."

The wind lifted around us, cold. The walls deepened to ruby. Carey put his arm around me in the last moments of light. "You see even at sunset why the Navajo call the desert a 'house made of dawn.' I bet that old woman wouldn't live anywhere else for all the electricity in the world. She got that land from her mother, who got it from her mother."

I pulled away to look him in the face. "How do you know?"

"It's a matrilineal society. Property is handed down through the women."

"That's like my family," I said. "Mama's family." I hesitated. "I haven't told you. But this has been hard. A couple of weeks before you and I left, Mama pulled this stunt to try and get me to stay. She deeded me our old farm."

"You mean the farm when you were little? At English Mountain? Wait a minute. She gave you—I thought that house burned?"

"Yeah. But there's twelve acres she hid. All these years."

"Shit!" he said. "I can't believe you didn't tell me!" He pushed my shoulder with his. "Oh, but we're mad at Faye, then, right?" He nodded. The sun set in that second. "What are you going to do with twelve acres? You're a land baron."

"Right," I said. "Such an heiress. No. I put an ad in the paper and put up a for sale sign. But I made out the ad before I saw the place. I listed it as farmland. But I should have known, it's all grown up with trees."

"But that's not a problem. You can cut down a few. Build yourself a house!"

"No. It'll sell to some developer, and they'll put up mobile homes. Welcome to Navajoland." I tried a laugh. But telling him had made me a little nauseated. I was glad I couldn't make out his features in the dark. I worked lightness into my voice. "You know how most places are getting subdivided there near the national park. Tourism is booming. Retirees are moving in."

"You're selling your birthright? No return of the prodigal? I mean, you need a place to live when you get back."

"It's not the same place."

"Glenna, you always talked about that place like it was heaven on earth."

135

"I guess that was my childhood I was talking about. Which is not a place."
I shook my head. "It's not the same." I couldn't think of a way to make him
see that it was like the canyon, still full of slaughtered peach orchards. If you
knew the history, if you'd loved a place like a body, it would constantly resurrect
every scar, every wound. How could the Navajo live in that canyon and not
have ghosts lifted up, always hounded by the faint scent of peaches?

When I was nine, Granny Pearl remarried after twenty years as a widow. Of
course, her new husband Ed had been "courting her," as he called it, for years.
That summer they moved in to Newport, sold her house and twenty acres, and
left Mama alone with Daddy and Dunn and me to make our own way with
Mama's inheritance—our house and adjoining property of twelve acres.

I mourned like somebody died. I was used to summer days picking berries
or daisies or purple clover on my walk to Granny's house, not a quarter mile up
the road. I had practically lived with her, spending plenty of summer nights,
and even school nights as I got older. Not seeing her every day was hard, and
I had my first taste of homesickness looking right out my bedroom window at
her house. The world around me was collapsing.

Even before the house sold, Mama forbid me to go inside. "I don't want
you on the porch. I don't want you in the yard. Don't 'but Mama' me, Sister.
You're liable to get hurt or tear up something. You've got plenty of room, and
if you're all that bored, run the vacuum."

Who listens to somebody forbid them from their grandmother's house? For
the first time in my life, Granny had locked her doors. I found an unlocked
window on the side porch next to the kitchen. The ground was high on that
side of the house, just two feet or so below the sill. I stepped over it like a high
threshold. The kitchen without its table and chairs was sad. The green linoleum
tiles buckled dark, except for where the stove had sat.

The fields outside sizzled with grasshoppers, but even in mid-July, the house
held a coolness. The fridge was unplugged, and a rank smell poured into the
room when I opened the door. I'd heard about kids suffocating in abandoned
refrigerators. I slammed it shut and tiptoed into the dining room, nervous as
a thief. The old china cabinet doors were open, nothing but sticky shelf liner
where jelly jars had left rings, and a mouse trap still pinched moldy cheese.

Whenever I stopped moving, an awful silence took over. There should have
been a hum of electricity, the sound of water in the pipes, the mantle clock
ticking, the broom sweeping the porch. In the living room beside the staircase,
a cherry side table Granny had always said would someday be Mama's. Three
cardboard boxes marked *FOR FAYE* in red magic marker. The first one was
nothing but old house dresses and cloth. Under Mama's name, Granny had

written *quilt scraps*, like Mama had time or know-how to make a quilt. She didn't even can vegetables anymore, but Granny had left behind her pressure cooker, canning tongs, a dented funnel, lids and rings and Mason jars, a stack of recipe books. In the last box were a couple of straw hats, garden gloves, spades, flower seeds labeled in baby food jars: spider plant, sweet William, forget-me-not, morning glory, abandoned flowers Granny said would never grow right in town.

The slam of the back porch door jolted me. I froze. Voices and footsteps moved through the kitchen toward the front of the house where I stood. I lunged two silent steps at a time up the stairs, avoiding the boards which creaked. I hunkered in the attic closet between upstairs bedrooms, and tried to hold my breath, but the harder I tried the dizzier I got. I broke into a sweat to realize I'd left the window wide open.

Through the slightly open door, I could hear Mama. She said something about the boxes, and then there was a man's voice. Not Daddy's.

"This is the house you's born in?" he asked. "Why's she wanting to sell?"

"Mama was born here, too," she answered. "In the room right above us."

"Why don't she pass this house on to you?" They rummaged through the boxes I'd left open.

"It'd take more money than I've got or she's got to fix things. Wiring's shot. Plumbing too. And it's got about no insulation. And she needs the money. Says she's retiring, tired of working this place like a dog." Mama said, "Look at this. There ain't much here I'll need in town either."

My heart plunged. Did she mean she was moving in with Granny and Ed?

"Aw, you might care more about it someday. A keepsake. We'll just haul it all and you can pick through it when you get moved in."

"You're right. There ain't a reason in the world to haul these up to the house and then to the trailer." I had no idea—not at that point—what trailer she meant. Granny and Ed had moved into Ed's house.

"They's some boxes upstairs somewhere too." I crouched in the closet, glancing around for a place to hide deeper, thinking of my excuses. I breathed into my cupped hands as they climbed the stairs. I could see through the crack in the door, Mama and a tall man.

"You're saving me a world of trouble," she told him. "I'd have to make ten trips in my car, what you can haul in one truck load. Glenn won't never let nobody touch his truck, especially me. Now, look at these dressers for Glenna and Dunn. Wonder if they'll even fit in those rooms in the trailer."

My legs trembled underneath me. In the musty smell of old shoes, my own anxious smell was sweaty and sour, like cider turning. Trailer. A trailer. What trailer?

"Ain't he going to wonder where these things is at?" the man asked.

"You think he gives a shit enough to pay attention to anybody else? Nobody but Glenna might catch on. I'm fixing to tell her, anyway. She won't say nothing."

Maybe I should have been proud, but I was sick-hearted and confused. They carried the dressers down the steps and came back for the boxes. Their voices came and went through the house as they took a few more small pieces of furniture. Then silence in a house that had always been comforting with its busyness. I sat for a long time. The sunlight in the hall was gone and the closet was dark before I could work up my nerve to go home and look at Mama without letting her see what I knew. What did I know? I was afraid of her secret plans. I was afraid to know who the man was or why she was with him.

The next morning, I woke up seeing what she saw, that our family, like the farm, was a wreck. Mama and Daddy had barely been holding it together. The upper pasture lay under two years' growth. Daddy had bush hogged just enough of the lower pasture to keep snakes out of the yard. Fence posts leaned into the road, the barbed wire broken in places, which didn't matter since Daddy hadn't replaced our cows after he got out of prison. The two old hens left in the chicken house didn't lay eggs anymore. Mama's garden was full of weeds and clods and un-hoed piddly rows of corn. Cucumbers she let grow fattened like hogs and ruptured and rotted. Circles of rocks were empty where she'd grown flowers. The tractor sat in a nest of Johnson grass near the slumping barn. In the orchard, yellow jackets stung all the apples to ruin.

Old people I knew talked about the way things used to be. But I was too young to be wishing for old times—the sweet scents of mowed hay and tobacco drying in the barn. The blackberry preserves Mama used to make. Or nights knowing she and I were lying awake after a day of canning beans or apple butter. Only sleeping after we counted each jar lid sealing with a metal kiss. I could still feel the loping giant swagger of the mule under me. Daddy let me ride as he plowed. I remembered the velvet touch of cow's noses and palming warm brown eggs into the basket Mama held and the sound corn stalks made in November wind. I remembered the time long before, lying beside Dunn on a blanket in the orchard while Mama and Daddy picked apples. He spun his fat legs like he was riding an invisible bicycle upside down, churning his little hands at the shadows and leaves. That joy was exact in my head.

Now all my knowing was confused and tangled. The paradise I'd loved was nearing its end. All that pleasure and safety and beauty long broken. And now I was full of the knowing of the brokenness.

The way Granny Pearl said Jesus would come back—at ten years old that's how I understood to wait for the signal. But after Mama told me the plan—that she

138

had a place for the three of us in town, that it was only temporary until divorce and peace and a way back—we would look at each other edgy and swept up in sickening excitement. She told me the best time to run would be on a Sunday, her only whole day off every week. That way she'd have time to get us out safe.

Most Sundays when she was off, Daddy would go fishing all day. The glitch was that he had started taking Dunn along now that he was older. And now that I refused to go with him after he'd nearly let me drown, Daddy dragged Dunn everywhere he went, as if he could sense he needed more than a partner-in-crime. He needed a hostage.

Every Sunday I woke up and listened to the house, knowing this might be the day that Daddy got a selfish streak and went fishing alone. It might be the day we could pack and run. Most Sundays Daddy would wake Dunn by six-thirty. They'd eat a huge breakfast and leave for the day. But one Sunday, as they came into the kitchen where I sat with Mama, my beautiful little brother vomited all over Daddy's waders.

Mama got Dunny into clean pajamas and back to bed. Daddy fussed and fumed. But he got his tackle box ready. He jingled his truck keys in his pocket and took them out every now and then. He stood in the doorway sipping coffee. I tried not to stare or watch the clock. I dropped everything I touched. I held my hands together so they wouldn't shake.

In the time it took Mama to wipe Daddy's boots clean and take Dunn's temperature, Daddy had started to worry over the clouds. He turned on the radio for the weather report. I stayed in the kitchen with him and Mama, staring into their coffee cups like dumb strangers. She was so still, so perfectly composed. A wind stirred up. I wandered from the screen door to the porch door and back again when sheets of rain in wider and wider gusts turned the orchard leaves to their silvery undersides. The rust edge of the barn roof hammered up and down, pitching a spoiled tantrum. I wished I had the power to tear it off in one huge blast and carve a jagged opening of dry light in the clouds and push Daddy out the door.

Mama told me to go back to bed, but I sat hopeful and dreading at the same time. She got up then, as if my stubbornness were her cue. She set in to fixing breakfast, coaxing Daddy with ideas. She said she would pack him sausage biscuits with a side of fried potatoes to take with him. But then she fixed him a plate. He ate and ate. He watched through the door again. And the storm started to slow.

He sat and half-dozed in his chair while the sky brightened, so I clattered pots and pans, helping Mama clean up the breakfast dishes while she packed him a lunch. I poured him another cup of coffee. When I'd all but given up, at nearly eight o'clock, he walked out the door. Maybe he looked back at us, a little worried, a little baffled, as if he were forgetting something he might need later.

The minute he was out of sight, Mama turned away from the door and put her coffee cup in the sink. She and I finished cleaning the kitchen, methodically, thoroughly, packing some of the dishes and pans as we went. She reached into the flour canister and the sugar and pulled out little plastic bags full of bills, mostly tens and fives. And then she sat me down and showed me her bank book. In case anything happened, Dunn and I would get the money in her savings account, two thousand dollars, more money than I could believe. But I knew she meant me to understand that what we were doing could get her killed.

The first day I ever moved, among so many moving days ahead, taught me that leaving is surprisingly dull, hard work. Without the truck, we could take only small loads in the trunk of Mama's car. We drove from Cosby to Newport and back three times. Each trip Mama and I strapped bedding, bed frames, mattresses, box springs, on top of the car, until we were worn out. Even if Dunn hadn't been sick, he wouldn't have lifted a finger. Feverish and furious, when he finally woke up and understood what was happening, he said horrible things to Mama. He lay in bed sobbing. He refused to talk. On the last trip she handed him a single black garbage bag and told him to pack what he could fit out of his room. His choice. She told him he had a half-hour, and not to forget underwear.

The trailer when I first stepped into it was a tidy playhouse. The empty rooms without curtains held light washed clean by the storm. But by supper the place was suffocating in the chaos of our boxes and stuff. Lonely confining rooms made our belongings look shabby. The few dolls I'd brought were stupid. My clothes hung self-consciously in my closet, like they belonged to strangers.

We sweated in ninety plus degrees, the hottest day of that summer, it turned out. Mama hadn't paid yet to have the electricity hooked up, so not even our box fan could stir the air. I was used to high ceilings, shade trees, a porch swing in the breeze. I was used to being outside whenever I wanted. But Mama forbid us. Dunn whined, "Why not? Why not? Why not?"

Because we will never be safe again, I wanted to make him see. *But we're safer than we were. Mama's safe now.* Mama watched out the windows through pinned-up towels, a prisoner of her new freedom. We ate bologna sandwiches she had packed in the cooler. We drank warm grape Kool-Aid. At dusk when the heat inside was unbearable, Mama pulled a small watermelon from the cooler and smiled weakly.

"Let's go outside, now it's getting dark," she said.

Dunn ran to his room, where he'd refused to go all day when Mama had begged him to try it out. I rolled my eyes at him, and Mama smiled a little. I was her ally, making every gesture to convince her, convince myself. Did she dread every car that went by the same way I did? We sat on the concrete steps and stopped chewing every time car lights came down the street.

I panicked when one of those cars swung slowly into the yard, but Mama knew it was Granny's Impala. She braked with a jerk and left the car idling and the lights on. Mama wasn't surprised at all. She'd had an accomplice she trusted more than me or the mysterious man at the house that day.

Dunn came running out of the trailer, thinking Daddy had come to rescue him. He stumbled off the steps and stopped. He looked back at Mama and then me, and then he ran on to Granny's car and hopped in the front seat with her.

"Well, I reckon Dunny is planning to stay with me and Ed tonight." Granny laughed into the dark.

"If his daddy comes to your house, can you handle things?"

"His daddy's done been up to my house. I fed him supper and listened to him read the letter you left and cry his eyeballs out."

"Don't you feel sorry for him," Mama said. "He's made his bed. He'll lay just fine in it." She spit her watermelon seeds out calmly, but her voice was shaking with anger. "He's hit me one last time. He's hit my kids one last time."

"If it's all that bad, get you a divorce on grounds. I've told you. You don't have to move out of your own house. I give you that house and land. It's beyond me what you're doing ten miles from home." Moths and bugs flew at Granny's headlights.

"Living in town, same as you. Close to work. Somebody's got to feed these kids. And they can walk to the grammar school, better by ten times than where they've been going." I hadn't thought, we might not be going home so fast as she'd said. Or ever. It hit me. We'd left our friends, the teachers we knew.

"Faye, all's I'm saying is it's your house. These kids need their home, especially if they ain't got their daddy. I've told you and told you to kick him out."

"You reckon God had it that easy pitching the devil out of heaven? This is the only way he'll know I ain't bluffing."

"How long you reckon before he figures out where you are? He'll come to the shop tomorrow."

"That's fine. Glenna and Dunny won't be at the shop. They'll be here at the trailer with you for however long it takes, like you agreed. They'll be safe where he don't know where to look."

The image stretched in front of me of the rest of our summer, Dunn and Granny and me sitting in the silent trailer, ten miles and forever away from home.

Granny slapped her flabby arm out the window and adjusted her mirror. She shifted into reverse and waved. "I reckon till you get your lights on, it'll be safe enough to feed these young uns up at my house. No need to starve."

She backed down the short gravel drive and into the street. Dunn's face looked back at us like a lost moon in the streetlight glare. The main street in Newport roared alive with cars. I sat and listened after Mama went inside. I could barely hear katydids in the trees down the street. There were no trees in the trailer's yard. Our yard. Houses across the street stared at us with windows like yellow, prying eyes.

"You know them soldiers," Mama said through the trailer's screen door. "Soldiers or anybody that's had a leg or arm shot off. They say for years they can still feel that limb like it's still there. It'll hurt after all them years. Phantom. Something."

She came through the door and sat beside me. "That's how I am without your daddy. You'll know what that's like someday with some man. Even when Glenn's not here, even if he was to die, it'd still be like that. I'd still feel him, like he was some part of me that got chopped off."

The trailer sank into full dark like a ship going down without any lights. Mama was only a silhouette as she stood up and walked inside, darker than the sky. I knew I was diminished, too, only an outline of myself.

UNBROKEN

"Looks like more rain." Carey pointed over the steering wheel at obvious gray clouds stranded over Arizona. Counting time by mile markers and scraggly brush on I-40 reminded me of working an hourly-wage job. The sluggish yellow distance dwarfed a long, toy-red train.

"I'm going to throw a clot from sitting." I unbuckled my seatbelt. "Don't wreck, okay?" I plunged into the mess on the backseat floorboard. It was a triumph to locate baby wipes to clean my feet. Dust from Mesa Verde and Canyon de Chelly drew fine lines between my toes and stained my soles like henna. I picked at the dirt under my toenails. Then there again, minding my own business half-a-continent away from home, a gut-punch to my memory: Mama and Daddy, Daddy and Mama, bound and tied to each other.

After all the trouble and risk to leave him, months after the divorce was final, after he burned down the farmhouse, Mama took him into the trailer with us. As if he'd struck a deal with the warden, he maintained good behavior. For a while. Whatever fish he brought home were already clean. He took a bath every single day. He carried his plate to the sink. He circled jobs in the want ads. He called Mama "Baby Doll" and "Sugar." They giggled at night through the thin, tacky walls.

Mama doted on him as if she needed to make up for all his wrong doing. She said it was none of my business. She rubbed his naked back while he watched *Dukes of Hazzard* and *Hee-Haw*. She had his supper on the table within an hour of getting home, after being on her feet all day. Worst of all, it mortified me to see her cut his toenails. She cradled his feet in her lap, culled the dirt from his nails, smoothed lotion on his calluses.

I asked, "Why do you lower yourself that way?"

"I ain't lowering myself," she protested.

"You really think for a second he'd do that for you?"

She sighed. "Sister, someday you'll have a husband. You'll see what a little thing it can take to hold two people together. Love ain't always something that looks even-steven to other people."

Husband, she said. *Love*.

Their happily-divorced-ever-after looked to me like bondage. But the power had shifted ever so slightly. Mama did have more control. Daddy could push her only so far because she wasn't legally his wife. Dunn became their blissful satellite. But I resisted the family orbit. I wobbled around Daddy's inescapable gravity, and I crashed into his temper. He blamed me for every betrayal, real and imagined.

By the time I was thirteen, to keep peace, I was spending most nights with Granny and Ed. Mama rationalized. She said since they lived near the high school, it was convenient. With me at Granny's the weather was calmer at the trailer. And I guess I was a willing sacrifice, because when Daddy and I mixed company, everything went sour, skirting his black moods. I couldn't seem to keep from provoking him. I took the helm Mama used to hold as the family back-sasser and troublemaker. I disrupted. I smart-mouthed. I pushed and tugged and tested Daddy's limits every direction I could.

But wasn't Mama aware how complicit she was, using me as her lightning rod? The more trouble I was, the easier he went on her and Dunn. Was it coincidence that she let me buy clothes Daddy hated, tight jeans and halter tops? She bought me blue eyeshadow, mascara, Bonne Bell lip gloss. She bought me fingernail polish for my birthday, and Windsong perfume. She let me get my ears pierced.

"You look like a slut," Daddy would say, but only when he and I were alone. I told him he looked like an old drunk. He would yank my hair until I pulled away and left strands webbed between his fingers. He slapped me or kicked my shins. I told him to burn in hell. I thought I might as well earn the bruises I had coming.

I never breathed a word to Mama, not then. Let her have her moment of peace. There were only two of us on the new battlefield, and I would take care of myself. I covered the marks Daddy left on me with clothes or makeup. I plotted my revenge, staring past his head at the crack that developed in the trailer ceiling, like a frontline on a map. I did not stand down.

Truth be told, I was relieved that he was killing off any remnants of childhood affection I had for him. By fifteen, I had become a study in apathy, learning better by the day. I never answered unless he said my name. I hid my true willfulness like the most valuable secret weapon in my arsenal. Will stronger than he could believe. I would make him taste the names he called me like bile in his mouth. *Slut. Tease. Little whore.* I would make his words true just to spite him. My power was my body, out of his domain.

For two years in high school, boys my age fumbled every chance I gave them, in all the cliché places—cars, basements, the closet in the yearbook darkroom.

Not one had come close to closing the deal. After three of my plainest friends called virginity quits, I knew I'd have to take charge of my own corruption. I wanted to get sex over with, and retribution was my biggest motivation.

Of all the males I knew, I picked Tommy Suggs, because at twenty he wasn't really a boy. And I picked him because he was the son of Daddy's old friend Sully, whom he'd fallen out with. Every night, Tommy rode his motorcycle home from work past the high school. After supper I would leave Granny and Ed in front of *Wheel of Fortune* and linger at the playground just across from the ball field. Tommy barely slowed on the third night. The fourth night I wore a white T-shirt, glowing in the shaded dusk, sitting on a swing. Tommy drove past at a crawl. He turned his bike around. He'd grown a sparse blond mustache since I'd been up close to him. He held power and freedom under every inch of his leather jacket.

He sat in a swing beside mine. The first thing he said to me was, "You're nothing but jailbait." But he grinned like that was part of the attraction. "Nothing but a tease."

He used Daddy's word, but on his round mouth it sounded like sweet talk, not a curse. "Little jailbait tease." He pulled my swing by the chain closer to his.

"I dare you to find out." I leaned into him and kissed him, hard, to hide my trembling smile. His mouth tasted like mustard and meat.

"I'll take you up on that dare any time," he said.

"Friday night," I said. "Right here."

"You still at the high school?" He looked a little worried. "Seriously, you're nearly eighteen, right?"

He didn't know *nearly* eighteen wasn't any more legal than fifteen. I nodded. "Where on Friday?"

"The football game, at the gate. Seven. You figure out the rest." I almost added, *I've got enough to worry about, lying to my mama.*

Friday afternoon she didn't notice I wore my shortest skirt, even in the chill. I set my overnight case on a chair so she'd see my flannel pajamas hanging strategically out of the zipper.

"You going up at Darla's to spend the night?" She was busy combing out a customer. I wasn't lying when I said yes. I would end up at my cousin Darla's house around eleven or midnight, after the game. I just wouldn't be going to the game. My Aunt Louise, with Darla, picked me up at the shop and dropped us at the stadium early, so Darla could warm up with the marching band. When her mom was out of sight, she gave me a hug in her hot uniform. Fat, acned Darla, near tears, with a romantic streak wider than her jealous one. Ecstatic that I'd asked her to lie her braces off for me.

At seven o'clock, Tommy Suggs pulled up on his motorcycle just like I'd said. Why was I shocked to see him? He didn't climb off, just motioned and revved his engine. Some kids stopped to watch me climb behind him. He reached behind us both with his leather glove to square my ass on the seat. The cold black of that touch ran down to my toes. He was protected, hands, skull, legs. No helmet for me. But in my thin cotton sweater, with bare legs and white panties glowing below my hiked-up skirt, more than anything I worried he'd know it was my first time on a motorcycle.

The bike jolted like a horse lurching out of a ditch and in seconds wind whipped my hair into a stinging frenzy. I held around Tommy's waist with one hand while I fought to gather my hair into my other fist. He went so fast I didn't know whether to laugh or scream. I couldn't control the speed or the direction, but I touched the power that did. He leaned around curves so hard I had to let go of my hair and lock myself onto him with both arms. My inner thighs gripped the rough denim on his hips. I lay tight against his leather jacket. Houselights and streetlights streaked in my peripheral vision. We flew past rushing trees and hills against the sky, useless generic landmarks.

When we stopped at a roadside motel, I knew there was no way I could find my way home. And nobody knew where I was. I was free. I was lost. My vulnerability was a vivid kick in the sternum. He slipped off. I balanced on the sole of one foot even after he braced the kickstand.

"You stay here." He shoved his helmet into my open lap. "Don't touch nothing."

"Where you going?" I called as he walked away. He turned back with a scolding look. "I can't stay out all night," I protested. "You said you'd have me back at Darla's before eleven."

"Hell, I can have you back by eight-thirty if that's all you want." He laughed.

He came back with a key and two cans of Coke. He reached in his pack for a quart bottle of beer. The room was hot. Even the paneling seemed to sweat. The radiator didn't change its hissing when I worked the knob. In the dim yellow, I couldn't see any way to open the window. There was just enough light to tell the curtains used to match the green bedspread.

"Here, I got this window open in the bathroom," Tommy called. "Come here a minute." His voice suggested he had a surprise. He sat naked on the edge of the tub, waiting for the water to warm up. He wanted to get the upper hand and dazzle me with his brazen gesture. No way would I show him anything but nonchalance. I glanced at myself in the mirror and altered my face to fit the tough gumption I needed to corral. I couldn't tell where the dirt on his forearms stopped and the tan started. His hands were dingy from the garage where he worked. The rest of him was pale as a baby. He chugged the beer. Green veins webbed beneath his skin. His belly as he leaned over to test the water had a soft roundness I hadn't expected, love handles, and welts where his jeans had cut into his waist.

I didn't see his penis until he stood up. I'd touched others, but always through jeans or in the dark, and I hadn't imagined they could ever be anything like the dejected sample in front of me. The hair on his chest and in a V low on his belly was the same color of his mustache, but the stub hung in a tangled nest of red. I thought of Opie Taylor.

Without a word, Tommy stepped to me and pulled my sweater over my head. He looked like he was studying a busted carburetor as he tried to unhook my bra. He finally turned me around and then pulled at my skirt. His body changed then. His stubble pricked the back of my neck as he pushed up my breasts with his palms. When he turned me around again and kissed me, his hands seemed to multiply, fast and coarse. Pressed high against my hip, his penis rubbed larger than I'd seen between his legs. I was too curious not to reach for it, even in the scalding light. When I held the length in my palm, he groaned. Something inevitable made me powerful. My touch and my body—no one else's—made him willing to take off all that leather, to be soft and white and naked.

Then I was naked too. My body changed too. I tried to slow down my breathing, as if I'd been running up a hill, tried to stop pushing my hips against his before I knew I could make such a motion. I'd been in the moment with other boys, when I was in charge, but not this way. He pulled me into the shower, and fumes like diesel oil rose off him in the steam. The water made us slick against each other, but my back sucked against the tiles. Then everything was over in such a dark flash of pressure, I couldn't tell when the quick, slight burn between my legs began, during or after.

Half-dressed, I lay sweating under the sheet. In the dark room I watched the television's crooked lines, the end of *Sanford and Son*, while Tommy finished washing off his day's grime and shaved. Orange neon glared between the curtains like a false sunset. Footsteps and shadows passed on the walk outside. I listened for a knock or a key in the door. I wished I felt different than I had before.

When Tommy came back in and lay on top of me, I didn't move. I hadn't expected any more contact. Beer breath made him smell like Daddy. But after I drank my own bitter swig or two from the quart bottle and shared his cigarette, I could only smell soap and wet hair. He kissed me in quick foolish spasms, grinning at me the way people mug for babies. Then he pulled away the sheet. His face was serious in an instant, and I could feel him hard against me again. He fumbled between my legs. He sucked on my nipples, and I willed away the warm waves rising through me. I'd had sex minutes before, nothing much, not really anything at all. I waited, bored and ready, for the kind of moment that had passed over like a shadow in the shower.

But the second time I had to struggle to keep thinking. My body wanted to go under, away from what I concentrated on, the light, the sheets, the ceiling. He rubbed up and down the length of me until my skin burned. I gripped at his arms and pulled at his shoulder blades, but he seemed to ignore every touch, even when I scratched his ribs. He acted. I reacted. I had lost the beauty of my power. I had no control, as if I weren't in the room at all, as if I weren't even in my own body, and there was only Tommy there, funneling in and out, until whatever I'd been, whatever I'd become seeped into the mattress and up my back.

For the ride home, I tucked a washcloth into my panties. I'd learned enough to tie my hair back against the wind. I used what I had learned about gravity and movement to grip the motorcycle seat with my thighs, leaning back against the dark and the curves instead of against Tommy. I blinked into the cold wind and hung on to the metal bar behind me until my arms and shoulders ached.

Without a word or a gesture, Tommy dropped me off at the foot of Darla's driveway in the dark, an hour before her friends would bring her home after the game. I hid in some brush by the mailbox, like we'd planned.

I stood because when I tried to sit in the weeds, it hurt. My pulse beat numbly in my crotch, as if the motorcycle were still vibrating between my legs. The fall dark was still, without birds or insects, even lonelier when the clouds uncovered a quarter moon. Later I had to tell my aunt Louise I'd started my period and needed a pad. No one had told me a man could make me bleed.

What had I imagined? That I could slip into power as easily as Tommy Suggs slipped into his leather jacket? Into me? Love and sex were not a motor vehicle. I'd seen them bind Mama like an addict to Daddy. She'd warned me. "You keep blaming me, Sister, for the life I've got with your daddy. Someday you'll grow up and see they ain't hardly ever a good enough reason to love somebody. But you probably can't do nothing to help it."

I hadn't wanted romance or love, though. I hadn't even wanted Tommy Suggs. I wanted to *be* Tommy Suggs. I wanted to confiscate his liberty, the force and speed that took him wherever he chose. I wanted to fly solo and never look back. Twice removed from being a virgin, I hadn't gotten one inch closer to free or an inch farther from Daddy. My head was as murky as the dark I stood in. I doubted love existed at all.

Carey slept while I drove, scanning ahead for the Petrified Forest. Ridiculous as I should have known it was, I pictured upright rock-solid trunks with stone branches. I finally understood at the first overlook in the national park that in Arizona most of the goods are over the edge. Below us the sunken plain receded in striated hills of steel blue, copper, bronze, pollen yellow, alabaster.

The Painted Desert was in full color, even under slate clouds with snaking jags of far lightning. A few icy drops of rain fell against our bare legs, and gusts stung our cheeks and hands. The other tourists raced past us in their motorhomes or to their motels on Route 66 or further on down the interstate. But we stopped at every overlook, waiting in the car through downpours, gone quick as they started. Far away pools of water like colored glass reflected a rosy light moving across the eroded badlands.

When the sky lightened, we hiked a steep path down across rounded pyramids Carey called teepees. The badlands. We avoided mud pits, but white clay built up like soggy chalk on our boots. We laughed how heavy our feet were and stopped over and over to stoop and scrape off the vivid white slog. How primeval and hard the desert looked, for all its softness. The eroding landscape so ancient and resilient, yet so fragile to the touch it seemed it might wash away in a single afternoon.

"This place reminds me a little—" I started, then bumped into Carey when he stopped to look back at me.

"No. I know there is no way you've ever been any place like this," he said.

"Yes. The zinc mines where I hung out in college."

"You hung out in a mine?" He walked on after he rolled his eyes.

"Well, not *in* the mine, silly. But where the slag heaps piled stories high, like white canyons." I stretched my stride to step into his boot prints. "In a dinky college town, in a dry county, there was nothing to do but drive around or sit in somebody's field drinking beer. There were two industries in that town—the college and the biggest zinc deposits on the planet. People don't know that about East Tennessee. To us that strange place was beautiful and safe."

But it was futile, trying to separate description from nostalgia. Carey went to college at Emory in Atlanta. He'd gone urban wild while I'd stayed in Hillbillyville. The bizarre, bald plain of white zinc tailings had held a scent of scraped stone and constant winter, like stepping onto the moon.

"Nights the moon was full, the whole place glowed."

"Oh, I get it." Carey laughed. "A sex pit!" He was right, but for me the place wasn't sordid. It was intimate.

"Not like you think," I said. "It was locals who knew the place mostly. I only went there with one person. Ever. He—oh, never mind."

"Go ahead," Carey said. He stopped short but didn't turn to look at me. "You went there with Mackie Hayes."

"Oh, my God! I did not go there with Mackie Hayes." The name bruised the air between us after all the years. Carey glanced at me and motioned to turn back. We headed to the Jeep in silence.

Our senior year in high school Mackie Hayes was my first long-term boyfriend, and Carey was hurt over and over, most of all by my neglect. And he was mean like a dog that's wounded. He said Mackie was just into me for an easy lay. We didn't speak for weeks.

Really Mackie's motives were way worse. I was an instrument of torture to wield against his rich and socially connected parents. And to be fair, I thought he'd help me exact a similar misery on Daddy. But in the cold war I had with my father, I couldn't tell if Mackie was an asset or a liability. Daddy knew the Hayes family had serious money, from hotels they owned way back. They drank martinis on the deck of their weekend retreat overlooking Douglas Lake. They vacationed in Hilton Head. I hadn't expected Daddy to be stunned into silence by Mackie's preppy presence in our trailer. A surprise: His status rubbed off on me, a protective barrier. We applied to the same colleges. By January our senior year, we were the school sweethearts, heading to college together, settled and headed for stability.

Our first break-up was almost a relief from all that mature exposure. I think Daddy was hit worse than I was. Boys usually dated me until we slept together. Sex ended relationships, in my experience, because no boy can focus on more than one hobby at a time. I was a brief intrigue until they joined a garage band, or until hunting season started. But Mackie came back. And besides keeping me, he also kept up his grades. He kept his job at the family business. He kept his routine. He'd get high on Saturday nights, and the next morning he would teach Sunday school.

"Whatever happened to him?" Carey turned to me.

I shrugged. "He runs a big motel in the Smokies. Married with a litter of kids."

"How do you always know the scoop on everybody?"

"Mama fixes their mothers' hair. Dunn fixes their daddys' cars."

"We should go to a reunion together when we're old." Carey laughed. "Talk about gossip. They'd all think you finally converted me. The only girl they said I'd go straight for."

I couldn't think of a way to respond. He laughed again. "We could wear the same clothes we wore to prom. Remember? You think they'd still fit?" He looked at me. "That powder blue tux. Your hundred percent polyester yellow."

"Hey! It was a nice dress!" He turned at the end of the trail and I blinked rapidly at him. "It brought out the flecks of gold in my hazel eyes." I hoped the lilt in my voice would end the conversation.

We climbed the final incline, in view of the car. "But do you remember the looks we got?" He fumbled for his keys.

"Yes." I sighed. "Because everybody assumed I'd be with Mackie." We got into the car and backed out, driving toward the Arizona distance with the windows down to the cool monsoon air, reliving two different sides of the same memory.

"I was terrified you'd end up marrying him," Carey said after a few minutes.

"You and I wouldn't even know each other now."

150

"Sure we would!" His voice was wounded. He pulled into the parking lot at the next overlook and shut the engine.

We looked out at the landscape, like a freshly washed alien planet, the hues and light swirling. A far curtain of rain grayed the distance, but rays of light struck the desert in pockets of gold.

What would it have been like, never to see Carey again, ever, after high school? He'd have had every right to hold me as an enemy forever, after such errors anybody might make at sixteen, seventeen. But I had been cruel to him in my choices.

He was a stranger in the car for several ticking seconds. What if I had married Mackie Hayes? What if Carey had been so devoted to Stan that he rejected my lukewarm friendship those years? What one small gesture could have rearranged the whole history between us?

"I was such a hypocrite. Or rationalizing," I admitted, "thinking I could be your friend while I was with Mackie." There was the smell of ozone, heavy in the air between us. I'd never come close to apologizing before. It was time, even though their fight hadn't been my fault. The years pleated together. "I look back and can't believe I kept seeing him. Even into our first year in college."

"We were so young." Carey was already forgiving me.

I looked at him. No. He had already forgiven me, all those years and years before.

Mackie had ambushed Carey. This much I understood the day after it happened. That Carey had been alone, and Mackie had been merciless. His knuckles were battered, and both of Carey's eyes were black. The bruises stained yellow around them, like jaundice, for weeks. I never saw the rest of him, but he walked like an old man for a week through the hallways at school.

"It's no excuse. *Young* is no excuse. I wasn't able to feel the brutality of anything back then. I didn't have room for awareness in me, to think of a beating as anything but temporary discomfort." My panic came in gusts, to recall blow after blow I had withstood. "My own family—"

"Glenna. You don't need to do this to yourself. You were traumatized as a kid. You needed shelter wherever you could get it. I wasn't your responsibility."

"No. This is awful to think of now. I did always want to protect you, but I let down my guard. I welcomed your worst nightmare into my life. I'm feeling now what I should have felt twenty years ago. We didn't even have a term for gay bashing back then, did we? I knew your parents threatened to press charges."

"What?" Carey looked at me. "You can't think—Glenna. Do you think—? Glenna, look at me. Mackie didn't beat me up because I'm gay. I mean, it wasn't a coincidence he beat me up two days after you and I went to prom together!" He looked at me vexed. "He wasn't a bully. Or not *just* a bully, anyway. I mean, he was jealous."

151

"Carey. Come on, obviously there wasn't anything to be jealous of between you and me."

He laughed with that wry squint he gives sometimes. "Glenna. Look around you. Who is still here, right here in this car with you? And Mackie Hayes is nowhere in sight."

And he was right. There was no one there but him, no other friend from so far back, or from any point in my life. None of the men I loved had ever stuck it out with me. No one had the stamina to deal with my shit. Of course, I'd assumed Carey would always be there. And that's the textbook definition of taking someone for granted.

Some people might say they don't remember a time "before." Before they had a baby. Before they got baptized. Before their first kiss. I'd be a liar if I said, *there was always Carey.* I do remember the time before Carey. My life was like that black-and-white part in *The Wizard of Oz.* Then there he was, a technicolor transformation, the kind when a zing goes through your head.

Carey stood in front of our third-grade classroom, the new kid. And I knew, he was my new kid. He looked me right in the eyes, and only then did he smile. What expectant wish had he seen on my face? I called him to me in my mind and held him dear. The world shifted a little on its axis.

In a way, the only way that's important, there *was* always Carey. There will always be Carey.

We stayed in the Jeep for one last overlook, scanning down slopes with deep erosion tracks. Jasper Forest Overlook held no forest, of course, nothing close to a tree anywhere. Carey explained, though, and I shifted my perspective. The petrified forest lay in boulders scattered on the ground, what looked from a distance like dark pebbles strewn down the plummeting cliffs. Sections of stone trunks.

Carey explained that massive floods felled and buried giant trees. Under pressure and time—aeons of millions of years—minerals fossilized in place of pith and bark. The rest was gravity breaking the horizontal logs into chunks as the deep, deep earth around them eroded away. Boulders shaped like logs tumbled out of the cliff sides as they gave way. I could see, then, sections of trunks poking horizontally out of the cliff edges, just waiting for gravity to break them off.

Later at Crystal Forest we finally stood eye level with boulders, some large as cars, chunks of tree trunks with petrified ridges of icy black auburn bark. Mineralized trees. Rain lacquered the interior rings, dazzling spectrums that had been hidden for millennia beneath clay—crystalline yellow and orange, amethyst and vermilion. The same minerals we'd walked on had intensified to hard brilliance over time. Beside a stone that dwarfed him, Carey looked like a boy. Even graying, with a few crow's feet around his eyes, his body held the boy

I'd known all those years ago. He turned to grin at me, pushing up his glasses like he had a thousand, thousand times, clarifying everything between us.

Road signs will stick in your brain. I couldn't stop singing that Eagles song with the lines about Winslow, Arizona, even when we were well past the exit. Carey dug around in his bag of tapes and said we might as well listen to the real thing. We pushed north of Flagstaff on Highway 89 into luxurious pine shadow. Beyond Humphrey's Peak, the highest in the state, plumes of smoke rose from a forest fire.

In and out of high desert and woodlands, I was impatient for the Grand Canyon and the lodge room Carey had reserved. I thought we were there when the horizon gaped open right in front of us, but he said it was the Little Colorado Canyon. Just an appetizer, Carey called it, as he pulled onto the wide roadside canyon rim. Navajo families were peddling jewelry and leather work under makeshift shade. They sat in lawn chairs beside coolers.

"Look." Carey bent to a tarpaulin layered in Navajo rugs. The wool was animal-hot in the sun. "The storm pattern," he said. "Always red, gray, and black. The four sacred mountains represented in the corners. And the jagged lightning design. But see this one mismatched line? On purpose. It's called a spirit line." He traced the intended flaw from the center to the edge of the rug. "A Navajo weaver always leaves this line, a way into the story she's telling."

"Nah," I said. "Anybody divorced three times will tell you, that's her escape route."

As I waited for Carey to use the port-a-john at the edge of the parking lot, every single vendor at each table asked the same practiced question, even a lone little girl keeping watch on a spread of trinkets. "Where you from?" Her dark face came clear when I took off my sunglasses.

"Tennessee." I smiled. "In the mountains. I bet you never been there before. I've sure never been here before." I ran my fingers across earrings.

"Two for ten dollars. The necklaces are eight. I made this one." She held out a necklace to me.

"Pretty." I took if from her and she picked up another and then another, one in each hand. "So, you ever been to Tennessee?" I asked. She shook her head, watching me with a hungry look, to see if she might make a sale, touching every piece I touched, reinforcing my choices.

For a moment I missed my job, helping kids navigate ways to admit their parents hurt them, ways their culture lets them down. With children, it's always been easy for me to be like a child, make myself touch my own hurts. Daddy always helped me be a good social worker because I had so much of my own history packed in that toolbox.

"Well, it's a long way," I said. "I'm getting homesick. I miss my mama." She didn't laugh, intent on her hopeful sale. I told her my name and she said she was Tiffany. "Tiffany, huh? You all alone out here?"

"There's my mom." She pointed to a woman walking toward us with a baby across her shoulder. She came to stand beside Tiffany, scanning the table as if she were making sure she hadn't been robbed, avoiding eye contact. The baby was only a few weeks old, in short overalls and no shirt. His back was covered with black down, which babies usually shed in the womb. I wanted to touch him. I wanted to touch him, and not in the way I'd touched the jewelry. And yet it was the same way, covetous of skill and beauty that was out of my reach. I set down the necklace.

"You make beautiful things." I nodded at the baby. The woman looked at him and brushed back his shock of black hair, then eyed her daughter before she looked straight at me and nodded.

Families with kids moved from table to table making bargains. I spotted Carey, the only soul I knew for fifteen hundred miles, maybe on the whole planet. Sensing she was losing her sale, Tiffany pointed. "Maybe your husband will buy you a necklace."

"Oh!" I laughed. "No, we're just friends. Since we were your age." She looked skeptical. "No, it's true. My whole life—" I had started to say, *my whole life I've loved him.* "My whole life," I repeated.

Whatever time doesn't shear apart, it strengthens. From my first rocky overlook, the Grand Canyon stretched like a mortal gouge in the world's hide. Westward across the Kaibab Plateau, the road followed the canyon rim in and out of Ponderosa pines and rangy junipers. Each view we stopped for, the evening sank into a deeper smear. The forest fire smoke stung the air and smudged the distance.

Carey was disappointed by the smog, but I could hardly believe the color and immensity, the pinnacles the Colorado River had carved. Through his binoculars, rapids were just a tiny white ripple in the serpentine teal. A mile below. I stood there and witnessed the river that far away, but I couldn't believe it was possible. Distances hazed and shimmered depending on where we stood. Even the farthest points seemed touchable, as if I were looking back at a memory. And yet those reaches were no place I could ever touch.

At Yavapai Point, the last stop before our lodge, the parking lot was overrun. We had to park way down the road and walk fast to catch the sunset. People sat along rocks as if they were stadium seating or leaned against the railing. A trio of French hikers, sunburned and barely dressed, milled in front of Carey and me, chattering and gesturing. Dark women in saris trailed men in turbans. Kids ran, calling in every excited language, as if they knew a universal translation like the night birds swooping and squawking over us. As the canyon sank from dusty orange into one muted blue, a shout went up, clapping and cheering, and people embraced. Carey and I were swept up, with our arms around one another. Everybody's home team had won.

By the time we found our wooded suburb of motel units, it was full dark. We devoured two cans of tuna chased with cheese crackers, then played "rock, paper, scissors" to see who'd get clean first. Carey won, which meant I could take my sweet time lingering later in shampoo and soap, but I fell asleep waiting on him, both of us zonked out by nine-thirty, with Carey's travel alarm set so we'd be up for sunrise.

Five-thirty Arizona time, I was already awake with a thrill in my arms and legs. Christmas morning thrill. I wasn't about to take time to shower. I jumped up and dressed in layers. Yesterday's T-shirt underneath a thermal layer of quarter-zip wool, and my down jacket on top. And my hiking pants that zipped off at the knee. We knew the day would heat up fast, but the desert dawn would be near freezing. Carey tugged on clothes he'd set out the night before. We grabbed our packs and coffee he made in the lodge-room coffee maker, and we walked into the cold dark. Bird call broke through the pines, but otherwise it was still.

Instead of crowds like the evening before, only a dozen or so travelers were up, huddled against each other or hunkered alone in fleece jackets and wind breakers. As the dark lightened, a few more people collected on the rocks and only spoke in whispers. We were ready for church to begin.

First light washed the canyon the same evergreen blue we'd seen at sunset, but the night wind had cleared the haze. We sat and watched the high canyon edge tinge gold, as the lower reaches glowed faintly. Brush flamed green in crevices on the lower butte slopes. The sun shot yellow high into the east, which purpled the western clouds. Carey tapped the bill of my cap and smiled oddly as he stood with his pack.

"I'm going down to a different vantage point," he said. I stood to follow. "No. By myself. I really need—I mean, honestly, I didn't think you'd be up for sunrise. I thought you'd sleep in and shower." He stammered. "I just—I need time. A minute. A few minutes."

"You didn't want me along?" I smiled, but he was serious.

"Just let me walk down here for a few minutes alone. A little while." He looked at me with the saddest expression I've ever seen on his face.

"Go," I said. "I'll wait right here for you, long as you want to be gone." I sat on a square rock, like a throne, to watch the shifting colors, my body stiff in the cold, not fully awake yet. But my senses were alert. The hot coffee piqued my vision and hearing—all of me alive while my body was as static as I could make it. I tried not to be curious about Carey or worry. I wanted to fix myself to let him be and not pry. But his sorrow hung over me. The morning turned sober in its glorious urge. I settled in to be part of the rock and absorb every second. This was an important moment that might never be again. No. It was a moment that would never be again. A moment without Carey and yet with him. Only he and I would remember, even if we weren't side by side as the sun flared at the horizon behind us.

The canyon wall far in front of me lightened downward by degrees, as if somebody had pulled a plug at the bottom of the canyon to empty the night. Light turned solid dark to shadow. Then ridges and hollows exchanged that shadow for color across the layered rock—pink, orange, ruby, light enough then to see the river waking a mile down to another eternal morning. And then the day was born.

I worried Carey might not find me where I sat unzipping the lower legs off my pants. The morning had heated up fast, so I'd moved down a ways, out of the sun, into the scrawny shade of a pinyon. He saw me right when I picked him out of a group walking to the parking lot. I stood and brushed off the seat of my pants, but when he got to me, he plopped down, legs folded beneath him. He took off his sunglasses, and I could see he'd been crying. He pulled out a bottle of water and offered it up to me before he took a drink. I sat back down facing him and screwed off the lid while he dug in his pack for breakfast bars. We ate and traded water back and forth without a word.

"I know you weren't Stan's biggest fan," he said finally.

"I didn't really know him," I answered. "Which is my fault."

"It's not anybody's fault," he said. "I wish you two had spent time together. But there was a stretch you and I weren't around each other much. Work and grad school. And then he was sick. And he and I circled our wagons, I know. Even his parents claimed I was hoarding him to myself. It's true. I didn't want to share him."

"That makes sense," I said. I didn't know how to keep him from crying again. He wiped his eyes. I tried to recall a time I had seen Carey cry. I cringed inside to think, again, that I had missed Stan's memorial service.

Carey could sense my guilt. He took a deep breath and exhaled. "I mean, I can't exactly say I know Kevin. He and I barely ever saw one another. But he seemed—I mean, he was right. He loved you. Probably still loves you."

I could only nod. I wanted to tell him, to find the words to say that he was wrong but right. That Kevin had loved me more than anyone, and I had loved him more than anyone. And so, the cruelty between us ran deep as pitch dark. I smothered.

"I can say I wish I *didn't* know Dawson." Carey laughed. "That's mean, isn't it?"

"It's fair. I wish I didn't either." I smiled to prompt him to stay light, to stand up and go away from this sad depth, the unknown cavity over the horizon in my life I hadn't faced yet.

But he turned serious again. "I mean, my sisters didn't like Stan either," he said. "They still think I'm just playing at being gay, though. They thought he was arrogant and materialistic. You can't say anything about him I haven't heard already."

"Carey, you don't have to go through all this or explain."

"No. I know. I mean, I love being on this trip with you, and I didn't mean to shut you out. It's just hard to be here—"

"With me. Yeah."

"No, I'm trying to say it's been great, but part of me is pissed off, I guess, that it's you here with me and not Stan. Or I'm feeling guilty for being here without him. We always meant to come here together."

"But you said you'd been here before."

"He was here as a kid and—well—with a guy before me. And I've been here without him. Before his lymphoma came back, we were sure there'd be time. Because this is where we started being together." He gestured. "Right here, at sunrise, this overlook is where we decided to be together."

"I'm lost."

"After we started—got involved—he was in this phase where he was seeing other men, several, and I couldn't stand it. It was dangerous. Those were dangerous times, you know? So many of our friends died. He was careful, and I was patient, but I'd had it with his free ranging." Carey grinned at the same time his eyes rimmed over with tears.

"You have to admit, Stan was hot. Let's just say, being monogamous hadn't been in his long-term plans. I thought he was out of my life because I told him I couldn't do the open relationship, you know? I needed to be—well, to be married, even if we couldn't legally. I told him he was the love of my life, my soulmate, all that ridiculous moony stuff. And he took it as an ultimatum. Done." He swept his hands together. "He came out here with some young pretty thing."

"But one morning the phone rang, pretty early. It woke me, and it was Stan calling from the big, fancy hotel here, the El Tovar, right on the rim. I mean, we'll see it today. It's like four hundred dollars a night.

"He said he needed to tell me two things. The first was to look for a package he'd be mailing from Arizona. The second was that he was done living pillar to post. That's what he said, 'pillar to post.'

"Then he said the words. I mean, I'd thought he was gone, out of my life. I'd gone to bed a wreck one more night, and now this. I was waking up to the words. I had a moment of that old cliché of thinking you're dreaming, you know? But I was awake. He said, 'I love you.'" Carey teared up again and choked back, trying so hard to get through his story.

And here I was, maybe the only person who had ever, in all of time, heard Carey say how his life with Stan started and took shape. He needed to tell me. He needed me to hear him. I split. Half of me filled up with Carey's trust. And half of me sank, to think I should have trusted him in exactly the same way. How could I match his bravery? Tell him about Kevin, my miscarriage? I was heavy as the heat, as Carey lightened and lightened, the weight of his story like a feather now.

"Stan said, 'If my plane crashes or I get lost in the desert or a scorpion bites me, I need you to know I love you.'" Carey laughed and wiped his eyes. "Sappy!"

"Not at all," I said. "It's beautiful. I wish—I really wish I had known how wonderful he was to you. I never knew he treated you the way you deserved to be treated. Now I know. Thank you. Thanks for showing me. I wish I could have been at whatever sort of wedding—"

"People don't understand at all. Gay equals promiscuous to them. But what if someone like me who is always a one-man guy just happens to be gay? I mean, the way that I'm also a one-woman guy." He reached over to put his hand on my head, tucked a new growth of curl behind my ear.

I could hardly bear not to cry, not to start crying and just wail. How long would it take an echo to come back from down in the canyon? Salt stung my gums, and I tightened my throat against weeping. "You're my guy that way, too, Carey."

"Well, not really, but that's okay. We're—" He hesitated. "We just are, aren't we? You and me. Me and you. We always end up at the edge of everything together." The Grand Canyon was on fire with mid-morning light beneath the pure blue.

"Okay. So." I let go of his hand. "What was in the package?"

"Oh! Right. A videotape. He videoed the sunrise right here." He lowered his voice to mimic and laughed while he cried a little. "'This is Stan talking from a thousand miles away to Carey. The sun is coming up at the Grand Canyon and there's nobody else on the planet I wish was here with me right now but you. I miss you. Life is unbearably boring without you.'

"And there's more. It's just godawful treacle, isn't it? I have the damn thing memorized. I mean, Glenna, I have a copy in a damn safe deposit box!" He giggled and dug into his pocket for his keys and held up the key to his memory.

"Well, as a woman whose house burned down—twice—I'd say that's just about the smartest thing ever."

"Yeah?" he said. "I save it for rainy, lonely Sundays. Anniversaries. And there's Stan's voice. He falls in love with me over and over forever. And now here I am."

"Here you are." I locked eyes with him and shrugged. "With me. I'm so sorry!"

His face folded up with grief and hilarity. He hugged onto me hard, laughing as he cried. "You in all your glorious dirt and grime," he finally said. "Girl. I mean, you need a shower," he said, sniffing. People walked past us and wondered why we were tangled together, laughing like grade-school girls. We lost our balance hanging on to each other and tumbled over into ancient dust, within a rock's toss of the vastness, but we didn't let go.

WAR STORIES

At Kaibab Lake, our campground host gave a grunt as he twisted in his lawn chair to make change. Tattoos of blurry indigo ran up his beefy forearms under pale shirt sleeves. Years and pounds after he'd pledged himself to the U.S. MARINE CORPS, the letters had worn thin as withering balloons. I had to squint in the awning shade of his RV to make out that he'd promised his left bicep to *Rosemarie*.

He handed me three crumpled ones out of a rusted cash drawer propped on cobwebby cinder blocks. A green parrot clawed a perch beyond his bald head where a sign warned, BEWARE OF BIRD. An occasional shriek broke the stillness. He asked for my license and printed my name in a receipt booklet, and my address—which I didn't explain no longer existed. Only a few campers and tents were already set up, no voices, no campfires. I scanned again through tall pines where Carey was unloading the Jeep at the site we'd picked.

"Sure is pretty dead." I attempted small talk with the top of the guy's age-spotted head. A patch of white hair at the back of his grimy collar was braided into a tail hanging nearly to his pot belly. White hair frothed on his legs below the tight hem of his coaching shorts.

"You wait. Six o'clock it'll be Grand Central." He licked his thumb and tore off the receipt. "That's for your dash," he instructed. "Check out's eleven tomorrow. Not one minute later."

Around five-thirty, he was right, traffic through the campground woke us from a deep, sweaty nap. As we cooked and ate supper, the place became a village. Long after dark, no vacancies left, car after car paused at the space beyond our campfire, where there was room for an unofficial set-up, but no table or fire-ring. People quizzed us and stopped at the host's trailer. Dead tired, with mad wives and hungry kids, they headed back toward the open highway.

It was easy for the guy to spot kids trying to guerrilla camp about ten o'clock. If their rattling VW van didn't give them away, his attack-parrot did. When he waddled past our campfire, they sent up a chorus of "Aw, man."

"We're at capacity, gang. You need to saddle up and move on." He shined a flashlight from spiked hair to bead necklaces. One boy tried charm, but the other two launched an all-out desperate offensive.

"All we want's a place to crash for one night. We leave first thing for Vegas."

"Look, there's no debate," the big guy said. "Rules are rules. Nothing personal, but I will call the ranger."

"But we're having car trouble," the hopeful heavy-set kid said.

"Be glad to call you a tow."

"You got a fucking million acres here!" A girl's voice came from the van. I hadn't noticed her, but he caught her in his light, and the red-headed girl standing beside her, crying as she ate SpaghettiOs straight out of the can. He shined his light long enough on her chest to read her T-shirt: *Zero to bitch in sixty seconds.*

"Sir," I said. The guy blinded me with his flashlight. Carey caught at my T-shirt as I stood up from my camp chair. "These kids really need a place to stay. If there's any way." He shook his head. "I can pay the fee. They seem pretty desperate."

"If they're that desperate, they can have your site."

"Glenna," Carey whispered. He stood and put his hand on my shoulder.

"Or I can call their parents," the manager said.

The girl who'd been crying sent up a wail. In a flurry her friends swooped her up like a precious belonging and hustled into the van. The transmission protested in a screech we could hear after their taillights disappeared.

I couldn't look at Carey as we sat for a few more minutes by our warm fire. I didn't answer when he asked if I was ready to call it a day. He stood up and scuffed dirt into the low flame, snuffing it to smoke.

"Carey! Maybe I want to sit up for a while."

"You mean, sit here mad at me all night?" He folded up his camp chair. I tried to make my eyes adjust to the sudden dark.

"I'm not mad," I lied. Who was I mad at? The kids, their parents? Myself?

"What was I supposed to do, Glenna? They're fine. They'll just have to drive a little farther than they wanted. Kingman is like three hours."

"You have no idea how bad it has to get for kids—"

"Oh, good grief, not getting a campsite isn't a tragedy. It might happen to us some night." His outline leaned his chair against a tree. "Now they'll have one of those college stories—"

"No way those girls were legal. They're runaways." I stood up and folded my chair. "I've worked with kids like that for nearly fifteen years. You didn't get their freak-out when he threatened to call their parents?"

"Maybe he should."

My eyes had adjusted enough to see him look up at the black sky. The Milky Way again. Our little campfire smoldering up toward it.

"Carey, remember what it was like. Remember figuring out it's not just kids that are assholes? Adults are worse assholes. With all the power."

I figured he was shuffling his memory. His parents sent him to a psychiatrist to cure him of being "queer." The coach of the track team singled him out for abuse, sicced his teammates on him. "Remember when you first knew my daddy was an asshole?"

Sixteen and crying in the high school hallway at my locker, Carey had touched the places on my arms and face that showed the blows Glenn Daniels had given me. We hadn't seen each other for the two weeks I'd missed school, so my cuts and bruises, my two broken ribs, were on their way to healing. We'd never talked about it since. We weren't talking about it still.

"Kids look like renegades because they use language at a toddler level. They don't even have words for what grownups do to them," I said. "Even our mothers, with their best intentions." My arms and hands started to tremble. I was tiny under the big Arizona sky. "They are—were—supposed to protect us. But my mother let me run wild too young. She let me get into trouble I shouldn't have until it was almost too late."

She hadn't protected me from my own father until it was very nearly too late.

"Everybody blames their mothers," Carey said in the dark. "Even when it's the fathers who do the bullying. Name-calling."

"Lions eat their own cubs, right. But mothers are supposed to keep that from happening. Those girls might not be out here if their mothers were doing their jobs. All over Newport and Knoxville I remove kids from mothers who were girls when they had babies, but it's no excuse. I've seen jealous mothers who lock their daughters in closets or basements. Or tie them up.

"One case I had, the girl's mother poisoned her until her skin rotted and her hair fell out. She nearly went blind. And a woman who sprayed acid in her daughter's face so her new stepfather wouldn't want her instead. Then the flip side is mothers who treat their daughters like some incentive package to get a man. I know a woman who held down her daughter while—well—Those girls just remind me how bad it can get. Everybody always blames mothers because that's the worst betrayal."

"Shit, Glenna," Carey said. "I never thought about you dealing with those kind of people."

"Those kind of people? Carey, I never ran away from home, but only because I had Granny and Ed to run to. But I *was* those kind of people. My people *were* those kind of people."

The honeymoon was long over at the trailer. Month after month after year after year, Daddy had gotten used to the divorce and settled back into playing dictator. Not just that. He suspected Mama at every turn. Interrogated her. He found out she'd kept company with Gus Potter when she first left him. I finally had a name for the man at Granny's house, the one who helped Mama move boxes and escape. A hell of a lot of good he'd done her. I would see him in town sometimes, or driving past, just a phantom for Daddy to be jealous of, I thought. The assumptions I made were those of a goody-goody. A girl as experienced as I was should have seen Mama for what she was—a woman. But more than that, a woman stuck and taken for granted.

Because she evaporated some weeks, logging longer and longer hours at her shop, Daddy rerouted his neediness. And his challenges, too. He picked at me like a scab. He was never able to be alone for ten minutes straight. If he couldn't keep Mama close, he'd keep me closer. He started refusing to let me stay with Granny. My junior year, I cooperated the way Mama begged me to. She said I had it in my power to keep the peace. I wore clothes Daddy okayed, threw away most of my makeup. Said *yes sir, no sir*. Unless I was at school or with Mama, putting in hours at the shop, he didn't let me out of his sight.

"No daughter of mine," he would say. "While you're under my roof," he said. I didn't dare sass that it was Mama's roof. He was waiting for me to slip up, and I couldn't have known how bad it would be when I did. The torture of the tension was enough to make me think about running away. But sixteen was in sight. I knew what sex was. What sex wasn't. There were no Prince Charmings to save me. After Tommy, before Mackie, no boy seemed worth screwing up my life. I could manage the marathon to college, like one of those soldiers counting down the hours, terrified to cross a landmine his last day with the troops.

I made straight A's. I made supper every night. And it worked for a good while. Daddy played nice. I played nice. And in pretending, I learned I could be a good daughter, even out of the habit of pretense. The side effect of my new act was that I also got pretty good at being Sister, like everybody called me. The very best part of me guarded Dunn.

He was a young thirteen, with barely a sign of the broadness and bull-head-edness he would inherit. And the lag of being left behind a grade was as good for him as it was for me to be the youngest in my class. He was little in the limbs, with small hands, but a wide, smart face. He had thick hair in a burr cut I rubbed like a worry stone. We were nearly constantly together that year, watching TV, falling asleep on the couch, reading, and playing games in my room. He slept in my closet sometimes where I'd built a fortress for him under the soft haven of clothes. We may have been teenagers in the external world. Together, we were little children.

Daddy envied our new bond, despised it. He seemed to relish making Dunn cry so that he could chide him even more furiously. "Sissy boy, what're you doing? You going to play dolls with your sister? Have a tea party? About time you got out from under the skirts around here."

Daddy made him join the football team. Dunn was the littlest player, facing blunt trauma every evening, and every Saturday morning at practice, and Friday nights when the high school had an away game. He couldn't stand up to anyone, but he could run. He learned all the quickness that would've made him a star quarterback in high school, but by then the doctor said he'd had too many torn tendons and ligaments, stress fractures from starting the game so young. Truth was, those hits may have been from Daddy's whippings.

I'd suffered enough bruises myself. But when I looked at the blue and purple-green welts on Dunn, I pictured Daddy laid out cold in his casket. I could see to it, lace his pinto beans with rat poison, rig up a pitchfork to spring through his chest like fangs. My own imaginary inventions scared me. The tortures that would neon through my brain without warning. How easy when he passed out drunk to slide his belt off. I was strong enough to jerk it around his neck until the tension cracked his windpipe.

Though I didn't have the nerve to murder, how easy to picture Daddy crushed in a wreck of beer cans and empty moonshine jars. But when Dunn rode with him, I waited for hours without breathing. So, while I was under Daddy's house arrest, I went along most of the time. As if I could protect Dunn just being in the same car. But I could make sure he wore his seatbelt. If Daddy had too much to drink, I rode up front. Dunn was angry I rode shotgun, but I claimed the danger seat for him.

The night of Dunn's last game of his first season, Mama worked one of her long Fridays, happy to wash her hands of all of us. Daddy took us to eat after, happy that Dunn hadn't fumbled or made any errors, though the team lost again. He made us order whatever we wanted, huge piles of fried catfish, baked sweet potatoes, steak fries. For a rare hour we just *were*, the evening like a beautiful bottle you forget is holding poison.

Headed home, Daddy turned into a joint he called the "Squat and Piss," notorious for cockfighting and arrests. I wanted to tell him Mama would be worried at home, that I needed to help her at the shop the next day. I wanted to say he would miss his TV shows. But nothing I could say would have made him take us home sober.

I'd only seen the concrete block building in daylight, with an empty parking lot. That night, trucks and motorcycles snugged up like pigs at a trough. The door was a massive slab off an old barn. Plywood boarded up the windows from the inside, like they were trying to keep customers from breaking out. Daddy opened the car door and stood with one foot out and one in when a man and woman stumbled out laughing. A few seconds of music and glasses clinking split open the cold air. Then the dark quiet, and Daddy leaned back into the car.

"I got to see a man about a dog." He looked from Dunn to me in the backseat. "You understand me, Sister?"

"Yes," I said. "Yes, sir."

"I don't think you do. You saying yes don't always mean yes. You hear? You so much as set one foot out of this car, I'll knock you six ways for Sunday. They's people in here—just keep the door locked." He told Dunn he was in charge of the loaded pistol in the glove compartment. Trying to scare him.

"Just aim and shoot. Sister you blow the horn, anything happens. But it better be a goddamn good reason." He looked at me again. "I'll jerk a knot in your tail." He slammed the car door behind him.

I wanted to ask how he would hear if I blew the horn. Or if Dunn blew somebody's head off? He disappeared into the reddish glow, and we were quiet for a long while, watching people go in and out. The door opened and shut, opened and shut, like the sideways blink of a giant, a glimpse inside his nightmare skull.

Dunn vaulted over the seat, into the back where I was, his feet high in the air, settling his head and shoulders on my lap. "I got to pee," he said as he stretched out.

"You lie." I poked him. "Hang it out the window."

He laughed, but then he lifted up with a serious look. "What'll we do? Really?"

"Piss in your football helmet." That made him laugh.

He squirmed. "Did we still have a horse when I was born?"

"Rayford. And a mule, Ted. You've seen photos. That one Granny has of Daddy holding you on Ted's back."

"But a picture don't mean I remember. Tell me." I told him about the farm until he fell asleep, which wasn't long. He'd had a hard day. But I kept the story going, a movie in my head until I woke up cold. My neck ached, both legs asleep. I covered us up with Daddy's coat on top of our own. When I shifted Dunn's dead weight, he whined, a scared sound. Awake he'd worry, so I withstood the tingling in my calves.

I woke up again at the sound of tussling, the car jostling. I swiped the fogged car window, surprised to see the gravel lot nearly empty, just a few cars in puddles of streetlight. Two men raised up beside my window, but Dunn didn't wake up even when I jumped. Like cowboys in a western, the men backed off then hunkered against one another grappling. They seemed to hang on less for payback than balance, tumbling to the gravel and then struggling up. They socked each other sluggishly in the ears and face and ribs. When one of them tripped and fell back, the other made a sprawling slow run to his truck, fumbling with his keys as he went. The one on his back pumped his arms and legs like a turtle, but when the other guy peeled onto the highway, he rolled over easy as you please and dusted off his seat before he lumbered back inside.

I wasn't too worried until a sheriff's car pulled next to us, quiet but with blue lights twisting. The deputy shifted his holster as he climbed out. The rescue

165

squad came to an eerie quiet stop behind us. Dunn pulled his body in a tight wad beside me and exhaled a frost of steam. I dried the smeared window with my sleeve to see them push a gurney into the smoky light inside.

For a long time, nobody came out. Then a string of men heaved one by one through the door. In the lurid blinding blue light tossing around us, they all looked like Daddy at first, but I couldn't clear the window enough to make him appear. They all got into cars and trucks and drove away.

Only two other cars were left in the parking lot. Every innocent person had been released. The only people inside were hurt or being arrested. Or dead. Lightning went through the top of my head, and I was surprised. I was not ready to live the rest of my life knowing I'd wished my own daddy into his grave. My breath shuddered out, bigger than Mama's cigarette smoke. I opened the car door and put one foot out. But Daddy's commands got the better of me and I sat. On the verge.

The cold was so quiet I could hear the ambulance lights clicking. And then the door to the place flung open. I shut the car door so fast that Dunn woke up, shifting with a grunted question. A man and a woman seemed to carry each other out into the air. She was wiping at her eyes and nose with a handkerchief, and there was blood on her dress. I was sure I saw blood. Dunn watched now, too, without a word between us.

When the last car pulled away, the patrolman held the door while para-medics pushed the gurney into sight with a heave. It seemed to levitate, bright and spangled in the revolving light. The sheet covered a thick body head to toe, a dead person. Daddy.

My hand was on the handle of the car door the whole time, but I was a block of ice. What could I ask? What could I confess? I'd wanted him dead, and it happened. The patrolman didn't look at us as he got in his car. His blue lights went dark and he eased out onto the highway. The rescue squad followed, and then all the lights vanished around a curve.

I climbed into the front seat and wiped the windshield with my sleeve. I slid behind the steering wheel and wiped the side window. There was one car left, which I hadn't noticed before. Neon beer signs flickered. I willed the plywood door to open, for Daddy to walk out. I knew instead I'd gotten my awful wish.

Dunn was whispering, "Don't, don't," to keep me from getting out of the car. I opened the door to get a better look, and listen, but the overhead light was horrifying. I slammed the door shut and climbed into the floorboard, as far as I could get from disobeying Daddy's final say. I wasn't ready for this inheritance, my terrible freedom.

A clattering sound, like dice in a closed palm was Dunn's teeth. He was crying into his coat sleeves, rocking up and back in his terror and grief. To know he thought Daddy was dead made me believe it. It was time to do something. I dug my shaking fingers into the glove box and all the little crannies, trying to find a dime to call Mama from a pay phone. Under the mud-caked floor mat, I found a coin and stepped out of the car with it. In the light it was only a penny.

Somebody inside pulled the plug on all the lights. The neon beer signs melted, and the whole place fell bitter dark. Dunn let out a yelp that turned into a wail. His eyes were dark and wide in the glare of the car light before he tumbled over the seat to follow me out of the driver's door. I stood on shaking legs on the pavement.

"It's okay. No!" I told him. I pushed at the driver's side door as he fought with the handle. "Stay here, Dunn, okay? Somebody's still inside. They'll let me call Mama." He howled as I turned and splashed full face into Daddy's chest. The surprise pushed me off balance, back into the car, but his fist closed around my wrist.

"What'd I tell you?" He shook me by the forearm. "'Yes, sir,' you said. Lying little bitch. Lie to me again."

The only word I could say was, "Daddy," which should have been a relief. Over and over, Daddy, Daddy. Not a scratch on him, whole and breathing his sweet beer breath into the night.

He stripped off his belt to whip me. He wrapped it around his knuckles for a better grip and held the ball of my shoulder with one hand and pulled down my pants with the other and lashed my bare legs and ass. I couldn't keep from fighting back. All that terror and guilt pommeled into rage. Dunn hollered and rocked the car back and forth. Daddy slammed the door in his face every time he tried to help me. He slapped at my face, and the slaps turned into punches as I tried to pull away and explain. He pulled my hair and smashed my face, my head, my back against the car.

I tried to tell him to stop. I tried to say, "We thought you were dead." I couldn't stop fighting back. I couldn't stop the unspoken familiar thought from coming out loud like vomit: *"I wish you were dead!"*

In the Arizona morning, the national forests vanished. I checked the map for upcoming spans of green, but on our route, from Williams to Kingman to Vegas and Death Valley, there was not a speck of forest, just miles of bullying sun and heat like a cocked gun.

Carey convinced me we should take a stretch of old Route 66. We were the only car that exited, out of hundreds. For twenty minutes, past desolate sheep farms, the only other vehicle was a ranch wagon hauling lambs. The driver turned to look at the specimen of us, on our way nowhere. I pointed out to Carey that we were coming up on the only entrance back onto I-40 for seventy miles. At a hole-in-the-wall called Seligman I made him pull over and look at the map.

"It's a historic route," he argued. "See? It's marked scenic."

I got out into the oven-like dry heat and stomped in front of the Jeep, only half-joking. "Stand here and look," I said. "Don't lock the keys in the car!" I slid my toe along a wide crack in the asphalt. "Nobody drives here."

"What are you freaking out about?" He climbed out, grinning at me behind his sunglasses. "There are clubs for people who drive this route."

"No. Look. Pavement like my Granny's kitchen linoleum. So holey you can see the layers from every decade. Here's red asphalt. It's *red*. From how long ago?"

"Oh, yeah." He bent to look. "Like the color of dodgeballs in elementary school! Whose bright idea was that, anyway? Like it's fun to make kids hurt each other?"

"Carey!" I snapped my fingers toward him. "Pay attention. There is grass growing in the road. Grass!" Brittle blades probed up, in suicidal patches.

"Glenna, there are fences and ranches. Route 66 is on the map. There are towns, for crying out loud." He laughed, but I shook my head. "Stop worrying."

I watched the dashboard clock as we set out again. We didn't pass another car for a half hour. The towns with pretty names, Peach Springs and Valentine, turned out to be skeletons. Old men sat in front of rusted-out, broken buildings and hand-painted cardboard signs. The apocalypse had left them behind.

The road tightened between acre-high piles of brown stones. And in that brief canyon, neither of us could wait any longer to pee. Without a bush in sight, we took turns watching the horizon line in both directions for any sign of a car. Everything butted up against nothing. The thermometer Carey had attached to the outside of the Jeep read 102 degrees at eleven fifteen.

Kingman blustered chaotic wind on a sterile planet, a clutter of chain motels and gas stations where 66 bisected with the four-lane to Vegas, a vein steady with RVs and cars headed in and out of the dusty mountains ahead. A shock of traffic after the miles to ourselves, but a weird relief. Over slow gray rises, in our little confined space, we joined the roving civilization.

Carey slept with his forehead against the window while I drove, taking in the high desert hills like bad medicine. Prairie dogs bobbed up along the roadside, and once in a while a dead coyote, nearly camouflaged into dust. I was starved for green, but there were only scraggly cactus and stunted grass. On ridge sides little tufts vied in equal spaces, each fittest survivor taking up so many precise square feet, as if Martha Stewart herself had climbed up to measure the plots.

Miles and miles and miles into the afternoon, even the sky took on a powdery dullness above mountains of bald rock. No vegetation, not a tree, not a stem. I doubted there had ever even been a seed from one rough peak to the next. The whole world turned to stone and glare as we entered mountains, the view constricted by hairpin curves.

168

Around one sharp curve, I jammed both feet on the brake, barely stopping in time behind a tractor trailer. Carey woke up with a "whoa-shit-fire." I braked hard again behind a whole convoy winding down the mountain. Hoover Dam opened in the chasm below us. "Oh," Carey breathed. "We're here so soon."

"I have to drive across that? I can't drive across that!" A slender curve of road crossed the dam, which held Lake Mead winking like a giant turquoise eye at the center of reptile rock.

"I forgot how amazing," Carey said. "Go! The guy behind us—" Cars blew their horns. I eased forward, but we were trapped on the steep road. The honking got worse. Carey leaned over and grappled the wheel away from me.

"Just ease up. We can pull over there." He pointed at a gravel turnout.

I swung over and got out on trembling legs. The heat pushed past me and into the car. My lungs were instant sacks of oven-hot air. Carey handed me a bottle of water out of the cooler. We stood there and drank, watching the lake and the twisting road below where tourists and kids darted through bumper-to-bumper traffic to see the view. My adrenaline was in such high gear, I expected to hear a wreck or screaming any second. Everybody below pinging back-and-forth like they were in a pinball machine. Carey was telling me how many workers in the Great Depression died from falling into the concrete or off the dam. When he started driving again, the car thermometer topped-out at 110 degrees, mercury at its limit.

The edge of Las Vegas was one giant construction site, plywood and naked beams and trusses. Armies of men in hard hats were laying shingles, stuccoing walls, backhoing foundations. As if it were up to them to make sure by the new century there would be no more desert wilderness. Cloned houses ambushed new cul-de-sacs, sprinklers watered sci-fi green sod, transplanted trees shaded adobe walls. A battalion of cars roared around us. Suddenly over a rise, the city glittered like tacky crown jewels. The sprawl was more terrifying than the heat. I gripped the dashboard.

I didn't see how Carey could talk and drive at the same time. "Best PR job in history," he said. "Las Vegas means 'the meadows.' Right. It's the Saint Jude of cities, getting its Disney facelift. Ten more years and all the old hotels will be demolished.

"I figure, let's check out Fremont Street hotels. Authentic Vegas, even though they've put the whole street under lights since I was here. A pedestrian mall. Shame."

Under the awning of lights, he pulled up to the first big hotel, rolled down his window and asked a valet how much. The guy held up his finger and dis-appeared through the whisper of double doors.

169

"No way can we afford this," I said. "I don't care how historic it is. A motel on the interstate is all we can manage. Look at us. You haven't shaved. We've got on the same clothes from yesterday. We smell like a campfire."

"At best!" Carey lifted his arm and blew air toward me from his armpit.

The guy dashed back and leaned into the car. Mint-cold air and cologne came off him in waves. "For you, thirty-eight dollars."

"Thirty-eight dollars apiece?" I was surprised it was so cheap.

"No, together. Special just for you." He opened Carey's door, and a second valet was helping me out before I could protest. A third guy was already unloading our luggage. In the casino lobby, cold as a refrigerator, every buzz, whistle, ding, slam, and slap overwhelmed me. I focused hard to keep some part of my body on every suitcase and bag. I read the fine print on the registration card Carey filled out.

"Are you sure you're not signing away your first-born child?" I whispered.

"They'd get the raw end of *that* deal." He laughed.

In the chill of our dim room, Carey belly-flopped on the king bed. I read the posted room regulations on the back of the door. "Look here. This says our room rents for two-hundred-and-sixty-five dollars a night. Somebody's trying to screw a hillbilly."

"Quit being suspicious over every little thing! I'm taking you for a martini."

"But Carey. There's a catch somewhere."

"Yeah. To get us in cheap so we spend thousands downstairs. You can't gamble if you spend all your money on a room." He rolled off the bed. "Come here."

He pulled me across the room to the curtains. Like a magician, he jerked the cord, and the dark room shrank back from the desert distance. A gajillion stories below, the streets and buildings shuddered and tilted. The floor sank under me.

"Shit!" I stepped back.

Carey laughed and pulled me forward again. One foot planted firmly behind me, I peeked across rooftops and houses.

"You've really never been in a building this tall?"

"Well. No. Not this high. On a mountain, yeah. But not inside. It's weird."

"Yes, it is," he said, laughing again.

"Don't make fun of me." I punched him. Cars on the highways stretching into the distance glittered like broken glass. As far as I could see, the gray stony jags rose up like a tidal wave rolling in to crush every decadent, spoiled thing.

"Shit." I couldn't keep from saying again.

Twenty-seven floors straight down, Fremont Street's casinos blinked under their roiling canopy of light bulbs. Glitter Gulch, Four Queens, The Golden Nugget, the neon cowboy angling out over the crowds above The Pioneer Club, Lady Luck, and Girls, Girls, Girls!

After we gambled and ate dinner and drank and checked out the neighborhood, Carey slept like a baby. I kept watch out the hotel window from time to time, feeling the city awake all night, twenty-four hours a day. Like a vampire heart. In the lobbies, in hotels all over town, roulette wheels clacked, dice tumbled on felt, cards slapped and whispered, slot machines dinged and whirred and vomited cascades of quarters. The city seethed billions of kilowatts into space. Even the McDonald's and the 7-11 were plastered in light bulbs. The late, dim moon over the mountains didn't stand a chance.

In the morning I was exhausted, but Carey said I had to see the Strip. He drove down the boulevard of palms, lorded over by kinetic billboards and towering fountains and casinos like big traps ready to spring. The giant glass pyramid, the Luxor, sat like some wild west alter-Pentagon with a hidden army of bartenders and bookies and dealers, strategizing decadence. Carey wanted to show me inside.

"No. We've seen it," I said. "I gambled five dollars and lost, like I do when I take Mama to Cherokee. I gorged on one buffet. I drank my first martini. I slept in a high-rise hotel. Now get me out of this hell-hole."

"Who, may I ask, urinated in your Wheaties?" Carey stopped for another red light.

"Look at all these people on the sidewalks. Like they're going to work. Gloomy gusses. I have yet to see the first person in this town laugh. What I'll remember is that half-bald old woman playing slots, propped up on a stool with her oxygen tank. She hits the jackpot and her machine pours out a shit-pot of quarters. But her face is a block of rock. She just slides in another quarter."

"One mamaw's entertainment is another mamaw's addiction."

"City of zombies. Let's go before they figure out we're still alive."

Like a stray mad dog, the suburban sprawl followed us for miles. And even after the last straggling houses, there was no wilderness. Along Highway 95, sign after sign barked orders at us: NO TRESPASSING. MILITARY RE-STRICTED AREA. Razor wire guarded the Nevada Test Site, atomic missiles waiting in the dark below the twisted cactus, palms, and Joshua trees shoveling up out of the sand like claws.

Death Valley burns. We trudged up the paved incline overlooking Zabriskie Point, and every inch of my skin felt the fire. I concentrated on plowing through the invisible smothering wall. Every breath I took sifted for oxygen through 123-degree air. Dry fire in my lungs. My heart seemed to need conscious focus to keep beating. My muscles weighed more on my bones. Flesh on my face pulsed against the tourniquet blaze of air. I was a walking fever.

For the first time, I stood in California. No giant trees in the fog, no roaring ocean, just bare-rock mountains seizing up around the hard, flat desert floor. Carey pointed out Manley Beacon, a hawk's beak profile, striated rock jutting diagonally above the valley. Like solid rock waves, other peaks mimicked the angular defiant shape of it. Like my nose. Like Daddy's nose.

All his features, all of him, had burned away to parchment. Nothing recognizable left of Daddy. How far past 123 degrees can a body stand? What is the last bearable degree before the linings of the lungs atomize and blood scabs up in the veins, boiled to clots?

What can a person bear?

The mountains pulsed against the sky, folds of stone that at home would be covered by loam and tangles of mountain laurel and rhododendron and trees. In Death Valley the earth's skeleton was raw bone, all the flesh seared away. Upheaved peaks in bared lines of blood rust, nicotine brown, gristle white, knuckle-bone yellow.

Nothing left of Daddy.

At Furnace Creek Visitor Center, we parked in mangy shade. A hot, hard wind shoved through the most unlikely willowy trees. I could smell running water somewhere. Three ravens rode the tossing limbs with their beaks wide open, stuck in silent screams. Carey dragged out the cooler, full of beautiful ice, melting fast. I rubbed a couple of cubes against my neck and cheeks and forehead. They disintegrated in seconds.

"Here." He held out a box of cereal and bowls and dug into our box for utensils.

"At two in the afternoon?"

"You want tuna salad in this weather, you're on your own!"

We sat side by side on the cooler, feeling the cold seep through the lid. A busload of Japanese tourists unloaded beside us, and one by one they pointed at us crunching our cool Raisin Bran. A couple of them snapped pictures of us. But their stares didn't trouble me like the ravens still gawking above us.

We toured the visitor center for nearly two hours, stalling until check-in time at Furnace Creek Ranch. Our room was small, but the air conditioner chugged against the odds. The sun pried at curtains, beating through the walls. The TV, lamps, walls, all seemed like mirages. Every human gadget was a struggling luxury. People just weren't supposed to be there. We'd landed on Mercury. Carey went for a bag of ice at the store to replace what had melted and came back with ice cream bars, already dripping in their paper wraps. We lay down and took a true siesta, waiting out the inferno.

In loose sleep I thought about the black-and-white photos displayed in the visitor center, of borax miners with their twenty-mule teams lined up against the Panamint Mountains. Behind the patient double row of mules and the men and the massive wagon, there was always one replacement mule. A spare because it was certain one of the twenty would perish. Pictures of women and children who lived year-round in Death Valley in the eras before air conditioning. A record 134 degrees. Once for a hundred thirty-seven days in a row, the temperature spiked over one hundred. In half-dream I revisited shadowy eye sockets and lean faces. They probably didn't even own thermometers, but they lived and died by mercury rising.

Late in the day the place cooled off to a cool 100 degrees. We headed back up the main road to explore a place called Badwater, the lowest point on the continent. The blast-furnace wind funneled between the ranges where Carey and I stood nearly three hundred feet below sea level. Miles across the salt flats, at the other extreme, Telescope Peak reared up nearly twelve thousand feet.

The last of the sunset pounded colors at Artist's Point into the rock, dusty turquoise and powder pink, pale yellows and oranges. Carey pulled over and rolled down our windows before he cut the engine. The motor and music died. He opened his car door and the chime ding-dinged its helpless sound. Then silence in the blue dusk.

"Nobody even knows where we are on the planet," I said. "If the car—"

"The Jeep's fine. Geez. You're a nervous wreck."

"I'm just saying somebody could get stuck out here. Has gotten stuck. We've got one bottle of water, and it's fifteen miles back. We're the last ones out here, Carey."

After we scuffed around and he took some photos, I think even he held his breath as he turned the key. The sunset happened high in the sky, a line of silver behind the mountain's jagged silhouette, like torn away light.

The next morning, up toward the pass through those same mountains, signs warned about the temperature, the extreme rise in elevation, the danger of overheating vehicles. Signs warned STAY WITH YOUR CAR. The ascent was unrelenting up steep, winding hairpin curves. To spare the Jeep, Carey turned off the A/C. We rolled down the windows and suffocated. Tanks were set up every few miles stamped, RADIATOR WATER. DO NOT DRINK.

We'd bought an extra gallon of water and a crazy-expensive bag of ice, but I felt as if I were being hunted, my skin papery in the heat. Sweat didn't stand a chance, drying the second it hit air. Carey and I had drunk a liter of water with breakfast and two lemonades at our gas stop. Neither of us had needed to pee all day.

As we kept gaining altitude the stifling air grew slightly cooler until we topped out. Panamint Valley—daunting as Death Valley—opened at the foot of the marbled basin of more gray mountains to cross. Easing down around steep curves, we sank into heat waves again. We stopped along the road at the valley crossing and looked at the miles and miles stretching in both directions of perfectly flat dry lake beds. From foothill to foothill, a heaved-open jigsaw puzzle of dry mud, the southern portion open to vehicles. The cracked earth was traced with tire tracks, circles that wound in a far tangle and vanished.

In minutes we were climbing again. Carey slung the car too confidently, too fast around long, thin curves that banked higher and steeper along the rim of the mountain pass. Outside the park boundary there were no guard rails, just a slim shoulder of gravel to skid on. Nothing to keep us from plummeting thousands of feet down bare-bouldered cliffs. When a camper fish-tailed past us, I looked over the escarpment and could not breathe.

We rode that cliff edge around a peak for probably ten minutes before Carey stopped at the first pull-out to give the engine and us a break. Behind us, the road we'd traveled was a narrow thread, a measly human interruption. The whole range behind was a marbled monolith folded into itself. I followed Carey to the raw edge for a better view, but unable to tell where the precipice was, I crept. Carey laughed as I sidled along in baby steps. I forced myself one step, one more, and then I couldn't move. Animal instinct in me flinched away.

"Carey, stop. We can't see if we're on the edge. Come on. Please."

In half a heartbeat, his boot sole scalped a line in the gravel. He barely kept his balance. I couldn't move. I couldn't stop picturing myself standing there alone where two people had just stood. It could happen that fast. He just laughed again.

"You don't have respect for fine lines," I said as I turned back toward the car.

"Come back," he called. "Aw. Come on. I won't go any farther. I promise. The view is great."

I slammed the car door and buckled myself in. Life and death. That quick. I wanted to scream at him so he'd understand the narrow places I'd suffered, so he would feel how terrifying to imagine the barest breath between burning and dying. I wanted him to have to carry around the line he'd reminded me of, the burden between murder and mercy.

Mama was tight-lipped at first as she propped me up in bed. As she cleaned me up, dabbing at bruises and cuts, she crooned an odd sound of displeasure that keened sometimes into something like a whimper. I don't know whether Daddy confessed, or Dunn had tattled. I'd been asleep or maybe unconscious, and I faded in and out at the barest sound of her voice as she tried to get me to stay awake. I could tell one of my eyes was nearly swollen shut as I tried to focus on her neck, her shoulders. I couldn't look at her face, afraid she'd know the menace in my heart. Not only for Daddy, but for her.

I watched my closed bedroom door, the doorknob. Past it, Daddy cried and paced drunkenly, said Mama's name over and over. He said my name over and over. He leaned against the door and breathed through the crack. The light in the hall cast ponderous shadows under my door. I could hear Dunny sobbing in the living room where he sometimes slept. Had my brother seen? When I refused to get in the car with Daddy, had Dunn seen the gun he held to my head? Did I have a witness to the will sizzling out of my body like electricity? Had he watched me give up the fight to be a daughter?

Mama kept leaning me up against pillows, trying to untangle the quilts on my bed. She handed me a bag of frozen peas. "Look at me, Glenna. Look up now, into the light. Follow my finger. Focus."

I struggled away, but she fought me. "Now keep your eyes open. I have to see if you're all right, Sister." Years later, I would blame her for not taking me to the ER. But that night, her cold hands on my sore belly and my icy fury meant that I would survive.

"Tomorrow?" She seemed to be asking the way. "Tomorrow, you don't act like nothing's wrong. You don't say a word to him if he's here. He asks you a question, you answer calm and simple. Through the door. You stay in this room until I'm ready to leave for work, and then we'll go get in the car, to take you to your granny's." She raised up to look at me with terrified eyes. "I might not be able to go with you like when we left the farm," she whispered. She was trembling. She meant she was relinquishing me. That I had to be the brave one.

How could I believe anything she had ever said? Trust any choice she'd made? Who would protect me? Gus had helped us leave the first time, hauled our stuff in his truck. Big deal. He tried hard not to look at us if he saw us in town now. She'd been an idiot to think he could help. That anybody could help.

Mama said, "I can't not go to work tomorrow, Sissy. But here, take this." She handed me a business card. "Last few weeks I've talked to a woman who's a social worker that knows what we need to do. Your daddy pulls any stunts, he so much as drives by your granny's and Ed's, you run and you call her to come get you."

"Why can't we go tonight?" I whispered. "Together?"

"No, it's this way. Let things calm down. Whatever happens, don't you worry about me. None of this wasn't never your fault. None of it. But it'll be fine. There's this friend of mine, he—"

"You mean Gus?"

I pulled back from her touch to my ribcage. She deflated and lay her body long against mine in the bed. We breathed like wrestlers do while she shook from sobbing. I knew then. I knew those long nights at the shop, she hadn't been at the shop. She hadn't been working. She hadn't taken special clients with chemo as she'd said. She'd been cheating. Not on Daddy. She'd been unfaithful to me. To whatever family I'd been trying so hard to save.

Her cool fingers pressed my swollen mouth closed while she whispered. She touched my bloody nose again and started crying all over. "Nobody oughtn't to have to survive this way." I wasn't sure if she meant me, or if she was crying for herself.

It's easiest to be saved when you least expect it. Maybe everybody gets rescued by what's always been right in front of us. It's easy to forget in the middle of the desert that its edges work both ways. There's the line you cross into the danger like a furnace. But there's also a line to step across to safety.

Around a curve, the Sierras razored snowy, broken points up into the sky like jagged silver glass. We drew closer and closer until I could see foothills. So long in the brown barren world of rock and sand, I'd forgotten the possibility of green. Green-gold cottonwoods flickered. Rocky towers sheered up, studded with the relief of evergreen.

I had forgotten trees. And then there they were.

At a place called Lone Pine, while Carey went into the visitor center to get camp info, I lay back in the cool grass and breathed in mountain air pooling down off the Sierras. On one side of me, a wilderness of boulders, and on the other, across a dividing line I could see grass stretched lush in mountain shadow.

When I stood up, brushing grass off me, I had to bend my neck back to look up toward Mount Whitney. I wasn't sure exactly which exact peak it was, the highest in California, highest in the lower states, but I knew those granite crags were the highest I'd ever seen, a salvation hovering above the desert's starved claim. I was washed and saved in the cool snow-melt air.

Some of the next days after Daddy pommeled me, I don't remember well. At some point late one morning I woke up and knew that Daddy was in Granny's kitchen. My bedroom door at her house was locked. I kept it locked every night. But it was just a hollow core door. I'd watched Daddy punch his fist through at least three of them at the trailer, which Mama would replace whenever she could save enough money.

But I could hear him wailing. When he cried, he was harmless usually. I raised the back bedroom window and pried the screen open in case I needed to jump and run. I felt under the lamp for the tiny knife I had taken out of Granny's kitchen drawer. Just a paring knife, but holding it in my palm, seeing it in the morning light, made me feel capable. Not safe, exactly. But I knew what I could do to him now. I was ready. I pushed the dresser in front of the door, just in case he broke through.

Every day around noon, Mama had been coming from the shop to eat a long lunch with me, brushing my hair and looking at my bruises, inspecting me the way a mother ape might look for lice on her baby. It was nearly noon, and I could hear Granny telling Daddy he should high tail it before Mama found him there. But it was too late.

For a long time there seemed to be several voices in the kitchen. Then there was just Mama's voice, in Granny's bedroom, just through the wall. She was using her Faye voice, the voice I imagined she used when she talked to Gus, her female voice. She was talking soft to Daddy in tones that forgot I existed.

I thought I would have to run away then, alone. I would have to give up on Mama, a ridiculous, weak woman. Her voice was soft as her perfume as she walked back and forth, absurdly soft. Somebody sat. I could hear Granny's bedsprings give. And Mama was loud enough for me to hear. Maybe on purpose. I'll never know, but I could make out everything she said, her words solid as rock. A mineral, hard love.

"From now on," she said, "this is between you and me, Glenn, like it's always been. I'm the one you're mad at, so stop dragging her into it. She ain't your whipping boy. She ain't your hostage.

"See? Now you got me using Glenna Jean like a bargaining chip, just like you do. But this is my terms.

"She stays here. She comes to the trailer only when she wants. And you don't ever come here again. You don't talk to her unless I'm with her. You don't visit her. You and her don't have any contact on your account. You leave Glenna the hell alone from now on, and Dunn too, or so help me God, I won't leave you again, Glenn." She breathed, but her voice never hardened from its promising lull.

"I will kill you," she said. "Dead. You ain't the only one can get mean. And I won't be drunk mean. I'll be sober and righteous. I'll run you over like a dog. I'll stab you. I'll strangle you in your sleep. I'll electrocute you in the tub. You won't know when I'm who I seem to be. I'll play sweet and next thing you know you'll wake up to a claw hammer in your skull.

"You ever lay a finger on either of my kids again, you're a dead man."

She took on every sin, every ugly wish I'd had that Daddy would die. She said the threats out loud that had kept my heart in tangled beats, the awful, blasphemous secrets. And she washed me clean with them. As far as I know, she never saw Gus again.

I knew I'd sleep sound. The worst we could say was said for now. Maybe the worst we would ever do to one another was done. My conscience was as clean as it could be. Through the wall between us, Mama's voice went on, and I drifted off to sleep in that cradle of her tone, the sound of her sweet-talking us all into surviving.

THE LONG WAY HOME

"Only maybe three hundred miles to the Pacific. As the crow flies." Carey pointed straight above our Lone Pine campsite to the Sierras. Distance had morphed into a vertical proposition, the horizon thousands of feet up.

"Maybe a homing crow." He grinned at my stupid joke. Side-by-side on our picnic table we drank hot tea and watched dusk work its way up the Alabama Hills, the setting of old Hollywood westerns. Far above the vast spread of brown boulders, the barest tips of the brutal granite crags were lit. A down-draft off the high snow scoured the last heat out of the cottonwoods and sagebrush. Our tent shivered near the creek we'd waded in like kids, squealing at the icy vise-grip of snow melt.

"This is the place they mean when they say, 'You can't get there from here,'" Carey said. "I mean, think of the desert we crossed to get here. Then Mount Whitney right up there marks the eastern boundary of Sequoia National Park. But to drive to the park entrance is at least a six- or seven-hour drive south. Through-roads are not a thing here. Lots of passes aren't clear, even yet.

"And you never saw that kind of cloud at home either." He pointed and sipped. "Lenticular." I'd already been keeping an eye on it, shaped like a huge angelic wing. The layers brightened from amber to rose, then to ember red as final dark took over the gray pinnacles. Then the first stars like ice crystals.

"And you're going to tell me I've never seen those stars at home either," I said.

"Well," he said, gesturing around with his arm. "Not like this." And we left it hanging, that always-something-else beyond what we could say or know, unreachable.

Next morning we headed north toward the only pass across the Sierras within a two-hundred-mile stretch. But not far up the highway, Carey stopped at a place called Manzanar, where Japanese American citizens were interned during World War Two. Anybody could see it was a perfect desert trap. The barbed wire and sentry towers he described would have been a moot point. Nowhere to run east or south or north except into murderous desert and crazy steep mountains. West was the Sierras, a wall of wilderness.

Carey swore the place was a national monument, and we could see it designated that way on the map. But there was nothing to show it. The only structure was a spiteful little pagoda-shaped guard post. We got out to walk around. Nothing but cracked ground and tufts of grass outlining where dormitories and buildings had been razed. A few scrub trees so dry they looked burned. A prisoner-of-war ghost town. One awful thing the government saw fit to leave intact was the scraggly, forlorn cemetery.

"God, I feel like vomiting, just to think of being stuck in a godforsaken place like this," I said. "Buried and forgotten."

"At least it didn't look so hellish back then. Manzanar is Spanish for apple orchard, which is how—Okay." He stopped. "You don't believe me. But up and down this whole huge valley there used to be orchards and farms. An agricultural mecca.

"But then there was an honest-to-God water war. You never saw *Chinatown*?"

I shook my head.

"We should have gone south a bit, not far from Lone Pine. A place called Owen's Lake, completely dried up because of the Los Angeles aqueduct. They take every drop of snow melt they can—"

"Oh, come on, not all the way the hell from this far north," I said.

Carey nodded. "Like Lake Mead for Las Vegas? The snow you're looking at right now, up above us, almost all of it ends up in LA. You'll cry when you see Yosemite, because they dammed up part of it, too. Hetch Hetchy. For water just for San Francisco. A hundred years ago, all along the eastern Sierras used to be like Eden.

"I mean, I can show you photos from the war. They parked thousands and thousands of Japanese here. They had to have food and water. The government stopped diverting water so much, and in just a few months the Japanese prisoners were raising cabbages and squash and potatoes.

"We need to go to a place Stan took me. Mono Lake, just near the entrance to Yosemite. I mean, Mono is saltier than Salt Lake even. But it didn't used to be, until they started diverting all the snow melt to LA. Stan told me—" He stopped with a little swallow. I was surprised by his sudden emotion. "Stan said the lake gets saltier and saltier and shallower and shallower because they starved it for so long decades. But I think they've just recently stopped that. Environmentalists stopped them."

He wiped his eyes and laughed a little. "Stan called Mono Lake the big blue margarita. There's this salt ring around the shore and brine flies suck it up. And all these sea gulls, like they stumbled in drunk from the Pacific. Stan called them the 'Donner-Party-of-Birds.'" He laughed but then sobered in another instant, crying a little again. I didn't know how in the world to comfort him. His grief churned up my own grief, hard, hard stones tumbling in my chest. I turned back toward the car.

179

"It's amazing there's even this much left," Carey said, following. "They should really make an example of it because it could happen again. I mean, loyal Americans under arrest for years. And we didn't just stick them in the backyard of hell, we robbed their farms and businesses. The government confiscated everything they'd worked for."

"They didn't get their homes back?"

He shook his head. I stopped to look at the parched ground and thought of the twelve acres on Genesis Road. "Like my family. The government took our land when they made the Smokies. Shoved us out and and instead we got pitiful secondhand—"

"Well, but somebody in your family got paid. For their land. Restitution."

"A check is not family land," I said.

"Well, and vice versa." He looked at me with some kind of meaning I couldn't read. "You said it, not me."

"I don't know what you mean," I said as we got in the Jeep.

"That twelve acres your mother is handing off to you? That's the only family farm you ever knew. And you said you're just going to sell it? You did say that, right?"

I looked out the window as he started the Jeep at the desert scraped bare of the awful human story. But who could put back decades of snow melt and streams and lake water? How could I muster up the will to resurrect a memory, especially when it was nothing but failure and loss? "It's not something I have the know-how to salvage," I said. "Can you see me raising a bean? One bean! Even weeds wouldn't stand a chance. Come on."

"But it's your inheritance," Carey prodded. "It's maybe not what you'd choose, but it's history. Where your family moved after being pushed out, one place to another. I envy it, your heritage. Most people don't get a second chance like that."

We were quiet as he pulled back onto the highway north.

"What about a third or fourth chance?" I said finally. "By then doesn't it all get kind of watered down? Look where we just stood, and all we can see is what doesn't exist anymore. That's what Genesis Road means to me. It's what doesn't exist anymore.

"And pretty soon everybody who was in prison here will be dead, and they don't know where they came from in the first place, anyway. That's American. We move on. That's everything we've seen and everywhere we're going on this whole trip. Move on. After the people before us screwed everything up."

I pictured Mama's land I'd scrambled through, a jungle compared to the farm I knew from childhood. Nothing left of what had been. Now it was a burden, the neediest place I could fathom. I didn't have it in me to claim it, much less heal it. I hadn't even been able to bring a baby onto the planet. I couldn't mother twelve acres back to life.

"But they would have gone back home if they could." Carey tried for the final word. "They would have given anything."

"Maybe not everybody has it in them to make that kind of deal," I said. "*Anything* is a dangerous offer."

In a little town called Bishop, we stopped to browse rusty antiques and eat a big, late breakfast. We sat there and swigged thin coffee like we had all day, time we wished later we hadn't taken for granted. Because later getting where we wanted wasn't an option. Through the plate glass cafe windows, under a sky hard and pure as blue glass, the Sierras backed the main street like sharp stone thunderheads. A banner across the main drag advertised MULE DAYS.

"You just missed it." The waitress refilled our cups as Carey quizzed her. "Sugar and cream? The biggest anywhere, thousands of mules. It'll be Christmas before they take those signs down."

"You happen to know if Tioga Pass is open to Yosemite?" Carey asked.

"They just plowed again after a late snow, five, six days ago. Yesterday I would have said you were lucky. But just heard the Lee Vining entrance is closed. There's a fire. People coming through last week had to drive the long way around."

"The long way around?" I interrupted. My heart was in my throat.

"Next pass north would be best, then?" Carey looked to her for agreement.

She nodded. "Sonora Pass. And come in the western entrance. But if the four-lane is closed you'd go east into Nevada."

"We just came from Nevada." I looked at Carey and felt sick. "Back through that desert?"

"It's fine." Carey laughed. "You have fires all the time out here, right?" He looked at the waitress for validation.

She shrugged and smiled. "Why not just stay here in Bishop and wait it out?"

"We've got reservations," I said.

"Well, Sonora Pass will add a day to your trip," she admitted. "But stop at Mammoth ranger station. Maybe they've got the fire out." She looked at me hopefully.

Carey wouldn't let me drive. He insisted on going the speed limit. He sipped to-go coffee and tapped his fingers to Led Zeppelin, "Going to California." Cars passed as if they knew to get a move on.

"She's right." I studied the map until my neck hurt. "Lee Vining's the only east entrance to Yosemite."

"I know that," Carey said.

"But even going around the Smokies, Carey, think how long that would take if a road is blocked. To go around Yosemite—if we have to go to Bridge-port—then it's all the hell the way around and come into the west entrance."

I bent to the map again. "God." I traced with my finger. "If it's the main highway, 395, that's closed? She's right. We can't even get to Sonora Pass. Two, three hundred miles around?" I scanned thinner and thinner lines on the map, unpaved roads into the desert and back again.

"I mean, the fire can't be that widespread," he said. But he glanced at the map, swerving.

"You're the one who said there aren't a zillion roads like at home."

He turned down the music and repositioned his hands on the wheel. "We'll figure it out, whatever happens. Our Yosemite reservations are for the next two nights. If we miss the first, it's just money. We'll still see—"

"No, you're still not getting it. We won't be there the second night either. Look at these little two-lane roads back east and then around through the mountains."

He shrugged. But at Mammoth Lakes he finally understood. Tourists rushed in and out of the ranger station, some of them giving up on the shuffling line. When we got close enough to hear the ranger, she shushed everybody to listen to the shortwave radio static, the latest road closings. She tugged at the thick braid of her ponytail, her face behind wire frames unreadable. A Girl Scout with wrinkles.

"Can you decipher all that?" Carey pointed at the radio and smiled his flirtiest at her. She slapped a map down on the counter and spoke so everybody could hear. She made a big X right where we wanted to go. "This road from Lee Vining is closed to Tioga Pass, eastern route to Yosemite. Been closed half a day. They're saying the four-lane is still open, but the fire is pushing toward it since the wind picked up. They'll probably make the call within the hour to shut it down."

"The through highway?" I pointed at the map. "This main highway?"

She nodded and pushed her glasses up. "Yeah, 395. You might beat it. But if you've got the time, I'd wait it out, maybe a day or two or the day after that, it'll burn out or they'll contain it."

I could read Carey's comprehension as he squinted at the map, the panic when he looked at me, and then he was ahead of me out the door, unlocking my car door first, peeling out of the parking lot as I strapped in.

We headed toward a slim window of opportunity at eighty, eighty-five miles an hour. Traffic dwindled in the two lanes headed south past us, then trickled, then all but stopped. The cobbled desert widened. Snow-thick western peaks shrank. And across a rise, purplish smoke boiled up behind brush-dotted slopes. The flume closed in on the highway ahead, edging up to choke off our route.

"We're wasting our afternoon." Carey slowed as we came in sight of traffic like a parking lot. Patrolmen set flares and directed cars one by one to a wide shoulder where they leaned into car windows and looked at maps. Car after car turned toward open Nevada barrens or U-turned back south where we'd come from. A few cars just beyond the blockade through the smoke disappeared.

"Look," I said, "they just let the last cars through. Goddamnit! We just missed it!" I jumped out of the Jeep and waved at a passing motorcycle cop.

"Get back," Carey called. "Glenna!" He was laughing.

"They just let a couple of cars through," I argued as I got back into my seat. "Maybe if we ask—"

"Because we're on vacation?" He couldn't stop giggling. He scanned the map as I sat on my hands and focused, like I could stare down the smoke boiling in front of us. "Look," he waved his hand across the dash. "We don't want the next pass, anyway. We want the east entrance, just there. It's not like there's much foliage. Once the fire burns across, just sage and bushes, no big trees, then we can get through. So what if it's tomorrow? Let's turn back. Settle in early. Find a place to do laundry."

But down toward the entrance there were big trees and swelling clouds of toxic gray. Firefighters in orange crossed the road and climbed the near hill. We inched forward until we were next in line to talk to the patrolman in his aviator sunglasses. A helicopter ferried a huge dangling red sling and unleashed its load of water on the smoldering hill.

"I mean, do we really even need to ask anything?" Carey said. Two women were railing at the cop about how they could get to work.

Carey traced his finger on the Nevada map, through dead space. "I mean, you win. You were right. The only way if we keep driving is hundreds of miles around to the west entrance. You want to do that? I mean, we're only like five miles from our turn-off. Not even twenty miles from Yosemite." He pinched his thumb and forefinger together. "That close." He fell into another inexplicable fit of giggling. "So close, yet so far."

"I don't see what's so funny. What the hell are we going to do?"

"Turn back, find a campsite in Mammoth, and wait this thing out." He tossed the map to me and turned the car around. "What people do. Make the best of it. Make friends with a ranger." He looked at me wickedly. "Or we could sit here and watch these gorgeous firemen." He laughed again until I wanted to smack him.

After the harrowing waste of time, we found a site in a campground on the edge of Mammoth Lakes. Big trees around us were a relief, like rain after a long drought.

"I mean, it could be worse," Carey said as we grappled with the tent. "We could be stuck in a June blizzard. Or have car trouble. Even if this lasts, we'll get to Yosemite. We'll just have to arm wrestle somebody for a campsite or stay outside the park."

"That doesn't make sense, 'it could be worse,'" I said. "Being stuck because of one thing isn't any better than being stuck because of another. Plus, I don't get why 'it could be worse,' makes people feel better when it could almost always be worse." I stumbled over mutantly huge pine cones and figured sleep was going to be pretty lumpy. "If you're going to play Pollyanna, do it right. *At least* there are trees and shade and it's cool."

"Ooh, no," he said. "I hate 'at least.' It always sounds so desperate."

"How the hell is 'at least' more desperate than 'it could be worse?'"

"Well, if I have to explain the nuances to you—" He made an exaggerated eye roll as he tugged the tent stakes out of their sack. "I'm sticking with 'it could be worse.'"

And he turned out to be right. That evening he decided he didn't feel like the restaurant meal he'd promised me. He didn't even want the soup I heated. He was exhausted and left me alone with a pinched fire of pine cones, their miniature balconies burning. I ate the last of the applesauce with both pieces of bread I'd buttered and grilled in the fry pan.

Not long after I turned in, I woke to him scrambling around the tent on all fours, trying to tug on his jeans. "Where's the flashlight?" His breath came across me in hot jags as he pawed in the dark.

"Here. Here." I leaned up and felt beside my feet for the long barrel of it. I flicked it on. In the slash of light his face was blanched. "What's wrong?"

He tugged at the tent door and tripped out. I leaned into the cold to watch him stumbling a zig-zag of light. I tugged on my jacket and fumbled for my shoes. When I looked back toward him, the flashlight beam careened up into the limbs in a dizzy circle and I heard Carey drop with a thud. I ran yelling as he collapsed. Before I knelt by him, he was struggling to sit. Our frantic breaths made white flumes in the dark.

"Get me to the bathroom," he whispered hoarsely. "Get me—" He lunged up but could only muster a crawl. A surprise of light blinded me, and someone was helping Carey off the ground. I pulled on my second sneaker with shaking hands and hobbled, following their voices. At the port-a-john the camp host was hugging her bare arms, talking to Carey through the door.

"Okay? Don't latch the door. Are you going to pass out?" she called.

"I don't think so." His voice came through muffled and strange. He moaned and I heard a thump against the fiberglass wall.

"Carey? It's me. Are you okay?"

"No," he said. He moaned and breathed harsh. I heard him heave.

"He must've eaten something bad." The camp host turned to me and said

I should get some water, a washcloth, a towel. I stood shaking. I was in my jacket and no pants, only my sleep boxers.

The door clicked and opened. Suffocating rotted odor of ammonia and waste washed out as the camp host held her light on Carey, his pants and underwear half-undone. She reached for him but he fairly well slid to the ground between us, as limp as if he had no bones.

"Either help me or go get a cloth. Water! Now." She handed me his flashlight and squatted down to tug Carey's boxers and his jeans up over his pale hip. I ran to our tent and couldn't find anything she'd said. I pulled on my pants with trembling hands. I finally found Carey's sandals and his car keys, and from the car I grabbed wipes, a bottle of water, and Carey's towel draped over the seat.

The camp host had him propped against the outside wall of the toilet. He was shaking like me, with chattering teeth. He pushed the water bottle back as she pressed it toward his mouth. He mumbled something incoherent and seemed to try to focus on her face. I was invisible to him, useless, standing outside the circle of her light.

"Didn't you bring him a blanket?" In the light, her shadow widened, motherly and monstrous.

Carey looked up at me. "I'm sick."

"You've got to stay hydrated, especially at this altitude," she said. She reached up and took things from me, pulled out a handful of the cool wipes and rubbed his face until his panting slowed. Then he nodded for a drink. But before he'd taken a good swallow, he was pushing back up, crawling into the toilet, and she followed him. Inside there was fumbling, moving, soft talking.

She stepped back out to lean with her palm like a blessing on the door. "How do you feel?" I realized she was talking to me. "He's worried it's altitude sickness, but he's got fever. Are you feeling hot too?" She stepped close and laid her cool hand on my forehead. The shock of it ran down my whole body. In the dark she could have been Mama. And then I was jealous of her easy motherly softness. I hated that she'd exposed my incompetent caretaking.

I had looked at her face when we checked into the campground. Even in the flashlight glow I could see again it was soft with wrinkles, but her hands were strong. Her flannel shirt was buttoned wrong over her sweatpants. She'd gotten to Carey in that urgency that pulls every good mother to a crying infant.

"You seem okay," she said. "You both eat the same thing the last couple of days?"

"Pretty much. Same stuff out of our cooler. We had breakfast at a cafe this morning. He had oatmeal I didn't have."

"Hopefully you won't get sick, because he's going to need you."

"I don't know what to do." My arms had gone weary from the release of adrenaline. My mouth was dry. "You think we ought to take him to an emergency room? How high do you think his fever is?"

She said he'd be fine for the night. But the woods closed around us. "Maybe he drank untreated water." She knocked on the toilet door again. "But even so, he'll be fine until morning. Then if he's still sick, take him to the clinic in Mammoth. I'm Evelyn. They know me there. You tell them. Evelyn."

Carey pushed at the door and she helped him out. "Get on the other side." She had to direct me. I leaned lightly as I could against his sour sweat and curdled breath. His weakness made him a stranger.

I only half-slept, with my back to Carey, stiff and ready to hand him off again to able-bodied earth-mother Evelyn. He mumbled in his sleep, arms around his belly. He sat up once, crying.

"What, Carey?" In the camp light glare he was wild-eyed from the fever or a dream.

"I can't remember." He was gasping. "What Stan looked like. I try and try and try. But I can't picture his face." His words rose into a sob, and he beat his temples with the heels of his open fists. I didn't know how to touch him, how to calm him. He wrestled away when I touched his face. He was manic, digging in his bag until he fished a picture out of his wallet of the two of them on a beach.

"Look at us," he begged. He pushed the shivering picture at me. I took it, but he grabbed it back and held the photo against his breastbone and lay on his back, knuckling at the tears running down his temples until his breathing smoothed and deepened. Like a motherless child.

When I was nine, I had chickenpox. Nearly thirty years later Mama still looks panicked when she tells about my fever, a hundred-and-five degrees. Ten miles from a hospital. I hallucinated—I can still see it—that my chest caved in, and I was being devoured by a gnawing nest of worms and spiders and bugs with pincers. But the real monster was Mama. She put my freezing, burning bones in a tub of cold water. She wrenched open metal trays of ice with a screech that shot through the nerves of my teeth, then dumped the cubes like ice bergs around the arctic of my shuddering skin. I hated her.

She smacked my hands away from scratching and put a pair of white cotton gloves on my hands. She held me down in bed a couple of times. Her rough hands betrayed me, but they were the same hands that brought me ginger ale and Jell-O and combed the tangles and scabs out of my hair and dabbed me with Calamine on cotton balls. She kept me from scarring myself.

I didn't inherit her capable hands. Mine are clumsy and hot. They kill house plants, mangle pie dough, ruin every stitch they try to sew, push people away, hang empty. My maternal instincts are nil.

All night I kept waking up, terrified. I had no idea what to do if Carey messed his pants or threw up in the tent. Or even if he just needed to tell me about Stan. Or worse, if he wanted me to talk about Daddy or Kevin or any of my life spiraling out of control.

"How's our patient?" Evelyn tromped into our site the next morning wearing her same flannel shirt and pink sweatpants, gray hair so thin I could see her scalp. She looked like a bag lady of the woods in her unlaced hiking boots.

She set a bottle of Gatorade by the camp stove where I was boiling water for the tea Carey had asked for. "Best not to give him caffeine," she told me. "He needs this." She pushed the bottle closer and swept the table clear of pine needles.

I was about to tell her I could manage when Carey pushed out of the tent like a hatchling.

"Well, if it's not Florence Nightingale." He grinned weakly. His hair was matted and spiky, his face sweet. He slumped on the picnic bench and looked up at her. *More like Florence Turkey Buzzard*, I wanted to say.

She beamed and leaned toward him as if she might sit down for breakfast. "You look better. Guess you both heard they got the fire under control?"

"Oh, wow, that's great," he said. "Thanks." So much had happened that for a split second I didn't know what fire she was talking about. He turned to me. "That'll make Glenna happy. She was freaking out yesterday."

"I wouldn't say I was freaking out," I resisted. I poured boiling water over the tea bag in his cup and pushed it to him.

"You should have seen her about to make a run for it past the barricade." He laughed. "One leg out the car door." Evelyn looked my way and laughed cautiously.

"I'm glad you think it's hilarious." I rolled my eyes at him.

"Oh, I'm kidding," he said. "I'm the one who caused all the trouble."

"No trouble," Evelyn said. "Not the first time or last that somebody yells for my help in the middle of the night." I couldn't help thinking that no one yelled for her.

"Last week a woman chopping kindling with a little ax cut her wrist down to the bone. Her husband was running around looking for Band-aids. Blood everywhere. But I got it stopped. Tied a tourniquet with her bra. Then he couldn't find his keys. He wasn't in any shape to be driving, so I had to wake Estelle and drive us to the ER."

"Who's Estelle?" Carey swigged the Gatorade, green as antifreeze. The cup of tea I'd made him sat steeping at his elbow.

"My daughter," she said. Our silence hung like a question in the air. She looked at me with piercing blue eyes. "You two haven't got kids?"

Carey and I tripped over each other to explain that we weren't married. She laughed and said, "I figured." To me her guess seemed more accusation than curiosity. She pointed a knuckle at me. "You're about the age I had Estelle. I was what they called an old maid, I guess. Back then, not being married—Well, my family thought Estelle was my punishment." She paused.

"She's what they called back then a mongoloid. Down's Syndrome. They said she'd never live. And if she made it, to put her away and forget she was born. Now I want to know how you forget a part of you that's living and breathing? Or even maybe worse, part of you that dies?"

Her eyes stared again right into mine, as if she knew the secret of the baby I'd lost, all the sadness tangled and locked up together, without an answer at the end. My face burned under her stare. I wanted her to touch me with her cool hands and sway me into a new time I couldn't yet reach, well and solid with faith I could also be a mother.

"You've had to give up a lot for her," Carey said, shaking his head.

"Oh, now, son, you've said that wrong-headed thing so many people say. Estelle is the love of my life. That's why I gave her a name that means shining star." She smiled so we would see she'd forgiven any misjudgment.

I had to wonder again through a fleeting comparison whether I could mother a disabled child—blind, deaf, autistic. Me who can't bear to touch a fevered face or go get a blanket and water, much less help somebody puke in a compost toilet in the middle of the night. I don't even carry Kleenex.

"Well, now here I've gone on and on with my whole life story when I just wanted to let you know you'll find the road ahead clear." She walked away and waved trivially as if the sun were in her eyes.

Limp as a dishrag, Mama would say, when we were wrung out from sickness. Before we were past Mammoth's city limits, that's how Carey slumped. The greenhouse morning sun exposed him in clothes he'd had on for two straight days, haggard from grimy hair to muck-dusty bare feet. He slept straight through the scorched sage flats where we'd turned back the day before. The fire had steamrolled across the highway, blackened brush for miles on both sides. A helicopter was still carrying loads of water to dump on smoldering ridge-line hot spots. It hovered low over a creek, then scooped its dripping load and lifted like an unsteady bee with pollen.

Nothing was stranger in that ash-blasted landscape than firefighters in their barrage of yellow gear and helmets. They looked like the firemen in the newspaper photos of my burning house.

We were near the entrance to Yosemite before I had to slow in a line of traffic. Carey stirred sluggishly. "We there already?"

"Next stop Yosemite." I patted his knee, proud I could give him good news. "You missed these Amazon women firefighters toting tons of gear."

He jerked upright and blinked befuddled out the window. "But I told you

I was going to Mono Lake. Glenna! We were right there at Lee Vining. You let me sleep—"

I slowed. "Oh, no. Maybe you mentioned—but you said we lost a day."

"But you can't even understand this part of the Sierras unless you see Mono Lake," he said. "Stan brought me there."

He leaned his forehead against the window with his eyes closed, rambling as if he were in a dream. "Stan and me at Mono Lake, with snowy mountains, and here's this huge blue lake in the desert, like some place on Mars, with these like stalactites or stalagmites. Which is the one out of the ground? G for ground? The water level going down uncovers them, like towers. Just a touch and they'd crumble." He put on his sunglasses. I acted like I didn't notice that he brushed away tears. Which I had caused.

Past Tioga Pass, at nearly ten thousand feet, we came into a melting world at Tuolomne Meadows. We pulled over and walked out into thick, ruddy grasses. I was afraid Carey might faint or fall, hardly a place to step that wasn't soggy along cut-through sloughs, rivers at their birthplace following the way down to foothill creeks. Round-shouldered mountains pushed far back from the high meadows, where the burnished marshes sang with thawing. Newborn water.

As I drove us toward Yosemite Valley, the meadows gave way to bald rock and granite slopes. Lakes and trees shifted around every curve. At one turn-out, Carey pointed out Half-Dome, the monolith so famous even I'd seen photos of its quarter-sphere, the sheer face un-mated for millennia. Something about it from miles away was maternal, a hooded feminine sweep of stone scarf sheltering the blank face without eyes. A Madonna at the center of the worn world.

Then it was like we sluiced into the valley, along the green-glass Merced River. Out of the woods, there, on the grassy flats, far above the traffic and sidewalks and bicyclists, the massive gateway El Capitan and granite towers, higher than I could believe, even as I was looking up at them, raring straight up, Carey swore to me, three thousand feet or higher.

As I slowed for valley traffic and the view, lush hardwood shade pushed river breezes, a scent like home, into the car. I glanced at Carey, shocked to see he had his hand over his mouth, weeping without a sound. He broke down then rubbing his stubble, as if he were making a terrible decision.

"These same trees I saw with Stan. The same rocks. The same water." His fever and sickness had provoked his grief. He wiped his eyes. "Maybe even the same sky. The same vapor up there. If I didn't look at you, I could almost believe Stan is driving, alive as you and me. More alive maybe. I mean, isn't he here and I just can't touch him? On the other side of the air?"

There was nothing I could think of to say, stagnating again in my helplessness.

"When he first died, I thought that. I thought if I could stop being in my skin, in my flesh, I could touch him. One last time." He wiped his face and choked out a soft laugh. "I know it's stupid. I was so out of my head, it seemed simple to just change dimensions—"

To think what an awful friend I'd been. To think that he'd been desperate enough to think of suicide.

"Carey, I think that's what everybody feels when somebody they love dies. Not that it makes you feel better. It probably doesn't." I wanted to beg for mercy, to say, *I wish I'd come to see you then. I'm sorry. I'm sorry.* "I'm so sorry."

He let out his breath in a shudder. I concentrated on the crazy traffic while he gathered himself in a stunned calm. He barely whispered, "If he's anywhere, he's here, I swear, like when he first died and I knew I couldn't see him or hear him, but he was somewhere. He's in this bliss everybody feels here. Don't you feel it?"

I nodded, but I wasn't sure. I wasn't sure I could feel a place that intensely ever again. Or a person. Where would I find any sensation of the baby I'd carried for only a few weeks? How did that grief compare to Carey's grief?

I pulled over and we stood beside the road looking forever up. Stone and gravity and snowmelt drew together to shape the valley with the power of a drenched, dripping fist of endless water. I'd seen so many waterfalls in the Smokies, but I'd never imagined a sound so potent it seemed to come from my own sternum. The valley thundered with waterfalls, some like scarves in the wind, some tiers of jettisoned river. Some of the tallest waterfalls in the world, Carey said. Hooves against stone.

"It sounds like a big loud heartbeat, doesn't it," Carey said finally. "Like maybe how loud it is when you're being born?"

We had come, truly, to the womb of the Sierras, like a lost home we'd never known. Trouble was, everybody else had found the same paradise.

At the campground, we found they'd given away our site, but they sent us to a possible fallback, Camp Curry, hundreds of white canvas tent cabins among pines and spidery Pacific dogwood trees. The glacier-carved valley's end was a cul-de-sac. Grocery, mercantile, cafeteria, swimming pool, gang showers, bike rental, infirmary, lodges, all crammed together below the monolithic elevations. And everybody running around like it was just another day at Dollywood.

We finally found a parking place, in a lot big enough for a baseball arena. Then stood in line for forty minutes to get one of the last available tent cabins. Then got an earful of warnings about flood zones, rockslides, bear attacks. Bear lockers were first-come, first-served and might not be available, but we had to have one. Under threat of huge fines, no food or cosmetics were allowed in our car at any time we weren't moving. Or in our tent. No storage for anything to eat, drink—besides water—or wash with. They even dissuaded against Chap-Stick and deodorant. Photos displayed cars ripped open by black bears. Then we had to stand in line at the store to buy a lock, in the lucky chance we could find a vacant bear locker to store all our food and shampoos.

"So, dang, we've lost a lot of money here," I said. "Forfeit the campsite fees for two nights, then rent a tent cabin."

"I for one am feeling lucky they had vacancies," Carey said.

"I know. But then buy a thirty-dollar lock? Nice grift they've got going on. Jack up the rule about food in a car. Why not let us take the risk?"

"Well, I mean, bears can smell like thousands of times better than humans, so we have to clear everything out."

"Carey, we've driven three thousand freaking miles. Everything we own smells like one big, gross Gorgonzola."

He groaned and held his belly. "Don't say Gorgonzola," he said, laughing again finally. But the thought of it went straight to my gut, and I wondered when I was going to come down with whatever had made him sick.

It took an hour to move into what Carey called Little Los Angeles. School kids on field trips scattered, families argued, dreadlock skateboard kids ate sandwiches off their car hoods. We decided we'd shower and have a snack and then lock away our food and shampoos and everything smelly into the bear locker we'd claimed. Then we ended up having to eat standing at the locker. And we didn't get clean. We were too tired to drive back to the real, true coin-operated showers. Besides no picnic tables and no fire rings, there were no showers in the Camp Curry bathrooms, just sinks and full stalls. Moms changing diapers, girls huddled at the mirrors, women in saris in line.

There was no privacy anywhere. We repacked our packs and hauled in one trip from the car only what was allowed in our tent cabin—pillows, flashlights, clean underwear—far down paths between the canvas cabins, looking for our number, 672. Carey was weak and weary, so we walked slowly.

"Welcome to paradise-in-hell," he said. "Or hell-in-paradise?" Inside the flimsy screen door to the white canvas tent, the barest essentials—a wood floor, bare bulb overhead, a twin cot on either side, worn white sheets and one dark green wool blanket each, a screen window above each bed with only a blind to scroll down against the noise and night air and mosquitoes we'd been warned about.

"So, Carey," I said. He flung his duffel and himself after it onto a cot, which nearly gave way under him. "Why you reckon there's a lock on the door? Anybody—or a bear, or, hell, even a mosquito—could just slash in and steal whatever or suck us dry."

"Anybody can break into our car, too, if they wanted."

"Seriously, I'd feel safer sleeping in the car. You're right. This kind of sucks, especially since you've been sick."

191

"I mean, the bath house has running water. I would have given a thousand dollars for a sink and a flush toilet last night." He reached up and pulled his window shade down against a group of boys running and yelling. He lay back and put his arm over his eyes.

We ended up with just enough time to get to Glacier Point for the sunset. Every mile I swallowed back my lofting stomach. Every curve and curve and climbing curve I tried to ignore my queasiness. I wondered how much of a fever I already had, how long before I'd need a toilet.

But I didn't want to break the reverie Carey held all the way up, with our windows rolled down to cool dusk air, drifting through pockets of bird song. Light spinning through the massive trees made a wheel in my head, a splendor of dizzying flicker. My gut undulated and gurgled, turn by turn spongy and gelatinous and then solid as a hot stone. I sweated with the glittering light and shadow, froze in the sun.

At the top, on Glacier Point, out in the open end of daylight, the cool air seemed to come from my pores, as if I were turning into granite and wind and snow. Cool sunlight came crashing down on everything, its fuzzy brilliance tracing the outlines of tourist families and stone stairs and metal railings.

Miles and miles across, the backsides of the mountains we'd been in front of the day before. The snowy stone horizon unfurled into canyon after sloping canyon. Half-Dome, so close now, hid her face from us. Then, from my fevered perspective, the dome looked like a gigantic woman's thumb, the flat nail to the north, and on the opposite side, the rounded, whorled flesh just starting its urgent push to light. The rest of her palm lay hidden under green, holding up the webbed life of every stone, every creature, every moment.

"Carey," I called him over. "Doesn't that look like a woman's hand, pushing up there?" I pointed. "Her thumb?"

"I can see that," he agreed.

I followed him to an even more dramatic overlook, along with hordes of families and tourists from tour buses. Magnificent shadows seeped into the monoliths below, gigantic stone the light burnished to gold. Lakes and waterfalls and tree trunks and the edges of rock went red.

I lost track of Carey in the crowds and got dizzier turning and turning to place him. I was a lost child. I wanted to be home. In my own bed. No. I didn't have my own bed. From so far away, it would take days and days to drive back across mountains and deserts and prairies, back where my mother would put clean sheets across me that smelled like hay, the clean of open fields. No. That was an old memory, from long ago.

Fevered homesickness left me disintegrated, legs and feet melding into the stone walkway. My hands were shovel-wings, my heavy head floating. I wished I could just soar off the thirty-five hundred feet of loft and set down in a yard I knew, in a town I knew, with people I knew. *Take me home.*

Carey's voice called to me, and I was found. Every step I took toward him I took with lead feet. Straight down off the overlook edge, the impossibly far valley and the rock and clouds swung to meet each other. I held the rail with a talon grip.

Take me home. Had the words really not come out of my mouth? I stepped back from the railing with my feet, but my hands wouldn't let go. The tilting world swam with waterfalls billowing and cathedrals of stone that might crumble apart.

"Look straight down at how level the valley is there." Carey pointed. "When the glacier receded, it left that moraine. You know what a moraine is? Glenna?"

I knew, yes, he'd told me. A moraine is the farthest debris a glacier leaves when it's pushed its limits, a wall nothing can get past. A dam. I couldn't say the words. *Take me home.*

"Glenna?" Carey stepped toward me in a flash.

"Take me home," I whispered. I let go of the railing, terrified I would lift and hover, but instead I landed on my back, nothing to latch onto, Carey's voice distant in the static-sizzling gray I could barely see through to sky above. Nowhere for me to go, there at the end of the top of the world, nothing to tether me. No child. No husband. Nothing from one end of the continent to the other to hold me in place.

Carey stared down the women in the bathhouse near our cabin and waited outside my stall while I went through the anguish he had the night before. Crisis management. I didn't know how I could sit on the toilet when I also needed to throw up. And I didn't know how long I could hold anything in while I was throwing up. He brought me my toothbrush and toothpaste, which I would never have thought to help him with after he was sick. He propped me at the sink and washed my face, then guided me back to the tent where I burrowed under amazingly icy sheets and the one blanket.

And then I didn't know anything else except that it was dark, and Carey was there. I woke up in a violent sweat, and Carey led me again with the flashlight up the path farther than I thought I could walk. I had to lie on the filthy bathroom floor more than once. I told him I'd have preferred the open ground he'd crashed into the night before. He held cool wipes on my forehead until the worst was over again.

"At least you know from what I went through, this bug'll be over soon." He smiled weakly at me in the mirror as he held another cool towel to my blotchy face. "And there's running water. And light." My face in the overhead glare was sallow, my eyes sunken in.

"Mama would say I look puny," I said and tried a laugh.

Long after the cot was too hard for my burning skin to stand, after the convulsions in my gut quelled, I froze, dreaming of a campfire. There was Carey. Carey's voice. Carey's hands pulling my sleeping bag around me. He opened the shade to study my face in the early dawn. His face was soft blue, the room in blue shadow.

"Here, you need to drink more," he said, pulling one of our camp chairs beside my cot. Water across the dry rock of my tongue. He had kept me drinking. He had covered me. On top of me our sleeping bags, both of them, zipped together, tucked around me.

"These were in our car, though." I loved their silky warmth and down, no more of the scratch of the wool blanket around my neck.

"I only left for a few minutes, I promise," he said.

"No, I mean, there are bears." I sat up and he pushed me down softly, laughing.

"Good grief. I had a flashlight. And there weren't any bears." He laughed. "Just some drunk rock climbers. Very butch." He laid a cool cloth on my head. "It dropped to nearly forty degrees, so it's not just your fever. You need to stay covered." His words were coming in puffs. He was wearing his coat.

"You'd make a good mother," I said. I didn't have the strength any more to keep from crying a little as I laughed.

He laughed and wiped my eyes before he stood up. "I mean, a fever makes anybody say crazy things, but don't go off the deep end, Glenna."

"No. You're good." I patted my leg, trying to reach for his hand. "You're a better mother than I would ever have been."

"Okay, now you're just having a little pity party. Go back to sleep."

"No." I tried to sit again. "I mean it. When you were sick. I'm a horrible person when I get scared. I was so scared."

"Okay. Hush now. Let's go back to sleep for awhile." He got up and opened the shade by his own cot. Blue fog outside shifted. He lay on his cot and pulled the sheet over his jacket. "You forget, I have experience." There was a pause across the dim blue.

"I took care of Stan for two years. I mean, you've just got a little stomach thing. He was an invalid. AKA diapers. I had to learn how to hook up an IV. For morphine. A catheter. But even early on, every day for six weeks there was radiation. Then chemo. Waiting for vomit. Cleaning up vomit. Getting ready for more vomit."

He sighed and shifted. "That's not the story I mean to tell. What I mean is that I would have lived like that every day forever if it meant I could keep him. But that's selfish. He was so tired at the end. But what got me through afterward was to know I'd done everything I could. That I'd loved him as much as I could."

I couldn't have convinced Carey that for most of us those two things could easily be exclusive—caretaking and love. I'd cleaned up plenty of old people, dying people, when I'd worked in nursing homes. It's easy to help anonymous people. Just a routine. A job. But nothing in it of love. Love is the hard part. The impossible part.

"Everybody thought we were lying." Carey's voice carried clear but quiet between our cots. "I bet even you thought it was AIDS. That was the worst at the beginning. But at the end it didn't matter. I guess it never mattered.

"But his ex-partners were hysterical and driving us crazy with questions. And my parents. It finally took Stan's doctor to convince our families he had lymphoma. I wanted to hang the results up like diplomas."

Carey's form took deeper shape in the brightening blue glow. But I had to close my eyes. I hung onto his voice to keep from falling off the planet.

"When his doctor said we should join an HIV-AIDS group, Stan went ballistic. But the doctor's reason was if we were being treated like we had the virus, we needed the same support system that actual AIDS patients had. And from the first meeting, Stan's whole outlook shifted. He stopped thinking about cancer and medicine and started thinking about wellness and joy.

"Maybe that was it, who knows, that kept him alive for months past the absolute limit the doctors gave us. He fought so hard the last weeks. I thought he'd die every day. But every morning—by then we had hospice—and he made the nurse get him clean and fix what hair he had left by the time I got up to feed him. He had his dignity and his beauty even then. Stubborn! That's what kept him here."

I lifted my hand out of the cocoon Carey had swaddled me in. I had the strength I'd been trying to find. "You're wrong," I said. "Stan stayed alive for you. Because you loved him. Because he loved you."

I could hardly breathe from the pressure of Carey's private memory. There was hardly room for me in the tent cabin. The wounds he'd carried around since Stan died. I'd never had an inkling because his peace seemed easy.

But his inside was as pock-marked as anybody's, maybe as crazy as mine, frozen and thawed and refrozen in a distraction of crevices and dead-ends. Everything piles up against the moraine. The silt sifts in layer by layer to soften the scars. But there is still the monstrous, thunderous, distracting memory.

"I never told anybody this." He was nearly whispering, but clear. "Nobody else was there when he died. He wouldn't let the nurse come. The last two days I tried to stay awake every minute. Like waiting for a baby to be born, but awful, but also a beautiful Sunday morning.

"I went to his bed to check on him when the birds started singing. He was wide awake, looking out into the trees. I don't know how I knew, but I knew it was the last time he was going to hear birds singing.

"He pushed the covers away except for the sheet, as if he was going to just get up and go to the window and float right out. And I thought that would be good if he could fly. He was so thin, but that morning he really looked strong enough to leave.

"I mean, I remember realizing that he was leaving. The sun was coming up, and I knew he was going to die right in front of me. And I was terrified. Terrified he would see how afraid I was. He just held my hands and helped me help him go.

"One second he was breathing." Carey's voice broke. His voice got loud with crying. "He was breathing. Looking in my eyes. Really hard. Then he closed them. And he relaxed then. I mean, he looked more like himself than he had in months. He was sort of smiling because—" he sobbed suddenly. "I'd been telling him about the first time we met."

"Carey," I whispered. "Come lay by me." The words I found finally were pure instinct, from long ago. What Mama used to say when Dunn and I were little, when she knew we needed her but couldn't accuse us of it. When she loved that we needed her.

Come lay by me.

Carey was beside me in two seconds, his body a cool comfort against my fever.

And he stopped crying the instant he was with me under the sleeping bags. We squeezed together on that narrow cot. I held my arm across his chest, out in the cold air, holding him. Then I stroked his hair, both of us filthy and weak. The cabin brightened and I pictured Half-Dome, that eternal thumb in the sunrise, holding up a forest as easy as a bed of moss for another day. The birds began to sing in the trees just when we were falling back asleep.

BRIDGES

Carey and I got our appetites back crossing California's farm belt. We stopped at highway fruit stands for strawberries and white nectarines and pistachios. And big cheap bottles of wine to take to dinner with his old friends we'd be staying with in San Francisco. Marcus and Sylvan. Their names sounded Roman to me, like sentries guarding the entrance to Carey's other life.

Farms shifted and open land rose and fell in waves, steep blond-grass hills with oak trees like giant heads of broccoli. For the first time since Vegas, we hit interstate, jammed twelve lanes wide as we closed in on the Bay Area, cars pouring in and out of hills planted with windmills, like pinwheel crops on long white stalks.

Carey beat time on the steering wheel to David Bowie's "Golden Years." "I can't wait to see people we know!" He flipped down his visor for the dozenth time and tested his smile in the mirror.

That "we." Instead of being flattered, it shook me. The "Berkeley boys" would be perfect strangers to me, and I pictured me and a trio of foreigners I couldn't reach. The closer to San Francisco we got, the farther I was from Carey's world.

Across the swimmy-high concrete slabs of the Oakland Bay Bridge, we pounded toward his old stomping grounds in anxious heartbeat rhythm. Shadows of riveted steel beams slashed the thin fog. I couldn't match the city's looming skyline with the manageable little peninsula on the map. It all straddled the San Andreas Fault, which we'd studied in social studies class way back. It had freaked me out even then to think about earthquakes. The book had photos of huge chasms in the earth. Crossing high above the bay, real danger seemed possible, even probable. My heart caught in my throat at the expanse below.

I'd only ever felt one tremor in Knoxville, a rumble that didn't even wake Kevin. Earthquakes happened to other people in exotic places, news footage of overpasses swinging like asphalt hammocks, yawning rifts in pavement. Now here I was, in those exotic places. Catastrophe could happen. Even the most powerful places break in two, bridges between people wrenched out of their sockets.

Carey knew his way around San Francisco like a lost dog finds its way home. Even checking the city map, I couldn't follow where we were any better than

I could follow the way he talked his way through. I think he was surprised how well he maneuvered side-streets in the tangle of downtown, crossing main arteries, darting in front of the cable car.

We topped out at intersections so steep they took my breath like a carnival ride. He toured me up the Embarcadero, past huge ships in dock, through the Marina district, down Lombard Street's pinched zig-zag. The blue bay and the red span of the Golden Gate Bridge came in glimpses as we drove back and forth and he pointed and talked, linking the present and the past.

There were his old haunts: Haight-Ashbury, the apartment he'd shared with Stan, their favorite Thai restaurant, their laundromat and corner grocery. Then he drove us through Golden Gate Park, a maze of palms and evergreens and twisted fronds, every plant in bloom with a million pouting lips. Without a word of warning from him, we came through the park to a boulevard along the coast. And across that road the whole western world stopped.

The Pacific.

Its lucid name held the exact opposite of surf I could hear above the traffic before Carey parked and shut the motor. I was stunned, shaking. There were no words between us. Carey smiled as if he'd created it all just for me. He took my hand to cross the highway, pulling me to the dark lion's roar of sapphire tide.

I carried my sandals to let the by-God *Pacific Ocean* pour around my ankles, up to my shins, drenching the hem of my shorts, freezing cold water. We couldn't keep from running in and out of the shifting surf, laughing and whooping. In a fracture between gestures, Carey caught me up in his arms. In that hair's-breadth of time it takes in any scenario, he kissed me. The first time he'd ever kissed me. And he hadn't just missed my cheek. And so, it seemed more than a simple token of relief that we'd arrived. I could taste the berries he'd eaten, his lips sweet and warm.

I tried to see if his tears were happy or from the wind. He held me so tight, I couldn't read his face. At the end of the continent, he was laughing in my ear and tugging me down the beach. Happier than he'd known he could be, I think. Happier than I had known. He ran us breathless, so it was easy for me to pretend his kiss hadn't registered seismic emotions, the whole corner of the world threatening to break off into the unknown blue.

Whatever brief spell we shared broke literally step by step. Carey let loose of my hand and lunged ahead two steps at a time up the polished oak staircase of his friends' Victorian apartment house. The smell of lemon oil gave way to sautéed garlic. He knocked at #3, where amber light poured around the red door, slightly ajar. The inner sanctum of the museum curator and the investment banker. Carey knocked louder to be heard above Diana Ross and the Supremes.

Shadows and big footsteps and the music quieted. A beefy, completely bald man in a white apron swung open the door and grabbed Carey, both of them shouting each other's names and laughing. Marcus it was, then, who lifted him off the floor and grabbed my upper arm with an oven-mitted hand, and then we were in the kitchen drinking sangria while he waved his knife and talked and stirred pots and tromped between stainless steel appliances in his red chef clogs, which matched the tile countertops, which matched the apartment door.

Carey recounted some of our trip while Marcus pinched off basil and rosemary from little red pots along the windowsill running the full length of the open kitchen and dining room. He cut lemons off a tree beside one of the columns marking the entrance to the living room.

I sat on the periphery in the nearest dining room chair and smiled as they laughed at old jokes, acting as if this were old hat. I was dizzy even before the second glass Marcus shoved into my hand, and from the smell of food and raging hunger. The high ceiling swam, and the dimly lit open rooms were a porch to the city lights spread beyond the wide windows. An expansive, expensive view of sky and water, and a sliver of the Golden Gate Bridge on fire with the sunset.

Sylvan came in right at dark just as the kitchen timer buzzed. His booming voice belied his size. Pale as a moth, he held a bouquet in one hand and lifted an enormous bottle of Cuervo Gold over his head with the other, so petite I wondered how he had the strength. He reminded me of a young Barbara Stanwyck, jockey-slight but rangy. He handed the bottle to Marcus as he clenched Carey around the waist, then he walked straight to me. Something in his eggshell blue eyes made me stand up.

"The woman revealed." He bowed deeply. "Welcome to civilization. I'm Sylvan, but friends call me Sylvie." I wasn't sure what that meant I should call him. He shoved an armful of irises at me and excused himself to change out of his suit and tie. "The Tennessee state flower," he shouted over his shoulder at me. "I looked it up!"

"Let me have those." Marcus bustled the flowers into a vase. He waved Carey and me to a massive table set with red-and-gold plates and bowls of roses. When Sylvie reappeared in a bright caftan, he seemed to take on all that beauty as a rival.

Marcus finished up kitchen tasks and brought the first course to the table, while Sylvan's preparations were more like a performance. As if he were dancing a solo tango, he lit the gas fireplace and set flickering candles round the room. His feet barely grazed the floor in what looked like satin shoes. But that was all prelude to the lingering kiss he gave Marcus as he pulled out a chair for him. They sat at either end of the table. Sylvan announced that the night called for stories.

"We want to hear about the Road, capital R. But we also want to weave

199

together the gap since last we saw you, Carey. Six years! And so much has changed." He looked at me as if I would make a big reveal on command.

I only listened and echoed their manners, unsure at first how precise I would have to be. I quickly saw the drama required spooning minestrone away from myself, spreading my napkin on my lap, never touching my salad with my knife. But we all dipped hunks of bread into peppery olive oil and curls of creamy Parmesan.

It was hard not to wolf my food. We hadn't eaten such a meal in weeks, maybe in forever. I was so wrapped up in the tastes that I didn't listen closely to the conversation. I had more than enough to be quiet and ignored. I only spoke to answer direct questions. Even so, my jaw felt sore from trying to avoid my accent. But still they asked me incessantly, *what?* I could hear Daddy saying: *You're a one-legged man at an ass-kicking, Sister.*

"Pasta con quattro formaggi." Marcus set the main course in the center of the table and ladled a serving onto my plate first. The pasta glowed golden thick. "Have you ever had it before?" Marcus asked.

I held up my wine glass and prepared to exaggerate my hick accent. Sometimes a situation calls for a hillbilly to mock herself so she can size up others. You stun people, and you can read authentic reactions. But one look at Carey's hopeful face and I couldn't bring myself to turn the joke back on them that tempted the tip of my tongue: *You really think we ain't got mac and cheese in Tennessee?*

The serving spoon went a little lax in Marcus's hand as he waited. He blinked. I took a sip of wine and nodded. "It all looks and smells amazing."

Across the table Carey looked relieved. I had successfully spanned yet another uncomfortable moment.

While Marcus filled our plates, Sylvie opened a bottle of wine he said he'd been saving for a special occasion. He made us all stand while we lifted our glasses in a toast to old friends. *Old friends.* Carey looked like a new acquaintance in the dim light. But all four of us clinked crystal in a fleeting union across the table.

Nearly ten o'clock, over dishes of raspberry sorbet and espresso, Sylvie dragged out the new bottle of tequila, along with a full liquor cabinet. Carey and Marcus stopped after the first round, but Sylvie slugged back shot after shot with lime and salt. He challenged me to drink up and coaxed me to make fun of "the academics," as he called them.

"So pooped from all their deep thinking. Art history and everything else history. A-history to Z-history, and all the F-freaking history in between.

"I want the moment here and now," he slurred, looking vacantly at me.

"So you're traveling cross-continent with Carey. Our Carey. Tell us about you two!" Carey shifted as if to say, *Let's call it a night.*

"You two have known each other, what? All your lives? And we all have Carey in common, the tie that binds."

I looked to Carey for agreement or support, though I understood Sylvie wanted me to collude in some kind of tell-all that would expose Carey.

"When we met, we were, oh, ten years old," I said. "He liked to jump rope." Carey laughed in relief or memory. Sylvie echoed too loudly.

He scrunched closer, so close he was blurry. "You're the shot in the arm I need. Someone entirely authentic. You are making me want to see the hills and hollows."

"They're called hollers," I corrected him. "And they'd eat you for breakfast, where Carey and I are from."

Sylvie rared back laughing against the couch and tucked his caftan between his knees. Carey was beaming at me or mortified. I couldn't tell.

"Well, you might find our city has a large appetite for *sweet little country gals*," Sylvie said. It wasn't just years of living with a drunk like Daddy that put me on alert. His mocking accent seemed to have an edgy meanness. "But Carey will defend you. He always defends his ladies. But she's nothing like Laura." He winked at Carey, who didn't meet my glance. "I don't think. Do you, Marcus?"

"Sylvie, be good now," Marcus warned, standing up. "Closing time. Give me that bottle." Carey held Sylvie in a steady stare. Something jittery but hard passed between them. And I let it. But it was hard not to ask about Laura. The phantom name I'd heard Carey mention a few times vaguely. He was flushed and statue-still.

Sylvie turned to me and launched in again. "You have to tell me absolutely everything about your trip. I swear, I am bored with this life, my job, this apartment. My God, I'm bored with my own body!" He stretched out his arms and looked at his delicate hands. "I swear, every pore, from follicle to feet, from hair to hiney, patella to—penis!" He laughed and clapped.

"Don't let him fool you, Glenna." Carey leaned across the coffee table to help Marcus collect bottles and glasses. "He's a rich old liar of a queen."

"The pot said to the kettle." Sylvie stretched his legs away from me on the couch and seemed to purr.

"Oh, please." Marcus jumped in. "You've never been bored. Has he, Carey?"

"If he ever was, it just meant a shopping spree. He always came up with another incarnation." Carey leaned toward me. "See, something you should know—"

Sylvan held up his hand at the revelation Carey was threatening. "Glenna, it is my vice to be the center of attention, but I am no liar." He stood, hands on slight hips. "I am not ashamed. But you may be shocked to learn that I was once—dare I say—a diva. By day a mild-mannered money man. By night, a junkie for the spotlight. I wore whatever it took—stilettos, false eyelashes, false everything. Oh! Marcus, remember that organza dress?" Carey and Marcus started to laugh.

Sylvie looked at me. "It was sherbet-colored, orange, raspberry, lime. And I wore it with these white Nancy Sinatra boots with three-inch heels."

Marcus turned off the lamp and motioned for Sylvie to quiet down. "You're scaring our guest. She's never met a female impersonator before."

Sylvie said, "Oh, please. Do not pretty-it-up for company, Marcus. I'm sure she knows what a drag queen is. The perils of pantyhose and eyeliner. Exfoliants and depilatories and razors. Not to mention the torment of bra straps."

"Well, those are not—" I started to disagree and then realized it was the sangria in me offering an opinion. But they were looking at me for the rest. "Those are probably the easy parts," I said quietly. Carey gave me a look I couldn't read.

"There is no job more cutthroat anywhere than being a pretend girl," Sylvie said, sinking across from me into the club chair with a sigh.

"Except—being a real girl," I said, tamping down the real challenge I wanted to throw out. I avoided Carey's look. I didn't want anyone, especially not Carey, to see my rising urge to say a thing or two about cramps. And failed pregnancies and miscarriages.

There was silence. Sylvie prodded against the rage he sensed. "Being a man is a dead-end job. Being a woman, I found exhilarating." He fell back into his chair with the tequila bottle in his hand. "But it didn't pay nearly as well."

That was his final jab, I thought. He seemed to shrink a little into his chair when I didn't come back at him. But I should have recognized him for what he was, with that acid tongue. I'd grown up with a mean drunk.

"But honestly," he said, "after seeing both sides, I could never straddle the gender divide again. No offense. Womanhood is a nice place to visit, but, really, who could stand to live there?"

I was relieved that Carey and I slept clean through Marcus and Sylvie leaving for work. We didn't mention the night before, but my brain ran in little circles around the name Laura. Late morning, we shopped near their Pacific Heights neighborhood and mid-day drove to Coit Tower for a 360-degree view, then afternoon at Union Square, then to Chinatown, where for the first time in my life I was a self-conscious minority. But I was getting used to feeling out of place. All around us a language I couldn't understand, people all shorter than me, every smell different from anything I'd smelled before, licorice and sandalwood and roasted pork. Chinatown held millions of secrets, but food was not one of them, on full display.

In a matter of hours, I could hardly match the me who now knew these things with the me who had lived until then without knowing them.

We met Sylvie and Marcus for dinner at a seafood place on the water. Sylvie pulled his chair next to mine and wanted to hear about "the city" through the eyes of a stranger. "I want details about the most exotic thing you saw."

I explained that Carey and I had mostly eaten our way through the city. All new tastes to me: white tea and dim sum, sour dough and Ghirardelli ice cream. Sylvie laughed as if he meant it when I said the sea lions barking at the pier were like sumo wrestlers.

"Oooh!" He gave a little shiver. "All those glazed duck carcasses hanging in the windows. And all the nightmare sea creatures in buckets right out on the sidewalk like giant live bait?" As I nodded laughing, he lay his hand on my forearm, the way a woman flirts. I thought the evening might be okay as long as nobody drank.

He insisted on ordering two bottles of wine and dinner for everyone, since, as he announced, he would be paying. He took charge of choreographing the back and forth of dishes until we'd shared from every plate—squid ink pasta, calamari in sweet chili oil, the local cioppino, tiramisu for dessert. He pouted when no one else wanted after-dinner brandy. He had two while the rest of us shared a French press of decaf.

He asked where we were going next. I was relieved when Marcus and Carey vetoed suggestion after suggestion. Carey reminded him we had to get up early for our tour, laughing that he hadn't been clubbing in years. "Remember? We were in our twenties then!"

"Nothing to remember, Carey, darling. I'll be in my twenties forever. Carey and I knew each other first." Sylvie turned to me, as if he were staking his claim. "Before he met Marcus. Before you met Stan, right, Carey? Even before Laura—"

"You were the first person I knew in the city, yes, Sylvie," Carey interrupted in a rush and cleared his throat. "I know I owe every connection to you."

"And don't you forget it." Sylvie slipped his arm through mine and strutted beside me to the car.

It was chilly in the morning air at the pier, waiting for our ferry to Angel Island, but nothing like the cold wind as the boat plunged across the bay. Still, we sat on the open front deck of the *Tiburon*, exchanging gum and sunscreen, wishing we had more coffee. I'd forgotten my cap, so Marcus loaned me a bandanna to tie around my hair. That, paired with my windbreaker hood, kept me barely warm. I huddled into Carey, as he pointed at Alcatraz and other landmarks. We kept a backward watch toward the headlands, hopeful for a clear view of the bridge, bound in fog like cotton batting. I could almost forget Marcus and Sylvie were with us as I stood at the railing with Carey, facing open water.

The sun ruptured the chill when we got to the island. Out of what Carey called the "micro climate" in the late morning, we were hot in minutes, peeling layers as we hiked from the visitor center to the historic immigration station.

"The place we're hiking to is like a west-coast Ellis Island," Carey explained.

"Well, it was a lot more—maybe rigorous is the word," Marcus interrupted. "And not so famous. Though it should be. And should be a national park, too."

Nearly two miles hiking up and over the island brought us to China Cove and the immigration station. Deep eucalyptus shaded the great long white barracks, where people from dozens of countries lived weeks, sometimes months through quarantine and documentation. In the empty rooms, Marcus pointed out the feature he was most interested in: Asian characters carved deep into the walls of horizontal wooden slats. The walls were like lined notebook paper, and some of the characters were as wide as the slats. They'd been puttied and painted over so often that some of the carvings were barely visible any longer.

I could tell Carey was in awe as he bent close to the symbols, as if he could tell what they said if he only peered hard enough.

"They don't know how best to maintain or restore them. Beautiful, aren't they, Carey? Some are haikus, poems. Messages to others who will come through," Marcus said. "Maybe family or friends—or even strangers. Just trying to make a mark and leave a trace. It's sort of heart-breaking. Everything is finally being translated for display at some future point, into lots of other languages."

Carey ran his hand lightly over the words, then pulled back as if he'd been burned. "Of all people, I should know better than to touch." He looked sheepish. "This really should be protected. I mean, seriously restored."

I stepped beside him and leaned closer to look. He surprised me by taking my hand. He held my index finger lightly between his finger and thumb and traced through the air to mimic each etched character, like we were Helen Keller and Annie Sullivan.

"Just imagine. Thousands of Chinese came through here across the years. I mean, people came from Australia and India and lots of other places, South America. Russia, even. But the Chinese were sometimes detained for months, or even years. The Exclusion Act was brutal. And now we're seeing the barest scratches—literally—that they left behind."

On our return hike, we stopped for a picnic in shade at the halfway point. We sat on a cloth Marcus had hauled all that way, and he and Carey divvied up salad Nicoise and baguettes and brownies they'd brought in their packs. Sylvie held out his pack as if he might work a magic trick. He pulled out a bottle of wine and four plastic glasses.

"That's against park rules." Marcus sighed. Sylvie shot him a look.

"Darling," Marcus said, forcing a smile. He wiped his shining bald head with a cloth napkin.

I accepted a glass to be polite, but regretted it when Carey passed, explaining the intestinal nightmare we'd just been through.

"But you're a girl with stamina, right, Glenna? Who doesn't play by the rules." Sylvie leaned in to pour more wine for me, though I'd had only a sip or two.

"Actually, I was wrong. She does remind me of Laura. Don't you think, Carey?"

"Sylvie, honestly." Marcus stood and dusted off the seat of his pants, re-adjusting the cloth.

"That's the third time you've mentioned that name," I said, looking from Sylvie to Marcus. Looking to Carey. "Who is she?"

"Somebody we all knew a long, long time ago." Carey wouldn't meet my eyes. "She's not important anymore." His comment hung in the air, the implication that she had been important once.

As we set off again, in the late pounding sun, just a few ounces of wine made me sluggish. And I was still drained from being sick, Carey was right. But even if I could have kept pace with Carey and Marcus, I thought they might want some time to catch up, just the two of them. So, I lagged back between them and Sylvie, who caught up to me fairly easily, even though he'd drunk nearly a bottle of wine.

I lost sight of Carey and Marcus around a long bend where the path topped out at a view of the bay and a city across the water.

"More wine?" Sylvie offered, coming behind me.

"We really ought to catch up with them, don't you think? The ferry leaves—" I glanced at his bare wrists. "Neither one of us has a watch. Don't want to miss our ride."

"Don't you care for dining or wining al fresco?" He laughed. "Do you like your pasta al dente? Do you like your men—" He had a smirk on his face.

"I love eating outside," I said. "Just where I'm from we call it a picnic."

"Where *ever* did Carey find you?" His laugh was obviously less with me and more at me.

"Asked and answered," I said, turning down the hill.

"Since you were babes." He followed behind. "And then you lost touch?"

"Not really," I lied. "We—I didn't really know Stan very well."

"Oh, Stanley. Yes. He wasn't much my cup, either."

"I never said that," I said.

"But since Stan died you and Carey had gotten reacquainted and—" He seemed to be working hard to choose words. "You two have rekindled?"

He'd probably never had an earnest moment in his life. All cat and snark.

He was red from the wine and sun, digging to provoke me to tattle something about Carey.

I let him dangle. But after a few steps I couldn't resist. "Rekindled?" I stopped to swig from my water bottle.

"Well, Carey's history—now isn't that a pun? Carey's history and he's a historian." The scalp beneath his thin blond hair pinked. I imagined the skin peeling later, him picking at it, and I couldn't keep from laughing.

"Oh, Carey must love that you love a pun. He's always been into the intellectual types. Not that you're an intellectual. That's what I can't quite peg. I admit you're a hard nut to crack."

"I can tell you never met anybody from where I'm from," I said. "So ask whatever you want." Any question he asked would say more about him than any answer I gave would reveal about me, or Carey.

"You've come thousands of miles, like nomads in a tent. You—pardon my lack of tact—but you are sharing a bed at our house, and I assume—"

"Oh, I think you're assuming the impossible there, Sylvie." I laughed without any humor.

"I assume, I was going to say, that you know Carey is gay."

I could barely keep from falling to my knees laughing. "I knew Carey was gay before *Carey* knew he was gay."

Sylvie's quick frustration showed. "You didn't let me finish. More precise would be to say that Carey's disposition is ultimately, well, he has been known to dabble in the zone between. Just ask him." Sylvie's curious rage made him spit a little. I couldn't keep from laughing again.

He took only a moment to gather his wits then. "Suffice it to say that Carey has a varied history, stretched very thin in places. Some of us are rather purists."

"You talk in circles, but I'm getting that you're not much of a fan of Carey's."

"Not true! He can live his life, but at what risk." His self-righteousness ended with a whisper. "Ask him about Laura." He leaned in. "Or you could ask me."

I turned away. The heat was nothing compared to the adrenaline flaring under my skin as I walked faster until I was nearly running. I turned back to see him, nothing but a troublemaker. But he'd gotten his barbs into me.

My spite for Sylvie won out over my curiosity about Laura. He was one of those people who thrived on making others feel little, stirring up conflict and worry. And he'd done it. Laura's ghostly presence followed me on the ferry ride back and through our last evening together. Even in the sleekest sheets and rich covers, our final luxurious night before more camping, I couldn't sleep for that name. *Laura*, like a dripping faucet or an itch. But whoever she was, she was Carey's business. Insomnia or not.

Our good-byes the next morning were subdued, even between the three golden boys. After I tossed in my bags, I settled in the Jeep to say my generous and sincere thank you. It had been a beautiful experience—the whole city. But I didn't need the hugs. Carey's promise to them seemed half-hearted, that it surely wouldn't be another six years between visits.

I was relieved he didn't invite them with us to the last place on his list of must-sees, the Japanese gardens. He asked a tourist to make our photo standing in front of the fat, serene Buddha, and then again as we stood at the apex of a steep wooden bridge. Across that bridge at a red pagoda, ivory girls in silk kimonos rustled to serve us spicy rice crackers and green tea. I held back my questions and focused on the sunny afternoon, the lustrous petals, angled limbs, the orange carp in the pond. Carey was silent, sipping his bitter tea, as if we'd had an argument and the rift was my fault.

"I guess I'll never see them again," he said finally.

"Marcus and Sylvan? Why not?"

"I think you know the answer to that." He looked at me and held up his palms like the scales of justice. "Old life. New life. Never the twain should meet."

He meant the struggle to bridge the gap between incompatible friends. Maybe he meant I'd made him ashamed.

"So, am I your old life or your new life?" I ventured.

"What?" He was baffled.

"You've known me the longest, so I guess I'm your old life, crashing into the life you carved out to be urban and hip and—" Sylvie's word for what I definitely was *not* came back to me. *Intellectual.* "I embarrassed you." I drank the last of my tea.

When I looked up Carey had tears in his eyes. "How can you possibly think that? If anything, I was ashamed of them, Sylvie, anyhow." He wiped his eyes. "Marcus. It was great to see Marcus. But how the hell does he live with that asshole alcoholic shit-for-brains?"

I had not seen such anger coming. I had to bite back my giddiness.

"I mean, of all the gall. He wants to punish me for shit that happened when I was a kid, basically." He stopped his rant and looked at me. "You have to know you could never embarrass me, Glenna. There are just things he holds over me—" He took a deep breath, and a tremor shook all the relief right out of me. I panicked. It hadn't been respect for Carey's privacy that kept me from asking about Laura. I was terrified of who he would become if he opened his storehouse of secrets.

"Laura?" He leaned up and nearly toppled our teapot. "Who he mentioned?"

"You don't have to, Carey."

"No, I should have told you years ago about her," he said. "But do you sit and tell me your mistakes with Dawson or whoever partner you had when? It's just not something I'm proud of. And it was an eternity ago.

"Honestly I hadn't thought about her in ages. I mean, I do *not* think of her. I met her my first week at Berkeley. She was older, probably like thirty." He shifted and looked into his teacup as if he might see the way to tell his story.

"She was brilliant and wild. And I was confused. She and I were—well, I don't know any way to say it except that I was *with* her. She's the only woman I was ever with. Just a few times."

"A few times," I repeated.

"Really, it's not enough to say I was confused. She was protective and—I mean, kind of a tyrant." He tried a smile. "That sounds sick. But we all make mistakes. I'm not ashamed. That's not why I didn't tell you."

"Why didn't you?" I thought of all my secrets. If someone asked me, if Carey asked me why I'd withheld them, what would I answer?

"I thought you'd be hurt." He laughed. "Like how egotistical is that? Like you'd think it should have been you."

"It should have been me." My words surprised him so much he leaned back sharply in his seat. They surprised me. And embarrassed me, too.

At the bottom of my cup, tea leaves like flecks of tobacco. I didn't want to risk what they might mean, so I picked them up on the tip of my finger and brushed them on my pants leg. I set my empty teacup down and could not stand the mystified look on Carey's face. I walked away from him, back across the wooden bridge, so steep I couldn't see him from the far end when I turned back to wait.

On a bridge, you are always between one place and another, everything an upcoming possibility. Halfway across the Golden Gate Bridge, in the rearview mirror, everything behind disappeared in the deep fog. There was nothing but being in motion again, and it felt good to be going *toward*.

"You ever hear about the longest bridge? Where is it—Michigan?" My words felt awkward out in the middle of the air, the way talking always is when you've argued with someone. But Carey and I hadn't really argued. It felt worse than an argument.

"Or maybe they do this on lots of long bridges," I said. "There are these people whose job is to drive all the fraidy cats who are too freaked out to drive themselves." Far below, scudding fog opened up to patches of blue water, like an upside-down sky.

"Seems like I did hear that somewhere."

"I want that job," I said. "Just driving back and forth on a bridge." I looked up through the red suspension cables like piano strings disappearing into the gray above. It was the last thing either of us said for miles.

Into Marin County on Highway 1, the wild open headlands jutted out of the fog. The winding road edged along naked yellow hills above the ocean, and then we moved inland a bit, into the scent of eucalyptus and pine, scoured clean by fog and ocean air.

By the time we entered Point Reyes National Seashore, the fog had burned away to cloudless blue. We walked for a little through an open field of California poppies, ringed by bay trees. Their lush darkness filled the air with fragrance out of kitchen stew pots. I thought for the first time in a long while of my burned up kitchen, my spices and cookbooks. But it didn't collapse me now to have such a thought. I breathed in the smell and could somehow love that it was brand new. Maybe because the scent was from living, growing leaves, millions of them, in the California sun.

"Here we go." Carey raced ahead to a row of blue metal posts along a rise of yellow grass where horses grazed. He touched a post and waved to me with a vague smile. "These mark the San Andreas Fault," he called.

"No way." I hurried to close the gap between us.

"Now. You're standing on the epicenter of the 1906 quake." He pointed to a line of dark grasses that marked the shifted ground.

"You knew this was here?"

His face shone like it had when we were kids, when he'd been proud to let me in on a secret. "I knew you'd freak out to stand right on the line. Remember, you were terrified of earthquakes? What grade?"

"You remember that?" I said, "You were obsessed with earthquakes, totally."

That beautiful open meadow, so fragile. Right under our feet, a hazard that could wreck whole cities. Maybe everything beautiful has its dangerous edge. A point of no return, no connection.

We drove roads to the shore under tilted dark trees that had been gnarled by a bajillion Pacific storms. At the sheer cliffs, succulents in flaming pink and orange and yellow hid jagged surfaces of rock. We warned one another back but couldn't resist looking over the edge. Sea lions barked so far below we could barely hear them and make out their brown, squirming mass.

Back in the car, for the long afternoon, we were silent, taking the coast highway north, just a narrow bevel cut halfway up the sloping blond heights. Carey pointed out in tight valleys there were stands of redwoods. Convertibles and motorcycles shaved past us. Carey put on tapes of old music, The Mamas and the Papas, Beach Boys, which I hated, but I didn't tease him or complain.

The sunset was only a failing brightness as we pulled into Manchester State Beach. The tide lay past acres of dunes and sea oats and hummocks of vetch below the viciously cold mist. I had pictured camping right on the shore and watching a brilliant day's end. But so much wasn't meant to be. I had wanted to be Carey's wonderful exotic friend who blended in with his boy pals. I had wanted to be the funny, beautiful conduit. I hadn't imagined instead I'd be possessive and defensive.

I had never in my wildest thoughts pictured a time or place Carey could be closer to any other female than he was with me.

He parked the Jeep to block the wind so he could get a shy fire going against the cold gray air. We hunkered in our down coats and passed a heated pan of canned salmon back and forth, not saying anything. After the decadence of San Francisco, the silence was harder to get used to than slim portions and yet another pit toilet. The quiet sagged between us. We turned in early, just after the moon pushed above low clouds. The wind was loud, plowing against the tent, and hard to distinguish sometimes from the roar of the surf. Neither one of us slept right away, lying close but silenced by the confessions we'd made after all the years.

One of us should, one of us would, finally, wouldn't we, bring up the rift between us? Several times in the night, when I woke, it felt as if a stranger slept beside me. I had a hazy sense that I should wake him up and apologize. Or explain. What would I be explaining? I hardly knew what I'd meant by telling him I should have been the only woman he was intimate with. It was stupid, I knew, the minute I'd blurted it out. It wasn't what I meant, and yet I felt, *how could you*?

Early morning, through dove-colored fog, Carey and I took granola bars and coffee down a trail head through sea grasses to the sloping hard beach. Nothing like the beach experience in San Francisco. The tide was far out, subdued and gray. The light was dull, and we were cold and listless, with another long drive ahead, and another day of not knowing how to mean what we needed to talk about.

Driftwood piled along the wide strand like a giant's pick-up sticks. Way down the way in the shining surf, a single figure flung a net into the waves. There was no one else in sight.

"Are these redwood logs?" It was a stupid question, just to fill the air.

"I would think they are, yes." Carey bent to rub his hands along the patina. I did the same. The long pallid timbers were soft and cold.

"Just wait till you see live redwoods. We might be there by lunch if we get a move on."

But the curves north of Manchester made for slow-going, up impossible hairpin hills. We swung up and plunged down, and sometimes we couldn't go more than twenty miles an hour. For lunch we snacked in the car on apples and cheese popcorn, trying to make time toward the redwoods ahead. What few pull-offs we took were pitched at an impossibly steep grade. The ocean curved like a lens, we were so high. Whitecaps flickered by the thousands into the turquoise and jade, a momentum that ended in explosions of spumes against jutting black rock, where the water laced into coves like the hem of a dress.

To look on a map and see how short a distance we'd covered was astonishing.

I'd been pretty cocky to think I'd driven the tightest possible curves on the planet. Even living in the mountains all my life, only one tangle I'd seen came close, the Dragon's Tail between Tennessee and North Carolina. A road motorcyclists think they own that leads to a pocket of virgin tulip poplars. A hundred-and-twenty-six curves in a thirty-mile stretch. But there, the road is focused within a tunnel of close, overhanging woods. The coast road was exhausting as much for the far beauty and distances as the curves. I was weary from looking at the gorgeous expanse.

But when the road turned away from the coast, mid-afternoon, it seemed suddenly too soon, even after all that torturous winding. Into the woods, the state highway came to a dead stop at a road sign: "End California 1. Jct U.S. 101." Past high banks of fuchsia blooms the mountain four-lane kept rising in elevation, and pretty soon we were passing logging trucks through the dense forest. The dim was claustrophobic after that open vista. We took off our sunglasses.

Deep wooded darkness settled ahead of us, and a fine drizzle started. Clear-cut scars opened up on steep ridges, big, sad, crew-cut meadows. Carey detoured us off the expressway again into a changed world where trees rose like the skyscrapers in San Francisco.

"Finally," Carey said as he craned his neck to look out the windshield. He rolled down his window. "Are we too tired to care?" He smiled vaguely and rolled down his window. "Surprise. This is the Avenue of Giants."

We entered a canyon of trees, fortress walls of redwoods whose towering crowns probed high into the scudding clouds. I rolled down my window too, to look straight up at the silvered sky, a mirroring ribbon equally as narrow as the road. We stopped as soon as we could and walked into the edge of the darkest light in the world.

A storm was imminent even in that living light, in the hush of the wind. Just a ways into the woods a cold pelt of drops pushed us back without our rain coats. Out of the massive cathedral of trees we got a good soaking as we ran along the roadway, scrambling into the Jeep to blast the heat. A jaunt that would have had us howling with laughter just days before.

Back on the road we came into darker and darker blurring swells of rain. Within the lashing there was nothing but the windshield and the frantic wipers and the bleed of red taillights ahead. We were at a dead stop in the wilderness of towering trees.

"Where are we, even?" I asked, bending over the map. I had to turn on the overhead to see.

"See? This scenic road that parallels the four-lane," Carey said. "We're right near a state park. Humboldt. I vote to stop there."

"At three in the afternoon? In this rain? I'm not sure the tent's that waterproof."

211

"Well, it's our best bet, I'd say." He checked the map over my shoulder. "And lots of people will be competing for a site. I mean, what's the use to risk the road right now? And the redwoods are what we came all this winding way for."

Around campground loops I was doubtful. But we found a site under a cluster of redwoods growing so close together their canopy wove a giant umbrella. Three hundred feet up. The length of a football field above us. I looked and could not absorb the fact of it. And yet it was true. The ground all around the fire ring and table was dry. Carey got a fire started right off in our grate, without any lighter fluid. I found two cans of soup we'd forgotten about.

"Before we eat, I meant to mention," he said, "there's a pay phone at the campground kiosk. I mean, it's been three days since you called your mom. You'll feel better."

I should have counted five, ten, a hundred. "Really? You're keeping tabs on when I call home?"

"Your mom is—she's probably worried, that's all I thought. Just looking out for you."

"Carey, I've been under scrutiny for two days. Like KGB surveillance. Like which fork do I use with my salad. Interrogated. Like a light bulb over my head—"

"Okay. Okay. I get it." He held up his palms. "Your business. Your timing. Jesus! I didn't realize it was so brutal of me to tour you around and show you a good time—"

"Leaving me behind so I had to walk two miles alone with that dickhead?"

"Whoa. I think you're being a little unfair." He lowered his voice as the campers beside us stopped talking, as if they were listening.

"You're the one who called him names," I hissed. "Which you should because he's no friend of yours."

"People change," he said. "He was really dear to me at one time. Really dear." His voice drifted a little. "But he's just never going to forgive me for Laura."

"Oh! Jesus Christ! Like we need to bring her up again? What the hell, Carey?"

"Seriously? You have no idea that you're being exactly like him? Holding against me something from—"

"No. Don't put words in my mouth. I do not care who you slept with fourteen lifetimes ago."

"That's not what you said this morning," he said.

I could have gone ten lifetimes without being reminded. It slowed everything we'd put in motion. I sat on the picnic bench with the cans of soup in my hands like weights.

"Carey, if there's anybody who's in no position to judge somebody for sleeping with *any*body, it's me. I blurted out some stupid shit that didn't even make sense."

"I'm not sure what you just now said even made sense." He slumped on the bench across from me. "Somebody, whobody, nobody?"

"Shut up," I said. He started to laugh.

I pulled the can opener out of the box and started opening the soup cans.

"So just so we're all done here—because we've got to ride together for like four thousand million more miles home—"

"Arrrgh" I laid my head on the table.

"Okay. We're going to drop Sylvie already. And not say his name ever again. He's a know-it-all bitch," Carey said. "He thinks his shit doesn't stink. He's got a phobia or some kind of sick hang-up. I mean, do you know how much he hassles any gay friend who's ever slept with a woman? It's like this compulsion he has to rub my nose in it."

"Like that's the worst thing you ever did?"

"To hear him tell it, yes. It was."

"Well, that is sick," I said. "Okay. We agree, Sylvie isn't our problem."

"I didn't know we had a problem. You're worried over something that doesn't matter. It's all in the past."

"The past, the past, the past. The past is never really over, is it? What I'm saying is I made it an issue and I didn't mean to. I'm trying to say I'm sorry. Whatever, whoever, Laura? I did *not* want to be her. Ever."

"I know that."

"Well, okay, then. I'm glad you know how ridiculous I feel. But since we're going there—and just making asses of ourselves—what did you kiss me for?"

"What? When we were on the beach?" He shrieked and stifled a laugh. "Did that offend you?"

"No," I said. "I just don't know—didn't know—what to make of it."

"Why do you have to *make* anything of it?" he said.

"I don't know. I just haven't been kissed in a long time, so go easy on a girl. And you've never done that before. And then I hated your friends. Well, not hated hated. Marcus was really great, but—"

"Stop it! Don't say his name! Beelzebub! And stop beating yourself up. We've driven thousands of miles with hardly a fuss. You're making too much of everything. You're just jealous. So what? How many times have I been jealous of men in your life?"

"Seriously?"

"Come on. Yes. I mean, nothing is 'anything' okay?" He made quotation marks in the air for the first time in two weeks, and for some reason it made me want to cry. I started laughing behind my hand. "Just like it's not 'anything' that I kissed you on the beach. And it's not 'anything' that you said it should have been you." He rubbed his hands together and crossed his arms over his chest. "I mean, can you imagine?"

"*Ick*," I said, and let my laugh go full force.

"Well, you don't have to be so mean," he said, grinning. "Now give me that soup and go call Faye or she's going to sic the California Highway Patrol on us."

I liked the relief of driving in and out of the dark redwoods the next day. I wanted to worship the blue patches breaking through the fog. It was sobering, though, to weave through pockets of poverty—fishing towns and dingy logging communities, and Eureka bulging with lumber mills and smokestacks. Carey asked if I could imagine when the forest wasn't fragmented. An unbroken strand from LA to Washington State.

Walking in the peace of Lady Bird Johnson Grove, the longer I stayed under those trees with Carey, the more I thought about how fleeting it all was. Ten years old. Twenty-six years ago. Thirty-six years old. Trees two thousand years old, older, and me just a blip beneath them. They spanned centuries, thousands of days before my life. Thousands of days after I'd be gone. And three hundred feet above us, a whole world in the canopy. There was the sound of eternal dripping, birds calling so high above they were invisible. Little lives that never touched the ground, just swept from tree to tree, vivid living going on that never knew the vivid lives we lived, our vivid, silly memories.

I dreaded coming out into the sun and parking lot and finding that I was grown up and lost and human. I would probably never see trees like this again in my lifetime, watching over us, like we were walking in the mind of God, connected to everything.

Once Carey and I stopped to sight down the length of a fallen redwood, from end to end nearly as long as a football field. It would take more than a century to rot, he said.

"It's actually called a nurse log," Carey said. "See? It's mothering probably an acre of seedlings and moss and ferns. And critters. Sure glad we weren't around when this thing fell."

"Oh, I don't know," I said. "That would be something to witness. Might be worth the risk. Maybe when these things go down, that's what starts all the earthquakes out here. A thing this big could set who knows what in motion." I turned to look him straight in the eye for the first time in ages, it seemed. I said, "This place is like being back at the beginning of everything that ever happened. A person could start all over again right here."

We walked on a ways. I stopped to press my hand against the bark of a tree, and he did the same, placing his broad, tanned hand just beside mine. He stepped ahead then and wrapped his whole body around as much of the nearest redwood as he could, stretching his arms and fingertips and laughing.

In some places the path was so narrow that one of us had to lead through the velvet green dark. I lagged behind Carey, bending to the redwood sorrel, like mutant clover as broad as my palm. The sun in high mist formed rainbows and great shafts of light made halos around the far redwood crowns. In that deep solitude I couldn't even hear the sound of my own footsteps in the thick, spongy layers of red bark that had flaked off the trees. We walked between pink blooms of rhododendron, lanky and high as average trees at home, stretching toward tiny slivers of sunlight. I walked looking up into the faraway green ladders of limbs, dizzy but looking up so that I couldn't see my feet or hands. I could almost believe I'd disappeared altogether. Nothing tethered me except what I could see and hear.

Around a curve, Carey was waiting for me, holding a bloom, as if he were a kid with a gift. But he was looking at the map, not at me.

"Okay. So. There's a couple of campgrounds really close, and other groves to walk in, and other campgrounds up the road—"

"I can see your brain going. I don't need the down and dirty."

He said there was a place that he'd always wanted to go. But the miles down an unpaved road might not be worth it. Even so early in the day, we probably didn't even have a shot at a campsite on the beach.

All he had to say was beach, and I was all in.

It took nearly a half-hour to drive down the steep, winding unpaved road, but it felt longer because of the anticipation. Two guys who were barely college-aged looked out of the station window at the campground entrance. The ocean pounded beyond, and my hope perked up.

There were only two sites left. We scouted, and I held our place while Carey went back to pay. By six that evening, our lives seemed reversed from just twenty-four hours before. No rain. No conflict, no oppressive dark wet. Just the roaring coast again. A place for us just yards from the high tide, tucked back into a little flat haven surrounded by some low evergreen brush. And as soon as we'd staked our claim, we raced each other to the sand.

From there we had our first real view of the namesake for Gold Bluffs Beach, tall yellow cliffs rising as a background to the campground, massive and rugged, their tops tossing in the Pacific wind with trees and brush. We walked one direction until we came to a creek we couldn't cross, then walked far, far, out of sight of the campground, the entrance station, and in the early evening fog ran right into a herd of elk grazing in the shallow dunes. Their alien forms stumped us to silence and awe for a few good minutes, and then Carey plopped down into the sand, dug his toes in and reached up to tug me down beside him. We sat cross-legged with the bluffs behind us and the endless ocean ahead.

"You kissed me first, you know." He looked at me in a dare. "It wasn't nearly as romantic as a kiss at the Pacific, but you did."

"I don't know what the hell you're talking about."

"Don't you remember when we got baptized?" he asked.

"What in the world made you think of that?" I laughed. "Wait. You think that's like a vaccine and maybe we need a booster?"

He laughed. "I think it's a once and for all kind of proposition. I was thinking. I feel a little weird because you were saying that I kissed you. But you started it," he said.

"I still don't know. What are you talking about?"

"You don't remember kissing me?" He grinned that Carey grin at me and picked up a small piece of driftwood and touched me on the head with it, as if I were being knighted. "The night we got baptized. I was scared to death. Absolutely terrified."

And then I did remember, a night I hadn't thought of in so many lifetimes.

"Oh, yeah," was all I could muster at the moment. I looked out at the pounding shore and then to the bluffs, glowing more vibrant each minute the sun shifted.

"We didn't tell our mothers," I offered. "Until the last minute, right before."

We sealed the deal with Jesus when we were eleven. One Sunday evening service when the invitation hymn started, we stepped out of our separate pews, where we sat with our mothers. Carey's mom was in some kind of glory. She had not only gotten my mother to bring us to church, but she'd gotten me, the renegade child, saved. We'd planned it and agreed, and Carey and I met in the aisle without even a signal to walk down to the front of the church, though I doubt we knew what it meant to make such a public gesture, walking down the aisle together in the name of the Father, the Son and the Holy Spirit.

Carey's corduroy pants made zippered sounds in the hush. I wanted to hold his hand. I remember wondering if that was how terrified people felt when they got married. The lights glared and everybody watched, two sinners repenting.

"What in the world do they convince little innocent children they're guilty of?" I laughed. "I guess we decided we felt ashamed enough."

"Or we were scared enough of dying to stand the embarrassment," Carey said. He unfolded his legs and stretched out in the sand with his head in my lap. We watched the sky and the waves and the bluffs altering color and light every shifting moment.

When the preacher put a hand on each of our heads, I wondered if my face was as pale as Carey's. Somehow, I answered yes, that I believed Jesus is the Son of God. Carey's mouth was quivering as he agreed to the same in a whisper. I stood closer, so sorry for him. I could feel his whole body trembling the air between us. Grown ups stood up at the preacher's gesture and sang us out of the sanctuary, with "Just as I Am."

I could hear the singing continue all the way in the basement where Mama hurried me into a baptismal robe. We waited outside the boy's bathroom for

Carey and his mother to come out. In the hall, our mothers pushed us toward the back steps that led up to the baptismal pool. They hurried back to the sanctuary to watch from the front pews.

On the landing, halfway up the stairs, Carey leaned back against the concrete wall, hanging onto the railing. Cold wind seeped under my robe, and I wondered if he was like me, naked except for his underwear.

"We have to get going," I said.

"But only one." His whisper was raw.

"We've come this far together," I argued.

"No. I mean, one of us has to go in first. He can't dunk us at the same time." Tears shimmered in his eyes, and he turned away ashamed.

There on that musty church staircase, under cold fluorescent glare, I leaned up and kissed him. My lips on his lips, the softest human touch. Maybe it was the simplest gift I ever gave anybody, just stepping forward and claiming without a word that I would sacrifice for him, that I would be his truest, purest friend. He understood perfectly.

We climbed the steps together to the baptismal font where the preacher stood waist deep in the water in his black robe, floating like a bloated frog.

When he reached for Carey, I stepped forward first into the tepid water. I watched Carey's eyes as the preacher talked, his heavy hands on my shoulders and head. I made my eyes say to Carey, *this isn't so bad*. I smiled. Then the preacher clamped a handkerchief over my nose and mouth and shoved me back. I had a fleeting thought that he might not let me up, and there was nothing I could do. For one hysterical second, I pushed back, and then I remembered that Carey was standing right there. He wouldn't let anything bad happen to me.

"What made you think about that night we got baptized?" I asked again. Suddenly he jumped up and dusted sand off his back and did a cartwheel. I jumped up and tried one myself and fell on my ass. He put his left foot on a dark rock and reached for my hand and pulled me over until I was touching a driftwood log.

"See, it's a game of Gold Bluff Twister," he said, lunging to put his other foot on a smooth stone. "Remember that, too?"

"I'm serious," I said.

He pulled away from our uncomfortable tangle. "I was just wondering," he said, "if you remember things the same way I do."

"I remember worrying that robe was going to fall off me and I'd be standing up there bare-ass naked except for my panties."

"Did you really think that, too?" He laughed. "God, all those people. I felt so stupid taking a bath in front of everybody. I was terrified.

"But you went first," he said. "You were so sweet to go ahead and show me it was okay. I mean, that was sweeter than the kiss on the stairwell."

217

I hadn't known until that second how hard I was wishing he would remember everything. I had the urge to put my hand to his cheek, lean up again and close the distance. His lips would be soft as a child's. His eyelashes fluttering against my cheek.

"You looked at me dripping wet, like 'see this isn't so hard.' I remember—"

He said the words *I remember, I remember* as he talked, like a mantra. Whatever happened in the bedrock of our lives, we could hold forever to that—*I remember, I remember*, fine as a web spun new over and over between us.

FIRE AND ICE

Not long after we'd settled in, blasts out of the surf shocked us upright. For a second, I worried about a tsunami. But the rangers hadn't warned about deafening volleys.

"Somebody's shooting fireworks." Carey turned on the camp light before I could stop him.

I lurched for the light and shut it off. "It's a gun."

"Don't be silly." He unzipped the tent and looked up into the sky. A rapid-fire of shots pushed him back. "I think you're right," he whispered.

I motioned for him to lie down. I re-zipped the tent. We were both breathing hard. "It's those dumb asses," I said.

Two truckloads of what looked to be a huge family had taken three campsites side-by-side. They'd set up speakers on the hood of one of the trucks and cranked mariachi music. Carey said I was racist to call them yahoos, but when they lit their campfire, he agreed idiots come in every color, with every accent. They burned big oily, hacked-up telephone poles and railroad ties soaked in creosote. Downwind from them, we choked on black smoke. A ranger finally made them shut off their music at ten.

"Those poor kids with them," Carey whispered.

"You don't get to pick your family," I said. "Or your bully."

We talked about what to do, whether to get in the Jeep and be ready to run. Or just hunker down. Every time the gun fired I sensed the whole campground wondering who'd save us if somebody really had gone around the bend. I thought about Daddy's nickel-plated pistol, always loaded. Who knows what to hate more, feeling helpless or feeling a little less helpless?

The gunplay never came with any shouts or screams, and only lasted a half-hour or so, ranging up and down the beach, never in the campground itself. We must have dozed. I sat up to hear a car easing along the gravel road. Blinding red and blue lights cycled through the tent.

"It's the law," Carey said. He clutched the sleeping bag at his throat, like somebody's grandma in a western.

"Okay, hide the loot," I said. Then we couldn't stop laughing, until we were shaking the whole tent. We shushed each other, trying to hear what various voices were demanding and denying by turns. Then we'd fall apart again, with hilarity and relief.

The sheriff had somehow known which site to check because in the morning one of the trucks was gone and all the men. The women and kids were eating a silent breakfast around a dead fire ring.

"I mean, it really was a gun?" Carey asked, as he started coffee over our fire.

"It's sweet you still want to believe in Tinkerbell."

"That sounds vaguely insulting." He laughed. "I mean, I'm not on high alert for gunfire, I guess."

"We make a good team," I said. "I'm not on high alert for fireworks. My first thought is *never* going to be, 'Oh, goody! What are we celebrating?'"

"It doesn't really matter." Carey sobered. "We were all at the mercy of a prick."

Near the campground, we hiked along a creek that flowed right into the Pacific, wading in it, through the murky depths of Fern Canyon, where twenty- and thirty-foot-high walls dripped dense with ferns. We walked inside emerald light, chilly in the fog. Neither of us said much, from lack of sleep and the absorbing quiet.

Back at the bathhouses we had cold-water wakeups and more coffee before facing the road. I waited at the Jeep while Carey gave his mom a call. And I waited. And I waited as sleepiness washed over me in the warm morning light in the Jeep.

I was nearly napping when he opened and shut the hatch. He handed me a granola bar when he got in the driver's seat. He started the car but stayed in park.

He started munching while he talked. "I'll drive you up and wait while you call your mom. But just so you know, the phone at the kiosk doesn't have good reception."

"Ugh. Carey, you hassle me every morning! I'll call her later."

He sighed and chewed. "Look, you're not allowed to get hysterical."

"Oh, shit. What?" I grabbed his hand to keep him from letting off the emergency brake.

"Calm down. I do not need *three* hysterical women on my ass. Two is enough." He pushed my hand away and we sat idling. "So, I didn't want to have to twist your arm. But your mother called my mother and sicced her on me. On your behalf, I just had a couple of long-distance come-to-Jesus meetings." He cupped his hands around his mouth and bull-horned at me: "For love of all that's holy, call Faye!"

"I cannot believe this," I said. "Mama got your mother to call you to tell me to call home?"

"No. My mother got a call from your mother that I, myself, was to call Faye *right then*. I thought something was wrong."

"You talked to my mother just now?"

He nodded. "And as I said, nobody's hurt, if that's what you're thinking." Inside my chest I flickered from fear to frustration to embarrassment.

"What the hell's she got her panties in a wad about?"

"Don't kill the messenger." He held his hands up. "Just call Faye."

"No. Just tell me," I said. My hands clenched. My feet, I realized, were pressed against the floorboard, a passenger in a car that wasn't moving, as if I couldn't brake hard enough.

He sighed and put his forehead on the steering wheel, steeling himself. "She should be the one to tell you." He looked at me. "You got a call about your land."

"A what?" It took me a second to understand. "Okay. So what? When?"

"Last week. That's how long since you called home. You're being a very bad daughter." He handed me his granola wrapper to put into the car trash bag, put the Jeep in gear and backed into the camp road. The bluffs rising above the road were less brilliant in the morning. But the Pacific was cobalt blue, an electric color. We had the day ahead of us up the Oregon Coast, two days, maybe three, skirting the continent as far west as land allowed. I wanted to follow the tide out, out, out, farther inch by inch, away from turning east, edging still away from home.

"Really? You know what's happening in my life before I do?"

"Not my fault. I can't even believe you're serious about selling your land, if I can just say. You are so wrong. I'm with Faye on this."

He pulled into a little space of worn grass near the ranger check-in station. "Carey. I have to think about this. I really do. I can't call her right now."

"Even though she's sitting by the phone waiting?" He shook his head. But he knows me. He eased out of the space and onto the road out of the campground.

I could take his disappointment better than Mama's lecture about responsibility. Dread knocked the breath out of me. The first choice I'd had to make since we left Mama standing at the trailer door.

"I mean," Carey started up again. "A man is hounding her about how much she wants for twelve acres? That she gave you? But she's left holding the bag? A painful bag for her, obviously. More painful than it is for you, Glenna. When all she wants is for you to have your family land? A gift of land, like serious real estate? *Real* estate, Glenna. Do you know how many people—? No. I'm done. I don't want to talk about it anymore."

"You—"

He held up his hand. "I said, I'm done. I might say something *you* will regret. Look for a phone while I drive. Or don't. It is literally your call."

A deluge north of Crescent City and weather reports from rangers made it obvious we ought to turn inland. The coast was socked in. Good-bye Oregon coast plans. Carey was morose enough, but I felt doomed by the surrender. We headed east and south to pick up the nearest highway north to the interstate. I told Carey it felt like we were headed home. An aching, panicked tired sank in again when he pointed out we were.

We had passed the halfway point in our trip. What I'd pretended might be an endless escape dwindled, finite. And responsibility for Mama's twelve acres had come calling. I had a serious choice to make, not just whether to eat tuna or ham, which campsite to choose, whether Carey was driving or me. The calamity I would have to face. Scant days and I'd be back in Tennessee to pick up the pieces of my life.

Right back where I'd started.

Into Oregon, through Grant's Pass, the drizzly forest closed around us, familiar like East Tennessee woods. A sense of peace mingled with my dread. Then out of the dark woods and rain, I-5 was a pure relief of speed. No access to a pay phone anywhere, as long as we didn't have to exit to pee. The interstate lay like a cool, blue vein on the map, a straight shot north.

I napped wakefully after our restless night of gunfire. It seemed, though, that Carey never stopped talking about the Oregon Trail and the settlers' Oregon Fever to get to the promised land. Eight months of hard-driving and accidents and cholera and frostbite and heatstroke. And the paradox of Oregon, the dream of the last wild place, settled by people who voted to have no slaves. But also no free Blacks. Oregon, a progressive state founded by white supremacists.

Whoever they were, they were pioneers. They did not look back. I envied that they knew they would never return to any place from their past. They reset the course of their lives. The grace of the future without any reckoning or regrets. In my rocking sleep our prairie schooner forded rivers, rolled on dusty tracks in a line of wagons strung ridge to ridge. We sailed with grinding gears up mountainsides and down. But home flickered its familiar images in the sun through branches. We drove out of the cold rain into brightness, closer and closer to facing up.

Carey reached over to slip off my sunglasses just in time for the last hour on the road. The brilliant evening lit up mountain valleys like those I'd lived in my whole life, spiky evergreens above glades of sugar maples and hickory and oak. Hardwoods. How long since we'd seen hardwoods? And fields of broom sedge and white clover and new corn in the fields and cows and the odor of grass and ozone. I was homesick from being on the road so long. Yet at the very same time I felt sick to know that I was *required* to go home, where I'd trade in the life of a pretend nomad for real, actual homelessness. Love and hate. Rock and a hard place. The big continental dead-end.

Of course, after my napping day on the interstate, once we settled into an econo-motel in Eugene, I couldn't sleep a wink. We nibbled out of the cooler and our scrambled food box full of stale chips and crackers and moldy bread. I said we should find a grocery, but Carey turned out his lamp and curled toward the wall.

"It's still early," I coaxed.

He had been kind enough not to point out the phone on the nightstand. He'd said his say-so and then truly left me with my conscience. I should call Mama. I sat on the other bed cross-legged toward him, as if he were my campfire. He grunted and pulled the covers around him.

"I drove all day," he said. The clock read 9:47. Nearly one a.m. at home. Mama would freak if I called so late. I turned the TV on mute and the whole journey pivoted.

I had stood in the Pacific. We'd breathed in air from other mountains. I'd seen the fire-bitten desert. We'd poured across the prairie. I had walked on top of a volcano. But now the inevitability of heading *home*, which needed a new definition in every dictionary. All that was mine in Tennessee was an eight-year-old car and twelve acres of abandoned, raggedy woods on Genesis Road, posted with a FOR SALE sign in bright orange, the biggest one I could find. And a mother who was furious with me.

And more furious every day. I was coming to a point of no return, yet I had to return. The afternoon I'd driven the stake, the fact of that sign kept my courage up, waiting for Mama to get home from her shop. Before she set down her pocketbook, I handed her the deed and a copy of the ad I'd taken out in the *Newport Plain Talk*.

Twelve+/- acres, woodland, at the foot of English Mountain, Cosby. Price negotiable. Sale by owner. Call Faye Daniels, Newport. 622-0013

"Glenna, what've you gone and done?" She held the paper between us like a bad report card. After I'd cut my hair, I wasn't sure I could still surprise her.

"That ad'll run eight weeks, while I'm gone with Carey and then some, probably. You'd better think of an asking price," I said. "It ought to sell maybe before I even get back, I hope. And I posted a for sale sign."

"Why in the world—?" She looked at me. "Wait. You went to Genesis Road? By yourself?"

My grief sizzled, and I had no mercy within that dark blame. "Did you want to make a mother-daughter day of it? Maybe rent a bulldozer and have a garden party?"

"You're awful hateful for somebody that says she don't give a shit."

"You're right." I settled down. "You're right, Mama." It was done, the sign up. "You see a golden egg where I see a dead duck. Why waste another breath?"

We never mentioned the land after that, not even during the calls I'd made from the road, most of which were quick. And lots of times I called when I knew she was at work so I could leave a message.

That's exactly what I did the next morning while Carey went to get ice to repack the cooler. Eight-thirty Pacific Time, 11:30 at home. She'd be at work, I was sure.

My icy stubbornness came blunt force against a burning urge to hear her voice, to make her understand. What would I say? Sell, no matter what the cost? Or never, ever dare sell that land? No matter what the cost.

I held my breath with every ring, and then left a cheery message that we were fine, headed to Washington.

"Say hey to Dunn. And Granny. I'll call again soon, Mama. Oh, we're mostly camping, and some campgrounds don't have a payphone." I stretched the truth. And that half-lie gave me the nerve I needed. "I know about the land, the offer. Carey told me," I said. "You really can do whatever you want."

When Carey came back and we loaded up the Jeep, he didn't ask how it had gone on the phone. He'd found a nearby grocery where we could restock for heading back east. Three thousand miles back. Like getting caught up a ladder and not wanting to back down.

I thought about watching with Mama the day Neil Armstrong was walking there. She had worried how those astronauts would ever get back to Earth. Getting somewhere is only half the trip. And once I'd gone spelunking in college. Way in the innards of that cave, we turned off our headlamps. Which way was out?

One of Mama's sayings came to me. *Caught between the Devil and the deep blue sea.*

Maybe because we'd stayed near Eugene's university district, a default memory of my burned house on Laurel Avenue near UT revived. Details of the renovation— its wood fixtures, charming nooks, even its odors—kindled up, like missing a lover's body.

Because I did love that amazing house. Carey wouldn't have been able to square that homebody woman I was then with the one denying her mother's inheritance. He assumed I didn't care about roots. But after losing the baby, and Daddy dying, and my house going up in flames, the hand-me-down of Mama's land seemed just another devastating loss-in-waiting. I couldn't bear to risk loving anything, any place, that much ever again. Or anyone.

My favorite times in the Laurel Avenue house, if I'm honest, were hours Kevin was at work or riding his bike, times I was alone, the first place since the farm that was truly home. That house soaked into my system, imprinted in me, if for no other reason besides the hundreds—maybe thousands—of sweaty hours I poured into it. I've never been so devoted to a place, spaces, the tiniest moments lived. Kevin helped with the painting, and he tore out rotted windowsills in the third-floor attic. But mostly he facelifted the outside. It was me who made the inside home. I helped the workmen sand floors and seal the oak back to a sheen. I laid tile in the bathroom and kitchen. It took weeks to strip paint off the banisters and refinish their grooves and bevels and newel posts.

But the thing I couldn't live with was the wallpaper, dizzy avocado stripes in the kitchen to match the fridge and stove we replaced. Like an archaeologist, I found four layers in the living room: a lavender print, yawning blue daisies, spiraling green ivy, and right against the plaster, a pale rose with delicate ivory flowers. When that base layer crumbled under my fingertips, I cringed. Some woman a hundred years before, when our renovation project was brand new, had loved that wallpaper. In her parlor, she'd rested from cooking over a wood stove and doing Monday wash. Or maybe she'd rested while a servant filled her every command. Either way, she'd loved that calming dusty rose. I felt ruthless ripping it down.

I was a woman like her, a hundred years later, housekeeping the best I knew how at the end of another century. I bought gallons of putty and caulk to fill in cracks. I painted the plaster walls in the parlor pale dove brown and the crown molding cream. But it didn't seem to be enough. To honor some spirit of homemaking, I searched book after book of wallpaper patterns until I found a nearly identical rose, with tiny ivory buds. And even though it cost a fortune, I bought some to line kitchen drawers and the pantry and closet shelves. Every time I put away a plate or a sack of cornmeal, I had a reminder that the place Kevin and I loved had been a haven for some other woman, and after her other women. For the first time since the farm, I could mark my belonging, a continuity I was part of.

Kevin didn't completely understand my drive to honor the longevity and life of the place, but he didn't mind. I replaced the busted pedestal sink in the downstairs bath not with a new, modern sink, but with a replica, as exact as I could find. I replaced dying forsythia and neglected peonies and crepe myrtles. Kevin wanted to cut all of it down, but I learned how to prune the lilac from gardening books. I had a tree man come and inspect the old dogwoods. I was determined to put down roots and maintain them.

I tracked down lamps to fit the era the house was built. I wondered what those other women would have thought if they'd come to visit. As if the legacy they'd lived there might help me mother a house. And I believed then, without a single breath of doubt, that like those other women—who were surely mothers—I was feathering a nest for children Kevin and I would eventually diaper and hold and bathe and draw with and do math homework with and have holiday dinners with, right there. That was why. That baby I planned on was the reason for all I did.

In Oregon, though, in the middle of awful sleeplessness, it seemed like I'd only been playing house, something a stupid kid would do. All of it a fleeting, hopeless domestic defiance of the damaged family I'd grown up in. Foolish full denial that—same as every other place I'd lived—I was just passing through. The fire cinched it.

The fire made clear to me that time will change every place. A home can't ever really be a home if you hold it accountable to freezing the past. A place can't anchor time. You're damned if you move into an old habit somebody else abandoned.

It's better to inhabit lightly. A house is just walls and a roof. A place doesn't really manifest good will or anything sacred or happiness or stability. Just the opposite. Wood and mortar are as fleeting as flesh and blood. I learned my lessons about the flimsiness of paint and wallpaper, just as bound to betray as a man or hopes for a child. Loving a place is nothing but a different kind of dangerous, lopsided marriage.

After the ponderous California coast, the Oregon interstate was a slingshot vortex. Carey sped through the Willamette Valley, past glades of tulips and fruit tree groves and exits for bountiful places people settle in forever—Springfield, Sweet Home, and Mount Angel. Aurora. Lean blue mountains resembled a jacked-up version of East Tennessee. Before noon, we were on the outskirts of Portland, half-an-hour from the Washington state line. At a rest area picnic table, we sipped coffee and surveyed our progress and our options and took the pulse of our stamina.

"Sensory overload," Carey said. "It's just too much."

"I feel the opposite in a way, like we missed something."

"Nah. Just the entirety of Oregon." He laughed. "We seriously could stop in Portland, City of Bridges. City that reads the most books per capita in the country. Or we could head toward Mount Hood. Like two hours away? Tallest peak in Oregon. Right down the Columbia River Gorge?"

He meant east. I scanned the map on our picnic table. East, anything east looked ominous. Directly east. Directly toward Tennessee.

"And miss Washington?"

"But if we see Washington, we miss Oregon," he prompted. "The whole route shows you why they call this the Cascades. Maybe America's best waterfalls."

"You've been already, so you don't need to go again."

"Well, but I've been lots of places we've seen. A place is different every time you see it."

I looked up and smiled. "That's what I've been trying to tell you. And Mama." Neither of us said anything. He was trying to let me be. "Twenty hours in Oregon is enough. How many times have you repeated what Stan said, 'You have to leave something for the next trip!'"

"Jesus. You're quoting Stan." He put his hand on my forehead.

We laughed and kept laughing in silly spurts. In between, Carey told me Lewis and Clark stories. The Columbia River was their big turning point, the legendary channel into the Pacific Ocean, where they knew—like me—that they were halfway through their journey. Now for the return. Which they couldn't just launch back right away. They'd run out of salt. I mean, they had to boil and boil and boil ocean water for months and repack and gear up.

Carey said he wished they'd stayed forever at the Pacific with Sacajawea, joined a native nation. Or he wished they'd died.

"You wish Lewis and Clark had died?"

"They're a love-hate thing with me," he said. "If they'd just disappeared, a long-lost mystery, this nation would be entirely different. How long until someone else would have gone scouting? Postponing until the Indians got their act together.

"We talk about reparations for the descendants of slaves," he said. "What reparations can we make to the Native Americans? We'd have to give them back the whole country. Every acre."

He pointed up the Columbia when we were crossing the I-5 bridge into Washington, funneling a blur of logging trucks and RVs, cars with bikes and kayaks on top. Halfway across the wide stretch of the Gorge, Carey slowed as much as he dared. We craned our necks to see, Mount Hood's volcanic cone guarding the eastern horizon.

But a glimpse of the pure placid snow-white of that volcano didn't prepare me for Mount St. Helens. Devastation started mildest at the furthest reaches when we turned onto the dead-end fifty-mile park road. The closer we drove, more and more cluttered carnage of downed trees radiated out from the blast, nearly twenty years after the eruption. Trunks like driftwood still littered the Toutle River's banks in tangled masses. Under a ceiling of high white clouds, hills greened with seedlings and grasses. Around every curve, wide open meadows where the land had been stripped of big timber. Elk ranged on a couple of peaks, an open prairie species taking over where forests used to dominate. Deep in the valley, at the end, the gray river glistened in dead mud. Nothing was growing yet on those barren flats.

The mountain looked harmless and shy, the top veiled behind a cloud. From the visitor center at Cold Water Ridge, we could see only the blue base of the dome. We stalled for the weather to clear and watched a half-hour video about the 1980 eruption, the famous stop-action footage of the cubic mile of ashy earth blown into a black cumulus, glaciers melted in an instant to torrential mud heaved into an ugly flood, churning with pieces of buildings and naked logs and roots.

When we got to the Johnston Observatory, for the closest view of the blast-ed north face, the clouds cleared. We could see right into the crater's crooked circumference, like a dark, rotted molar. Flumes of straggling mist below the edge were warnings of another eventual eruption. A new dome was forming inside the crater the old dome left behind. Between the mountain and us lay the heart of the blast zone, lifeless pumice plains.

"I remember from when we were in school." I turned to Carey at the outdoor railing. "I didn't remember that sixty-two people died, though."

"Some because they were ignorant," Carey said. He lifted his face to the cool wind, which seemed to come right off the volcano.

"Or stubborn. Not a bad way to go, maybe. Like that old guy, Harry Truman. He knew he was making a life-or-death choice. But he'd lived here nearly his whole life. He didn't want to survive into the apocalypse."

"Well, not an apocalypse," Carey said. "A natural disaster, sure."

"No. His personal apocalypse. Two-hundred-thirty square miles plowed over. He didn't want to be alive to see the place he loved obliterated. Everything he'd known is gone. That lake—Spirit Lake—where he lived, is mostly buried."

"But it's not like the place just vanished."

I laughed. "Carey it's exactly that. Vanished."

"You're not looking. There's life all over the place. Fish and animals, the elk." As we walked back to the car he couldn't stop pointing out wildflowers and new trees, green stubble interlaced with the white flesh of dead trees.

"The elk shouldn't even be here, you said yourself. Plus, he knew he'd never live long enough to see it recover at all. He didn't want to see it like this. This is all new. And even fifty, a hundred, two-hundred years from now, it'll never again be the place he loved. He knew the place he loved would never exist again after an eruption."

Carey was quiet for a minute, and then he stopped walking. "I didn't mean to be so bossy," he said. I turned to him.

"Oh, don't coddle me. It's okay you've been bugging me about Mama's land. It helps me think. I'm not Harry Truman, but that land of Mama's is a different place on the planet now. And, hell, I'm not the same either. I was ten. A ten-year-old kid, Carey, when we left that land. You can't go home, right?"

What had I expected to find when I went to that dead-end? Mama's daffodils still blooming to greet me? Her clothesline full of clothes flapping a big old welcome? My sunlit, open memory was romantic. I hadn't expected a foreign place, obliterated, grown over with maples and dogwoods and kudzu. A wild, lost place.

I was a trespasser there.

"I'll stop preaching," Carey said. "But one last thing. With what you've been through, I wish you wouldn't make a rash decision. Not from way out here."

"I don't see how it's rash. For twenty-five years that land was already lost to me. Like if you thought somebody was dead for a quarter of a century. You've done all your grieving. You've remarried and moved on. And then you find out, that person is alive after all. And maybe they're old and decrepit and you have to wipe their ass."

"But it's not like that, really," he said.

"Carey, I couldn't even take care of you when you had a little food poisoning! How am I going to nurse twelve acres into shape? It would take a maternal genius."

"But you don't have to touch it. Just don't sell. It's *yours*. You told me your great-grandfather bought that farm after he got booted off land to make the national park. That's family history. But the actual land is, well, it's land, Glenna. An actual place. It symbolizes your roots. Appalachian roots." He started the Jeep and we looked out through the windshield at a hawk harrying some birds above a big stretch of blown-open meadow.

"I don't need a symbol for my roots. And there's a creek, if you want history, that runs through the Cosby part of the park, named after that side of my family. Dunn Creek. But I don't have to own it to know where it is, where it goes."

"There's a creek in the Smokies with your family name?" He nodded. "Pretty impressive."

"Oh, what's impressive? White men get shit named after them all the time. Who named these mountains all these white names? Mount Hood, Mount St. Helens, Mount Whitney? They had Indian names before. They'll have some other names way in the future."

He got excited and started rattling off details about Tahoma, the Indian name for Mount Rainier, what's lost to others who used to abide.

Did he understand? I needed to hold the fullness of my story to myself. I didn't tell him—couldn't really say—what it was like as a kid to wade in that creek that has my great-granddaddy's name, Granny Pearl's granddaddy, Eustus

Dunn, who was dead even before Mama was born. A man my brother is named for. I've risked drinking untreated water out of Dunn Creek, raw and cold with a zest of metal, like blood would taste without the salt. I've stood by that rushing water and walked trails nearby, knowing I was retracing footsteps of people I came from, who led hard, hard lives, who could not have imagined their descendants would be removed and live an outside life, a city life, a mobile life.

I don't have to visit a patch of ground, and I certainly don't have to own it, to know what's been lost to my whole family. Lifetimes. The Lewises and the Clarks take and take, Carey was right. Or maybe it's no one else's fault, not white male supremacy or the landed gentry or the government or the patriarchy. Maybe my own genetic code had kept me from living on land that's rightfully mine. Holding what belongs to us in my family has always been like trying to hold creek water in our cupped hands.

The stories go that for all his bitterness, my great-granddaddy Dunn was most heartbroken to find out once he and his wife and kids were resettled, none of them would be allowed burial in the family plot. There were several family cemeteries like ours left intact after the Great Smoky Mountains National Park was established. But after removal, nobody else had access to be buried. I've heard Granny Pearl say many times that Eustus Dunn died of a broken heart. He was an old man when she was born. Her grandmother Hester was much younger, and she married again after his death. He's buried alone somewhere on the farm on Genesis Road that came down through my great-grandmother Hester to Granny, and then through her to Mama. And now to me.

When I was a kid, we used to visit his gravestone, way up behind the barn, with a metal marker of some kind, flush with the ground, smaller than a sheet of paper. It's surely lost forever now. Hester is easy to find, buried with her second husband, Granny Pearl's stepfather, in the big Methodist cemetery in Newport. But if I tiptoed over every centimeter of that twelve acres, I might not run across my great-grandfather's grave. Probably a sunken-in plot covered up in wild grape and kudzu and mayapple. He's there forever somewhere, more alone than anybody deserves.

The entire rest of his family, his mother's people and his parents and some of his sisters and brothers who died as infants, are buried in a little cemetery just off the trail past the campground in the Cosby section of the national park. But Eustus Dunn didn't have the peace of knowing he could rest beside his mother and daddy and kin. I've been there so many times, whenever I've hiked that trail, stooping to look at the broken-off, moss-covered stones that mark the people who are the reason I live and breathe.

Granny Pearl swears it's true that two of her older brothers carried their daddy, Eustus Dunn, to that cemetery the last two springs he was alive. Old-timey churches in the mountains—and other places, I guess—have "Decoration Day" every spring, to go and clean their ancestors' graves and even plant flowers. He knew which stones marked his parents' graves, though now they're obliterated. He was feeble and bedridden from a stroke, but he had his mind, and when he asked to go, there was no money for a wheelchair, even if one had been able to make it up the steep trail to the graveyard. His two sons took turns carrying him on their backs part of the time, until they got tired. Then they would heft him in their arms like a baby. Two miles in, two miles out.

Tourists find their way there plenty of days, thousands of tourists over the years. The place has become a spot on the historic list for the Smokies. People with license plates from Michigan and Illinois, Texas and Ontario, people from everywhere on any given day stop and look at my ancestors' graves. All but two sun-bleached headstones are broken and unmarked, lines of illegible blue lichen replacing the names.

But even if they could read the names, none of them know the story of the two sons, grown men, who hauled their grieving daddy all that way and back just so he could cry and cry over bones that no longer held up the bodies he had loved, bones covered by galax and moss and mushrooms and bloodroot and birdsfoot violets, where saplings will grow into trees which will take over someday, and nobody will remember there were ever graves there at all.

Carey and I stopped on our way out of Mount St. Helens at Coldwater Lake, the crystal blue waters which started forming in that space on March 18, 1980. Strange new life born out of the devastation. Now it's a beautiful oasis in the gray landscape. Birds called from reeds at the edge as we walked around the boardwalk.

Carey pointed at the blown-out top of the volcano again. Through the clouds the gaping hole in the mountain looked fragile, a broken eggshell some giant creature had pecked its way out of. "I don't know," Carey said. "I mean, there's a paradoxical beauty here. Maybe in some ways more beautiful than before."

"What's gone is gone."

"There's something amazing in its place, though." He looked at me, pushing his sunglasses up onto his head, staring at me with those earnest eyes. "Just call your mother. Tell her to tell any caller you're thinking it through, until you get home. That simple. It won't hurt you to wait."

"Carey—"

"Tell me. What? Tell me what that would hurt."

"The place is a myth."

"It's not everybody who can own a myth, though." Carey smiled. His look shifted and he pointed to the ridge behind me. A herd of elk grazed there on the new growth between rotting dead fall. I knew he wanted me to see life that wouldn't have been there if the damage hadn't been catastrophic. And I did see. But down the steep rise, among the new green of tiny firs, the bleached stumps of blasted trees looked for all the world to me like gravestones.

Somehow, the damaged world of Mount St. Helens hit me even more keenly driving through the forested foothills around Mount Rainier. All of that same kind of beautiful, ancient vivid green had been there then, too, before the blast. I tried to imagine the towns along the Cowlitz River, Morton and Mossyrock and Randle, covered over in mud flows and ash if Mount Rainier ever blew.

I regretted saying it aloud because Carey hyped up the nightmare scenario. "Rainier, man, right now there are millions of people in the possible blast zones, not just the pyroclastic flow. Huge populations in Seattle and Tacoma, but little communities that would be done in. There's this town Orting that sits where they know major lahars—the mud flows—were bad before, thousands of years ago. Because Rainier is a giant compared to any other volcano, as far as ice cover goes—two dozen really massive glaciers, huge snowfalls, with like hundreds of inches every winter. I mean, you'd have raging floods of melted mountainsides."

We camped right about dusk in Ohanapecosh, a low-elevation section of Rainier, and when night fell, the woods were so deep I couldn't distinguish tree silhouettes unless I looked straight up into the clouded night sky. The dark was pure and silent, and I kept trying to listen for a volcanic roar beyond the creek beside us. I slept ready to run for higher ground in case of rumbling. That's what the park brochures advised, in clear, scary print.

The next morning on the way up the mountain, we walked in a grove of "patriarch" trees, thousand-year-old western hemlock, red cedar, Douglas fir. Untouched for a thousand years in a volatile world. Feathery green wavered on black limbs like the millions seared away at Mount St. Helens in just seconds. So far, we'd seen nothing of Rainier's peak, just miles and miles of evergreen with bursts of open sky. As we rode curves after our hike, I matched Carey's leaning-up squint-for-squint through the windshield, hoping low-scudding clouds would clear off the mountain.

I looked at the photo on the park brochure of the mountain dome lit sunset pink, harmless as a scoop of strawberry ice cream at the end of the day. But when we got to Steven's Canyon, climbing up and up the road carved into talus steeps, it came to me that we were already on the mountain, so vast that I'd been looking for only the most extreme measure of it. Like a flea, I was looking for the doggiest part, when all along there I'd been, riding that dog's hide already.

We stopped for a picnic at a silver lake, so beautiful I didn't notice the clouds opening up. Carey grabbed my arm. In fewer than ten seconds, the misted specter of Rainier's volcanic dome appeared and then vanished again. And I understood only maybe three seconds of the whole vision. It didn't seem possible that a mountain could stand that high, and on my own I don't think I would have recognized its white bulk as mountain, more of an optical shimmer of cloud behind cloud, an ice cumulus. A monster.

At a place called Paradise, we reached the tree line, which was also a snow line. A surprise of high drifts was plowed back from the parking lot of the alpine lodge, the end of far white imperceptible from the start of the glaciers rolling up into the clouds which obscured the mountain still.

The second the Jeep stopped, I jumped out with a whoop and dug my hands into icy, dingy snow. Carey opened the back of the Jeep and after digging for just a few seconds tossed me my down coat and gloves. He pulled his on as he ran past me up onto the packed ridge of snow and pelted me with snowballs. We rushed each other, plowing into a low swell of snow, smashing the cleanest snow we could find into each other's clothes and hair.

"Shit, I'm soaking wet now." I laughed until I couldn't catch my breath. He pulled me to my feet.

"Would you like a nice, hot shower?" He looked up at the clouds, but he had a shit-eating grin on his face. "No problem because—drum roll—I booked a room for us in the lodge." He took off ahead of me toward the Jeep.

"You lie!" I shouted and chased him. He was pulling our suitcases out of the back by the time I reached him. "Just what made you think it'd be okay with me if we stayed here?" I feigned a pout.

He counted off reasons on his fingers. "One, we're sick of being in the car. Two, we're sick of camping. But mainly because—" he raised an arm and gave his best game-show host stance—"Baby, we are in *Paradise!*"

Truly, the lodge was heaven. Our room was rustic and cozy, but to us it was heaven. I spread out socks and panties to dry that I'd washed in the sink and stood in steaming water and brushed my teeth and ran a comb through my growing mop of hair. Carey pulled me to the window when I was finished and showed me that we had a slant-wise view of the peak, or where it would be if we could see it, hidden by darker clouds than before.

The long post-and-beam lobby was bookended by roaring fireplaces. In late afternoon people sprawled in club chairs and on the carpets, reading and writing postcards, watching their kids play checkers before dinner. It might have been 1920. It might have been the future. Carey wrote a postcard to his mom and handed me an extra one to write Mama. I did it to get him off my back, and because I really was starting to feel guilty. I thought I might call her right then, a time she'd be home. But I still couldn't bring myself to actually do it.

After a supper of trout and pinot grigio, when we were feeling right civilized, Carey and I sipped more wine and watched through the grand lobby windows as the snow went gray. Every little while we'd step out the main doors and look up, shrug and come back inside. Mist unraveled down the mountain as families and mountaineers moved in and out with their gear. A bright red fox snapped past the window into the trees like a spark. The buzz through the long room was that Rainier might show its face for the first time in two weeks.

By sunset, word spread that the Tatoosh Range to the south had cleared. Carey and I pulled our coats back on for the tenth time and joined a small group in the cold dusk. The lowest clouds really had lifted, and the snowy spires washed orange, then lilac against the sky dusted with stars. Down in the firs, birds whistled to one another.

"Sounds like they know something we don't," I said. "And the stars are clear. I can't believe I'm standing here freezing, waiting for a mountain to show up. Like waiting on a man."

Carey spooned up against me, holding on as if the slow wind might blow us down the valley. Everyone else drifted back into the lodge, and there was not a soul to hear the birds except us. Behind us Mount Rainier still hid in the stalled clouds.

I slept lightly in my twin bed, making vigils at our window in case the mountain came clear. At midnight, I woke to altered light in our room. An almost full moon burnished the sky, shimmering through the waning sheer of cloud. The mountain's vast, inevitable glow, a ferocious immensity, pressed up into the sky, like an echo of the moon's glow.

When I tugged the covers off Carey in his bed, he grumbled, but he hurried to the window. He couldn't have been fully awake when he pulled his coat on over his pajamas. We both jammed our bare feet into our boots and ran down the hall, through the lobby doors and out into the cold. The sky gave birth to the mountain as we watched, the frozen light increasing. We stood looking up until our necks hurt. The few people still awake and aware like us went back in, but we waited until the last strand of cloud was gone, not even the tiniest wisp washing over the rounded crest. The whole mountain, forged by heat and sealed by cold, outshone the moon, thundering white.

The next morning, we feasted on French toast and pancakes and hash browns and eggs over easy and bacon. And thin coffee, but we drank loads. We spruced up for our two days and two nights in Seattle—the real true jumping-off place, the end of the line, the dead-end. The farthest north and west we would go. A little trill in me set ticking by the luck of seeing the mountain, the enormous power beneath our feet in that volcanic potential. We reorganized and packed up our dry laundry and all the mess we couldn't believe we made in just one night. We loaded the car just at checkout time and walked around sinking deeper into the snow than we had the day before.

Every time we looked up from our little walk in the snow, I could not fathom the presence of the mountain, could not hold the vastness of the ridges and glacial patterns in my imagination. And then as we drove away, down to the road that would take us to Seattle, I would look over my shoulder, or up through the windshield, or even in the rearview mirror, and the mammoth alien hulk of it surprised me every time. Rainier seemed, in the clarity of that morning, the shape of whatever mysterious, dangerous, placid, amazing, potentially beautiful, unknowable, insurmountable task my life had become. My real life. Not my play life on the road, not the full-blown journey of my denial, but the actual treacherous, impossible climb up, and up, and up. To what?

People died on that mountain. People got up there and avalanches plowed over them right at the last footstep they achieved. People spent their lives wanting to get there, and they failed. People drove all the way, day after day, to arrive at the mountain clouded over and invisible to them forever. But some drove all the way across country, and the mountain cleared for them, for the first time in two solid weeks of gloom.

"I wish it was about two or three weeks from now," Carey said. "The snow would all be melted enough to open the road to Sunrise, which is Stan's favorite place. So close to the mountain. A whole different view than here."

"It's good. It was all good." I stopped and shaded my eyes, thinking this was as close as I would ever get. And it had been exotic and profound. So now I would go back and live with Mama in the trailer and get fat and old and lonely. She and I would sit in our recliners and have our lifelong standoff about the twelve acres on Genesis Road, too stubborn and scared to log it or farm it or live on it or even lay eyes on it again.

"Good. Good. This was just a preview," Carey said. "Are you ready for decadence and pampering? My favorite city ever." He said we'd go to the Public Market and watch the fishmongers throwing fresh catch at each other and eat the best clam chowder and Rainier cherries and fresh figs and white nectarines.

"I want you to taste all my favorite things. Oh! And these chocolate-dipped macaroons. And cheese curds. We'll pick out our own fish to have grilled right in front of us." He stopped. "You look worried."

"This will cost a fortune. And I've been careful, but I've run through a lot of insurance money just paying off the balance of the mortgage and—"

"Don't think about that now."

"You're the one who's been telling me I have to think about it! Land is money, if we're pragmatic about it, and stop being sentimental."

"No. I mean, I've been asking you to call Faye and just talk. One thing at a time. One step at a time. Wonderland Trail is just one step at a time, with a hot shower at the end. And maybe a foot massage. Maybe good, good things."

"Or maybe you settle in your first night in the tent after all that hiking and it's raining like a nightmare and storms and lightning and blizzards. And then the volcano starts to blow." I thought of all that fury and ice, the paths of the glacial rivers coming off Rainier raging with mud and trees, a ruin great enough to break off half the state of Washington from the rest of the country.

And twelve acres. Twelve little acres at the foot of English Mountain. And I had run away from that land, all the way across the country to stand on a damn volcano. What harm could twelve acres do to me?

From Pioneer Square Hotel, we walked vacantly around, getting the bearings of the old part of Seattle. We set out on foot for downtown, where the myths of the city turned out to be understated. Past a ridiculous number of coffee shops and homeless people and crowds of pedestrians in every color speaking every language, past Ethiopian restaurants and totem poles, and tea shops and Thai restaurants, past hat shops and scarf shops and Indian restaurants, we took the monorail to the city center, backwards, watching the decadence of glass and traffic and people growing smaller and smaller.

Centered in a sprawling city carnival, the Space Needle looked at first like a huge disappointment, like the defunct Sunsphere in Knoxville, just another burned out star. Parents and kids trundled around with cotton candy where I'd pictured elegance and glamour.

We got in a long line for tickets. "So, this was built for a world's fair, like Knoxville?"

"I know what you're thinking," Carey said. "I promise it's worth the entry fee. And we get a refund if we eat lunch in the restaurant. Best twenty-dollar salad on the planet." He pointed over our heads at the tubular framework suspended over the beveled hourglass base. "It's no urban myth. The restaurant really does turn a full circle every hour."

On the ride up the glass elevator, the tackiness fell away, and in a *whoosh* the city and Elliott Bay and islands spread far around us. It was the closest thing to flying I had experienced, like a bird zooming straight up. I would have paid to soar and sink and soar and sink like that over and over, dull and calm and mesmerized. Never moving east. Never going home. Just up and down all day. Every day.

"You think they need another girl to run that elevator?" I asked Carey after we stopped. He laughed and tugged my hand, pulling me through crowds in the circular hallway museum. And then out the door onto the viewing platform, which circles the whole structure. The blue water and sky sparkled. To the south, jets were taking off and landing. Glass high rises, giant shipping cranes, and the piers were a toy foreground for Rainier, a white planet on the southeastern horizon.

The wind coming off the Pacific whipped us to a chill as we walked around. I'd forgotten there would be other mountains west of us. The Olympics reared their peaks like dazzling icicles, sharply opposite Rainier's soft dome. East and west, bookended by mountains that face each other eternally across the blue distance. A marriage of volcanic fury and ice.

"Take a good, long look," Carey said, pointing west. I shifted my pack on my back. "This is as far west and north as we go, I think, don't you?"

He had tried to break it to me gently, but I'd been looking at Seattle on the map for days. I'd known this was the pivot-point. The road had run out from under us, and I was exhausted. We walked around a few more minutes and he took some photos then asked a couple of tourists to take a picture of us together, there at the wide place in the road as Daddy used to call it.

"You're shivering. Let's—"

"Wait" I said. "Wait. Let's just stand here and freeze for a minute. It reminds me about a story Mama told me after Daddy died, which she'd never told me before. Can I tell you?"

"Here in all this cold wind?" He hunkered down and put his hood up.

"What I'm thinking about is that maybe I don't get to decide," I said. "About all that's going to happen to me. I didn't get to decide most of what's already happened in my life, really. Did I? Mama always said that about Daddy. That she didn't get to decide. To love him."

He squinted at me. "That's true for most of us, isn't it?"

I nodded. "I guess. That we don't choose who we love? Or who our parents are? The big stuff. So, if I decide—If I decide that land is mine, that means I want it, that I claim it. Why don't I want it? Mama is the one who always tried to tell me you don't always get to decide. But I thought it was just her excuse. That she didn't choose him."

"But not choosing *is* choosing." Carey opened the door, and cold suction pulled at us. "Even if you don't choose, you're making your choice."

"The bravest thing my mother ever did is something I've never done," I told him. "She flew in a plane."

It might not sound like much to most people in the modern world, who cross time zones like they're going to buy a carton of milk. So many times in my life I've looked up to see a glint in the sky, a plane so high it looks like a grain of sand, and I think about that open-hearted, big time in my mother's life and I can hardly fathom it.

Even when Mama tells the story, she can't believe she was ever so young and full of courage. But the future makes people foolhardy. And love. What force made my mother willing, at nineteen, in 1960, to get on a plane all by herself and travel across the Atlantic to Germany, where Daddy was stationed with the Army?

A few days after we buried Daddy, Mama and I sat on her front stoop and shared most of a six-pack. She'd never told the story quite the same way before, with grief in her voice, for times gone. But as we sipped, the story got generous and warm, a confession of the most powerful sway she ever experienced.

I hadn't been that drunk in years, trying to make my body a place where a baby could thrive. And I think Mama hadn't had more than a sip or two at a time in ages.

So was her story true, or was it just safe to believe it now that Daddy was dead? She could compartmentalize him now that he was gone. She could frame the portrait of him she loved, along with the portrait of herself she most wished were true.

She says she tried to focus, as the plane took off, on picturing Daddy's face, how happy it would make him to see her again, to sleep in the same bed with her, and not be lonely. And she thought selfishly, too, she admitted. She had missed his whiskers first thing in the morning, and then the feel and smell of him clean-shaven.

She said she knew he would love a fresh apple pie and her fried chicken that he hadn't tasted in months. She thought about how she could make a little barracks house into a home, hanging curtains she'd made herself and folded in her trunk. She was dreaming, too, already about how glad she'd be to take them down in a few months and fly back home to her farm and her family and her house. She was already homesick on that plane, thinking about the garden she would plant and animals and kids she might have on the land where she was raised.

"Me and your daddy," she said, "hadn't seen one another for four months. That's a long time for newlyweds. Your Granny Pearl pitched a fit. She was sure I wasn't ever coming back. She cried and cried.

"But big as Pete, I took the bus to Knoxville, and from there to Atlanta, and I climbed right onto that plane. And you have to remember, it wasn't a plane like they is now. It was a big lead bus in the sky. And I hadn't never been no farther than from Cosby to Virginia Beach on my honeymoon.

"And just like Glenn, he wasn't there to meet me. I got a taxi to take me to the base, but the driver was German and didn't know what I was saying. I finally pulled out a picture of your daddy in his uniform, and then he figured where I was headed."

In a lot of other tellings and retellings, the story detours at this exact point. Mama gets distracted talking about the food she hated that she could never get used to—rye bread and warm, dark beer, sauerkraut and bratwurst. She'll talk about how she nearly starved and couldn't find anything to cook, and she was so skinny when she got back home, from morning sickness with me. Sometimes she'll tease me that I must be part German. Sometimes she tells about other wives she met, hanging up clothes in their courtyard, or she'll talk about how she went all that way just to be alone ninety percent of the time, with Daddy on maneuvers or out playing cards.

She has never told exactly the same story twice, because that's how people where we're from tell a story. But I also think she is seeing it new every version, seeing the past unfold again. Because the past is a living thing.

But there was a part she told me sitting there on the stoop which she'd never told me before. She focused on the view out the plane window when she was way out over the Atlantic, midway between her old life and her new, between home and Daddy, between the place she'd always found comfort and the crazy, terrifying future.

"Up there in the plane," I told Carey, "I think time stopped for Mama, and she could see just for a few seconds where she was from and where she was going. And she knew she was free of all of it just for a rare few hours out of her whole life. Up in the air she saw things perfectly clearly. I wish that would happen to me."

She described it to me that day on the stoop like she had gone to heaven and come back with news of beyond. "We was up above the clouds," she said, "like a mattress. Layer after layer of clouds. I couldn't bring myself to look out that window for the first hours. I couldn't eat nothing, I was terrified. But about halfway, I must've fell asleep. The pilot woke us all up in an announcement saying something about the sky had cleared and it was a rare sight, and we ought to look out.

"What he was wanting us to see was Greenland. It didn't even look big from way up where we could see, just ice. Mountains of ice and icebergs. Sharp and white. There wasn't a cloud nowhere then. And, Lordy, I knew water could be blue, but it was so deep and dark it didn't even look like water, and it didn't look cold. It looked tropical blue, like you could live there forever."

When Mama got to that part, her voice was wistful, but not to see that strange sight again. She was thinking of her and Daddy, young, braving new frontiers. The whole world was at her feet, and she hadn't yet made one wrong move that she knew of. All the years stretched out like promise ahead.

Sitting there after we'd just buried Daddy, she sounded proud that she had gone to such great lengths to keep promises she'd made, against all odds.

"The blue of that ocean," Mama said, without one spark of regret, "was just exactly the color of your daddy's eyes."

BOUNDARIES

Across Snoqualmie Pass, stately evergreen forests swept us east, no matter how many times I checked the rearview as I drove. I couldn't shake the feeling I'd left something behind. After two nights in Seattle, we'd lingered a third day, eating all the Rainier cherries and cedar plank salmon we could hold. I had breathed in my last lungful of Pacific air. We'd watched ferries leaving for Alaska. There was more West, going on without me. Through the shrouded afternoon, it took all my self-control not to make a U-turn every time we passed an exit.

We came to a region Carey called the Scablands, where the Columbia rolls through deep chasms. The wind funneled and rocked the car so much I had to wrestle the steering wheel. Everything tugged at me, *turn back, turn back*.

The sunset, bold and mesmerizing behind us, washed across peppermint fields in eastern Washington. Even with the windows up, we smelled the bright cool before we saw the emerald waves. Irrigation contraptions stretched their shimmering curves. Signs on fences labeled the divided crops for miles and miles: *alfalfa, soybeans, barley*. Carey rolled down his window and flung both his arms out into the wind and howled at the moon coming up in the east.

"Okay. Time for you to drive again." I pulled onto the shoulder with my flashers going. "Let me howl for a while!" But any howl of mine would've been frustrated at the markers mocking me, each mile closer to my complete lack of a plan.

My life was as fluid and untethered as that dark wind we plunged through. Farmhouse lights sprang up one by one, just as stars populated the cobalt sky. My only destination was the narrow space between the road's white lines. Shutting Carey out of my periphery, I imagined how it would be to travel that stretch of road alone. Alone through the thousands of miles gone by. We had survived all the blow-outs between us so far. But for a woman who's had her share of finite relationships, it was easy to think even Carey might disappear, the way those stars would blink out in the morning.

What if Daddy hadn't died and Carey hadn't shown back up in my life? What if we hadn't come to the edge of the continent together? The mishaps, road weariness, the lostness we'd put ourselves through, all of what I'd been running from. In that growing dark, the horror of losing the baby smacked me in the chest. I turned to make sure Carey was still there. I didn't mean to gasp.

"Jesus!" He swerved and glanced at me and then into the rearview. "What?"

I let my hands, crossed over my heart, fall to my lap. How could I say the hardest, truest, ugliest parts of myself? And risk the way he thought of me?

"I would have sworn I saw a deer. Sorry. Just a shadow of something in that field." It wasn't a lie. All those shadows I carried with me followed like ghosts. Had I thought I could leave them in some western ditch? My security had always been in secrets, sliding cool and forgotten as fish trapped under the weight of ice. But being secretive hadn't protected me. A secret is less barrier and more prison, I was finding.

What would Carey say if I asked him to share that weight and darkness?

When we were kids, I was terrified Carey would learn about my family and pity me. You're never on equal footing with someone who feels sorry for you. I was halfway glad his mother wouldn't let him come to our trailer. We always hung out at his house. Years back, we learned how to maintain a solid threshold between us. But it only takes a step to cross a threshold. But a step toward or away? A step deeper or farther? And then what happens?

Ahead there were timelines and state lines. Montana, Wyoming, Colorado still between me and whatever I had to face. At some inevitable mile marker, I would know when it was put-up or shut-up time. Carrying secrets or leaving them. That line of silence I would find the gumption to keep or cross.

Out of Spokane, late next morning, the mountains across the chimney of Idaho looked like a softened repeat of the Cascades. A fine rain settled along our route. The steep woods folded close, summits misted over. Evergreens by so many millions had a blurred effect, like a misaligned design of tiny triangles. We stopped for early lunch in Wallace, self-proclaimed silver-mining capital of the world. There was even a rack of sterling jewelry beside the diner's carousel display of pies.

We walked off coconut cream and blueberry crumble in and out of antique stores and knickknack shops. In a historic brothel, two sisters had set up a shabby consignment store—vintage clothes, estate jewelry, old china and silver service. We decided with one conspiratorial look to take their two-dollar tour.

On the main floor, in the old saloon, instead of crown molding a pressed-tin border of half-clad women reclined in repeating positions. Someone had painted their hair for tacky variety, blondes, redheads, the full range of brunette, colors flecking off. Upstairs was storage, tumbled cardboard boxes and empty display cabinets in cramped spaces where prostitutes had taken their customers.

"A lot of rooms," Carey said.

"A lot of business," the guide said. "Twelve, fifteen, up to twenty girls at one time. On the books they kept." She sounded proud. "And there were several houses like this in town." She shut off the light in the upstairs hall. The wooden stairs creaked as we followed her back down.

"So back then—well—that career choice was legal?" I asked.

"Idaho wasn't a state," Carey chimed in. "And career choice?"

The owner stopped and looked back at us on the stairs. "Lots were widows. The mines were dangerous, don't you know. People were free to survive best they could."

As Carey drove, I imagined living in one of those tiny rooms with low ceilings, barely a breath of pasteboard between the hourly ruckus. Dressing and undressing, cleaning up how many times a day in a space barely big enough for a bed. Boot steps on the stairs, the shuffle of men downstairs waiting their turn. Miners smelling worse than the mules they rode in on.

"It's weird to think of legal prostitution," I said. "But I always wonder why it's illegal for women to do what they want with their own bodies."

"You think they want to?" Carey sounded surprised. "Hey, look, only a couple more miles to Montana. Wahoo."

I looked out at the mountains ahead. "Don't you think that's possible? I'm just saying why isn't it legal if somebody chooses? Sex in the porn industry is legal, on film. I think the difference is men make a killing off porn. Producers, directors, distributors. But with prostitution women could be free agents. It's just nobody wants that."

"I mean, you'd legalize prostitution?"

I shrugged. "Those rooms creeped me out. And human trafficking is a horror, especially for girls. But if prostitution was regulated? If women kept all they earned and were safe? Like in Nevada. Shouldn't they be free to make money however they want?"

"But what I mean is," he said, "it probably isn't 'however they want.' It's always been out of desperation. That or marry a rich man. Which is a kind of prostitution."

"Better than starving," I said. "How weird things have changed. Women had the freedom to charge for sex, but they couldn't vote. But now women have all these rights except what they do with their bodies."

"Oh, women totally have more power over their bodies now than back then. Birth control." Carey said. "Legal abortion."

"Not for long, if some joker gets in the White House," I said.

"You think it's okay?" He looked at the road, braving his own curiosity. What would he think of me if he got the answers I had lived?

"Who thinks abortion is okay?" I said. "But it's a luxury to think it's a moral issue. It's a health issue."

"I'm kind of surprised you—" He waved his free hand in the air. "Well—I didn't mean to bring up—" He was trying to tread lightly. "It's touchy. I mean, for everybody. But especially, knowing you wanted—*want*—to have a baby. I'm surprised you're pro-choice, is all." Carey's expression was determined and concerned. Earnest. He didn't know if he wanted to know.

"You mentioned desperation. As long as there's desperation, there has to be legal abortion. You go for an abortion—"

"I mean," he said, daring a look at me. "Are you saying 'you' as in generic you, or like a capital *You*, you?" He pointed at me.

"*Me*? Of course not." My denial sounded guilty. But I was glad to be able to say the truth. "Listen," I said. "I was careful, except the first few times, when I was way too young. And when I wasn't careful, I felt lucky. Except it turns out having fertility problems is not actually luck."

Crossing the Montana line right then should have been a great subject changer, along with the rain that started hammering the car. We should have been doing high fives and whooping it up. We should have been paying attention to the slick highway and the thick dark clouds ahead.

"You do have a problem? I mean, getting pregnant?" Carey slowed to a safer speed while cars and trucks zoomed past on long interstate curves. The mountains were blotted out by rain.

"Kevin and I tried six ways to Sunday. I think you guessed from what I've said. Medical interventions. Procedures."

"Would you have done it, though? When you were younger?" Carey's blunt hypothetical cut into me.

"How can I answer that, Carey? You mean when I was fifteen or sixteen?"

"Well, just, I mean, do you think—" The Jeep was a prison through louder and louder torrents. I couldn't jump. I couldn't swim. I couldn't weasel out.

"I can't say a-hundred percent I would *not* have if that's what you mean. But if I had, it would be my biggest regret. Can you imagine having an abortion or even giving a baby up for adoption, and later not being able to get pregnant?"

"You know women who have?" He took his eyes off the road for a second to gauge my answer.

"How could I be my age and not know someone?" I wanted to ask him, *How can you be your age and not?*

Red lights splashed across us. We skidded and cringed when Carey slammed on the brakes, waiting for the truck behind to slam into us. When we came to a stop, its grill blocked the back window. That close. Westbound traffic stopped beyond us.

And at the end of the steep curve we'd come around, the east-bound lanes were a parking lot. Bleary red and blue emergency lights. Patrolmen in yellow ponchos laid flares along the danger zone.

"Everybody's driving like a maniac," I said.

"Oh, I meant to warn you. There's no speed limit in Montana," he said.

"Shit. How do they not have a speed limit?"

"Some kind of twentieth-century Manifest Destiny, I guess," he said. "It's your right to go as fast as you can and hold it on the road. And then the state pays for all these metal crosses to mark where people die in wrecks."

The rain came harder while we were stopped, until it was almost one sheet, one constant sound. Midday fell into dusk, so the lights ahead seemed brighter. Carey cut off the wipers. Then a few seconds later, he shut the motor.

"I mean, who did you know who had an abortion?" Carey asked.

"Sheesh. You're like a snapping turtle."

He shrugged. "We're not going anywhere. But even if we were going anywhere, we're going there together." He laughed. "But you don't have to—" An ambulance crossed the median ahead. The wreck had just happened. Just minutes earlier, it could have been us.

I thought I might as well start with the worst. "It all started to go wrong with Kevin when—" I hesitated. Why did every story start and end with Kevin? "Like I said, we tried to get pregnant for ages, which is really stressful and awful, and then this, well, opportunity—" I unhooked my seatbelt and turned toward him. "My cousin Darlene's daughter. You remember Darlene?" Carey nodded. "Her daughter Cindy got pregnant. Seventeen. She knew Kevin and I were desperate to have a baby. Everybody knew."

We were all at Grandma Ruby's for the last Christmas Kevin and I were together. The house was crammed full of Daddy's family, but somehow Cindy and I ended up in the back bedroom stretched across a quilt, looking at old photos. When I found one of her as a baby, she started to cry.

I propped a chair against the doorknob to lock it. "How far along?"

She sat up and wiped her face and said, "Daddy'll kill me, and then Mama'll dig me up and kill me again." She'd taken an early pregnancy test. I tried to convince her it might be a false positive, but she swore she knew. Six weeks, probably less. I kept my voice cool and detached, like I do with clients in my office. But it was myself I was trying to calm.

I admitted to Carey I instantly put my needs into the equation. Her problem was my gift. A family member, pregnant with an unwanted baby. I was already picturing Kevin and me in the delivery room with her.

As if I'd willed the words out of her, she asked, "If I did have it, would you keep it?" I wanted to jump up and go tell Kevin we were having a baby. "You could raise it and not worry about whether I'd done drugs. And Gary hasn't either," she said. "He's just a fucking asshole, is all."

"Well, luckily that's not usually genetic." I was glad for her weak smile. "So you're broken up?" My most selfish question yet. "Any chance you'll get back together? He might want the baby. Did you tell him?"

She nodded and started crying again. "That's why he broke up with me. Same boring-ass story as everybody else."

I was a big jangling nerve of hope. I had to stand up. "You really need to think about what you're saying," I told her. "I'm really sorry about Gary. And I'm sorry you have to go through something you don't want. But there are lives at stake here."

"That's why I'm telling you," she said.

"Didn't you tell her yes, of course?" Carey interrupted, excited, even though the end of the story was so obvious. Or at least the only ending I was willing to tell. "I mean, yes. She wanted you to have the baby. So why—"

I took a deep breath, which sobered him. "Like I said, I tried to think about what was right for her and not get my hopes up. She wanted me to fix everything, but I was trying to be clear, even if she gave us her baby, it wouldn't all be fixed. I was trying to be professional. It was the kind of thing I deal with at work. But inside I was Jell-O. I told her if she wanted to give the baby to us, she had to be sure. Only she could decide."

Carey was silent as we both looked ahead at stalled traffic. The flashing lights of emergency vehicles swarmed across the median to the westbound lane, racing past with victims.

"Looks grim," he said. "Did you ever think, just a few minutes different this morning, five minutes less to eat lunch, that could be us up there wrecked?"

"I already played out that scenario. It doesn't do anybody any good. And if we'd been there instead of them, maybe a wreck wouldn't have happened. What if we'd left earlier and that saved everybody?"

Carey gave a humph. "I never thought of that," he said. "We're talking about free will here, I guess. I know how the story ends. I mean, you and Kevin got divorced not long after."

"That wasn't because of Cindy." I took another deep breath. My hands were trembling in my lap, clenched together. "That's on Kevin. And that's a whole other show, as they say."

I told Carey I could hardly wait to leave that night and tell Kevin, but on the drive home, after I'd spilled Cindy's whole story and unfolded our future, Kevin didn't say a word.

"Isn't this almost too perfect?" I prodded him.

Kevin said, "I think we need to think about this a good long while, Glenna."

"What are you talking about? Every single thing we want just fell into place."

"No. Everything we want did not fall into place."

"You're actually telling me you're not sure you want to have a baby."

"No. That's not what I'm saying," he answered.

"I don't know what we need to think about, Kevin. Cindy's pregnant. She's a good, clean kid. She doesn't want to keep her baby."

"Does she want to *have* a baby?" Kevin asked. "Does she want to give birth?"

"I told her to think about all that. She's taking it really seriously."

"Glenna, this time last year she was wearing braces. She's a majorette. She's a kid." His words put me in her skin for a minute. But that only made me furious with envy. I wished I could go back and be her. But I would have been terrified, just like her. And then I pictured her years ahead, my age, and me with a teenaged kid. Her teenaged kid. My cousin Darlene the grandmother of my kid.

"And does the father want the baby?"

"I asked her all of that." I was angry that Kevin's sense of the downside had seeped into me. "I told her to think about all that."

"Cindy gets your permission to think about this life-changing choice, but I have to make maybe the most important decision of my whole life in a split second?"

"Just explain why you're not excited about the possibility, Kevin? Why do you have to deliberate? Just one time in your life, why can't you just go with your instincts and feel what you're feeling?"

"No. You mean why can't I feel exactly what you're feeling." He pulled over to the shoulder and turned on the hazard lights. "Did you ever stop and think that maybe these *are* my instincts, Glenna? Maybe I *am* feeling what I'm feeling?"

I couldn't say words. I couldn't admit he was right.

"For one thing," Kevin said, as if I'd asked him to make a list, "Cindy is family. It's too close. She'd be at our house constantly with her mother. Maybe even the boy's family. They'll end up wanting to be involved."

"What's wrong with that?" I shouted. "It's her baby she's giving up."

Kevin was infuriatingly silent. The flashers clicked while Christmas travelers passed, thinking our problem was something as simple as car trouble.

"I have to say this carefully," he said nearly in a whisper. "You need to think about the words that just came out of your mouth: 'It's her baby.' It would always be Cindy's baby, because she's not anonymous to us. That child would never be ours."

When Carey reached over to take my hand, I jumped, remembering the way Kevin had reached for me. But this time I didn't embarrass myself with sobbing. The Montana wilderness held its breath. Ahead of us a helicopter hovered for a moment and then settled onto the closed oncoming interstate lanes.

"That's a bad sign," Carey said. "Somebody's hurt really bad. Closest hospital is probably Missoula."

Figures ran hunkered in the rain under the beating blades. A few minutes later the helicopter lifted like clumsy debris in a storm. Brake lights flickered out two by two. Cars ahead budged. Carey started the ignition and we buckled up.

246

We moved with the reverence of a funeral procession past the scene. Shattered glass, crumpled fist-sized pieces of metal, scattered paper and clothes. We were just two people in a cavalcade of humans passing the wreckage, as if nothing in the world had gone wrong.

We had already moteled it five nights out of the past seven. Carey said civilization was oppressing our sense of escapade. We were going through more Lewis and Clark territory, and we needed to "feel it." Otherwise, we might not have risked camping during what turned out to be only a brief break in the rain. As we staked the tent fly, the cloud we'd been eyeing let down a curtain across the Clark Fork. The evening went yellow. Trees thrashed in the sluicing blur.

"Hurry," Carey yelled as I tossed our sleeping bags to him. He shoved them into the tent and then ran back with me to get one more load. "Don't worry about locking!" All the other campsites were empty, of course. We ran as the storm shifted louder. Rain pounded into the river, like horses' hooves. The visible line of it moved toward us, churning the water's surface. Big drops splatted. Under the fly's vestibule, Carey held the zippered door open for me and crawled in behind, and zipped us in, just as rain clobbered the tent.

In the early evening, what would have felt claustrophobic to some was liberating. On our own again, out of traffic. Shoes off. Cozy. Nobody in the world knew where we were. Something cut loose inside, sheer luxury to roll out our sleeping bags. Trapped by softening rain. We lay back and watched rivulets run off the tent, little shiny balls of shadow and light.

"I'm hungry," I finally said. "Can you believe it's after six?"

"Hold that thought. Especially here we don't want food in the tent. Remember, they have grizzlies in Montana."

"A bear's a bear in my book," I said, "once it's big enough to eat you."

We lay quietly awhile, and I thought Carey might have dozed off. But he rolled onto his side toward me. "I know I should drop the subject," he said. "Because it's obvious Cindy had an abortion. And that had to be part of what—well, that was hard."

"I promised her I'd never tell anybody, ever," I said. "I feel awful." And I did. I had spilled somebody else's secret to deflect attention from mine.

"But who am I going to tell, Glenna?"

"That's not what matters. It's her story to tell," I said.

He sat up like a hound catching a scent. "It's your story too."

"Only if it doesn't leave this tent, Carey. Not another soul knows."

"Not even Kevin, right?"

"Well, he had to figure it out," I said. "But he made his bed, so to speak."

"That sounds lonely," he said. "So that's what led to the divorce? Because you wanted to adopt and he didn't, and she had an abortion? And you blamed him?"

"Good grief. You sound like a bad *Lifetime* drama!" I sat up and flicked at pools of water weighing down the fly. "It's more complicated. And less complicated." How could I tell him about Cindy and keep the baby I'd lost a secret, when the two were tangled so grievously?

"Cindy was terrified to tell Darlene and Carl. You know how religious they are. And she didn't have a dime. And the boy—the father—was this rich prick on the baseball team. But he was terrified for his parents to know. He said he could maybe sell some baseball cards to help pay. How awful is that? What else could I do?" I took a deep breath and looked at my hands in my lap. "I took her, and I paid for everything."

Carey gave out a little sound like humming, like he had a headache. "She offers to give you her baby, which you think is your lucky chance, but instead you pay for her to have an abortion?"

"I know," I said. "It sounds ridiculous. And I understand regret. I do. But it wasn't my decision. You remember that cross in Texas, that abortion protest site?"

"Onward Christian soldiers," he said.

"That place pissed me off because, what about the personal stories and the reasons we all have, the women we've known? As much as I regret what she did, I have to live what I believe, I guess. And I believe it was Cindy's decision. And the more the weeks went by—because this wasn't a split-second decision, Carey. This was weeks and agonizing weeks. The more time went by, she couldn't go through with her offer."

Carey's face had a look I'd never seen, sort of overwhelmed with patience and sympathy, but confused. As if he could see I was telling a half-story, half-truth. But there was no way to say out loud to him how awful I was, all the selfish evil I'd done.

I'd taken my own pregnancy tests just weeks after Cindy told me she was pregnant. And then I no longer needed her baby. Abortion or not, it didn't really concern me.

If nature had gone the way it should, Cindy would have been seven or eight months pregnant. And I would have been about five months along, just starting to wear maternity clothes.

The morning I drove her to the clinic, I told her to tell her mom I was taking her shopping for a graduation gift. I had a little makeup bag already wrapped up in my backseat. The real gift was maneuvering Cindy past protesters and through paperwork. I had to explain what going to the gynecologist was like. She'd never been. I described the paper gown, the stirrups, the speculum.

But how could I tell her then what it would be like, what it would mean, to take a potential life? To lose a life? I couldn't have imagined that in just a few weeks I would know. I was so smug. I was pregnant. And I was helping a scared young woman. I was being non-judgmental and open-hearted.

In the waiting room her hands shook. She jumped whenever names were called. She started to cry when the nurse came for her. I stood, so she'd stand and walk across the room, but she waited there beside me.

"You're going in with me, aren't you?" Her pupils were huge with fear.

"I think they won't let me," I said. I led her to the nurse in the doorway.

"Please, please go with me, Glenna! I can't."

I motioned the nurse to wait. "You have to be brave and make this final step on your own, Cindy. You have to believe this is the right thing for you. If it is, you're free to walk in there. If it's not, you're just as free to walk out." My heart beat a little faster for her, for the line she was crossing alone.

"No. I'll do it. I have to do it." She stepped past the nurse into the hallway.

The nurse whispered, "You can come with her."

"No. This is as far as I go." I stepped back and the door shut in my face.

All I could say to Carey was that thin version. I explained that it was Cindy's choice, and somehow, I was the only ally she had. Luckily, she'd just turned eighteen that week. There was nothing for me to sign. No runaround. I put my money on the fact that each person makes choices they have to live with, right or wrong.

"But how sad you felt you had to put yourself through that."

"It really doesn't make any difference who wrote the check, does it?"

He shrugged and lay back down. "Maybe not," he said. "But the money's not the thing, is it? And you and Kevin never talked about it at all?"

I shrugged. "He didn't care enough to ask about her."

Carey hummed again, a judgmental tone. I had explained as little about the ruin of our marriage as I could. And Kevin came out looking worse than was true and better than a different truth. Kevin didn't have room in his worries for Cindy as I shoved him out of the house, out of my life, for all the harm he'd done.

"He was out of the picture, Carey. I'd already filed for divorce. Not because of Cindy. He had a battalion of his own secrets. He made bad, bad choices."

But I held Kevin accountable for the choice Cindy made. Here were two women at the end of the twentieth century trying to find a way to bring a life into the world, and I convinced Cindy—and myself at the time—that Kevin stood in our way. I made him the fall guy in my version. I told Cindy that Kevin didn't want to adopt. I told her he didn't want her baby. And then she blamed herself for our divorce. And I let her.

I had traveled so far to try and forget my duplicity and the miscarriage. If I squinted into the blame, it felt as if my role in Cindy's decision brought on the miscarriage. Like I had it coming to me. Now memory churned like the river and the rain. Carey slept the perfect sleep of the righteous. But I'd stirred up my own troubles again.

The next morning, we spread out the soaked tent and damp sleeping bags in the back of the Jeep. Even our waterproof gear had gotten saturated. Something dank had seeped in.

Near Deer Lodge, Montana, the rain gave way to empty clouds that hid the Rockies north of us. We'd come into sparsely treed foothills the color of faded leather. Like Monopoly pieces, red-roofed buildings fronted the folded hills. Carey had talked up the place, a national historic site devoted to ranching, one of the biggest operations ever. We were barely in time for the ranger-led group, gathered on the porch of the frame house.

"The Grant-Kohrs Ranch," the ranger was explaining, "now covers fifteen hundred acres, but at the height of prosperity, the owners grazed cattle across ten million acres from Colorado to Canada. Barbed wire and feed domesticated the open range. Cattle operations like this one were in existence for thirty short years."

Inside the house my eyes took a few seconds to adjust as we filed into a dim Victorian parlor. I was still trying to fathom having the run of ten million acres. Now barely a hundred years later, highways and interstates cut it all into pieces. The ranger crossed into roped-off rooms and instructed us to gather on protective floor covering. The house hunkered down as wind howled around the eaves. The place was no mansion, but rich brocades and lace and polished wood held a sheen of wealth, and womanhood. The dining table was set with fine glass and porcelain. A pristine oasis of civility.

"Augusta Kruse was just nineteen when she married Conrad Kohrs," the ranger spieled. In the brochure, Carey pointed out her young face and her husband's old one. She had worked her eastern-bred fingers to the bone to separate her refined portion from frontier filth and cow shit and blood and sweat, all of which made her fine things possible. Through the house, past prim, sturdy furniture and poster beds, the sanctuary of the kitchen held her collection of crystal vases. The window looked onto a flower garden. She'd outlived her husband by decades, sculpting tame bouquets, as if it only took a few petals to stop the wild roughness at her threshold.

One room in the house was designed by Kohrs for men only, where deals were made, whiskey decanted, cigars smoked. Sunken leather chairs and luxurious wood held the arrogance of Biltmore in Asheville. Carey agreed and whispered that they were built around the same time. The house was a castle fortress by Western standards.

"There's an archivist on site," the ranger was saying, "who deals with Mr. Kohrs' diaries and business records. The entire second story of the house is devoted to that work, so it's closed to the public."

He paused and pointed to a photograph of Mrs. Kohrs, matronly and old, nothing like the young girl in the brochure. "The personal history of Augusta Kruse Kohrs, however, is to be seen only in this home she created, in the furnishings and spirit of these rooms. Before she died, at ninety-six, just after World War II, her daughters and granddaughters followed her wishes that her extensive diaries be burned."

Carey gasped. People turned to look at us. He had his hand against his mouth. I honestly thought he might faint at the thought of all that history gone.

"It's the deliberate destruction," Carey said as we followed the others out of the house. "It's arrogant."

I squinted at him in the bright wind. "She didn't want us knowing her business."

"But how selfish," Carey said. "She committed malicious, historical suicide. Out of, what, spite?"

His words struck me, and I lagged behind for half a step. *Spite. Out of spite.* My silence was spite, growing monstrous every day. I'd lived for months on the rationale that Kevin didn't deserve to know Cindy's story. Or about the baby I'd lost. I was bravely private and heroic, wasn't I? Why burden Kevin or Carey or anyone?

But in truth, my life was stifled by the power of a haughty grudge. That's how Carey saw Augusta Kohrs. For him her diaries were the bones that held up her life. Her stubborn silence demolished her very self. Forever.

I stepped beside Carey across a puddle on the way to the bunkhouse. "She probably didn't want to be judged, or put her family through the rummage of it all."

"Why'd she write it all down in the first place, then?" Carey said.

"For herself. To look back on and help her remember. It was her life. She was free to do what she wanted."

"But it's criminal," Carey protested. "History is bigger than an individual life. Just think of the collective loss. People complain we only know about the lives of men. Whose fault is that?"

The sky brightened as we peered into the dark bunkhouse, not fifty feet from the main house. A huge contrast. The rooms were like stalls for animals, windowless with dirt floors.

"Obviously she felt entitled," he said. "Look at the difference right in front of us. The tour said not one word about the anonymous cowboy." He walked over to an educational plaque. "Says here a pair of boots cost a month's salary. These guys were slave labor. Welcome to the romance of the West."

"It's tragic," I said. "I wish cowboys had kept diaries."

"Don't be sarcastic. I'm serious."

"I'm not sarcastic." I took his arm. "I'm serious too. It is tragic, for history, for us. They probably didn't even know how to write."

"But she did. She was—" He was angrier the more he dwelled on it and couldn't let it go. "I mean, I'm talking about vandalism. What would people think if she'd burned down the house?"

I cringed and let his arm go. I didn't mean to stop in my tracks, but my legs froze.

Carey turned to look back at me. "Oh, God. Glenna, I'm sorry. I didn't think." He was pale. Mortified. But he couldn't know how deeply, how far back into my past his comment cut. All the way back to Daddy's spite long ago. Burning down our house in Cosby just to ruin Mama's life.

"You can't exactly compare a diary and a house," I said. I didn't say, *and a person*. "Those are not the same." But even as I argued, I was wavering inside. Which was worse? Those diaries recounting thousands of days of a woman's spectacularly unique life, which might enrich generations to come? Or my daddy dying in a fire? Or my little life? My house? The line between sins and tragedies blurred in the flitting sunlight, pouring over the hills between shadows of clouds.

In all of it, I was my daddy's daughter. Spiteful. Holding my secrets like a lit match.

Between Livingston and Gardiner, the Montana sky coagulated, and above the ruff of hills a white shawl of fog exposed the blue shoulders of the Absaroka Range.

"It's snowing," Carey said, just as I recognized it. "Look. There!"

Snow on the ground at Rainier, pressed in curved, dirty drifts, was paltry compared to falling, heavy, nickel-sized crystals. I pulled the car into the mouth of a rutted ranch road and got out to watch the muted air fill with living white. Tall roadside grass clotted with it, like soggy cotton. Except for the motor and windshield wipers, I couldn't hear anything but cows bawling and the snow-flakes landing. Lights in barns and houses flickered, where the wilderness left off and civilization started.

Gardiner was a tame thoroughfare of tourist shops and motels, advertised as the "Gateway to Yellowstone." But the town stopped like a line in the sand. Past the last-ditch strip of postcard shops and restaurants, maybe fifty yards separated the town from the boundary of Yellowstone. I drove through the stone archway that reads: *For the benefit and enjoyment of the people.*

"Kind of an odd slogan," I said. "If the reason it's here is people, then how is it wilderness?"

"Same with the Smokies, isn't it?" Carey said. "If they hadn't tamed it a little and nobody experienced it, then nobody would fight to protect it. Wilderness needs people. To protect it from all the damn people."

The snow ended as abruptly as it started, around a steep bend in the road.

The river rolling along our route tugged away from us, churning and gone. Over a rise, just about the time we crossed into Wyoming, I made the first of dozens of roadside pull-offs in Yellowstone. There in the vast valley, skirted by storm-colored mountains, below pine bluffs, the strangest patch of earth I'd ever witnessed. A pristine iceberg steamed but didn't melt away.

Until we closed in, I didn't notice the suburban sprawl of buildings next to the icy-white hillside sending up its flumes. On the lawn beneath trees flanking the Mammoth Hot Springs visitor center, mule deer grazed, so common that tourists weren't even stopping to snap pictures. Besides our hotel, a store and gas station made crazy commerce with wild animals and steaming earth. A misplaced town square.

It was nearly four by the time we checked into the hotel, buttery yellow, built like a rickety old dorm, with long hallways and big windows. By four fifteen, we'd stashed our stuff and hit the park road again, stopping in the sulfurous humidity wafting off Minerva Terrace. It looked like a broken off chunk from another planet had just sizzled out of the sky and crash landed.

Standing close, I could see that what looked blindingly pure white from far away was faint copper-penny pink, sherbet orange, pee-in-snow yellow. We climbed a boardwalk around the springs and mounds, gurgling and slurping stinky belches, the smell of rotten eggs. Tourists' footsteps shook the boards, and little kids ran up and down, holding their noses and complaining about the stink. Carey and I couldn't keep from laughing at them, and Asian tourists striking entertaining poses in front of the springs.

"It looks fragile as Alka-Seltzer," I said. Water steamed in cascades down the snow-stack mineral stair steps, the tops scalloped like giant white-blazing bottle caps. "Like it would dissolve."

"Travertine," Carey said. "Hard as a bullet."

From the top of the boardwalk, we looked down on an area sculpted exactly like the springs, but dead, black-and-white as an old photo. I pointed at the black trees like claws around the ashy terrace.

"A dormant spring," Carey said. "The springs grow so fast they cover up the boardwalks. New fissures can open any time. Be sure you don't step one toe off the boardwalks. Seriously, people get boiled alive, burned up."

"Oh, no. I'm sorry again!" he said, swinging to face me. I patted his shoulder. "It's okay, Carey. I have to get used to it." But I knew I'd never get used to the way any mention of heat and fire brought Daddy to my mind's eye, flayed by flames. Seared to ashes.

With over a hundred miles of roads in the park, Carey wanted to cover as much distance as we could. "Great," I joked as he started the car. "After a bajillion miles, a scenic drive before dinner."

And then it was anything but scenic. The last thing I needed was to see

253

the burned forests in the north part of the park. Miles and more square miles of black woods. Charred blotches of bark like bubbled tar, most trees scoured down to bald yellow innards, so that the lodge pole pines, straight and seared of limbs, looked like a fresh crop of telephone poles.

Carey thought the destruction was beautiful. The way he thought Mount St. Helens was beautiful.

I decided to read to him from the brochure and stop looking at the horror. "It says, the park is more than two and a quarter million acres. And the big fire in 1988, eleven years ago, burned eight hundred thousand acres. Forty percent of Yellowstone."

I couldn't keep from looking up then at the devastation. "And they're still debating whether it was the right thing to let it burn?"

"They made the choice," Carey said, "to let the fire burn for a long time, days I think, before they intervened. The fire policy then was based on the idea that lightning strikes and big fires have always been natural, and man should stand back and let nature run its course. It's a big political debate, to clear underbrush or put out fires. I mean, we just think we can control fire." He said it as if he were teaching me a brand-new lesson.

For a mile or so, the wooded plateau opened up to a relief of colorful wildflower meadows and stands of healthy trees. Still, far ridges were a puzzle of burned and unburned woods. Next to the road, black carcasses sprawled in new growth and greening underbrush.

"Well, from what it says," I said, "they used their power to draw a line where they saw fit. None of the buildings or lodges burned. But it gives an account of the animals that perished. Some people think the low number is propaganda. The controversy is if they kept structures safe, why couldn't they save the wildlife."

"The question I think they mean is, is wilderness more important than civilization?" Carey slowed to see the distance over a rise.

I thumbed through the pages and ran across the park service's fire policy in bold headings. A political sound bite about deadwood and scouring wilderness clean for its own good. About man letting the wilderness have its own destructive way. I couldn't read those scalding words aloud, and they hung in my mind like smoke: *Fire is nature's way of cleaning up the dead so that the living can get on with things.*

Carey slowed around a bend where cars lined both sides of the road and pulled over to see if there was a bear or bison. Birds as yellow as beacons perched on reeds called in sharp, pretty voices across a small lake. People steadied their binoculars, and one man stood on top of his van with a camera the size of a Howitzer.

In Yellowstone, I could see already there is a hierarchy of animal sightings.

And a mad dash competition. We couldn't drive more than a couple of miles between traffic jams. Sometimes there were just tourists scattered along the road, ranging into the meadows, scanning the distance for the slightest glimpse of fur—families of badgers, marmots, elk. It didn't take long to realize most people wanted a big open-air zoo, animals to gawk at.

Traffic thinned after we crossed the highest point on the park road. We stopped at a roadside picnic table for dinner. The air was sharp off of dingy snow, and big ravens blew in like leaves to eyeball our sandwiches. Limbs creaked. Carey read off sites on the map named for animals: Dunraven Pass, Blacktail Deer Creek, Panther Creek, Swan Lake, Wolf Lake, Otter Creek, Buffalo Creek, Grizzly Lake, Chipmunk Creek. He pouted when I said, no, I didn't want to play a game to see how many animals we spotted.

But I got pretty swept up looking for bison, though the region we were going through wasn't one of their big ranges. At the Grand Canyon of the Yellowstone, a broth of green winked 1500 feet below, a mix of fresh water and boiling mineral runoff. Vent holes poured steaming rivulets down the canyon walls. I pointed out to Carey that the pines looked like they were marching single file down the vertical ridges into the river. He said the canyon colors were cornmeal yellow and pumpkin-gut red, muddy dijon, tomato pink. We gave over to the urge to name everything in human terms.

We tromped through white mud that clung to our boot soles, like we'd tromped through at Painted Desert, to viewpoints of the canyon falls. But the curtain of water, spilling like liquid green glass, was nothing like seeing my first wild bison.

We had finally come to wide open meadows. Out in the far fields, whole herds of bison, so different from the fenced-in bison I'd seen in Oklahoma. Carey and I squinted through the jittery tubular dark of his binoculars. Their hides were molting, the long reddish pelts uncovering new, velvety brown. We watched until they were lit to a shimmery, shaggy outline by the low sun.

On our way back to the hotel, around a tight curve, Carey stopped where two male bison had ventured into the turn-out. He edged the Jeep beside the near one. I had no idea how monstrous they could be until I was face to face. The bison right beside me was as big as the Jeep. Carey rolled down my window and leaned across me with his camera. The bull let out a rumbling breath and rolled his huge eye at us, black as an eight ball. He sidled closer, inches from my window, as if he were daring us. His musk rose, a brutal heat. I shrank back against Carey, who stuck his camera farther out the window.

"That's enough," I managed a whisper. "We shouldn't be so close."

"He's right by the road," he said. "It's not like we're in his territory."

"That's exactly what we are, Carey. This is all his territory. He's rolling his eye again! Stop clicking." The bull pawed the ground, never breaking his giant scissoring chew. He stepped so close I felt the vibration of his weight. His hump blocked the sunset. "Carey!" I whispered louder.

"Okay, okay." He set his camera in my lap and eased the car out of park. A waiting car pulled into the space the second we got back on the road.

"You said people get hurt doing that," I chided. "Chasing after wild animals."

"We were safe in the car," he said. "Probably. And wasn't it great?" He laughed.

I backhanded his shoulder. "Now. Where are the bears?"

"Not enough excitement for one day?" We both lurched forward as he slammed on the brakes. Cars were stopped in both directions. In the gap a bear lumbered across the road like a baby crawling.

Carey tugged at his camera with one hand while he steered us onto the slim shoulder with the other. "Watch, Carey, watch!" The bear broke into a sudden trot, and its waddling, dark hind end disappeared into a thicket of saplings.

Carey gave me a stunned grin. "You said you wanted a bear. Tah dah! I never saw anybody conjure a grizzly. Now say, 'I want a stack of twenties!'"

"Good grief, that wasn't a grizzly. That was a black bear cub like we have in the Smokies." He argued, but I pulled out the park newspaper with animal photos. "See? How to tell a coyote from a wolf, elk from mule deer, black bear from grizzly. See, rump higher than shoulders, long, straight snout, small frame. No hump. You didn't even see it. Had to grab your camera, like an average touron."

"I saw it," he protested.

"Did you notice it was wearing an earring," I quizzed. Carey looked skeptical. "A green ear tag," I insisted.

"Oh, yeah. They catalog all the animals they can. Wolves, especially. Give them names. Follow their routines and movements. Bison are controlled because the ranchers are afraid of disease." Traffic loosened and we moved. "I mean, if they cross park boundaries, ranchers can legally shoot them. Grizzlies are tracked with satellites."

"You're lying," I said.

"No," he said. "They collar them, and the collar has a sensor, or they embed a chip under the skin."

"That's science fiction. Too bizarre," I said. "Too sad."

"But it protects them. Their environment."

I pictured unsuspecting bears waking up from tranquilizer darts, lumbering off under constant surveillance, doing intimate bear things, numbered like prisoners, with nicknames and dossiers. "We only pretend we have wilderness. If we control everything, then it's not wilderness anymore."

"You don't think this is wilderness?" Carey said. "Ten minutes ago you were scared."

"Not if it's all being cataloged and supervised. Something domestic and tamed by definition can't be wilderness." The wild otherness I'd felt in that bison's power, its enormous sloping girth, the sable hide and patches of tawny scruff shedding off. It was wild, which I understood from the urge to keep my distance. "I don't know," I said. "Maybe once a person steps one foot inside the wilderness it stops being wilderness. We take over the whole place, paving roads and building hotels. It's kind of like an amusement park, isn't it? Maybe wilderness is a myth," I said.

Carey shrugged. "Maybe wilderness is in the eye of the beholder."

On one hand, it makes sense that the world's oldest national park has hospitality down pat. But on the other, there's a false sense of civilization to match the false wildness. Through our lodge window we saw the dusk-lit bluffs, mountains and sky. We took showers and walked to the general store for a snack. Past postcards and gifts, racks of expensive sweatshirts and caps with Yellowstone emblems, we came to freezers lined with Ben and Jerry's, shelves stocked with Oreos and chips. And every kind of liquor and wine and beer.

"You want a rum and coke instead of dessert?" I teased Carey.

He pulled down a fifth of Myers's dark in one hand and seesawed it against the pint of Cherry Garcia in his other hand. He looked down his glasses at me. "Why choose?" He laughed.

After ice cream, we sipped in the civilized hush of the lodge's map room, surrounded by rich honeyed paneling and burgundy velvet drapery. Under twenty-foot ceilings, I studied the marquetry wall map of the U.S., dark walnut and oak and pale ash designating man-made boundaries.

We were in our room and asleep by ten o'clock. I woke up not long after to what I thought was the irritation of rain dripping on the tent again, *pick, pick, pick.* Then I felt the big dark room around me. I listened hard. There again, *pick, pick.* "Carey," I hissed. I leaned toward the space between our beds and froze when the scribbling, scratching started again, holding my breath to listen.

"What is it?" He moaned turning over.

"Listen. Shhhh. There's a mouse!"

He flung off the covers to sit on the edge of his bed. In the dark he cocked his head to hear the frantic skittering. "Oh, shit, it's in our food box." He flicked on the light and the noise stopped. He tiptoed across the carpet and leaned over the box. I stood but stayed by the light and the bed. "It's in the Pop-Tarts," he whispered and pushed the box with his toe. A tiny body with oversized ears leaped like a cartoon over the edge. I screeched and jumped backward onto the bed. The field mouse slalomed under the nightstand and twice around the perimeter of the room before stopping behind a corner dresser.

"Oh, shit! Oh, shit!" I bounced from foot to foot on the bed, flinging my hands in the air. "Get it out! Get it out of here!"

Carey bent double laughing. "What's wrong with you? You're acting like a girl!"

I stopped mid-wail and blinked at him in the bald overhead light. I covered my face with my hands and started laughing as I climbed off the bed. "I'm in my sleep. Who was I there for a minute?"

"Good to have you back." He laughed again, and we bent toward the dresser. Both of us lunged back as the speedball mouse rolled between us and vanished under the door to the hall.

"So that's how he got in," Carey said. We rummaged through the food box and tossed the package of Pop-Tarts with the nibbled foil corner. We pushed all our luggage onto the high shelf in the closet and shut the door. Carey got back into his bed.

"Well, that won't stop him." I crammed towels under the closet door, then pulled extra pillows from our beds and jammed them in the two-inch space under the door. But not twenty minutes later that mouse or his cousin probed back in. I listened to its pitiful hunt and Carey snoring.

Guilt washed over me, a well-fed, warm intruder. I was glad when the mouse somehow got to the Pop-Tarts we'd thrown away. It's wrong to feed wild animals, but I had the urge to unwrap it for the poor thing, suffering rules and walls.

The next morning as we packed up to leave, I told Carey about the reappearance he'd slept through.

"Shouldn't we tell somebody?" He pulled on his jeans and pushed his hands through his clean hair.

"Tell who what?" I leaned around the bathroom door, mouth full of toothpaste.

"The hotel should be informed they have mice," he said. I laughed so hard I strangled before I could spit and rinse. "What's so funny?" he asked.

"Like they don't know they have mice in Yellowstone? Mice don't know doors from shineola."

He laced his boots. "So you're saying we're the ones trespassing here?"

"Carey, darlin, I figure it's lucky they don't have *bears* roaming the halls."

Yellowstone altered in the morning light. Flounced clouds broke apart to a robin's-egg blue, a nearly freezing morning. I drove through Golden Gate, a portal in the mountains. The escarpment glowed alchemical. Like Lot's wife, I turned for a last glimpse of the steaming chalk-white of Mammoth Hot Springs, burbling and bustling like a mythical city in the valley's chalice.

Carey kept bursting into mini lectures from the book he was reading. "I mean, we saw a few thermal features yesterday, but we just skimmed inside the caldera."

"Put the book away, Carey. You're missing the day!"

"But the caldera covers a thousand square miles? One thousand square miles of geothermal activity. Ten thousand features, more than any other place on the planet. Fumaroles and mud pots and geysers."

"Oh, my!" I said.

"Listen, there's this one limestone cone built up at the edge of Yellowstone Lake where fishermen used to boil the fish they'd just caught. Alive one second, cooked the next. But the scientists decided the bacteria in the cone might not be too healthy."

"For the fishermen or the fish?"

He faked a laugh-snort. "Seriously, I just mean, you wanted wilderness. How much wilder can you get than this whole place is an active volcanic site? It all might explode any second and wreck the whole planet."

At Norris Geyser Basin, across a vast plain, in the cold air, steam vented furiously from underground fire. Boardwalks ranged out onto the stark plateau between dozens of smoke-white flumes. All the tourists looked vulnerable, even the few like us who were dressed for the cold. The rest had on everything from tube tops to flip flops. Carey loved the geriatrics, men in ties and women in Sunday shoes and panty hose. He joked about geezers among the geysers.

My catty comments were about the women wearing what Mama calls "parachute suits," neon aquas and pinks and oranges. Like big old mylar balloon people.

Another boardwalk had civilized the floury-white plain where little pools shone like extraterrestrial ponds. Porcelain Terrace, an acid barren boiled down to white. Fountain Paint Pots blubbered pressure-cooked mud. Putty-colored blobs lobbed up to smack and sink into steaming pores on the belching surface.

Everything wild, dangerous, seething and shaking. But people had tamed the place with signs marking every last puddle, gurgle and farting vent: Jewel Geyser with its shivering chandelier. Sapphire Pool, Excelsior Glacier. Grand Prismatic Spring was saturated with colors of the rainbow, ringed and ruined by a boardwalk and the tromping footsteps of thousands of people.

There was a mini metropolis built around Old Faithful and its whole groaning, spewing landscape. Buses of Koreans and French and Japanese people were unloading into the restaurant and the timber lodge. At the visitor center there were actual posted eruption times, like tide charts, so everybody could schedule their day.

We squeezed as close as we could among the midday throngs on sidewalks and grandstand benches flanking the park's prize centerpiece, nothing more than a bubbling spring. They ate snacks and chatted like they were waiting for the homecoming game to start. Old Faithful gurgled in wider surges as tense minutes lapsed, seething up two or three feet in the air, then receding, time after time. Then the geyser stopped teasing and ruptured into a short wavering vertical white plume. The tourists clapped and stomped as if the spout would respond. The chill wind blew the gush away from us, wider than it was tall, the ground shuddering, a force that had the power to kill us all.

The crowds *oohed* and *ahhed* and then cheered as the turbulent flare burst up and held its wavering pose, up, and climbing up and up onto itself. It curved away from its cone like a long quill quivering, right on schedule. Towering. As it finally sank and waned—just like they do when movie credits roll—people checked their watches and stood to leave. They shut down their cameras, put away their video recorders and hustled to beat the crowds to the snack bar. Carey and I slipped onto a newly vacant place on a bench and watched until the geyser had shrunk back to its hidden, silent self.

Past the park's southern lakes, I felt a release from the powder-keg landscape. Whatever threatens below the surface has nothing on the tensile power of the earth's skin, holding in all that volatility. It exhausted me to think of the turmoil and regret and grief I'd been holding back, the enormous forces at work underneath the surface of my life. And the strength it took me every day to hold in grief and stories. The caldera even below the lakes let out little lapses through ruptured vents and holes and fissures. All the tension in the world finally finds miniature weak spots to take a random breath.

Carey said again if the caldera ever blew, it could possibly ruin the whole planet. Nuclear winter. Ice age. The wreckage of every living thing. The clouds glowered again, threatening rain as we drove along Rockefeller Memorial Parkway, south toward the Tetons. We put our caps back on and rolled our windows down to let in the clean, moist smell of unburned trees. Early evening fog spilled out of the woods.

Then even above the roar of the motor, Carey braked at the sound of pounding. I thought for a split second maybe Yellowstone really had blown a gasket. Out of the mist, just as Carey came to a full stop, wild horses clattered across the pavement right in front of us, dark and tall like phantoms. A whole herd. Piebald and golden and brown in their gloss. And then just like that they were gone.

"Did you see—?" Carey said. "Or—"

"Shh. You can still hear them," I whispered. They stomped and snorted through the woods. A line of cars behind us started to park along the road, and people got out to look. At the back of the line, drivers who couldn't see the mystery blew their horns. Carey moved timidly ahead, and for miles we both scanned the woods for that beautiful wild vision of flashing manes and tails.

In the Tetons, we camped in more rain at a place called Colter Bay. Mountains—the most spectacular mountains—hid behind the weather. We couldn't see farther than the rain-drenched trees around us, and then the dark tent. In the rainfall I fell into a dream about my house. I dreamed there had been an awful mistake. People kept asking if I'd seen the site. How did I know it was my house that burned?

I went back to make sure the firemen had been right. There it was. In the row of Victorian houses, my house sat with its passive face to the street, abandoned. The yard was overgrown with tangles of kudzu and weeds. Behind burned trees the front porch tilted. The door was held wide open by a stranglehold of vines. Lizards skittered in and out. Mice and snakes scurried away at my first footstep on the mossy floor. A bear lumbered out of my line of sight into dark recesses.

Inside then it wasn't my house but a cave, the wide, yawning mouth protesting. *Where have you been, woman?* Neglect in every inch. The walls had been swallowed by limestone and travertine, dripping with sulfurous water. Rivulets trickled and steamed. Green life grew from the stairs. Roots hung from the mildewed cavern ceiling.

Then a shadow in my mind shifted, like a dead tree being pushed aside. There Daddy stood, palms folded—not into fists, but held together in front of him, as if he were about to sing. And then I realized he was holding something to show me. He was trying to say something from the edge of distant burned-out woods, and I had to look through binoculars to watch his mouth. I could never make out what he wanted to say.

I held my hands in front of me the way Daddy had, and something wild wriggled there, beating its life against my palms. But it was a secret. I shouldn't look. Daddy stood at one side of the meadow with his secret. And I held mine, standing on the other side. We never unclenched our hands to motion or signal, and neither of us budged one inch closer to the other. I watched past Daddy's shoulder as the steaming landscape shifted into the wooded overgrown farm we'd left to ruin so many years before, a fractured, wild place like no other place on the planet.

When I woke up, my hands were sore from being clenched together. "Hold out your hand," Daddy would say to me when I was a kid. He'd gently drop from his loose fist a ladybug or lightning bug into my open palm, or my favorite, a bristly balled up caterpillar. He called them woolly worms. If we stood patient and still as stones, the woolly worm would slowly open, like a breath tickling my palm. Daddy would read its black and orange bands for signs—of a late fall, or a harsh winter, an early frost.

"He's got him a thick coat, don't he?" He'd laugh. All those signs he knew, an innate knowledge of seasons and how to read the land and sky in all their weathers. My daddy had a naturalness inside him that fewer and fewer have.

What it must have been like for him to lose Mama when she took Dunn and me and left. Hurt bad enough that he would go so far as to burn the farm down to say, what? His love? Was the fire he set vindictive punishment or a smoke signal of devotion? If you don't say the words, if you can't let go of the sense by telling truth, then maybe it's easier to wreck the world.

I'd been living on my own terms. My will be done. What landscape was I burning behind me? Carey said the twelve acres were mine to do with what I chose. A free woman with choices, steps to make. How did I know what to choose from the future if I refused to speak the past? The pocked skin of earth, it couldn't keep back the turmoil beneath without releasing its rotten-egg stench and burbling fury.

Not saying the baby I lost, not saying aloud the hurt Kevin had done, I had believed my silence would heal me. I'd get back to Tennessee whole in a new way, liberated, with all my misery in a nice, tidy little sack, like rocks in a bird's craw. But I'd been living the way Mama lived, hiding away from a place she loved, refusing even to acknowledge the land, our past. What had it cost me, shutting myself away from the place I loved? Like trying to fit a lid over the wilderness, a box around the moon.

EVOLUTION

Sunrise convinced me: Bring your hardest hardened criminal to the Rocky Mountains and you're likely to get your confession.

If I hadn't needed to get up and pee, I might have missed the day breaking wide open and swept cold, the Tetons sawing up into the clear pinking sky. The rain and every cloud had vanished, and left only pure light, insistent as a rooster.

That kind of clarity pretty much demanded tattling on myself. Secrets are a coward's refuge. Time to go big or go home. But then, I was headed home either way. Chicken or warrior, I would be knee-deep in my future soon enough.

I shivered from the cold and an ecstasy of adrenaline as I hurried from the bath house to the tent in my unlaced boots, hugging my coat around me. One other person stirred near our campsite. There was the scent of coffee and pine smoke. I couldn't fathom what words I would say first to Carey, expecting him to be sitting like a Buddha, waiting to hear me.

Of course, when I unzipped the tent to crawl back in, he hadn't stirred a centimeter. His face, swaddled in the hood of his sleeping bag, was tender with deep sleep. But his boyishness was fading. It wasn't just the two-days' growth of beard. His thin frown lines were set, and creases around his mouth. I could see where age was taking him, both of us heading toward forty and into the second half of lives we hardly recognized.

Not many people in our generation know one another from childhood and on and on. Maybe that friendship was too much to ask of him, of myself. I couldn't guess how little it might take for us to lapse apart again. Before, on my lousy part, it had taken only Stan. But Carey had been sweet to admit that he hadn't liked Dawson or Sam much, either. Maybe we didn't have room for one another in each other's real lives. Maybe this journey would be a last place for us, a mobile long good-bye. My dread of going east, I suddenly realized, was partly the dread of going my separate way from Carey. I needed to start making my peace. But there was no coming to peace without trusting him to know really, truly all that had prodded me to travel west with him.

With tiny quiet motions in the tent's vestibule, I laced my boots and zipped up and found my wool cap. As I zipped the tent closed again, I held my breath.

Carey didn't budge. On the park map I drew a circle around a nearby short trail to a place called Swan Lake, then weighted it with a rock on our picnic table with a quick note: *I'm off to see the Wizard. If I'm not back by 8, send a posse.* To scare away early rising bears, I talked and whistled between bites of apple and slapped my thighs while I hiked.

And I tested right out in the air the way I might start my monologue. Was it a confession? "I didn't tell you everything." Or I might say, "I want to tell you something I haven't told anybody else." It's a self-conscious thing heading into new territory.

Other than the noise I made, there was only the sound of the woods and meadows waking up—bird call and the wind shifting. The small lake lay in a cove of cool shadow where water lilies quavered, like they might start making a tone. Dawn came indirectly, in sun on the peaks. And on the mirror of water, the fire-pink mountains, burning their rock-solid rightness on the surface. Swans swam across the glow, skating around the reflection of marble crags. I talked to them a little and kept waiting for them to trumpet, but their white bodies glided guiltless and silent.

Carey was busy when I got back to camp, looking for a spare battery for his camera, counting out rolls of film for the day. The surprise of a perfectly clear morning made him chatty before caffeine. I made coffee on the camp stove and ate two bowls of cereal while he talked to the guys in the next site about places they'd camped in Wyoming and Colorado. He looked at maps with them while I packed our sleeping bags and started taking down the tent. The morning went nothing like I'd imagined.

But at so many junctures we were in sync. We agreed in less than three minutes which route to take, a tough choice—south into Utah instead of across Wyoming. Without a word we both left on our coats and rode with the windows rolled down in the wash of cold. We didn't get very far very fast. Carey stopped at the slightest pull offs to take dozens of photos. Granted, the Tetons did morph with every curve.

"Doesn't it, Glenna?" Carey started the engine for what seemed the hundredth time that day and looked at me. He pointed. "Looks like the peaks are melting into the lake? The tectonic plates still shove the granite up a few inches a year, though. And with no foothills, they pour right into the lakes. We're so lucky. If it had kept raining, we wouldn't be seeing this. So lucky. "Les Grand Tetons." He laughed at his forced accent and pulled back onto the road. "You know what it means, right? French for the *great teats*." He slowed and looked up through the windshield as we came around a curve again. "I mean, can you imagine any prissy English explorer getting away with that?"

x

264

"I really didn't know that," I said, trying to laugh with him. "They don't look like breasts. Not to me. There's nothing maternal about them, anyway."

"I think it was kind of a joke," he said. "Like Madonna in her cone bra, you know? Bawdy in a cartoonish way. And I'm not exactly an expert, but I think guys don't really want 'maternal.'"

"Teats. Tits. Breasts," I said. "Those are all different, right? These mountains are just so—well, the mountains we're from? Now the Appalachians are motherly and round. The Tetons are—well, they're like God's voice."

Carey slowed the car and looked at me as if I had made a discovery. He laughed. "Old Testament God, though. Like they could smite you."

I could only shrug. Was that what I felt in those peaks, facing this high horizon? A threat? A tectonic pressure daring me, or else?

"I always think the New Testament God is much nicer," he went on. "With Jesus as his buffer zone. A real fishes and loaves kind of guy, who knew his wine."

"Always up for a picnic." I played along. He grinned that Carey grin. And I could see in his face that space in the universe inviting me to *be*, move past whatever might happen because of the saying and telling. It wasn't a bear or swans or the mountains or sky or some deity I needed to speak toward. Here was the boy who had always known me, my friend against all odds. He needed to know my grief. My guilt.

"Yeah, but don't forget." I held my trembling hands in my coat pockets. "Before you could sit down to eat, you had to sing for your supper. Say you're awful and start fresh, all over again. Only then, the big drawback is everybody knows how awful you really are."

"But when we were kids, getting baptized together, the package deal sounded great," he said. "Didn't it?"

He slowed at a turnoff. The Tetons had already shifted in the mid-morning light, pure stone and age, the sky an afterthought.

"Hey, let's get a picture together here," I said.

"Great. Yeah. We haven't taken more than three or four photos together this whole trip." He rigged his camera on the car hood, set the timer, and we stood beside white aspens with the Tetons behind us, listening for the shutter to click. After a few shots, we looked at the mountains, like marble waves, their giant slow motions evolving to the blue-dark color of the whole planet, the color of Earth from space.

"They look so permanent," Carey said. "It's too weird to think there was a time before they ever were. And then millennia to get worn down to the way they are now. And then eroding back to nothing in millions more years." He waved his hand. "Just give it time, I guess, and time will move mountains. No wonder they say that, right?"

I got in the Jeep while he put his camera up to his eye and snapped a few more shots of the the craggy, overpowering jut of that horizon.

Those photos we'd just taken, inside his camera, would show split seconds of our lives. Faster than a blink. What would it be like for Carey, picking up the prints in a few weeks, to see our faces together? And who would find those photos years ahead, maybe one lost picture stuck to a cough drop at the back of a drawer? What would somebody think of those two people squinting into the sun?

He got back into the car and put on his seat belt. When he reached for the key in the ignition, I blurted, "Wait." He stopped to look at me.

"Okay? You look, so—kind of freaked out." He took his sunglasses off.

"I didn't tell you. The truth about Cindy. I mean me. That it was my fault. I let so many bad things happen because I was selfish and mean and—"

"You're not selfish and mean."

"I shocked you yesterday. And there's worse—"

"Me?" He put his fingertips to his sternum. "I'm unshockable."

"No, you were shocked."

"I mean, surprised? Maybe? But you did a truly selfless thing. Putting Cindy before yourself."

"No, see? Carey? You can't—I can't let you think that."

"I don't judge you," he said. "Or her. I'm for a woman's right to choose."

"It's not about that," I said.

"I mean, at first," he said, "I admit at first it made me sad that you couldn't adopt. But you didn't want to use her. If you had twisted her arm to give you her baby, that's terrible. She needed you. And it seems almost kind of noble."

"Oh, Carey! Noble? Please listen. I blamed Kevin for not wanting her baby." I looked at the peaks ahead of me, a focus for the anguish. "And I let Cindy think it was entirely his fault. He was out of my life, though, and I could have had her baby. At least—" My own words stopped me. "See? Like it's a consolation prize. It was a *baby.*"

"Well, she could have found some other couple to adopt if she'd wanted."

"But I think I was jealous she might do that very thing. So maybe on some level I convinced her."

"To have an abortion?" he asked. "She's the one who went through those doors. I mean, yeah, you helped her be brave."

"That's what I made it sound like to you. And to myself. On a good day I can convince myself it was bound to go the way it did. With or without me. But I could play bystander because I was getting what I wanted." I took a deep breath. "Because, by the time Cindy had to decide, I had—I'd missed two periods."

Carey waited to understand for a heartbeat. I could see confusion disappearing from his face, as if the bones under his skin were softening.

"You're pregnant?" He screeched. He lurched to unbuckle his seatbelt and swung around in his seat to face me, to reach for me.

"Oh, no!" I pushed my palms toward him. "No. Carey." I shook my head, and his face went dark. I couldn't look at him. I looked through the windshield again, at the rocky, jagged peaks with snow lines and glacial pockets. "I'd be showing by now. I'd be about five months along."

"You lost a baby." He said the words I couldn't.

Now that the time had come, I couldn't answer a simple yes, or even nod. I was brave enough, finally, to look at Carey again. Tears had pooled in his eyes. For once I didn't mind his pity. He would see pity wasn't justified.

"How can that happen?" His face crumpled and he felt in his pockets. I reached into the backseat for the roll of paper towels.

"It was fairly early, which is common, from what I read later. A first pregnancy a lot of times ends up in miscarriage." I shrugged like it was nothing, taking on the role of soothing him. "Maybe upwards of like twenty percent of all pregnancies. Sometimes the baby dies—the embryo—right away, even. Maybe it doesn't attach. But the symptoms that it has, well, failed, don't show for two or three months. The, the symptoms, you know, the spontaneous—" That morning's blood and gruesomeness came back to me. I had to stick with facts and technicalities, or I would be wrecked. Statistics kept the landscape in focus. "Some women don't even know they're pregnant. But I took an early home pregnancy test. Hell, I took five of them. I hadn't even been to my OB. It was so early. But I know I should have. I should have gone—"

The world tilted, then, the peaks falling forward toward me. My own voice condemned me. My words made the blame real, the deep realization I had barely let myself consider.

"It's my fault my baby died." I was cold and shivering. "Isn't it? Because I was stubborn? Spiteful. I was out of my head furious at Kevin. I couldn't stand to see him, even. And I just sat there in that house. Smug." I looked at him and whispered, "Carey, what if I'd gone to the doctor right away?"

"Stop blaming yourself. They told you. The doctor said these things happen."

"No. I read that. After. Nobody—nobody—"

"Glenna." He took my face in his hands. "You didn't go to the doctor even after?" He pulled off a paper towel and wiped my face. I hadn't realized I was crying. For the first time in ages, crying.

"Really, it was so fast, Carey. It was over. Nothing anybody could have done. It was gone. One morning. It woke me up, and it was over so fast. About two weeks after Cindy—"

"I can't believe you didn't go to the emergency room. Or call an ambulance, Glenna. Women die from this kind of thing." He held his hand on my head, like a blessing. "Glenna, honey."

I took the towels from him and scrubbed my face dry with a hard swipe. I didn't deserve to cry. I could hear Grandma Ruby all those years ago, defending Daddy, begging me to forgive him, to cry for him: *You ain't got a heart.*

"I couldn't have gotten to the phone, Carey. For a long time I just lay in the bathroom. I couldn't stand some stranger in my house. Really, the only person I thought about calling was Cindy. I kept wanting to tell her. Because she would understand. I was alone like she was alone when—"

"Don't. Don't talk anymore. You're wearing yourself out. It's all okay. I'm so glad you're okay."

"But let me finish," I said. "You don't know how I keep thinking. I keep thinking I got what I deserved."

"Why would you—why would anybody deserve a thing like that?" Carey said. "Nobody deserves to lose a baby. It's not punishment."

"But every day I *know* it is a punishment, though. Because, you have to see. When I took Cindy—I knew I was pregnant that morning I took Cindy. I had what I wanted. It was okay for her to have an abortion because I didn't need her baby."

"But I know you. You weren't thinking those things."

"I don't know what I was thinking. I wasn't. I was so angry at Kevin and hurt. Hell, I wasn't even feeling. I was numb. I thought I didn't need anybody else. I didn't need Kevin or anybody. Because it was my baby. Mine. All I had left."

I looked at Carey then, with clear eyes, with all my meaning, and I could see my sins were dawning on him, just then.

"Kevin didn't know I was pregnant. I was planning to tell him. I swear. I was about to tell him. Every single day I was just on the verge of telling him. I was waiting to sign the divorce papers. Like maybe the baby might be a sign we should stay together, you know? And then, well, it was so confusing. And he—" I stopped. It was too much of a tangle to talk about Kevin yet. "Just—it was *my* baby."

"And so, you never told him about the miscarriage at all." His face showed that he understood almost everything.

"I never told anybody, Carey. Until you. Right now. Nobody knows about the baby. I never even told Mama. Not anybody. Just you."

We rode in exhausted quiet, right past Jackson Hole, where we'd planned to stop for lunch and a look around. A stupor took over me through the winding woods along the Snake River. I wasn't paying close attention until the mountains were gone and Carey was driving us along a dead-level highway through endless high plains of sagebrush.

There was nothing now but distance. Pronghorn antelope moved like quick birds. In single file groups they grazed with surprised masks and twitching white tails. For a long time, the only other landmark was the Wind River Range. I focused on that little line of white-capped blue following far beside us. The nobbed plain sped past, while in an optical illusion I was lock-stepped in slow motion with the mountain range. In minutes, seconds, the peaks receded and disappeared in my sideview mirror, like a coin edge slipped into a child's bank.

Naked sky. Naked earth. No trees, no hills, no shoulders of mountains. No safeguard in sight. Only random tiers of snow fence and barbed wire between us and the curved edge of the planet. Not since Texas had we been exposed to so much wayward, domineering sky. And the range. Rolling like there would never be anything else again besides emptiness.

After hours that felt like days, Carey said we ought to eat something, that I must be hungry, because he sure was. We pulled off the highway for peanut butter and jelly, and then when we set out again, he tried to manage the quiet in the car with some levity. He was juggling the moments between us that had shapeshifted into a new dimension. He made a game of timing between cars. I half-heartedly helped. He figured after a half-hour we passed only one vehicle every four-and-a-quarter minutes on average, mostly campers and motor homes. They rocked us with brusque bursts of air, a split-second vacuum. All those blurred faces headed where we'd just come from.

I looked at the map. Soon they'd catch their first glimpse of the peaks, and in less than two hours lose sight of the high Rockies because they were blocked by foothill ranch lands. They would pass cowboys pressing their herds across greening folded uplands near Pinedale, the last town before the tight-bellied hills of the Gros Ventre Range, where the sun falls like coins through thick dark forest. In four hours, they'd be in Jackson. In six hours, they'd be startled, convicted, maybe redeemed, by the stark granite faces and throne swales of the Tetons, locked down in glaciers that had been in place in some form or other since the Ice Age.

I craved the blue morning hours in the solitude of that sun-drenched stone, before I burdened Carey with my burden. I should have held tight. If I had stood there long enough, maybe I would have been purified without saying a word. Words I couldn't take back. With the patience of aeons, I could have recontoured every rift of myself. By myself. But I didn't have aeons. Human time is impossible to gauge against bedrock time. I had only words and memory and the erosion of my weakness. And now I was bound to Carey in a different, new way, already transforming.

Hitting traffic and construction in Rock Springs was the biggest jolt on the road since the wreck we'd seen in Montana. Carey drove through jackhammering and shadowed hard-hat faces, truck grills stacked with orange cones like mechanical rhinos. Crushed gravel dust mixed with steam from tar rivers. Whir and drill and grind for twenty minutes, then back to the lonesome rush of the plains.

Past a long curve, the earth sloped away to the west and opened a deep vista, miles of alternating valleys and swells, bounded by a blue mesa horizon. Down in the vast, dry maw, the only human thing was an insignificant pale line, a dirt road. My stomach melted in my abdomen. My skin pricked, as if I needed to find cover.

"Badlands," Carey pointed to the far chasm, swerving. "I've always wanted to see this part of Wyoming. Just think how many geological zones we've passed in Wyoming alone. I mean dozens of different eco-regions. Do you see those soft mountains there, and mesas?"

"I see them. That's all there is, is seeing."

He looked at me. "You've had about seven thousand miles of distractions," he said. "And you weren't really distracted, were you?"

His knowing stung me and cradled me at the same time. We rode in silence again while I looked at the map. The highway was bound for a place called Flaming Gorge, a huge spraddling tuber where the Green River is dammed between Wyoming and the wilderness of Utah. When the road curved, we topped the edge of a basin and there was the wide empty puzzle-piece mirror.

Closing in on the dam, motorcycles and SUVs took over the road, and big 4X4s pulling boats—everybody towing something. In the dam's narrow channel, where the Green River turns back into itself, a mini metropolis with parking lots and picnic areas, speed boats on the wide, winking reservoir.

Carey pulled into the visitor parking lot. "You think you can drive awhile, after we stretch?"

"Another damn dam, you like to say," I said.

"What?" He blinked at me. He undid his seat belt without turning off the motor. "Oh, yeah." He was nodding, but he didn't budge. I couldn't see his eyes through his sunglasses.

I'd never known Carey was so down on dams until we got to Yosemite. He explained a new environmental movement for eradicating the worst dams on the planet. His top picks were Hetch Hetchy in Yosemite and Glen Canyon in Utah. He railed that rec areas like Flaming Gorge are the worst, that they make people upstream into dickhead yokels, fishing and boating, never understanding the consequences.

"Aren't we getting out?" I unbuckled my seatbelt.

He held on to the steering wheel and looked out the windshield. The air conditioner was still running. "Carey?"

"At first I thought—I guess I feel so heartbroken for you." He shut the ignition and in seconds the swampy green-house heat smothered me. He opened his door but faced me. "But I can't stop feeling sad you didn't call me, I mean right away. But then it slowly dawned on me. Glenna, hell, I mean, we've driven nearly seven thousand miles, and you didn't say a single word. Not in all that time."

My whole body flared with the heat of the day, and his disappointment.

He got out of the Jeep and grabbed his elbows in his hands over his head, stretching. "So, you're not up for a little break?" He asked. I shook my head.

Next time I could focus on the day around me, he was halfway across the dam overlook, pushing among tourists. When I stepped out of the Jeep, my legs nearly buckled. On the lake there was a boat, just a tiny speck of white on the green water. Tawny bluffs angled way above the surface of the lake, scraggly evergreens on the narrow ledges.

Carey was looking down the side of the dam where the water is unleashed, flowing free again. He'd told me about the devastation of TVA dams, the huge damage and extinction we'll never calculate because back then, just after the Depression, no one did environmental studies. Never heard of such a thing.

Carey wanted to turn back time and undo dams, just like he wanted to undo the place I had holed up, the thousands of miles, way down inside myself. But I couldn't retrace all those miles and find a sooner place to tell him my losses. He had made a career of looking past the obvious facts and dates and events into the tangle of things, the deeper repercussions. Anybody who thinks dams can just be dismantled right and left has to be a little sanctimonious. Leave it to Carey, an idealist, to believe there would be anything to salvage, even if you could peel back all that water.

But I'm a realist. I know, if you demolish a dam, and erase the beautiful lake, everybody has to see the devastation created year after year down beneath, the big, drowned scars. The yawning ruin where there used to be a placid sanctuary reflecting an easy sky.

Dinosaur sculptures in garish colors smirked as we drove through Vernal, Utah. Big billboards advertised Dinosaur National Monument. Businesses seemed psychedelically happy to serve park-goers.

The ranger at the entrance station to the monument had been alone in the hot sun way too long. And Carey and I hadn't said much since we crossed Flaming Gorge. We both jumped when the guy leaned into the Jeep with a park map, with his loud "Yessir, yes ma'am, a good number of sites vacant at Green River campground. Cottonwood shade, right by the river, in view of Split Mountain, named Split Mountain because over the millennia it was *split* by the Green River!"

We picked a site without much deliberating. The cool air under powerfully tall cottonwoods was a surprise. The river in the late evening light passed fern green, just like its name says. We walked to the shore and watched it roll by for a few minutes, but decided it was too much like watching the road.

Carey had the tent halfway completely staked by the time I'd gone to the bath house and checked out the facilities.

"You hungry?" I tried to sound flip. One of us had to start talking again. I bent to help him finish tying down the fly.

"Not much," he said, grunting as he stood.

"After nine, ten hours in the car and nothing but a snack, you're not hungry?"

"Not much, really," he said again, stretching.

I couldn't keep from shaking my head in a blinding frustration.

"What?" he asked. "What's funny? I'm not hungry." He headed back to the car for more unloading.

"Nothing's funny. Is this how you treated Stan whenever he pissed you off?" I opened the passenger door and got my pack and the bag of car trash to toss.

"Who's pissed off?" he said. "I'm tired. It's been one of our longest days of the whole trip."

"Come on. I've been waiting for you to finish what you started for two hours."

"What did I start?" We stood on opposite sides of the the hatch.

"Carey. Stop answering questions with questions." My hands were shaking from being hungry, and now mad, facing my judge and jury. "I should have known better and kept my life to myself. I assume you want me to apologize for holding out on you."

"How did you hold out on me?" He started digging through his suitcase and setting clothes aside. "Do they have hot showers here, by the way?"

"Agh! Questions! You said, basically, how could I go seven thousand miles and never trust you. But at least you're more evolved than most men. It took you a few hours to make this all about you."

"What's that supposed to mean? I don't get what you seem mad about, Glenna." He sat on the bumper of the Jeep.

"I'm mad? You're the one giving me the silent treatment. I should've seen it coming." I pulled the cooler out of the car. "You can starve if you want. I've got to eat."

He tried to take the cooler from me, but I turned to the side and then sideways in the other direction to deflect him. But he wouldn't let me pass, up a little step of cottonwood roots. When I tried again, he took the cooler and set it on the picnic table.

"You're more male than I thought."

He stumbled around me and blocked my way back for another load. "You can't just say some shit like that and walk away, Glenna. I'm more *male* than you thought? What the hell does that even mean?"

I stepped away from him. "You've got the same foot-in-mouth testosterone every man has. Everything eventually comes down to how it affects *you*. So, it's not enough that you're the first person, the only person I ever told?"

"That's ridiculous. Is that really what you think?"

"You said, and I will repeat—and it was you who stormed off across that damn dam—that I went seven thousand miles without telling you. When I should never have told you or anybody." I shoved around him and pulled the food box out of the Jeep. He blustered behind me and grabbed the box out of my hands and threw it on the ground. Potatoes and cans of tuna and salmon and boxes of graham crackers and cookies and cereal flew in a crazy pattern all around us.

"You can't think that of me," he said. "What have people—the men in your life, I mean—what have they *done* to you? Look at me. Look. I am *not* those men. I didn't mean what I said in any way you're thinking. I meant that I truly cannot imagine what you've gone through all by yourself. Or how." His shaking voice scared me. He started to cry. "What you feel from me is that I'm sad for you, Glenna. No. I'm devastated. I mean as sincerely as possible how awful it is that you've coped with this—tragedy, it's a tragedy—alone. All alone. You thought keeping this locked away was your only option. It has crushed me all day to feel one little percent of what you must have been carrying."

His eyes got big, and he turned and walked away with his hand over his mouth and sat on the picnic bench. "Jesus. You're right. Foot in mouth! I can't believe I keep saying the wrong thing. 'Carrying.' How could I say that? And what I said about fire. I keep trying to think of how, what to say. All day I didn't know what I can possibly say."

His words buffaloed me, crushed me. I bent to pick up a couple of potatoes off the ground. "I didn't know. I'm sorry, Carey. I am."

"Stop that. Stop and listen to what I'm saying," he said.

I raised up. I wanted to throw the potatoes at him for being right, for being faithful and true, but I stood there holding them in my shaking hands.

"You don't need to apologize. To anybody. Or not to me, anyway. Especially not me. It's just so hard to take in everything. How did you *stand* it? Do you even know how scary sad it is that you didn't even go to the doctor? You didn't even tell your mother?" He came over to hold the box and help pick up what he had spilled.

"But that's not what you said."

"Well, what am I allowed to say? You tell me. I guess I *am* judging you. But you think a good friend should just gloss over everything and say, *Sure, you're behaving normally?*" He wiped his eyes with one hand while he held the box against his hip.

The sun was lighting only the top of Split Mountain then, the dark coming on fast, and a chill in the air. People in other sites were looking at us as they tended campfires and went in and out of their trailers to get ready for the night.

"Carey, what can I do except say again I'm sorry? Telling you was wrong. It didn't help me, and it just made you feel awful too. I held back because of this exactly. I worried it would wreck the whole trip, and wreck me, and just look at your face. I told you things you want to fix, but that's not what I want. I can't stand to travel another mile with you if you're going to look at me like I'm so pathetic and pitiful!"

"I don't think you're pitiful," he said. He set the box down, and we sat across from each other at the table. He handed me an apple. "No, that's a lie. I think this is all pitiful. But you can't get mad at me because you told me. You can't hold it against me now that I know, and if you do that's on you." He sighed and pulled out a foil wrapper of Pop-Tarts and opened it to find crumbles.

"And one more thing. I can't help if I do judge you for telling the wrong person."

"But I don't know how I could ever go back and fix things with Cindy if she knew. There's nothing—"

"Cindy? I'm not talking about Cindy!" He shook his head. "Jesus Christ, Glenna. Do you really not know that you should have told Kevin first? You have to tell Kevin. Not just for him. Think about what it's doing to *you* not to tell him."

"I'm fine."

"Okay. You're fine, but Glenna, Kevin lost a baby too."

His words made me limp as a rag, as Mama used to say. Carey could see the effect, the dawning that happened to me. He got up to sit beside me and handed me a corner of his Pop-Tart. We munched in the dark as a wind purled across us.

"Will you build a fire?" I asked.

"Obviously, the man is the one who builds the fire, with his massive evolved ego!"

He shoved his shoulder against mine, then leaned his forehead to my ear. "You have to tell Kevin," he said. "That's me talking as your dearest friend. You will never be okay again until you share this awful thing with the only other person who can understand, Glenna. I can't be your substitute. It doesn't work like that."

I opened and closed my mouth. "I can't go home," was what came out. "I've been trying all day long on the road every day to figure out what I can be if I go back there. What will happen. Please. Don't make me."

"I totally get now why those twelve acres are so heavy," he said. "You can always come stay with me awhile. You know that. But I think you finally have

274

to do this for you. Even if you hate Kevin." Carey shrugged. "We've got two thousand miles to go. Plenty of time for you to practice on me whatever you need to say." He put his arm around me. "And this time I will try to listen."

"I don't hate him," I said. The words actually sounded true out in the air.

Carey convinced me to take the tour of the fossil quarry before we packed up our stuff the next morning. We were up, grimy and sleepy-faced, to beat the heat of the day. But it was already hot. I doubted there had ever been a drop of dew as far as we could see. We drove to the central parking area and ate granola bars while we waited under a heat-soaked metal roof for the shuttle bus up the ridge to the dig site. High bluffs around us blanched like an over-exposed photograph.

We thought we might be the only takers for the first tour. But minutes after we parked ourselves on a bench, a family pulled up in two big campers. The kids poured out in unbelievable numbers. Like clowns out of a tiny car, Carey joked. They scrambled to see who was fastest to the shuttle pavilion. The echo of their screaming and scuffling—twenty or so kids in all sizes—was deafening. Carey called them magpies. They ran and grabbed at each other from behind three wilted mothers in dirty sneakers and old-fashioned broom skirts. Their hair was pinned under their bonnets identical to the hefty granny's. All hers, three grown sons with bellies, their wives, and tow-headed kids.

"Mormons," Carey mouthed, as he punched a vending machine selection.

"How do you know?" I looked again at the parents, sober as statues amid the teeming kids. Carey rolled his eyes as he took a swig of juice. "They could be Pentecostals. Or Mennonites," I whispered. "Or maybe they're just having a family fashion crisis."

He laughed so hard he strangled. He held out the bottle for me while he coughed and wiped his nose on his sleeve.

Seeing them made me jealous, truth be told, the selfish bounty of so many kids. Enough kids between three couples to fill an elementary school classroom. One of the toddlers peeked out at me from behind his mother's gingham skirt. We played a smiling game until the matriarch shot me looks.

"Whoever they worship," Carey whispered in my ear, "they need to tie a knot in it. It's the worst conspicuous consumption. That holier-than-thou 'replenish the earth' bullshit. What they're really after is survival of their own gene pool. They just want to clone more of their own kind. Plus, who wants to buy that many pairs of Wranglers?"

He looked at me with wide eyes. "And there I've done it again, foot in mouth. Just cram my whole leg up in there. You want to buy that many pairs, don't you?"

"Nope," I said. "Just one would do me. And it ain't about the gene pool."

The linked cars of the shuttle tram pulled to a lurching stop, and the crowd made a languorous chain. The driver helped the grandma. Carey held me back by the sleeve and pointed to the last empty car. He wanted a buffer between us and the squabbling brood. We climbed on, but the motor drowned out everything as we started.

He had to lean close for me to hear him. "You thought about adopting before." His tone was a question. "You could, without Kevin—"

"Maybe not the time or place." I had to shout. "Later?" He nodded. In the open cars ahead, the kids slapped and punched and laughed, survival of the fittest. Rivalry and competition. Everything a game of one-up. Who saw the quarry building first?

It sat like a modern mistake jutting out of the earth, three glass walls with a ski-jump roofline. All of it replaced the cliffside they'd removed to dig to the dinosaur bones. Carey was quizzing the ranger before we set foot inside the building. We entered on the second story, into the hushed chill. We looked across a railing to the dug-out wall of half-excavated fossils, buried millennia ago. They dwarfed us all.

I was distracted by the kids, though. On the first level, I could see one of the boys had gone too far. His father pinched the nape of his neck, like Daddy used to do to us. A rough paw on skin left pale from a recent summer crew cut. While the other kids ran wild, the boy hung on to his dad's hand and looked up with wet eyes for judgment. For love. The boy was minuscule and soft in relation to the stegosaurus and brontosaurus fossils in the chiseled stone. His burred hair would be soft even in its stiffness, I knew. I wanted to touch it, my want more gargantuan than the massive jaw and thigh bones, the links of huge vertebrae.

"Hey, Glenna." Carey came behind me and led me toward the displays down the stairs. "What would some of the fundamentalists we know think about this place? Like my mother?"

"Oh, your mother is not a fundamentalist," I said.

"Look in the dictionary? There's her picture!" He tugged me to a display. "The inerrancy of the Bible, Creationism—or Intelligent Design—there's a stampede of stupidity coming, and she's waving the banner. Falling for that new crap in her church. People used to have more sense. We're *devolving*. You know, she really believes the earth is only about six thousand years old."

"What?" I had to laugh. I looked back at him. "Nobody really believes that!"

"Yep. Her preacher told her. Because according to the Bible, God created the earth about 2500 B.C. They can prove it, counting on their fingers. I mean, all the science, hell, the whole Enlightenment, to them it's mumbo-jumbo. She honestly asked me once if I believed in dinosaurs."

"Like Santa Claus?" I laughed again. "What'd you say?"

"I told her, 'Um, yeah, Frances. I've seen their *bones*.'"

We came to a plexiglass case holding the zippered spine of a slope-backed dinosaur, its tail curled in a reticulated whip.

"She can't argue with that," I said.

"Oh, sure. Her preacher says fossils are a conspiracy cooked up by the paleontologists. Or he would if he knew that word. Or some of them believe Satan put fossils in the ground, to fake us out. The Devil uses his power to make them *appear* around 145 million years old. I mean, the Bible doesn't say anywhere, 'And God said, let there be *dinosaurs*.' To them that means they can't be real."

I hadn't seen him so hilariously riled up in awhile. He bent to peer into the next plexiglass case, pecking as if he were trying to wake up a snake. "Mostly they're afraid of *that*." Inside a clock simulated the five-billion-year history of the planet, with twenty-four hours delineated on its face instead of twelve. Human beings have only been around for ten thousand years. Human time on earth was represented by only two minutes, a nearly imperceptible ratio. Two minutes.

What did any of it matter, then? No wonder such a thought scared everybody straight into the arms of Jesus. What was my life, or a life I could have given life to?

When I turned Carey was laughing. "What?" I asked.

"I'm remembering. A couple of summers ago, I took kids for a British history course in England. And we went to Stonehenge, maybe the most recognizable prehistoric site. I mean, *iconic*, right? And this religious right kid in full-on denial mode said to me, 'I don't believe in prehistory.' Like it's not right there in rocks bigger than tractor trailers.

"I mean, people like my mom are terrified," he said, "to imagine the world before humans. If you believe, you have to believe there can be time after humans. And it is sobering to think that nearly everything that's ever lived, except roaches and alligators and mosquitoes, has gone extinct."

"Has not," I said. But just as I protested, I knew he was right.

"Glenna? And thinking we're at the top of the food chain? We're so not." His face clouded. "Viruses rule the food chain. Anybody who saw friends die from AIDS like I did? No. Humans are expendable," he said. "But why does fact intimidate their faith?

"And they get the most arrogant, unbelieving scientists on center stage. But I know plenty of academics, physicists, chemists, who are believers. They've seen the face of God in their work. Study literature? There's God. Study math? There's God. Study history? There's God."

Everything he was saying took me by surprise. That he believed in something that couldn't be calculated or documented. How had I not known that?

"I mean, why does it always have to be either or?" He said. "Us or them?

Right or wrong? Science or religion? Evolution or creation? What's more cosmic than evolution? Evolution *is* creation."

Past the Colorado border, Carey let me know I had just two more new states to enter—Kansas and Missouri. Three if we drove through a squiggle of Illinois. Determined to make camp at Rocky Mountain National Park by dark, we ate as we drove. Over every long rise, around every bend, the earth's surface managed a chameleon act, yellow ocher and adobe pink, juniper-covered buttes, and buckling, burnt-brick craters.

Every endless inch of desert was more beautiful because we were running out of it, lifting onto range land. Hay-yellow hills arched high as tidal waves above ranch houses between Craig and Steamboat Springs, a big jolt of civilization with its shopping centers and gas stations. The ski slopes carved green canyons through steep mountain forests.

But what I watched for, intermittently, clear above the mesas and plateaus, were the Rockies again, with their convicting pull into the cleansed blue heights.

Past a stretch of red rock, into forest, we passed square miles of blue lake. Carey said, "That's the absolute last we'll see of the desert." The motor whined without let up against elevation changes. Lodge pole forest tightened around us, denser as the mountain curves got steeper.

"Well, we're not through the mountains yet, so don't be talking no prairie."

When we came to the national park kiosk, we traded drivers, and I loved steering the Jeep up around hairpin curves, as if the sway of mountain roads was memorized deep in my bones, winding up into the trees a familiar sensation, although it was a place I'd never been before.

We crossed the Continental Divide for the fifth time on the trip, and the last, Carey said.

"Stop it," I said. "Naming all the last times. You're seriously harshing my buzz."

"I'm just balancing where you left off," he said. "All those first times. First volcano, first glacier. First sight of the Pacific. First redwood."

"But it's depressing, naming off the last things. Last geyser. Last of the desert. Last big gray rock. Last dead juniper."

"Okay." He laughed. "You'll be glad, then, that there's another first for you up ahead. One last biggie." A few minutes later, we came to the tree line. A stagger of scarecrow-ragged evergreens canted as if they were yearning for just one more foot of terrain. Then the tree line was below us and there was nothing above us but sky and blowsy clouds skimming the top of the planet.

In a few more miles, Carey said, "Tah-dah! Tundra."

A little skiff of ice crystals purled across the parking lot I pulled into. Up a bald trail people hurried in all kinds of summer clothes. Before we even opened the doors, Carey and I dug out our coats again, and caps and gloves. At the back of the car, I pulled on my waterproof pants over my shorts. I wound my scarf around my neck as we climbed the open path across the naked, pocked, raggedy ground, laughing. Laughing for no reason besides the bright cold air. Laughing because we'd woken up that morning to eighty degrees and now it was sleeting. Laughing at the muscular wind that pushed us forward across actual, living tundra.

But I had to stop every half-minute or so in the thin oxygen. Carey had warned me that at 12,000 feet, just walking would wind me. Laughing set my head aching as if a raw V pressed inside my skull. It was a little bit like having a hangover, dizzy as we went like sails full of wind.

Walking toward the rounded edge, past big pillars at a place called Rock Cut, I had the sensation we might walk right on, beyond the high curved horizon, receding layers and layers of mountains, ten, eleven waves of dark green, velvet blue, purple, stunned with snow caps.

Three hundred sixty degrees is always a powerful force to reckon with. Water in hollows of rock reflected sky, a pale wash of gray. As I turned and turned the whole world jolted, just a little sigodlin. Catty-cornered as Granny Pearl used to say.

Daddy would love this. Against my will, before I thought to think them, those words were in my head, ignorant of time and death and anger. Solid ground turned into a dizzy precipice, and I stopped, expecting to see Daddy out of the corner of my eye, right there with me on the tundra.

A day when I was a kid. Just like that, a memory sprang up out of the murky primal gunk in my brain. An April day when I was a kid, Daddy drove us all up into the Smokies, the highest elevations, to see a late, hoary snow. Icicles like jigsaw teeth decorated rock overhangs. Diamond strands of ice encased every twig and bud, everything white and glistening as sugar crystals. There was not a sound except the crackle of that spun glass. I hardly dared to breathe, as if gravity might unleash me from my perch on Daddy's shoulders and I would float away.

He held to my thighs, taking giant steps that shook me, listed my stomach like a seesaw tilt. I was a new person from the one who lived low to the ground. There at Newfound Gap, there was no ground, no ceiling. He held my legs under his biceps, and I circled my arms around his neck. Together we were the highest creature in the world.

Carey shouted above the wind and broke the spell. Turning back, we faced an icy blast in our faces. Infinitesimal crystals of sleet pelted us. No more wind at our backs. We pulled our hoods tight and hunkered as we walked. I had to slow and catch my breath. Carey paused with me and jumped up and down in the cold.

"You go ahead," I shouted over the wind. "I'm right behind you!" He nodded.

We went a few more steps together and then I had to hunch over at a halt again. I saw, then, the dull uniform blur of the tundra transformed into miniature lives, the ice crystals peppering the ground and bouncing among a zillion tiny blooms. Bending closer I knew some secret was coming to me, out of the vastness, the finer connection of one detail at a time, one step at a time.

Close up, the tundra was a garden, a wildflower bed, all of a piece but in a fractured infinity of color, the way grains of sand make up a beach. No blossom was any larger than a cross-stitch x, but between the porous rocks, cankered with black lichen, tundra moss and blossoms padded the ground almost entirely, a quilt of teensy flower faces. Fairy buttercups bloomed from impossibly minuscule red buds, smaller than peppercorns, and these spilled into webs of tiny ferns. Mossy cushions with sage-colored fronds, miniature imitations of parsley and cilantro and artichokes. Plush pale pink anemone petals, prim purple and white bells, dollhouse bluets.

A million tiny Edens. All those possibilities. Such tender things. But stubborn. Survival of the stubbornest. And I wondered then how rarely the tundra blooms. How brief a season. And how rare that I was there to see it. What a cruel place to survive. What a secret little space we all inhabit, so fragile, so unlikely, each of us.

I started crying before I knew that I was going to. I was tired and I wanted to lie down and sleep on that plush shoulder of the planet. I turned back several times to keep the cold from slapping me in the face. My eyes blurred from wind and turmoil. Walking with my gloves over my mouth and nose, I was light-headed, with barely a toehold tethering me to gravity. A thread of pure determination tugged me, crying the last wind-lashed hundred yards to the car, where Carey was waiting inside, out of the wind. When he saw me coming, he got out of the car and cocked his head as if he wasn't sure it was me. Frozen rain and condensation left his eyes blurry behind his glasses, but I could see their dark seriousness. I could see that he saw me clearly. And I saw him.

All the feverish cold release I'd felt in the Tetons washed over me like rapids. When I got to Carey I cried and didn't feel ashamed. I cried the way I should have cried at Daddy's funeral. The way I should have cried just to miss the stupid tour at Graceland. For all the disappointments. The way I should have cried for my ruined house, my ruined marriage. My job. The deep wound between Kevin and me. My baby.

Our baby.

Carey drove while I cried and stopped and cried again. He did not try and stop me. Just handed me tissues and paper towels. He skipped the first song on the mixtape he'd planned for Colorado—"Rocky Mountain High"—which he'd jokingly threatened me with earlier. Skipped to Linda Ronstadt, "Desperado." He played Bonnie Raitt singing "I Can't Find My Way Home," and Pure Prairie League and Little Feat and John Prine, songs I never would have known he liked from high school days, from before high school. The sun glowed on snowy peaks as if it were mid-winter.

I cried more. I cried because I couldn't turn the clocks back. Cold wind whipped the car around a veering sweep to face a gorge of steep, dark woods, pinched around a river far below. Down the canyon a bristle blanket of trees, millions of trees, and across that divide the streaked snow, where boulders the size of cars had crashed to a stop. So far away they looked benign as pebbles down the snow-skid, a place so steep probably no one had ever set foot there. Such a precarious way down it terrified me, so vast maybe nobody could maneuver through and survive.

I cried for the farm on Genesis Road we lost when I was a girl. I cried for all the hurt Kevin had heaped on me, the wound he'd made right through the center of me, like a shotgun blast I had to find a way to undo. I cried because nobody could change that damage but me.

At our campsite in the foothill meadows, Carey and I sat in our camp chairs exhausted, looking up at the peaks where we'd stood not an hour earlier. Moraine Campground around us may have been barreled across by glaciers, but rocks didn't hold dominion here. Just like in the tundra, green swathed the granite. Ponderosa pines whispered, brick-red trunks heavy with jade-heavy branches, like gigantic bonsai. The sky billowed, a pale muslin sail. The meadows were healing over with summer, softness binding the whole in ways that rock can only envy.

While we set up the tent, I kept my eye on the Coleman stove, trying to use up the food we had left—some fried potatoes, a can of black beans, apples in butter. At intervals like the bird call around us, Carey and I made small talk. We sank into the evening with nowhere else to be.

"I mean, you're okay now?" He got brave enough, facing away from me, hell-bent on his third attempt at a fire in the fire ring. The kindling we'd gathered was damp. I pulled out the bag of tortilla chips, a firestarter trick Kevin had taught me. Carey shoveled a few of them under the kindling, and they caught.

"I'm fine. I promise you, I'm finer than I've been in a long time. And I know you wonder what the hell happened, and you're being so careful not to ask. I don't know if I could explain it if I tried. Just one of those mysterious things, I reckon."

"Oh, it's everything all at once," he said. "You hit pause for several weeks, and you have to dread hitting play again. I mean, every mile is closer to dealing with so much."

281

He sighed and broke more twigs. "At least that's how I feel," he said. "Maybe I'm projecting. Like I could bawl my eyes out too, to go back to the same damn lonely house. And Stan still won't be there. But then, at least I have a house to go back to, so I've got no right to bitch about how bad I really, really don't want to go home alone."

I poked him with a stick of kindling I was toying with. "So you're going to miss me?"

"Like somebody cut off my arm," he said. He blew into the kindling and one of the larger logs caught. He leaned back and squinted one eye to inspect the little fire he'd finally built. "Yeah. I dread saying good-bye. It's like somebody punches me in the gut when I think about it."

Evening light stretched across the Ponderosa pines, and the birds had gone quiet. Now all we could hear were the spring peepers in the rain-soaked meadows and creeks. Yellow flowers glowed in the waning light.

"I was thinking about Daddy," I said. "At first. In the tundra, I mean. I don't know. He would have loved to see that, and for once I didn't mind him showing up."

"He shows up a lot," Carey said. "I mean, I think even I can feel him with us sometimes."

I thought for a second that he was teasing. But he wasn't. "I have to say, that's kind of too freaky to think about," I said. We both laughed.

"He's your daddy, so I'll just stay out of it. I'm sure there are good memories."

I leaned closer to the little flame. "You know, he held a gun to my head. It seems like not that long ago, really. It was just a little pistol. He said, 'By God, I'll take you with me someday.'"

"Jesus, Glenna. Listen to you, 'a little pistol.'"

"I know. But what else do you do with that? What am I supposed to do now that he's not here, and he can't take me with him? But he nearly succeeded, I feel like. He made me mean. And, shit, he took my damn house. My house where I lost the baby."

"Jesus," he said again. "I don't know what to say."

"You don't have to say anything. I don't even know how to say my own— sludge. The sludge of my life. How to build any kind of future out of what I've been given to work with. And those goddamn teensy flowers. Did you see them?"

"Flowers?"

"The damn flowers all over the tundra. Billions of little blooms. And I could have missed them just like that." I snapped my fingers. "Why in the hell did they make me think about my daddy? How many years of therapy could that take to figure out? I don't have that kind of time or money."

"Hell, they'd be paying you to hush." He giggled a little.

"I could be the ruin of therapist after therapist who just can't take it anymore." We were both laughing then, ridiculously, trying to keep quiet. Voices through the campground carried so easily, the air clear and light.

"Only you were strong enough to put up with me for a whole lifetime, I reckon," I leaned back in a stretch.

"Strong's got nothing to do with it." His face in the firelight was shining and peaceful. He didn't look at me, just kept poking a stick into the flames and blowing lightly every now and then, his other hand cradling another stick of wood on his knee.

He looked past my shoulder just as I heard a noise in the meadow. The fire was dim enough and the moon bright enough in the twilight that we could see mule deer grazing.

"Look, Glenna!" Carey whispered and pointed. I focused on a disturbance in the herd. A coyote slunk between clumps of sage, pale and camouflaged against the brush. But he could only crave a nip of mule deer babies. The mothers stamped and stamped louder and louder, more of them circling frantically, methodically. They held dominion in a collective commotion, and then in one surge they chased the coyote off. He sidled away, tail tucked between his legs, his fur steaming in the cold damp rising.

"Maternal instinct," Carey mumbled. "Keeps the planet going. But I can't."

"Can't what?"

"Keep going." Carey stood up and stretched and folded up his camp chair. After he'd gotten settled in the tent, I kicked a little dust into the fire and crawled in. I turned off the camp light and put on my silk long johns and my warmest zip-up sweater. I felt for my wool cap in case I needed it in the night.

"I want you to know that I was serious," Carey said as I climbed into my sleeping bag. "You've got the rest of Colorado and Kansas and Missouri to unload. Or not. And then we'll call. At least once a week, right? I mean, there's no limit on these ears."

"It won't take two thousand miles," I said. "But I've saved the saddest for last."

"Well, that's going to keep me awake all night," he said. "And how is that even possible that there's something sadder?"

"Kevin has a kid." I turned toward him and sat up in my sleeping bag.

"What?" He sat up and turned on the camp light. "I knew. You lied when you said he didn't cheat! I knew he—"

"No. No, no. Last year he found out that his old girlfriend had a kid. A little boy. And he didn't tell me, so technically he didn't cheat. But it was way worse. He wasn't exactly faithful." I lay back down.

"Oh, my God." Carey stretched out, too and turned off the light. "Oh. God, Glenna. Seriously?"

My adrenaline pushed me upright again, to face Carey in the dark tent.

He was looking at me even though he couldn't really see me. We were two outlines. We were darker than the dark.

"Yeah," I said. "So, Kevin dated this woman Sheila for a couple of years before me. They broke it off a few months before Kevin and I met. And we never saw her because, well, they broke up because she wanted to move back to Nashville. And then about a year ago, evidently, she moved back to Knoxville, and he found out she had this four-year-old boy. And he put two-and-two together—"

"Wait. She hadn't told him?"

I cringed to think about the secret I was keeping from Kevin. A miscarriage was the only thing I could give him from our marriage. Familiar jealousy rose up in me that I'd tried hard to squelch, so I could stay married.

"I blamed him that she—the two of them—took something, well, sacred from me. I could never give Kevin his first baby." I didn't add, *I couldn't give him any child.*

Carey said, "I mean, he might never have found out. Did he have a paternity test? And, Jesus, this is right about the time Cindy—"

"He was juggling shit I had no idea about. I don't know about the paternity test. But it's his son. He looks just like photos I've seen of Kevin as a boy."

"Wait, you've seen him?" Carey leaned up on his elbow so that I could see the outline of his head.

"Yeah, a glimpse." I couldn't yet. I couldn't tell Carey the rest. "I'm so tired. And I'm really not that interesting, my sob story."

"It's not a sob story," Carey said. "I can't imagine, finding out that kind of, well, it's kind of a miracle that fell in your lap. A kid just like you wanted, falling into your life."

"Not our life," I said. The ground under me was hard but seemed to be spinning. My heart was pounding.

"I mean, it's a betrayal, but not a betrayal he meant." Carey pleaded Kevin's case.

"He meant it," I said. "Intentional. First-degree betrayal. He hid it from me for months and months. All the time we were trying to conceive."

"Oh," Carey said, as if someone had punched him. "Oh. I see now."

"Yeah. I'm taking these infertility shots and going through awful procedures. Sadistic doctors. And nothing worked. And the whole time he had everything I wanted. We wanted. But all to himself. He didn't need Cindy's baby. You see?"

I was trying to keep my teeth from chattering, with shaking hands, reliving that betrayal in my head. The day I found out.

"The best thing that ever happened to him. Maybe the best thing that could ever have happened to me. But I wasn't good enough to be a mother to his son."

"I'm sure that wasn't it," Carey said. He lay back as if he were calculating with me what the reason could have been. In minutes his breathing slowed, so I was surprised when he said, "What's his name?" For a moment I thought he was talking in his sleep. "Kevin's little boy. Do you know?"

"Tobey," I managed. "He's blond. He looks a lot like one of the boys we saw today, the Mormon kids? Really lean and long."

"It's a cool name, really," Carey said. "Nobody uses it much anymore. Tobey."

"Tobey." I repeated. My voice surely carried his name out into the meadows where the mule deer were circled together for warmth, the steam of their breath rising.

CROSSROADS

Before I had the name Tobey to pin to his betrayal, I doubted Kevin's fidelity. On good days I thought fertility injections and volatile hormones were making me paranoid. In my logical mind I couldn't believe he would be unfaithful. But I lived with a perpendicular sense of everything between us. Any given moment, like a hot flash or a spasm, my imagination might seize up with scenarios: Kevin and a woman in a dim hotel room, a jacuzzi lit by candles, room service and chocolate strawberries. I was even jealous of naps he might be taking with what's-her-whore. I drove to work and home visits and juvenile court, the grocery, unable to remember how I got from one place to the next. I sensed Kevin was splitting his life in two. Our life. And I was right.

Carey drove us through late morning past Estes Park and toward Denver, the peaks hidden by clouds, everything hazy and vanished. He agreed Kevin made terrible decisions, but he asked what difference it would have made if Kevin had told me about Tobey from the start.

"You mean if he'd come home with flowers and a Hallmark card and said, 'It's a boy?'"

"No, Miss Smart Ass. I mean if he'd said, 'I need to tell you, I found out I accidentally impregnated my previous girlfriend.'"

I told Carey, "It's not as if I haven't thought of that scenario. Somehow, if Kevin had made room for me when he found out?" I really believe I would have been the world's most grateful stepmother ever. But there were no sweet hypotheticals. There was only what Kevin said, after I'd routed out his months of hiding and lies. That stubborn, solitary capital letter *I* did us in, independent and selfish as a marble column: *I have a little boy.*

That fall Kevin behaved like a kid who's sure the adults are going to tell him no. Easier to ask forgiveness than permission. He went out Saturdays alone, volunteering for trail maintenance at the national park. But he came home with no mud on his shoes. No lipstick smudges or perfume showed up on his clothes, no random strange earring fell out of his pocket. But I found food in his pack he'd never eaten before—organic animal cookies and fruit roll ups, juice boxes. I found receipts. Not from Victoria's Secret, but from Toys-R-Us.

A ticket stub from the zoo. He explained a toy drive, a field trip with students he'd forgotten to mention, a chaperone gig he couldn't get out of.

There was a check to the lumber store for three hundred dollars. But not a speck of sawdust in our yard. Kevin said he'd volunteered the lumber for some maintenance at a nearby state park. Later I found out he actually had donated the lumber and his time. Two weekends in a row he'd helped build a jungle gym at Tobey's preschool.

Later, after everything came out, it was hard to stop imagining every hour, every minute, every step Kevin and Tobey had taken together. Covert operations without me. Nothing, no abuse, no yelling, no gun-to-the-head ever wounded me like being cast out of my own marriage, my own dreams. My own future.

Kevin who'd seen me with a pillow stuffed under my shirt to look pregnant, who'd seen me cry and rant and work so hard to give us a child. Out of all the people on the planet, Kevin held and loved the one thing I wanted to love, and he refused to let me have even a little part in that belonging.

The only glimpse I'd had for myself, with my own eyes, went the way the worst betrayals always go. The shock to the cerebral cortex. And then the heart rearranged forever. The shiver that runs through terra firma and threatens everything you've ever believed about everybody. The one infidelity I would never have guessed.

The evening after I saw Kevin with Tobey, I didn't exactly plan an ambush. I was a raw nerve, half-terrified, half-lunatic with grief, waiting for Kevin in our dark bedroom. He'd lied and told me there was a late parent-teacher conference at the high school, not to hold dinner. Third time in a semester. I didn't turn on the light when I heard him on the stairs in his sock feet. But I stopped pacing and sat on my side of the bed, facing away from the door. I couldn't bear to see his outline.

His shadow fumbled for the lamp but missed when he jumped at my voice. "It's just as well to leave the light off, because you've already kept me in the damn dark for so long," I said. "What's his name? Can I at least know his name?"

He sat on his side of the bed, facing away from me. I couldn't stand to feel his weight sinking into the bed we'd shared. I stood and opened the curtain and looked at details in the dim yard below. The neighbors still hadn't thrown out their Christmas tree, shriveled under their porch light.

"Tobey," he finally answered. "His name is Tobey." He turned to me in the dark. "How——?"

"How did I find out you spent your afternoon with a child? I followed you and saw you with him, Kevin."

He shifted and stood and turned on the light. The yard below disappeared behind our reflections in the window. "You followed me?"

"Don't even pretend you've got the right to ask questions here," I said. "Don't you dare." I turned to see the blur of him, the shape of his head and beard. A stranger, a monster, coming into focus as I wiped my eyes. "Tobey." I tried to keep my voice steady. I tried not to cry, but my rage was spilling over. My wound deepened. "It's a sweet name. You've had time to get used to it, right? How long?"

"I was going to tell you, Glenna. It's just been so hard. I was waiting—"

"Yeah, I've been waiting too, every twenty-eight days. I guess you got tired of sharing the wait. I've been sitting here all afternoon, and the simplest thing I come back to over and over is that I shouldn't have to ask why you're sneaking around behind my back with a toddler."

"He's four. He's Sheila's."

"Sheila-you-dated-before-me, Sheila." I stated the fact I'd already guessed. "And so he's—He looks like you."

He nodded and tugged at his beard. He took up more of the bedroom than he'd ever seemed to before. He looked me in the eye. A very brave move. "I should rephrase. He's Sheila's. And he's mine. I should have told you that I have a little boy."

"You've had all this time to play Daddy with her?"

"Jesus. Glenna. There's nothing between us. I hardly speak to her."

"You don't have to throw me a bone," I said.

"I promise, there's nothing you have to worry about. She's as lunatic as ever. That's one reason I didn't tell you, because I have no idea if she's going to let me share custody. She's getting married, so I'm treading lightly here. It's so complicated. And then with us trying to have a baby. All you've been through, and an upset like this? I didn't want to get your hopes up. Again."

"Yeah. Please protect me. I'm so fragile. I couldn't bear, oh, let's say, the stress of, like a dozen medical procedures and filling out a living will and surgery. And where were you? Oh, right. At the zoo. At his school, at the playground."

He came around the bed toward me. I pushed a bedside chair between us, the way I've held my bicycle between myself and a barking dog.

"Glenna, honestly, I wanted to wait and see what's the legal deal. Not just the emotional ramifications. This is still a shock. To me! And you know how I told you Sheila is. Turns out she's been diagnosed bipolar, and she's trying. She's taking meds. She's not an unfit mother, just a hippie-chick. But she changes her tune ten times a day. I don't know what to trust. At first, I didn't half-believe he was mine, but just look—"

"How long, though?"

"Only—well—" He backed up and rubbed his face. "Not that long."

"When?" I yelled. "When, when, when?"

He grabbed the chair and pulled it away from me and stepped so close I backed into the wall and nightstand. "Glenna, please. Don't make a catastrophe out of this. You have to believe I've been trying to spare you."

"From what? Having everything I ever wanted?"

"But this is not everything we wanted, Glenna. Just like with Cindy. What little time I get to spend, I have to beg Sheila. You think she'll let me introduce him to my wife? I've had to be so careful. The lawyer says my rights aren't clear yet. I could take her to court, but I can't afford—"

"You've seen a lawyer? Here I sit, an expert in custody. I deal every day with parental rights. I know the only adoption lawyer in Tennessee, and you don't even consider that?"

"I can't talk with you like this. I don't want to get into all that right now with her. It's delicate."

"Oh, by all means, protect Sheila's feelings. Because she's so aboveboard." I looked at him. "How long? When did you find out?"

"Jesus. Okay. Less than four months."

"Fuck you, Kevin. Fuck you. Four fucking months? While I've been taking stupid hormone shots. Having sex with you every day until I never want to do it again. Lying there with my legs up in the air, hoping and praying. And you watching me at my worst. While you weren't who you said you were. Wasting my time."

"How was any of that a waste of time?" he said. "How does this change that?"

"This and that. This child, you mean? That baby we're trying to have?"

"If I'd told you earlier, you'd have been in a shitstorm mood just like now!" His face reddened as he tried to climb up, force his way out of the hole. The bedroom shrank, hot and fierce.

"You think this is a mood? Getting betrayed is not a mood, Kevin!"

He paced around the room, long legs taking him all the way to the door in three strides and back. "I dreaded exactly this. I knew you'd pitch a jealous fit."

"You said I don't have a reason to be jealous of Sheila."

"Jealous of *me*, Glenna!" He stopped and lunged toward me again, flailing his arms. "You're jealous of everybody with a kid. Jealousy like cancer. And now it's got to be your worst nightmare, that your own husband has a kid. I dreaded telling you. Yes. Dreaded. Because I knew you'd ruin all the good, the joy I get. I wanted to enjoy this just a little while."

I stopped shaking for the first time in hours, then. There was nothing else to be afraid of. "You don't know anything about me," I said. But he did know me. And that was the worst of the very worst.

I went to the cedar chest and pulled out covers for the guest bed. He stood with his arms out, but I dumped them in the hall. I slammed the door behind him. I was fairly certain he could see what I did—that our marriage was over.

Along the downhill winding roads to Denver, I told Carey about the odd relief of that sleepless night. Having an answer lifted a huge burden. I wasn't crazy. But at the same time there was new chaos. Kevin didn't resist. He made a choice—Tobey instead of me. Not once did he try to argue his way into staying. He took the next day off work and packed some stuff while I was gone, as if he couldn't wait to get out of the house.

"That hamster wheel of regret and stupidity and being duped and all those feelings? And to hear him admit how awful I was. He thought I would ruin his relationship with his son."

"Don't go there," Carey said. "He said that in the heat of the moment."

"No. He was right. When would have been a good time to tell me, Carey? It's taken me months to see, he *did* deserve time alone with Tobey. It's sacred, that father-son bond. Parent and child. I know that now. I only—I was only pregnant for a little while, and I feel the weight of that life. But this? A four-year-old. Vivid and alive. And I was—still am—so jealous I can't stand it. How can one of the best things that ever happened to Kevin feel like the worst thing that happened to me? How selfish is that?"

We were quiet around turns as the morning brightened a bit, the lowlands coming clear, but clouds still scuffing the crests of peaks we knew were beneath, always below the gray. Finally, I could come to some kind of pass, some knowing about myself, with perspective, with the distance.

"Kevin was right to be scared to death of me, wasn't he?"

"Glenna, don't think that. He was confused."

"I was a crazed maniac. Somebody he didn't recognize. I didn't know myself. And I can't blame hormones for everything, or desperation. People get desperate for lots of reasons. It's not an excuse. It was wrong, the way I found out, a freak chance. I deserve what I got, for basically stalking him."

Carey had a doubtful look. "You were worried. Anybody would be."

"No. I followed him, and that's wrong. Not really on purpose, and I didn't mean to snoop, but I did follow him."

Everything so far that looked suspicious had fallen out of his pockets or had been listed on joint credit card statements. I'd never confronted or accused him. I found out about Tobey in the most benign way any suspicious wife could uncover a secret.

That Friday, I got off work after a half-day. I drove to the high school to surprise Kevin, take him to lunch, something I'd done a dozen times, same as he'd shown up lots of times at my office for an impromptu picnic or a long lunch. I truly didn't mean to uncover his secret.

When I pulled into the faculty lot he was pulling out. "He didn't see me," I told Carey. "I blew my horn. I don't know how he didn't hear. I did wave. Honestly. He drove right past me like I was invisible. Which pretty much says everything."

I merged into traffic behind Kevin and followed, a little breathless. If he'd looked in his rearview for more than a glance, he'd have seen me. It was sneaky and fun, so I pushed down that gut feeling about the unknown I might stumble into. I thought about pulling beside him and blowing my horn, but I wanted to see his expression when I caught up to him at whatever restaurant he was headed to. The January sky was clean blue. Early crocuses bloomed. It made me a little giddy to pretend we were driving to a rendezvous, thinking things might escalate into backseat steam. I let myself think we might get pregnant, just because of my silly whim.

I had the first jealous inkling when he drove past a couple of nearby lunch haunts with veggie menus he liked. And he was driving fast. By the time I could have gotten around to wave him over, he was in the entrance lane. And then I was following him onto the interstate. It looked like he might be running away, leaving his whole life behind.

"So where did he end up?" Carey asked impatiently.

"A daycare center. Where Sheila agreed to let him visit Tobey every Tuesday and Friday. Even though it's way out of his way. He had just enough time to drive there and visit for a few minutes. Sometimes he picked him up and drove him home if Sheila needed. That's why he was late from work so many times."

I pulled into a space on the street when Kevin finally pulled into a parking lot in a busy residential area. I'd never been in that part of Knoxville before. Bare limbs shaded my car, but not enough to hide me, and for the first time I sensed I was doing something risky. Kevin locked his car and crossed the parking lot. Then I thought maybe he was going to a new dentist. Or eye doctor. My head was a muddle of confusion to watch him open the gate to Noah's Ark Daycare. He walked past murals of smiling cartoon zebras and giraffes, lions and monkeys and elephants. My heart pounded like a clock. An alarm.

When Kevin rounded the corner to the playground, a little boy broke free from the arc of a swing and raced right into his arms to be lifted up into the blue sky, one clean unbroken, certain movement. They hugged and leaned away from each other and laughed. I hadn't seen Kevin laugh like that in so long. I'd never seen him laugh like that into a child's face. *His* child's face.

My mind struggled to see someone else there, not Kevin at all. Someone who looked like Kevin and wore his clothes and borrowed his car. Someone else holding a beautiful, gold-fleshed, blond boy, a walking, running, talking, laughing, breathing boy. Who looked like Kevin and tugged at his beard and held onto his neck.

Kevin carried him toward the door to the building, listening to words I couldn't hear, that little voice saying secrets. Secrets to keep from me. Kevin talked into the boy's ear, kissed him on the forehead, the cheek. He touched his hair.

As he opened the door to go inside, he hefted the boy higher onto his chest. They were the most beautiful sight I'd ever seen. I wanted them to be mine. I wanted to be walking there beside them, holding and held. They were so close, but as untouchable as a snowflake under glass.

One last glimpse. One last glimpse as they turned to go inside. One little hand shining against the broad back of Kevin's sport coat, little sneakers flashing in the sun, knees latched above Kevin's hip. For one moment I swear I could feel the excited, tight torso of that little sweet body against me, the warmth under his shirt, his little ribs. I could feel his heart beating, new and wondrous in the world, his breath in my hair. I looked into the blur of his eyes. I could smell the sweet sweat of boy, his legs wrapped hard against me, the precise, solid heft of him, his little hand on my back, holding me.

I'd always pictured Denver on a tilt with its mile-high status. I was wrong. After miles around curves, down out of the high peaks, I felt like we straddled the middle of a seesaw. For Carey, Denver opened like Dorothy's Emerald City, busy and shiny and happy. The minute we checked into the hotel room, he set down his suitcase in the lobby and pulled out his list of questions for the concierge. I had our room to myself for what turned into a wrangling, pissy phone call with Mama. The city streets I could see from our window screwed into an off-kilter hassle as she bossed me long distance. Carey came in just before I hung up. He threw brochures and maps on the bed where I sat. "Anything wrong at home?"

"Anything *right* at home?"

"Whoa," he said and pulled back jokingly on invisible reins.

"Ha freaking ha, with your cowboy humor," I said. He sat on the bed and put his arm around my shoulder. "We need afternoon margaritas," he said. "Forget the stories. Forget the acreage for a little bit. The struggles of a land baroness."

We found an urban cowboy bar and ordered expensive margaritas at a window table looking out on the 16th Street Mall, tourists and businesswomen in sneakers and maintenance guys and boys on skateboards. A frenzied traffic jam of human bodies.

"I did all the leg work, you know?" I said. "Taking out the for sale ad. But hell, I don't know if the deed really has my name on it or not. But she gives me this damn guy's name and phone number."

"The buyer from before?"

"I guess." I pulled out the notes I'd scribbled. "She forced me to take this number for—Morton Phillips. She can't wait for me to deal with this shit when I get home? No. I have to take care of this when I'm a thousand miles away. Why can't she just sell? It's not like it means anything to her."

"Doesn't it? Does it mean anything to you?"

"That's what she wants to prove, right?" I said. "She wants me to do her dirty work. She would have sold the place years ago if she had the nerve."

"Oh. I see. You're calling her hand. Trying to get her to prove she doesn't care about the place any more than you do?"

"I'm not trying to prove anything," I argued.

"Yeah," he said, with his infuriating nod. "You two are playing the longest long-distance game of chicken I've ever seen."

The whole afternoon, I tried to get hooked on Denver the way Carey saw it, but I had to concentrate to stop drumming my fingers on my thigh while he tried on cowboy shirts and hats, while we wandered the new maple halls of Denver's mammoth public library and the gold-domed capitol with its murals and stained glass. I followed his gaze up and down, back in his slow-burn academic mode, pointing out historic buildings and describing endlessly all the things cattle and gold can buy. A city looking back at the frontier but already taking a step into the next millennium.

The next day I was still trying to keep pace as he led me through the lower downtown, LoDo, in and out of stores that smelled like black pepper and sweat, with creaking dust-pressed floors and old ceilings, decorated for modern retail and clerked by kids in headsets. At the museum I walked behind him through rooms of urns and paintings and beaded native artifacts. I pretended to pay attention when he bragged about decadent cowtown chic. All I could think about was running out of time, the way we had run out of mountains.

Our last evening there, he treated us to fancy Mexican. We seemed to have hit on a theme, so I told the waiter to put margaritas on my tab and keep them coming.

"You had any fun at all here?" he said. "Probably out of steam after—well, you've had a lot to unload."

"It's fine. Haven't you had enough of my unloading? I just shouldn't ever call my mother. How am I going to live with her until—what other choice comes up? I've been trying to call when I know she's at work, so I can just leave a message."

"I figured that out ten states back," he said.

"Am I awful?"

"Do you hear me having long conversations with Frances?" He shook his head. "We owe our mothers *every* everything. Our lives and genes. And in return they drive us insane. My mother will never ever believe I'm not going to get married to a 'nice girl' and have a bunch of babies. The me I am wasn't in her plan." He looked behind him for the waitress.

"Maybe I shouldn't be anybody's mother. I'd just wreck another life."

"You'd be—will be—a great mother," he said.

"I'm not so sure anymore. Never was sure. I just thought about what I wanted. Maybe I should give up on having that role in anybody's life. I don't know if I'll ever even try again."

"Celibacy? It's not all it's cracked up to be," he said. "Take my word for *that*."

"I may not exactly have a choice," I said.

"Oh, everybody's got *that* choice." He laughed. "Come on, you and I could get laid tonight if we wanted. Within the hour. Go out on this cowtown and throw down with some cowboys. Saddle up. Move 'em out." He slung a fake lariat.

I couldn't keep from laughing at him. The first sips of margarita had kicked in. "Rawhide," he whispered coyly. We both nearly fell out of the booth, laughing.

As we walked back to the hotel after some late evening shopping, he knew exactly what I meant when I asked, "You think it's that easy?"

"Sex with strangers? Yeah. The rest? Not so much. We're in the middle of our lives, is what I think," Carey said. "We had this idea that right about now we'd be on autopilot, coasting for the duration. By now, work and family with a partner and a place to live would all be figured out."

"If only one of those things was set," I said. "Just pick one."

"But it's kind of exciting. I don't mean like in college being at sixes and sevens about who to date or what career to pick. But in a more devastating, dramatic kind of terrifying way." He laughed.

"Really inspirational, Carey. How about some uncertainty with your tequila?"

"You know what I mean. You and I have some serious losses behind us. And death. It's easy to whine that shit didn't go the way we wanted."

"Sorry," I said. "Eight thousand miles of whining."

"Not you. Or not only you. I mean everybody our age, at this stage. Halfway through life. Nobody on their wedding day thinks, 'I'd better start planning for the divorce tomorrow.' Or the funeral. Even though it's in the freaking vows! The built-in tragedy ahead for everyone. And nobody figures on having a kid who's deaf or has cerebral palsy or gets addicted to drugs.

"We don't figure on having to figure it all out over and over. Think about all that time to be a wistful teenager. And college! How much time just sitting around self-discovering? Twenty-two years to develop the tools we needed for adulthood. Get that career going. Get that mate.

"But nobody gets a master's degree in What-the-Hell-Just-Happened-To-Me. Nobody teaches a class in how to sit by your lover's deathbed."

"Or go through three divorces" I said. "And everybody else gets a redo."

"How you figure?"

"All those other losers who are divorced or fired or alcoholic?" I said. "Even they have a kid. Even my daddy had kids. And suddenly it's their turn again. What does it matter if their life turned out shitty and disappointing? Their dream to play major league ball or be an actress didn't work out, but maybe their kid can pitch. Or be a rock star. Their kid could be a supermodel. Maybe their kid could be president. And none of that's a reason to bring a kid into the world," I said. "But it's a pretty big perk. And the natural way of things. Those people our age with kids don't have to look behind them constantly and wonder what could have been. They're too busy looking ahead to the next chance."

"It's redemptive. Having a kid," he said, nodding. "I mean, I get that."

"But when you can't have that, well, you and I just have to get up and dust ourselves off for the rest of the ride, I think."

He looked at me earnestly and said again. "Rawhide."

Nowhere we'd been was any flatter than Colorado east of the Front Range. My mind could have blown a fuse, rummaging back through Texas, watercolor washes of Arizona, the high plains. I was a forest animal, skittish in the bald open. Or one of those cowboys in the old westerns, dashing from one stronghold to the next. Sky and earth divided into barren halves. At a rest area, I climbed onto the hood of the Jeep, scanning west as if a magnet pulled me backwards, the natural direction for a barren woman.

What was it I thought I'd see? A skim of white cumulus lay on the horizon. Then like an electric sizzle, I saw it wasn't a cloud line. It was the Rockies stretched pale and thin, the whole range dividing who I'd been from who I might become. The start of the West. The end of the West.

Those mountains were a long-distance message, the cusp of what lay in either direction. And every intersection had always been like that. I just wasn't always good at recognizing directions. Choices.

But there were hills in Kansas, rolling and lovely. From the Smoky Hills, where we caught a quick night in our first commercial campground, to the Flint Hills, we took back roads. Every town seemed lulled in a valley, caught between modern upkeep and the worship of old days. We stopped in Council Grove, named for a treaty between the Osage and white pioneers to open up the Santa Fe Trail. Ruts still run like a seam in the land, near the intersection of two scenic highways, a true crossroads where pioneers left messages for each other in the hollow of an oak tree. Now it was a stump on the lawn of the Council Grove post office. Carey stood on top of it.

We found one room left at a bed and breakfast. Too hot to camp, we'd both decided. I'd forgotten how awful humidity can be. After the cool mountain meadows, ninety degrees in Kansas sizzled with insects. Sweat crawled down my back while we walked to the town museum, to look at flintlocks and bonnets and an actual Indian scalp. Carey took the brutal thing for granted.

"But don't you wonder?" I asked him. "If that fight went the other way, would this town hang up a hank of blond hair?" I leaned close to the glass of the case, even though I was grossed out by the patch of shriveled human skin still holding the dull hair together. "You think it's male or female?" I asked him.

A big statue near the town square, "The Madonna of the Plains," honored women pioneers. "She's about as feminine as a bison," I said.

It was easy to imagine massive granite thighs and hips under the granite pleats of her skirt. A granite child hung by her side, looking up desperately into her face, but ignored. No Madonna has ever been less maternal. Her eroding face was manly and stern. Her hands, holding a granite baby, were coarse and large as her booted feet. She looked unwaveringly westward.

"Nobody who came a thousand miles to walk across Kansas was that sturdy," Carey said. "I'm talking rail thin. I mean, did you see any women in any photographs that look this beefy?"

The women in those photos at the historical museum, slack and spent, most of them held bodies of dead children or stood beside caskets they had to bury along the way, in the wilderness, without a marker. At least I knew the location of my burned-down house. If I could stand to be there, I could visit where I'd bled out the only baby I would probably ever conceive. The life I'd failed to protect, not sturdy enough for the long haul.

"She's the kind of mother you'd want, though," I said. "Ready to take scalps."

"And feed the planet," Carey said. "Look at those boobs."

Next morning our tires on the road held a solid tempo through the simmering heat and constant green of the Flint Hills. There was suddenly no more endless wheat. Or corn. Or sunflowers. No irrigation or heavy farm machinery. Rocks and trees and cows pinned down the rolling prairie.

"I promise you," Carey said, "you won't be disappointed in our detour. The Flint Hills aren't majestic or grand. But it's the absence that's the something. You can already see the difference. Wide open space is why the tall grass prairie is being made into the newest national park. And I mean—"

"Carey, cut the sales pitch. We're already here."

"I mean, I want you to understand. Everybody freaks out about whales and spotted owls, but nobody cares about plants going extinct. Okay, the rain forest gets rock star attention, but grasses—" His face was burnished with sincere excitement.

"Only about one percent of America's native tall grass still exists. And most of that one percent is right here. This is the only place on the planet you get a sense of how the pioneers saw the plains. There's this book about the county we're in right now."

I made a smart-ass comment that from the looks of the place it must be a short book, but he said it's a monster. "The author picked Chase County because this—right here—is as close as possible to the geographic center of the U.S., where longitude and latitude mark the middle of the continent. And see those rocks jutting out of the hilltops? That's what the pioneers called flint. Without that, right under the surface, the tall grass would probably all be extinct because this would have been plowed over and planted and domesticated, too. The flint keeps this place wild."

I tried to see wilderness in front of me, the quiet cross-section of primeval America. Who could know what Genesis Road had been like in its virginal state? Then it struck me that it surely would have been wooded. And now it was returned to woods, the way it had been long before plows and farming altered it. It wasn't a mess of jungle. It was transforming to its natural urge. It wasn't a shameful place. It was resurrecting.

Over steeper and steeper rises, we came to the biggest town in Chase County—Cottonwood, population under a thousand. All the businesses were closed for the afternoon, the only lunch place and a couple of antique shops. Nobody braved the afternoon heat except in and out of the courthouse on a rise at the very end of the main street. The building was as stunning in shape as it was size—three square stories of limestone, not so much sheltered by its tile roof as decorated, like a big old gray cake with red icing. A bell tower with clock and flagpole centered between quadrangled dormers, edged around with wrought iron, as if somebody wanted to fence in the cornices.

Carey said, "That looks like a prissy fortress some gay-Paree tornado set down here by mistake."

But armed as it looked, he wasn't daunted one bit. He climbed the limestone steps, walked right into the middle of a workday. Typewriter keys clacked, phones jingled, and footsteps creaked on wood floors. I was used to a modern courthouse, not one without security guards. Carey tugged me into the first office we came to and asked the clerks about a tour. They gave us free reign, and he set out two steps at a time up the spiral staircase. He'd already been to the top floor and back by the time I'd used the restroom on the main floor.

"Ready to hit the road?" I looked up at him leaning over the banister, beaming.

He shook his head. "You got to see this." He turned and lunged back up the steps ahead of me. Up and up, I didn't catch him until we came to the top floor. "You ready for this?" he asked. He stood on the threshold of an open doorway and stepped aside so I could see. "Amazing, right?"

The interior of the old county jail was aluminum or stainless steel, even the floor, dense sheet metal quilted together with studs. Medieval looking. The cell block itself took up a quarter of the open chamber, a cage of rooms.

"State law closed it down in the seventies, the sign says. But just think, this was the working jail for over a hundred years. Remodeled not long before it closed, I guess."

I stepped inside. For some reason hay was scattered on the shining floor. To soak up piss or blood, maybe. A rank smell still hung there, as if the last prisoners had just been bailed out.

"Look at this." Carey touched the walls in the common area. They were concrete block, not metal, but someone had taken the trouble and expense to paint them the same robotic silver. "It makes the place feel cold," he said. "I mean, sort of numbing. Like somebody studied the psychological effects."

Set between two barred windows, even the picnic table in the common area was metal, bolted to the floor. Names and dates carved into the surface had raised up rust, fine scratches scabbed over.

Carey started laughing at all the graffiti. "'One day I smoked dope for a whole year,'" he read aloud. His laugh echoed weirdly. I shushed him, but he kept reading all the "fucks" and "fuck the mans" and "fuck everythings" and laughing until we were going back and forth, like it was a contest. He read off names like a roll call: Eugene, Frank, Angel, Martin, Sven, Bill. A tally of thirty lines stacked neatly in six cross-hatched rows. Beside it in tiny capital letters THIRTY DAYS. "Look." Carey waved me close. "'Nixon SUX'. And 'Nuke Hanoi Jane.' There's history here. 'Free Leonard Peltier!'"

I sat at the picnic table and touched the rough braille of names there and on the bench. "I wonder if Daddy carved his name on some surface when he was at Brushy Mountain," I said. "I used to wonder when I was a kid what the 'state pen' looked like."

"Not as nice as this," Carey said.

Through the opaque glass of the windows, the day was smudged to blue and green. No details. The faint glow was a taunt of color.

"It'd be hard not to see outside. For even a day," I said. "Think about weeks, months." For anybody used to wide open Kansas it would be like starving a little every day. "I've never really been inside a jail before." I turned to Carey. "I've been to juvenile detention or holding cells, but not like this."

"Tell me again what your dad did. Moonshine, I know. But they put him away a whole year?"

"Shit. Sounds like a bad movie. Is that really my life?"

"You're not embarrassed, are you?" Carey leaned on the table. I could imagine him in that stance at the front of his classroom, his arms crossed. "It's not a reflection on you or your family. I mean, what a paltry thing to outlaw. It's punishment for a cultural difference. I mean, it's a penalty for tax evasion, is what it comes down to."

"Well, it was a felony because he crossed state lines. He was stupid." I stopped. "Don't you think it's embarrassing? You'd be embarrassed."

"It's just whiskey." Carey shrugged. "There's worse stuff than earning money for your family. Now it's meth and marijuana. Every generation has its whipping boy. I mean, people have done a lot worse."

"Yeah. He did," I said.

Kansas was an open ocean after ten minutes in that jail, the wind so freeing it seemed it might lift us off the prairie and into the blue. Graveyards brought us down to earth. Along with signs put up by the warring sides about the new, tall grass national park.

"One man's progress is another man's invasion," Carey said.

The spreading oak shading the site's parking lot was gigantic. In relation to other prairie trees, it seemed mutant. But it was dwarfed by the historic ranch house built from the same limestone blocks as the courthouse, nearly as high as the cottonwoods in the sloped yard. But big as the house was, it was dwarfed too. The whole property took its status from the limestone barn, which a woman in the courthouse had bragged is the second biggest in the whole state.

The air inside the vast, open barn was cool as a cave. Rangers had rigged up a slideshow about the history of the Z-Bar/Spring Hill Ranch and the old one-room schoolhouse at Fox Creek. Carey sat in a folding chair for the next show, but the sunlight and green drew me out. "Sure, you can walk anywhere on the property," the ranger answered when I asked. "Up behind the house there's a trail head. Follow through the fields, all the way to the school. You have to cross the creek, but it's shallow enough. Or you can drive. But it's a nice walk."

Carey said he'd watch the program then drive to pick me up at the school. I set out up the hill through wild grasses, shushing like a taffeta dress. In the middle of my life, in the middle of America, I walked mown swaths through the click of grasshoppers and prattle of birds. I knew I was probably close to the school when I could hear frogs singing in the creek the ranger had mentioned. The summer grass was getting so tall in some places I had the sensation of being a kid again, walking through fields of broom sedge and Timothy hay nearly as tall as my head. Through a stand of trees, across the creek, the path was crossed by another mowed path. I stood there looking in four directions knowing I could not make an educated guess which way I should turn.

I listened again for the creek, and decided to go off the grid, launching out through the tight, high, itchy grasses, like when I was a girl. They gave off the golden swelter of the day's heat. I got swimmy-headed and turned around, so dizzy it scared me for a second. I'd forgotten to bring water, and I soon lost the sound of the creek. I was so hot and sticky, breathing hard, my heart working from climbing up and over the hills, the grass so high I couldn't get my bearings. I stood there lost until I made the decision to sit a while, and then I lay back in a nest of tall grass. A cool wind tossed through the grasses all around me, with the sound the whole treading past makes, sneaking up behind, such whispery footsteps you underestimate its power.

One hot afternoon, the last summer we lived on Genesis Road, I flattened my back against the cool kitchen wall behind the door to the front porch and eavesdropped. Between the hinges I could barely see a little slice of Mama. She was sitting on the porch swing with a bowl in her lap, breaking and stringing beans. Grandma Ruby's voice and Mama's went back and forth, wavering against the fuzzy sound of the black-and-white TV Mama had rigged outside, so she could keep tabs on Haldeman and Erlichman and John Dean.

It was a summer of treachery.

As usual, Grandma Ruby was defending Daddy, excusing him because he'd grown up suffering through her Papa's bullying. She thought the rest of us ought to let him off the hook like she had.

"It's Papa's fault Glenn's how he is. His and mine." She was crying. "I ought to have took him as far from Papa as I could get. I thought I was doing right, that he needed a man in his life. It's his Daddy's fault, you want to know the truth. Running off. But life wouldn't have been no harder broke and hungry than it was on me and Glenn living with my papa. You got to understand. He beat Glenn like he beat me when I was a girl. I'd stood it. I figured Glenn could stand it better, seeing he was a boy."

By the time I was born, Daddy's Papa Sims was an old, shriveled up man. He died when I was four, and in my faint memory he had nothing in common with my own bullying daddy. But once I saw in a box of Grandma Ruby's old pictures labeled *Papa and Glenn* of the two of them working a field of tobacco. Grandma Ruby's daddy looked big even beside the mule. Daddy was an unrecognizable boy, his hair so blond it was the brightest, whitest thing in the photo. He nearly disappears next to his papa and the plow and the mule, bleached out by the sun. How could Daddy ever have been that weak white shadow?

Tears and bribery and guilt, Grandma Ruby pulled out every weapon in her arsenal to get Mama to pity Daddy. She wheedled Mama to confide in her. Was she really thinking about taking us and leaving her sweet Glenn? I crossed my fingers and held my breath that Mama would stick to the plan she and I had made. Our secret. I knew the getaway money was in the flour and cornmeal. I knew we could not trust Grandma Ruby.

"He's got in his mind someway that you're going to take them young uns and hightail it." Grandma Ruby sniffed. "If he's wrong, it's up to you to make him see. A man's got to be able to trust his family," she said. "He's in a state, laying up at my house, I'll tell you, Faye. I never seen him like this before. Crying and moping."

I could see across the cluttered kitchen, through the far window over the sink, the overgrown fields, the tangled collapse of the orchard. And Daddy *run off Lord knows where*, Mama always said. I didn't believe for a second he was at Grandma's house. He was avoiding work and Mama and obligation. The mountain's late day shadow spread. The second hand on the wall clock pocked. Everything moved but me, a waiting mouse.

"It's my daddy's fault he's high strung and needs that peace he gets with a beer after work, Faye. You know that."

"A beer would be fine, Ruby," Mama said. "So would work," she added. "But he can't stop at one. He can't control hisself no way, and I got two kids half scared to death of him the minute he pulls the tab on the first can. You tell me what're you going to do about that? What's he go being like his granddaddy for, if his own life as a boy was so awful?"

"You never seen him as a boy," Grandma Ruby plowed on. "It's hard to believe now, but he was the least little bit of a thing. And he's still that boy to me!"

Mama stood up. I swear I could feel her movement through the wall. "You and me both, Ruby, we got to stop making excuses for him. You and him got to face some things. Me and my kids need a normal kind of life."

"But what's that mean, Faye? You got to lead him to that. He's just in a stage after being in jail and—"

"That was four years ago. And nobody knows any better how hard it was because me and my kids lived ever day of it. That was our year too. Our life too. And if Glenn can't make it all the way home—well, I'm tired of waiting."

"But he's got so much on him," Grandma Ruby said. "I know he's hard on Glenna and Dunn, but it's brung back a lot of hard feelings I do believe, them being the age he was. They remind him of when he was their age and my daddy—"

Mama laughed, but I could hear it wasn't a real laugh. "Now you're blaming his own kids for the beatings he gives them? Why does he beat me, you reckon? Go on and blame everbody but the man hisself. You ever stop to think, that that's his problem? That he don't take responsibility because you find some excuse ever time?"

Grandma sniveled. "I spoilt him rotten. I did. I took the heft of things off him because I felt sorry for him. But you don't know how it was. You never met Papa before he was senile and decrepit. But I'm going to tell you a story. No, now you sit down and listen." There was a pause. Mama didn't budge to do as she was told.

"All right, stand there, then. I ain't never told nobody how Glenn broke his leg. And I venture he never told you hisself neither?"

The swing creaked on its chains when Mama sat back down. I held my breath. The secret I'd wanted to know. The questions I'd asked Mama, but never dared ask Daddy about his crippled leg.

"He talks a bunch of horse manure," Grandma Ruby started, "telling a different story every time about how he broke that leg. How a bull chased him. He fell out of the barn or a tree. But he broke his leg being forced to be a man before his time. My daddy like to drove Glenn into the ground. Worked him like a man twice his age. He worked mules to death, Papa did." She sounded victorious. "But Glenn wouldn't never give in. Stubborn. He did whatever Papa said."

Her whole story couldn't have taken more than two or three minutes. But the planet stopped spinning, the way it does when any tragedy is unfolded as calmly as a picnic blanket. He was a boy my age, nearly ten, no bigger, no stronger, without the muscles he would get in the future. But there must have been some inkling of his bullheadedness or fury to keep him going. And that I could understand too, right then. Because that part of him was in me. He broke his leg falling off the first tractor he ever worked on, the first big machine that made Papa's mules obsolete. But his papa wasn't very good at driving it. He made Daddy try, but he got tossed off, somehow. Daddy's right leg twisted when he landed, and a hairline fracture spun a helix through his thigh bone. But the left thigh, the one we all knew about, his shorter, stunted leg, that one ripped open with a compound fracture.

"That leg wouldn't have got infected. He'd have healed just fine if Papa had brung him on to the house. But Glenn laid up there in that hayfield three hours before I knew something was wrong. Daddy took it personal. He said Glenn was just being shiftless, trying to get out of work. He cut the rest of that field while my boy laid there bleeding in that blistering sun. Papa come in for lunch and told me to fetch that worthless son of mine.

"He wasn't but a little thing, but I like to never got him out of that field by myself. Had to drive into the field, far as I could. He was about out of his head. Thought he was in the ocean. He'd heard men tell about being in the Navy in the war. He asked what shark had bit his leg off. "My daddy never come to visit even one time the week Glenn was in the hospital, burning up with fever. Blood poisoning like to killed him. Alls he said to Glenn when I brung him home was what he'd cost him. He had to hire two grown men to help him with the rest of the haying. Two men to do the work he expected of a boy. And he decided he'd make Glenn pay them men with the money he saved up from hogs he'd raised and all them cords of wood he chopped to sell."

Why didn't you pay them your own ugly damn self? I wanted to run out on the porch and scream at Grandma Ruby, who always wore the newest fashion and drove a new car every two years on the spot, from money her second and third husbands left her.

"You understand? Them hard times he lived? He oughtn't to had to live through that." Grandma's voice was like the preacher's, low and soft just before the invitation hymn, to come to Jesus, forgive your enemies. Take the sin of the world onto your shoulders, beg on your knees. Be glad for the beatings you've taken. Amen.

I wanted to rush out and tell Mama to hang on. You can forgive your enemies, but not if they share a bed with you. Not if they're not sorry.

Mama stood up. "You're right, Ruby. No child ought to have to go through such a thing. Being beat and hurt and damaged for life." I held my breath until I was dizzy with adrenaline. She couldn't tell Ruby our plan to leave. She couldn't let pity get to her. I was ready to rush onto the porch and sacrifice myself. My chest was sore from being still. Where the wall I leaned against had been cool, it was fiery now. Sweat covered me.

"I reckon," Mama said, "you see my own kids' daddy is about to damage them for life. And you resent how I protect my kids, who oughtn't to have to live through that kind of bullying," Mama said. "What I see is, you didn't do like a mother ought to. That maybe you're jealous I'm doing better by my kids than you did by Glenn. Even if it means protecting them from their own daddy."

Before I could budge, Mama stepped through the porch door and caught me hiding and listening. Her mouth opened, but then she motioned for me to duck as Grandma Ruby followed her to get in the last word. But all she did was grab her purse, and in a minute, I heard her start her new car. I came out into the open, believing then that no matter what, Mama wouldn't give me away. All our secrets were safe.

Distances between Kansas towns became briefer, the towns themselves a little bigger as I drove a two-lane through the bronze light between day and night.

"Looks like the yellow brick road," Carey said. He faked a laugh and punched my shoulder. I rolled my eyes. "But we're still in Kansas, Toto," he said.

"Oh, shit. I wondered when the Dorothy jokes would start," I said. "You're just about to Missouri. Better cram in all the Oz jokes you can."

Out in the dusk cool, between pastureland rolling south and acres of wheat burnishing the crest of northern hillsides, I pulled into the gravel driveway of a farm. "I've got to have a snack," I said. "That'll tide us over till Lawrence. Then I'm going to chomp down on some beef, as God is my witness. No, wait. That's Scarlett, not Dorothy. Wrong heroine."

Carey thumbed the air, pointing at cows grazing right next to the fence. He whispered behind his cupped hand, "Ixnay on the eefbay."

I laughed. "So that's not pig Latin, I guess. It's cow Latin?"

We got out and laughed while we rummaged in the back of the Jeep through the toppled food box underneath our souring bath towels and plastic bags of stinky clothes.

"Apples and bananas and cookies, oh my!" Carey was giddy. "There's nothing left but mashed fruit and stale Oreos. 'If I only had a steak!'" He sang at the top of his lungs, and the younger cows jostled and flinched away from the sound of him. He stepped onto the empty highway and danced a few steps. At the back of the Jeep, with the few slices of bread that weren't moldy, we built what I swore would be the last peanut butter and jelly sandwiches of my life.

"A moratorium on PB and J, girls!" Carey shouted. The braver cows looked up from their chomping and lumbered closer. They pressed their boxy jaws toward us.

"Looks like somebody else is hungry." They rubbed against each other and whuffled their big nostrils through the bars of the gate. The smell they gave off was the condensed heat of the day, comforting and sweet and rank, a grassy smell. The smell of childhood. I held out my free hand and rubbed a couple of wet broad noses. I tossed the last crust of my sandwich at their hooves when I was done. They stepped back and the most skeptical slung her head. A strand of snot flew over her shoulder.

"Not so smart, cows," I remarked to Carey. "But look at those big, beautiful eyes. I used to love helping my daddy with his cows. He could bawl just like a cow. They'd come running. I swear, I think they loved him. He used to sing to them. Elvis." I looked up to find that Carey had stepped across the highway.

"Maybe he loved them, too," he called back.

I stepped across the road beside him, into the wheat growing right up to the shoulder of the highway. "Didn't seem to have trouble butchering them for T-bone steaks," I said. There was no fence. If there were any native grasses still dormant under the surface, the golden green wheat had banished them. But here and there little communities of sunflowers held their yellow faces just above the tops of the grain, moving in a wind I could barely feel across the hairs on my arm. Close enough to hear, but out of sight, a train wailed.

In the cross-cut blade of low sunlight, then, I noticed a house behind a thicket.

Less of a house than a ghost made of sun-bleached boards. Carey was looking up at the weather vane above the windows, broken out like missing eyes.

"This is the kind of light I remember," I said. "But there's not even that much of a house left on Mama's land."

In that between time that lasts only a few seconds some evenings, the day turned over. I took a deep breath of the past, like an ache in my lungs. One step closer and I bent into the wheat to run my hands up the stalks. Way out in the tassels, cicadas rasped like they do high in the trees at home. The train and the whine of the jar flies noising together carried a homesick sound.

"I did like the tall grass," I said. "I'm so used to seeing everything cultivated and planted and grazed. But those hills of tall grass were like the fields at home people let go fallow. Or mountain balds. But they don't stretch like that for square miles."

"Far enough so you got in a good long hike," Carey said. "I didn't think I could catch up with you, but then I got to the limestone school before you."

"I lay down in the tall grass for awhile," I said. Looking up into knee-deep grass, I thought about that day my daddy lay broken in the wheat. The sun curled inside my skull, and the grass seemed to breathe, as if I stretched out on the hide of a sleeping, warm animal. "You know," I turned to him. "if you lie down like that and look up at the grasses and sky, you all but disappear. If you don't look at your hands or feet for awhile. It's a weird sensation."

"You'll get ticks," he said. "That's what Frances would say."

"Well, your mama ain't here," I said.

We got back in the car, but I wanted to try it again, lie down in those grasses so high no one could have found me. I had been lost and found in the wavering breath of that field. I wondered what kind of person could leave a little boy in a field like that, broken and thirsty and lost. Was that the place where all my daddy's fury started? Maybe that very day, lying there in that field, his hot wrath had revved up. Who should I blame for that far back, that deep? I tried to think how long it was between that little boy hurt and the man in prison. I wondered which time seemed longer to him, three hours of pain in that hot field or a year away from Mama and Dunn and me.

And what had I let mark me the way that day had marked him? Could I understand that day and still blame him? There had to be more in me than just sympathy for the boy he'd been, abused and stunted by forces out of his control. I had to feel more than a miserly pity that he'd been bullied into being a bully.

Carey drove the rest of the way to Lawrence, and I drifted in and out of his lecture about it being the place the Civil War actually started.

"I mean, people came in droves to vote Kansas free or slave. A bunch of strangers lit into it. And no small skirmish. It was a massacre. Border ruffians wrecked and burned the whole town." He went on asking and answering his own questions about Dred Scott and John Brown and Free Soilers and Jayhawks and abolitionists. "I mean, and if you think about it, the Civil War was really the start of the Civil Rights Movement, right here in the middle of America. Everything came to a head right here."

And so it did.

That night in Lawrence, in the first crease of night, I fell into a dream like the Kansas sun. The town was burning in a massacre, people running and screaming. And then it was my house again, burning in a rage and no one able to help, no neighbors or firemen who weren't trying to put out other blazes. In a panic I thought maybe everybody I knew was in my house in the fire. I rummaged through all the names and faces I knew. Mama. Carey. Dunn. Kevin. I reassured myself, calculating over and over that nobody I loved was inside. I watched the new paint peel off the Victorian molding, the turret room smoking like a steam vent.

It seemed as if I could be inside the fire and witness and not be harmed. Fire licked the lattice and ate my irises to black ash. I heard the dulcimer Kevin had given me rupture. Our brass bed groaned as it melted. All the sentimental stuff, my photos and handmade baskets and all my recipes floated in spirals of smoke. The china from Sam's mother shattered like wind chimes. The dress I wore to marry Kevin, its hem like flaming handkerchiefs. As soon as something came up in the inventory of my memory, I watched it burn. The pattern on the stainless flatware Mama gave me ran together like lava. Three wedding rings in my jewelry box melded together, hissing like little snakes. I could see the quilt Granny Pearl's mother had made when the family lived inside the boundary of the national park, before it was a park. A few squares of moth-eaten wool from her daddy's Confederate uniform. It scorched and disintegrated patch by patch, as if I were looking down on fields from high above.

I was flying above the flames, looking down, then. It wasn't my house I saw, but our farmhouse smoldering. Everything burned as I stood alone. I looked down at my hands and feet to be sure I was still there. Not a human sound. Windows that had been blankly staring at me blew out in black shards. Then inside the train roar, like a million screaming mouths, one scream careened into me like a sword. A little boy struggled up toward the top of the roof ridge.

When he saw me, he stopped the furious scream and started to cry. The roof crumbled. He scrambled up the pitch as it caved in behind him. I thought I recognized him, but he was obscured by smoke. He looked back at me once and held out his arms. He stamped his feet, not impatiently, but thinking he could work up a momentum and fly to me. If he believed, if I believed, he could fly. Maybe I could catch him. He strained toward me just as his hair lifted in the thermal updraft. The flames whiplashed ferocious blue-orange spires, gnawing the roof, sharp at his heels like a fanged mouth. He took one last inching step and looked at me as if I had struck the match.

I seized up in my sleep. The choked-off screams were mine just as Carey grabbed me. I didn't fall. His voice pulled me away just as the fire knifed toward the boy, and then there was only darkness and Carey.

"It's okay. Wake up! Wake up. You're dreaming," he said. "Just another nightmare. Come on. Wake up good now. Jeez. You scare me to death doing this." He rubbed my back and told me to breathe. "The closer we get to Tennessee, the worse this gets."

"I'm sorry! I'm sorry," I said.

"It's okay. I just feel bad for you. Just talk to me." Carey moved around to kneel in front of me on the mattress. "My mom always says you need to talk to break the spell of a nightmare."

How could I say that I saw Daddy there, a burning child? Scrambling and falling into ashes and no way ever to see him again, to say what we needed to finish. Daddy. That doomed boy on the roof looking at me, blaming me. So clear, a moving image of the boy he'd been in photos taken half a century before, a little blond boy, doing nothing but trying to escape the roar that chased him from boyhood to the end of his life.

"I would know his eyes anywhere," I said. Daddy's eyes. Blue. And there within them a question, full as a voice inside my head asking, *what would you have given up to save me, Sister? What would you give?* "Oh, no. Oh, no," I said.

"Be still, now." Carey held my forearms, and I was still. But I couldn't stop shaking my head as if there were a swarm of bees tangled in my hair.

"Tobey," I said. "It was Tobey there, too." And it was. The beautiful boy, falling into the nothing that had come of Kevin's life with me. Because of me. Tobey. The only child I had ever refused. How many strangers' children had I tried to save, earning my living? How many families had I fought to save, but my own, I just let go out of fury? And this one boy I could have given up my pride for. I didn't fight for him for a second. I had blamed all my failures and loss on a boy, the way I'd blamed the whole burned down past on my daddy. "I'm sorry! I'm so sorry!" I came to myself rocking back and forth, so dizzy the room spun.

"It's just a nightmare, Glenna. Don't apologize," Carey said. He knelt on the bed with his forehead against mine.

I wrenched away. "No. I'm so, so sorry."

Hadn't I looked away at the last moment, right as the fire got them? But I couldn't stop the image now, over and over, the roof ridge sagging like a swinging bridge between us. The black-hole wind cracking open and the fire swallowing itself in darkness. I hadn't been able to see the dream through to the finish.

But I knew the ending. I knew what I had to do.

I didn't want to wake Carey again. At five in the morning, I used the pay phone in the hotel lobby. I thought Mama would be up, seven Tennessee time. But I

307

didn't realize we'd crossed into Central Time. It was only six a.m. her time. She panicked, so ballistic it took me a couple of minutes to convince her I was okay. "Where did you say you are?" she asked for the third time.

"We're in Lawrence, Kansas. Nearly to Missouri." The light through the hotel's lobby doors was blue-black from the streetlight. I could see traffic on the street.

"Still in Kansas? Is it all that far to take two days across? I just got postcards yesterday—was it yesterday? What's today? From Washington State." I heard muffled talking. "Lord, Sissy, we've woke up your brother." She whispered as if it would make a difference. "Go back to bed, Dunn. He worked late last night. What? She's in Kansas."

The night clerk looked across his desk at me as if he could hear the confusing exchange hundreds of miles away. "Mama? You still there?"

She was laughing. "He's about a smart ass. He says to ask if you seen any Munchkins."

"Tell him just a couple of flying monkeys." I couldn't help laughing, nearly giddy to think of them there in the half-dark, not mad at being woken up, just anxious to hear my voice and tease me as if I were right there with them.

"I wish to God you'd call your Granny Pearl. I told her you called two days ago, but she don't believe me. She's sure you're killed. Send her another postcard. Did you send her another one? She's got the damn things plastered all over her fridge. 'Course you'd probably get home before a card would get here. Won't you? Kansas isn't all that far, is it?"

"We're headed to St. Louis next. Carey's got friends we'll stay with there."

"Lord, how many people does that child know? He never met a stranger."

"I don't know how long he'll want to stay. Then we'll probably stop at Reelfoot Lake, maybe Nashvillle." I implied we were taking our merry time. I didn't dare admit I wanted to be home as much as she wanted me there. If I opened that possibility even a nudge, she'd badger me into hijacking Carey and driving straight through. It could take as little as one good, hellaciously long day. And that sort of land-speed record didn't sound like such a bad idea at the moment. "Listen, Mama, why I'm calling, you didn't get a call back, did you, about the land, from that Phillips man?"

"Yesterday. He called yesterday morning. He works third shift. I found out his Mama went to school with Grandma Ruby. She was a Carter. You remember Jeannie—"

"Mama, listen. I've only got five or six minutes left on this phone card. You didn't do anything, did you? You didn't agree to sell, or sign anything?"

She sighed. Even that far away, the sound of it shamed and relieved me. "I swear, Sister. I have talked till I'm plumb blue in the face. I told you, I give

308

you that land. It ain't mine to keep or to sell." She paused. "And I ain't your damn real estate agent, neither."

"Okay, then, if you wouldn't mind going ahead, though, and call the paper and cancel the ad."

"Glenna Jean. Lord help! That ad ran out week before last. You have lost all track of time on earth. But you'll have to let me get that Phillips man's number. I gave it to you, I thought. He was asking when you was going to call and I told—"

"Mama." I tried to interrupt her, but she had already put the phone down. "Mama!" I shouted. The night clerk looked at me again, as if he might have to stop a ruckus. I waved him off and pictured my minutes running out like an hourglass. I wolf-whistled into the phone, the way Daddy taught me to whistle when I was little, if I ever got trapped or lost or somehow left behind.

"Ow! Sissy. Lord, what're you whistling for. You'll have to call back. I can't find the number."

"Mama, I don't need his number. I don't need you to do anything but tell him and anybody else, we're not selling." I started to hang up with those words. There was a silence from her end. "Mama?" I thought we'd been cut off.

"Well, I'll just tell him if he calls that you'll be back in a few days. Can I tell him that? And your granny wants to know you'll be home soon, too."

"Tell her not to worry," I said, meaning all of them, Grandma Ruby, too, that I'd left hurt and grieving without me. *Tell her I love her*, I wanted to say, meaning all of them. Meaning Mama. But the words were so naked. They'd always been too naked. I couldn't remember anyone in our whole family ever saying, *I love you*. In the brief silence of thinking it, cold washed over me to imagine never saying those words. Never hearing them once in the house I grew up in. Never saying those words to my own daddy. Then I flushed hot at how near I was to saying them. Just words. But how amazingly hard it was to lift my tongue into that new language. "You don't need to tell Mr. Phillips anything. Except no sale. We're not selling."

"Who's we?" Mama laughed. "You and that mouse in your pocket?" It was a saying of Daddy's.

"I thought maybe you might want to move back out there," I half-teased in return. "You can get a new trailer and your address could be Genesis Road again."

"Now, what in hell would I want to go and do a thing like that for? And pay you rent money?"

"No, that land is—"

"Sister, get it through your thick skull, child. I give that land to you. If I wanted to live way out yonder, I'd of moved out there years ago. I thought you might put you a house out there. You got any insurance money left to—"

"And drive an hour and a half to work every day?" I interrupted.

"So, you're going back to child and family services?"

"You know, that's one thing out of about a thousand I'm not sure about, Mama." I started to laugh, and I hoped I could hide that I was crying, too. Mama laughed, too. "Tell everybody—besides Mr. Phillips, that is. You can tell him to jump in the lake—" I laughed again, "that I'll be home soon as I can. That's all I can promise."

A recording came on to say my time was nearly up.

"I love you, Mama," I blurted out in the nick of time.

"You know I love you, too, Sister." Her voice was uncluttered, dry and clear as the prairie sky. She didn't hesitate. Not even for a second.

CONVERGENCE

Carey and I never made the stop we'd planned in Independence.

Just over the Missouri line, in a sudden downpour, I leaned over to watch him point out the Truman library on the map. I didn't see road construction signs until the tires jolted in a rough whine on the graded road. The Jeep shimmied and I jerked the wheel. I'd been driving slowly, but sharp braking on an oil-slick patch spun us into a skid. We tore through three or four orange cones and swiped a barrel before we rammed at a slow tilt into what Daddy always called a chug hole.

And there I was again, Glenn Daniel's daughter after all, surviving another crash. Nothing worse for either Carey or me than sore slaps from the airbags and the grab of seat belts. And guilt that I'd scared him to death and ruined his car. But he was silly with relief, laughing and hugging me, holding my hands in his, scanning up and down my arms, peering as he pulled our seat belts away and tugged at my torso, holding my face in his hands. Neither of us had a scratch.

We got soaked standing in front of the Jeep, as if looking long enough would lift it out of its angled, cock-eyed misery. The tow truck got to us before anybody else, after folks who stopped to check on us said they'd call in the accident. Carey refused to let me stand there while he was dealing with the guy. I had to step up high to climb back into the Jeep and slide over to the passenger side, which was wedged against a concrete barricade. I propped myself upright in the slumping Jeep and watched them through the drizzly windshield. I didn't know if I was shivering from rain or from the slow melt of adrenaline. Traffic slowed as people gawked.

"It's the axle," Carey said, as he climbed back inside. He flapped his arms lightly to shed water off his raincoat. I held up my finger at the sound of the first sirens approaching, and he nodded he'd heard. "It's broken in two. No wonder. They left a damn crater in the road. You'd think they'd fill it. Or post warnings."

"I'm pretty sure those giant fluorescent traffic cones were my warnings," I said.

He laughed, but I could see a strain on his face. "I'm so sorry about your car, Carey. Really, I'm so, so sorry."

"Stop with the sorries. That's what you said after that nightmare last night." He looked at me and grabbed both my hands. "Nothing to be sorry about. That's why they call them accidents. And that's what insurance is for." He leaned across me to dig into the glove compartment for his registration and other papers. His hands were trembling. "We're both okay. Pretty lucky trip overall, don't you think? Except for the food poisoning." He laughed as he looked through the paperwork. "Oh, and the forest fire."

"They'll want my license and stuff too. Since I'm the one who wrecked everything." I reached for my pack in the tumbled back seat. "Don't forget the dust storm or monsoon, whatever that was, on route 666. That was wild."

"But we didn't argue. Not too awful much, did we? For two people sharing a tent for how many freaking days!" He faked hysteria with his hands in his hair.

"Just a couple of bitch slaps," I said. In the rearview, a highway patrolman was laying flares, and another was writing up something in a notepad. "This guy is making his report. Tell him it's my fault," I said.

"Not too many rainy days, either," Carey said, still cataloging how lucky we'd been as he reached for my license. "Really great weather almost the whole time. I mean, until today. And, hey, nobody robbed us! And we didn't fall off a cliff. Or get burned making campfires."

"Or get raped by that bison. Not for lack of trying." I punched him in the shoulder. "Or bake our brains out in Death Valley. No bear attacks."

"Seriously, think about it. Not one spider bite or bee sting. No scorpion stings. No rattlesnakes. Probably not even a sunburn. Pretty sweet to travel eight thousand miles without any real mishaps."

"Carey, honey, I don't know about you, but my definition of mishap ain't what it used to be. I figure I've had my quota." I motioned that I was going to climb out after him. "Has it really only been eight thousand miles?"

The whole shebang was my fault, but it was Carey's car, so I butted out. He didn't need my two cents to add to the confusion that ended up being the worst part of the wreck. He and the tow-truck driver talked logistics as we rode along in the pouring rain. First Carey said maybe we should call the airlines, to see about tickets home, which terrified me. My first flight. Would this be it?

Then when we got to the shop, the repair folks said a diagnosis on the Jeep couldn't be done that day. How long would it take to deal with insurance if it was totaled? Should we rent a car? Should we get a motel and settle in even if repairs took several days? But why sit around bored in the rain in a miserable industrial part of some nothing Missouri town?

From what I'd seen of Daddy's mangled cars, I figured the Jeep was totaled. Carey called his insurance company from the pay phone in the waiting area of the garage and went back and forth about various scenarios and estimates and prices, wrangling. The tempo of the conversation got more and more tense, and Carey's worry wrinkles were setting in. But the anxiety drained out of his voice when he finally called his friend Neal in St. Louis to tell him our drama. Neal offered to drive and pick us up, rather than have us skip the visit we'd planned.

I looked up at Carey from the bench seat in the garage waiting room. "This guy is coming all the way across Missouri to pick us up and tote us to his house?"

"Well, he lives west of St. Louis, really, so it's not the *whole* state. Maybe a little more than three hours? Four? But Neal always was a mensch." Carey shrugged. "You'll love him. He's the kind of guy who would donate his kidney to a stranger."

I got it then. The relief I saw on Carey's face wasn't about expense or details or his car. He'd been worried we would have to rearrange our plans and not see Neal.

"Oh, I'm slow on the uptake," I said.

Carey picked up his pack to dig for more quarters. He'd started with four rolls, for laundry and calls and vending machines. He looked at me as I handed him all the coins I had. "What?" he asked, looking sheepish.

"Nah. Nobody would be driving all the way the hell that far to pick up some old bald friend with bacne who's gained fifty pounds." I laughed at the red rising in Carey's cheeks and his smile. "He thinks you're pretty," I sang. "And you think he's pretty right back."

And Neal truly was a beautiful man. We were on our second round of peanut butter crackers from the vending machine in the garage when he pulled onto the lot in a white Lexus, a knight in shining armor, one of the darkest men I've ever seen, with an accent from—I would later learn—Algiers. He was an amalgamation of French, British boarding school, Midwestern wry humor, and African chic. And he was at least six-five.

My trip alone with Carey was suddenly done. But we were both regaled and swept up and joyfully fine to no longer be a solo duo. Maybe being rescued is like finally getting to eat when you're starved. Even the most mediocre sandwich is going to taste like manna straight from heaven. But Neal was actual manna. He took us to a cafe that served true barbecue—Memphis style—the first great meal we'd had since Denver.

Aside from the stunning driver, I was ready to fall in love with his ride, just move right into that heated leather backseat. After the frenzy of hugs and introductions, whatever puzzle of our stuff we couldn't fit into the trunk we piled up next to me, our packs and coats, the sleeping bags in their stuff sacks.

After we ate, I was weary enough to lean against the soft smell of all our days on the road and close my eyes. By the time we pulled onto the interstate, I was an afterthought. I listened while Carey and Neal exchanged reunion stories and rehashed the lost years between them. They came to the common bond I hadn't known they shared. Neal had lost his partner too, from an HIV-related infection just days after his thirtieth birthday. But in twenty minutes or less they'd dispensed with the pity party about hard times. While they drove into the future, I slept across Missouri.

Way past midnight, the two of them were still talking in Neal's cluttered dining room, where he'd been going through boxes of photographs and letters from friends he and Carey had in common. Carey was stunned and then beamed about the stack of cards and letters between the two of them. I sat with them awhile, mostly because I wasn't about to turn down the best bourbon we'd tasted in weeks. Drink and the history laid out on his cherry table made me dizzy, names and faces of their friends, so many dead and gone from what Carey and Neal called "the plague."

But the bourbon only fueled my insomnia. In Neal's huge suburban house, I lay awake in my own big bedroom in the middle of a king-sized bed and missed Carey. Every time I closed my eyes, I saw the gray-silver blur of the wreck, the slow-motion crack-up coming. I'd gripped the steering wheel so hard my forearms were sore. I had pushed both feet hard as I could against the brake. Like so many calamities, in the end it was one inch or another either way, to prove nobody is in control. People walk away simply because. Or they don't. People die, simply because. People lose babies. People survive.

The mahogany bed took up only about a quarter of the room, filled with antiques and bookshelves and a couch fronting a bay window with orchids. I ended up being more comfortable on the couch, but that just led me to click through channels until I felt stoned with lethargy. I hoped Carey would see the light under my door, and would stop by before turning in. I heard the two of them saying their good nights down the hall. Two doors shut. Hours went by as I dozed until I couldn't stand it and turned off everything and got into the bed. But I couldn't fall asleep without Carey, not after sleeping in the same room, same bed, same tent with him for weeks.

In all my thinking about what my life would be like when I got back to Tennessee, the most difficult part to imagine was going through every day without Carey. Whatever real life I started up after the trip, the hardest rhythm to learn would be living without our little domestic routine on the road, silly squabbles, the reunion we'd patched together out of my burned down life. Carey was faithful and known. And he knew me.

On the premise to myself that I had to pee, I listened outside his door on my way to the guest bathroom. I couldn't tell if he'd turned out his light or not.

As quietly as I could I turned the knob. I just needed to see his dark form safe and breathing. The scent of his soap came to me like a warm touch.

Neal made Belgian waffles for a late breakfast, with raspberries and maple syrup. But it was the fresh roses and lit candles—before noon—that confirmed my instincts about his intent. Carey raised his eyebrows at me across the table, already set when I came into the breakfast room. He seemed oblivious overnight our trip had turned into three's a crowd. And I was the crowd.

But Neal seemed oblivious too. "Did you sleep okay, Miss Glenna?" he asked as he set my own French press of coffee beside my plate.

"Oh, sure, who wouldn't in that big old bed?"

"That belonged to my grandmother, from Jefferson City, Missouri, the capital," he said. "But I think she only haunts the room a little from time to time. Maybe when there's a woman in the house."

I looked up at him and he and Carey laughed. "Carey knows the story. That my mother refused to take any of her mother's furniture," Neal said. "No lie. She believes spirits inhabit heirlooms. So, I got everything. Missouri is just another place Southerners brought their weirdness to," he said. He pointed at the French press. "Just when the timer goes off in a second, push that plunger."

Neal was too hilarious to be so fetching, I told Carey later.

"That's a great word. 'Fetching.'" Carey said. "I want to fetch me some of that."

"Seriously," I waded into the obvious water. "How in hell is he single?"

Carey feigned indignation. "Don't you wonder how I'm still single?"

"We all know the answer to that. No one can live up to Stan. Not till now."

While I spread out the tent and sleeping bags to air in Neal's driveway and then took a restless, sore nap, the two of them went shopping for ingredients for supper. For four hours they clanged pots and laughed over glasses of wine. Salmon, asparagus, a cheese soufflé that fell and nobody cared. I came into the kitchen to ask if I could help, but then ducked back before they saw me. Neal's hand was lingering on Carey's shoulder as he sipped from the ladle Neal held to his lips.

After dinner they dallied over amaretto and pound cake and strawberries they'd dipped in chocolate. Forty minutes passed that I didn't say a word. Neither of them noticed. When Carey volunteered the two of us to clean up, I thought he wanted time alone to spill his giddy secrets. But he set into the task of loading the dishwasher with sober concentration.

"How does he keep his girlish figure?" I prompted finally, as we carried the last load of dishes from the dining room. Candle smoke drifted. Neal started music in the living room. Not a recording. He was playing the piano.

315

"What?" Carey said.

"Are all your friends gourmet chefs? And performers?"

"Oh, I don't think this is a normal day," Carey said, brushing his hair out of his eyes. "He just wants us to feel at home."

"He wants to get in your pants," I said.

"Glenna!" He slapped me with one of the rubber gloves he was putting on. But he was pleased.

I bumped him aside to put a bowl in the dishwasher. "You're blind if you can't see what's going on."

"He's just being generous, I told you. He's always been this way." Carey tugged at the gloves, trying to appear unimpressed. But he had a soft smile on his face. He took a last swig from a wine glass and bent to put it in the dishwasher.

He raised up and gave me a serious stare. "Do you like him?"

"What does it matter? Plus, I don't know him enough to know if I like him. It only matters if you like him."

"Glenna, what I mean is, he has bent over backwards not just to help me." The piano playing stopped, and Carey dropped his voice a notch. "He's helping you too, taking us in like this. For however long it takes to fix the Jeep. He's made that clear."

"Oh, I'm just chaperoning for now. Wake up and smell the waffles. It's like damn Valentine's Day around here." I started drying the silver he'd hand-washed and set on a towel. "Look, Carey. Real silver. I know you guys are gay, but nobody uses the family silver just to be nice. You'd better pay attention and seduce back a little."

"I'm not talking about that right now," Carey said. "I'm talking about you. And I'm not asking whether you approve. And don't say it doesn't matter. I'm asking if you like him. Without me in the equation, even. I don't know—I need to know."

"Carey, if anyone could make you as happy as you've been today, that's all I care about." A soft note sounded from the living room, music underlaid with scratches, an old vinyl album, and we were taken back to another time.

He shrugged, but his face was lit, hopeful. "I think we've mostly talked about the hard stuff we have in common. It's a relief, to talk to another person with the kind of baggage he and I have. That's all it is, don't you think?"

He looked up from the sink again, hoping I'd confirm what he was terrified to want, feelings he was terrified wouldn't be true. "I lost Stan and he lost Paul. That's our main connection. Maybe that's too dark a reason to connect with somebody."

"So, losing Stan and Paul, that's what you've been laughing about all afternoon? And that's why he's playing the sexiest Miles Davis in there now?"

"Miles Davis," Carey said. "He knows I love Miles Davis." We blinked at each other, and he turned back to the hand-washing, plunging into the suds for more silver. He jerked his hand out of the water, the glove sliced open on the food processor blade.

"Are you cut?" I said. "Oh, shit. Are you bleeding? Here. Take off those stupid gloves. Since when are you afraid of dishpan hands?"

He held up his bare hands to the light. "Look, Ma, no marks," he said. "You were saying about *stupid* rubber gloves?"

"Yeah, like I was saying, remember always, always to wear rubber gloves." I faked a sober face. "And always use a condom."

For a second, I thought I'd gone too far. I'd opened up an unspoken worry, political and private all at the same time. And scary. But he slapped at me with both wet gloves, slinging water everywhere until I grabbed one of them away and hit back. "Truce!" he cried, wiping his eyes. "Ow. It hurts to laugh. Are you sore, too?"

"From a little car crash? You are such a pussy."

"I wondered how long you'd have to know me before you picked up on that," he said. He poured us both a clean glass with the last of the wine from the bottle, and we made a silent toast, a wish we didn't want to tell aloud, because it might not come true.

Carey and I rode with Neal to work the next morning, just a few minutes from his house. He had all-day meetings at his law office in St. Charles, where Lewis and Clark set out nearly two hundred years earlier. Shops along the brick-paved streets wouldn't be open until ten or eleven, he told us. But he'd made the generous offer of his Lexus for the day, so Carey could drive us into St. Louis. In morning traffic, it took nearly an hour to get there, past miles of tract housing, video stores, fast food and convenience gas stations. After the plains and prairie, it was culture shock to be back to the smear of one human contraption after another.

Until we were parked and on foot, we could see the Arch only in fragments, eclipsed by rooftops and bridges and brick corners. We crossed a busy street and there it swung up into the sky, whole. Its impossibly high slender silver span pitched above an open park that sloped right down to the Mississippi River, where a couple of gambling riverboats were docked.

After the cramp of traffic and sprawl, taking a breath felt freer in that expanse of trees and grass and water, the tail-end of the prairie, the "Gateway" of the West where not that long ago the West we know hadn't even begun.

Viewing the Arch from beneath offered a dizzying perspective. I touched one three-sided pillar of brushed metal, already hot as a stove in the morning sun. The metal was scratched high as arm's length with graffiti and initials, which reminded me of the prison in Kansas. But the Gateway Arch was the opposite, free and wide open, a portal to what is yet to come.

The muddy smell of the river whipped on the wind through the heat. How many days since we'd crossed it from Memphis into Arkansas? How many stories and solutions and resolutions? How much mileage to bind me to Carey, Carey to me? I had been a new creature heading west, and I was newer heading east. Along a concrete barrier wall a Girl Scout troop sat swinging their legs, reflected in the bright metal of the Arch. I followed the curved line up and up into the deep Missouri sky where a white wad of cloud moved like a dirigible. I staggered into Carey.

"Whoa. Felt like the ground was moving," I said.

"It's maybe the Arch," he said. "It's built to sway, several inches. Six hundred thirty feet of hot steel swinging in the wind. You ready to go on in?" He waved the brochure at me and grinned.

"You think I'm falling for that?" I laughed. He looked confused. "Come on Mr. Urban Myth. Like there's a restaurant in the torch of the Statue of Liberty?"

"No!" He laughed. "There's a museum underneath, in the basement." He led me to a spot beside the leg where I could see doors down a long sloping entrance and crowds going in and out. "But you know, too, right, you can go up inside?"

"Now you're just shitting me," I said.

"No, no. See those little windows?" He tugged at me again until we were in the right spot to see. I squinted up. In the apex curve, two dark rectangles like slitted crossed eyes. "There's a sort of ratcheting elevator. On a system of cogs."

"No way I'd go up in this thing."

"It's one of the physically safest shapes in the universe," he said. "From what I've read. A parabola. Remember geometry class, junior year?"

"That was on graph paper. Not stuck and rotting in some tiny mole hole at the top of—" I leaned my head back again and pitched dizzily until Carey grabbed my arm.

We followed other tourists down the long ramp angled beneath, through automatic doors into cool air. From there it was an escalator ride further underground to a lobby and a dark museum commemorating Jefferson's plan for expansion, Lewis and Clark's journey. The first curved wall was marked 1803.

"You go inward." Carey swept his hand in a horizontal arc. "Into the circular layout, chronologically. We could spend days reading letters and journal excerpts."

"*You* could," I said. I scanned the nearest cases of worn clothing and remnants of gear. A stuffed bison, an Appaloosa pony, and a huge bear marked stations like points on a compass, and in the middle of the concentric circles, a statue of Jefferson. By the time I'd done a quick run-through, Carey was just reading panels on the second ring of walls.

He found me after I'd gone through the gift store. I was watching a film in the lobby of the cramped tram ride to the top of the Arch.

"Would you really ride up in that?" I asked. "I'll wait for you."

"It's perfectly safe." He cleared his throat, and I could feel him looking at me.

"Sort of—well, sort of like flying. Which is four times safer than driving."

"Doesn't mean I'm taking off any time soon."

He laid his arm along my shoulder and leaned toward me. "Come sit down with me a minute." He took my hand to tug me over to a bench. He patted the seat beside him, but I wouldn't sit. He sighed. "I just want to run this idea by you." He was still holding my hand, as if he were proposing.

"Carey. You are freaking me out."

"The mechanic called before you came down for breakfast."

"Did they work through your insurance? Is it a rental deal or can you settle—"

"Look, Glenna," he patted the bench again, and I sat. "The guy is worried he'll get in trouble with the insurance company. The Jeep's not a complete wash. He can't say technically that it's totaled. The front axle is a pretty routine fix, from what he said. The wheel's bent. Some other more major front-end damage is the question. It needs body work. Painting. But the frame and engine are fine."

"I can't tell if that's good news or bad." I sank down beside him.

"It's good news to me," he said. "Maybe not—well, you might not, I mean—" He reddened as he stammered. "I mean, he can get all the parts, eventually. He's confident about the body work, which could take a while. Maybe six or seven days. Maybe more. Maybe, I mean, more like twelve."

"Twelve days!" People in the lobby looked at me.

"I could have it towed to a different shop, I guess, instead of that little place. But he's certified."

"Carey, sell the car. The frame has to be bent. I've seen cars of Daddy's that looked in better shape that were goners. We can rent—"

"Stan bought me that Jeep," Carey said quietly. "Plus you and I took the trip of our lives in that Jeep. I just can't leave it." He looked at his sandals.

I felt the ground swing under me the way it had when I looked up at the Arch, giddy and unsettling, and exciting. I could feel his excitement.

"I swear, the car isn't really an excuse," he said. "Even if we hadn't wrecked I'd want to stay. Of course, the car made it easier for Neal to let me stay. And admit he wants me to. I mean, to stay. And you have to try not to be mad at me because I'm going to take care of everything. Just, I mean, I won't be driving you home. I've got frequent flier miles—"

"Oh, shit, Carey." The breath punched up out of me and I had to stand up. "We're only like nine hours from home. Maybe ten. You're just going to not finish our trip? Just rent a car and then you can fly back here and get the Jeep."

"You want me to drive you all the way back to Tennessee in a rental car, drive back here alone, then drive back by myself?"

"Well, I can drive it myself, then."

"There's no reason for that, though. It's silly. Renting a car one-way would cost a ton. A plane ticket is free on my miles. Plus, the flight is only an hour. You'll be home like that." He snapped his fingers. "It's the least I can do."

"Do you really think if I can't handle an elevator in the Arch that I can fly in a plane? There's no way in hell. I'm too old to learn to fly."

"Just flap your wings?" He grinned again. He knew he'd won the match, hands down. I'd gone on and on about how anxious I was to get home, played all my cards before I saw any of it coming.

"Be serious," I tried again.

"I think this is very serious," he said. "Neal and I are serious."

I sat back down. I could feel the power of possibility arc through the air, Carey's sense of surprise that this far in life, he'd found a place to be.

"I want you to be happy for me, Glenna."

"I am," I said. "I really, really am. It's just all tangled up in so many things. It's the kind of thing a friend tells you about on the phone, you know?"

"I'm glad you've been here to witness it, though, or I might not believe it. I'll always remember that you were here when this wonderful man—I mean, it's so fast. But we've written letters for years and years. So, it's not fast at all. But, I mean, last night after we'd all gone to bed, I went back downstairs." He put his jaw in his palms as if he might be able to push the smile off his face. "It was nothing, really. Neal heard me and came to see if I needed anything, and it just happened."

"Ew. In the kitchen?" I feigned offense.

"Don't be daft." He pushed against me with a grin, wiping his eyes. "We didn't do anything. He just kissed me. It's all, it's just sweet. And so surprising."

"There's no surprise, Carey." I nudged his sandal with mine. "So, I'm booted out while you play house?"

"I don't mind if you stay. Neither does Neal. But what I mean is that I know I can't expect you to. I've been feeling how antsy you are since Denver, even before. And, not to sway you, but if you aren't here, I may stay until the semester starts. So—" He took my hand again. "There are three or four flights a day direct to Knoxville."

"I just don't see any way in hell I can get on a plane," I said.

"I have one word for you. Xanax." He stood up and took my hand as if it had all been decided. "I've got some, no problem."

"Are you serious?" I stood up. "All this is making me woozy enough."

Walking hand in hand past the video displays in the museum lobby, we stopped to watch a different film, documenting the building of the Arch in the

320

'60s. Construction that took two and a half years was time-lapsed into seconds on the screen. Side to side the separate base pillars went up, the south leg a certain height, then the north side, and up and up until the builders' last step, to make the two halves of the Arch meet in the middle of the air, hundreds of feet up. Inches, even bare centimeters off, and it wouldn't have connected. The cranes placed the last section of the Arch, a fraction between perfection or failure. Happiness or grief. Found or lost.

"Wow." Carey breathed. "All those blueprints. Fifteen years of planning. And it could have all been ruined by a little gap."

How easily could I have missed Carey in my life? Or anybody else? How narrow a chance do two lives have to meet, just two out of all the others? How does anybody know how to stay put, sturdy and faithful, but with enough sway to withstand tornadoes? We make imperfect matches. Messy overlaps. The best humans can do is give a little reach, hoping gravity pulls us back together soon enough.

I watched the video of the Arch going up a couple more times while Carey bought postcards. Each time it was suspenseful. It seemed effortless, but miraculous, those two halves of a whole meeting way up in the middle of the unknown.

Carey put his arm around me. "Ready?"

"That's how a baby gets formed." I turned to him.

"What do you mean?" He stepped toward the screen to see the two sections meet again.

"We all form back to front," I said, reaching to touch the back of his scalp with both my index fingers, bringing them around until my fingers met at his nose. "Back to front. The skin and bone come forward from each side. That's why most of us aren't symmetrical. And why babies are born with cleft palates. It's hardly ever perfect."

I rubbed the soft divot under my nose, above my lip. And Carey touched his, as if he was looking in a mirror. "I forget what that's called," he said.

"It's a sort of scar. Kevin told me," I said. "Where the two halves come together." I ran my tongue under my upper lip, then my lower. "You know that connective tissue? Fine as a thread. Even under your tongue. And there's a seam in the roof of your mouth. That ridge in your hard palate."

We started laughing at each other as we made faces probing our tongues around the insides of our mouths.

"You look like you've got a dip of tobacco," he said.

"But feel. You can feel the attachments, right?" We stood face to face testing the insides of our mouths with our tongues, as if we'd lost wads of chewing gum.

"Stan would want you to be happy. He'd be happy you're happy," I said. "I want you to be happy."

Carey nodded but didn't stop rolling his tongue around the inside of his mouth, prodding for evidence of how in the world life could have come together just this way.

In the chaos of socks and knotted panties in my duffel, clean and dirty were inseparable except by sniffing. The next afternoon, Neal showed me how to use his washer and drier, and I did a couple of loads of laundry for me and then a couple for Carey while I sorted out only what I absolutely needed when I got to Mama's.

Carey came into the bedroom while I was at the height of confusion, cross-legged on the floor sifting through clean laundry. "I swear," I said. "Count the national park T-shirts. I dare you. And how much of this did you buy for me? These pants, and both of these sweaters. I never thought having stuff would ever be a problem again after the fire. How'd I collect so much in such a short time?"

He shrugged and sat on the edge of the bed to help fold clothes. "You don't need to do that for me, Carey." I dug into my backpack, for half-eaten candy bars and receipts. I'd already weeded through my cosmetics kit, tossing battered bars of motel soap, everything I'd hoarded like a half-starved refugee.

"You really think I can pare all this down for the plane by tomorrow morning? I can take a carry-on and one 'personal item?' Is that what you call it?"

He nodded. "You call Faye yet?"

"What the hell am I going to say? I know she wouldn't want me to drive the rest of the way by myself, but I can't tell her I'm flying. That would freak her out enough, but then I have to tell her I'm flying because—get this, Mama—I wrecked Carey's car."

He laughed. "Well, just show up and surprise her then." He stood up to go and turned back at the doorway. "I mean, you're going to call Kevin, right, to pick you up at the airport."

I couldn't have been more shocked if it had thundered inside the house. "If I can find his phone number in all this mess of shit, yes. How'd you know?"

"Who else do you want to see so bad that you're willing to fly?"

Tobey, I thought, before I knew what I was thinking. I nearly said his name aloud.

After I'd admitted my plan, it was real. I panicked that I really wouldn't be able to find Kevin's number. He always insisted on keeping our number unlisted, so students couldn't find him. In and out of snapped and buttoned pockets, little hidden zippered places in my suitcase, I finally found in my purse, where I'd already checked four times, the little slip of paper Kevin slipped into my palm at Daddy's funeral home visitation. When I held it up to the light in my trembling hands, the faint pencilled number was erased for breathtaking seconds. In that blinding space I found my deepest wish. Kevin's number surfaced pale but salvaged, his familiar handwriting. His name that used to be my name.

I felt like a thief, with the weight of the phone in my hand. All I had to do was dial. Eleven digits. Easy. But it took three tries before my shaking finger got it right. Then all I had to do was hope that he was out playing music. Then hope that he was not out playing music. That he was out listening to a band. All I had to do was listen to the ringing. All I had to do was leave a message. All I had to do was hang up quick. Rent a car and show up at Mama's, and never see Kevin again.

"Hello." He answered on the fourth ring, his voice as clear as if he were beside me. I sank and sank and sank into the bed. I slipped off the edge and sat on the floor.

"Hello?" he lingered on the o.

"Kevin?" I couldn't think of words to say beyond his name. Would he know my voice? He used to swear if he were blindfolded in a room of fifty women, he could pick me out, by taste and smell alone. Not a hundred? I'd always teased. Not a thousand?

"Yes, hello," he said hesitantly. "This is Kevin Hamilton."

"Kevin? It's me." My voice was barely there, or too loud. My head was so light my ears were ringing.

"Glenna Jean?" What could I hear in those two words? Everything and nothing. We held our breaths across the distance. "Well, Glenna Jean." And all over again, he knew me.

"Yeah." My diaphragm cupped around my lungs and heart. Dishes clattered in the kitchen downstairs and night birds answered one another in the trees outside. Neal and Carey were laughing. I couldn't breathe. If I breathed, I would cry. All right. I would talk to Kevin without breathing then. I would breathe later.

"Glenna. Where are you?" Kevin's voice saved me. I held his voice in my mind like the focal point women use during labor. And he coached me through.

"Well, what did he say?" Carey motioned excitedly that I was next in line at the airport terminal the next morning. I didn't know he could be so lively at five thirty, as if everything were normal. My head was bleary from worrying all night about flying and crashing. About all sorts of crashes that might happen. Anxiety settled like ice, slowing everything I did, speeding up everything and everybody else. In less than an hour I'd be up in the sky, which was still dark.

Neal had gotten up with us at four, not just to say good-bye. He sent me off with a packed breakfast and coffee, a business card with his number and address, a kiss on the cheek. He grabbed Carey and me for a huge triple hug and said I should come back soon.

"It's more what Kevin didn't say," I said. "He didn't ask me what I'm going to do with my life or where I'm going to live." The woman across the counter looked at my ID and then at my face and then at my boarding pass she'd printed up. She looked at the tag on my suitcase and squinted at my carry-on duffel and backpack. I followed Carey's reactions, gathering that all this was normal procedure. I wasn't about to be patted down. Bells and buzzers weren't about to go off and declare me unfit for travel.

"I asked him how Tobey was," I said. "That was hard. But once I said the name—I blurted out if I could meet him. And he didn't seem one bit surprised. Can you believe that? He said he's told Tobey about me. Isn't that crazy? And Tobey keeps asking where I am, he said. He didn't even ask why I called him to pick me up at the airport instead of Mama. Mainly he didn't say no. Not once."

"I know I'm being nosey here, delicate subject." Carey picked up my duffel and we moved out of line. "Let's go through security and find your gate. Did you tell—"

"I'm waiting till we're face to face to tell him about the baby," I said. "I need to see him when I say it, you know?" I stopped and turned. "If anything happens—" I stopped and caught hold of Carey's wrist.

"Nothing's going to happen to you, Glenna, dear heart." He laughed at himself for the oddness of the phrase, but tears welled up in his eyes. "It's a beautiful clear dawn. Nothing else can happen to you. You're on a mission."

"But if something did, you have to tell Kevin about the baby. You have to make absolutely sure—And Mama, too."

"Here, sit down a second." He motioned to a bench. "I have some things to give you."

"Carey, you've given me too much already. Everything. You've paid for more than your share, just so I can keep my insurance money. It wasn't fair of me to let you."

"Shut up," he said, digging into his pack. "Remember rich old Stan fondly."

"And I thank you by wrecking your Jeep."

"Like that's not the best possible thing that's happened to me in three years?" He handed me a little box. "Really, if you hadn't wrecked, it wouldn't have been dramatic and romantic and lovely, so shut up and open that."

I lifted the lid off the white box and inside there were no earrings or a necklace. There was a blue bear.

"Do you remember looking at Zuni fetishes? In Santa Fe and some other places?"

I lifted the carved bear up, the beautiful blue stone crackled with white and black lines. On the bear's back was a tiny arrow carved out of brilliant turquoise, tied around its body with a strand that looked almost like hair, and in its mouth another piece of turquoise carved in the shape of a fish.

"See, the arrow symbolizes a burden, but the bear carries it proudly. Because, well, that's how burdens are. They become part of us. But, well, struggling is rewarded and fulfilled, too, with dinner that it fought to catch, the fish. I'm bungling it, but the meaning is beautiful. Even if they make up that shit to make a sale. There's a little card in the box."

"It reminds me of the Rockies," I said. "Like the Tetons."

"And here's this," he said, handing me a small suede sack after he undid the knot. "I didn't buy this. It's the most useless thing I brought. It was Stan's so it seemed—" He choked and fought back crying again.

I pulled out a compass, beautiful, even with its scratched glass and mottled bronze housing. "Oh, Carey, I can't take this!"

"Yeah. No." He pushed it back toward me and then smiled. "Or it's a loan, then! That way, we'll know it's a sure thing we'll see each other again. Soon. Whenever you need to find your way. And then we'll pass it back and forth. What do you think? I just want you to have it now, and then you can give it to me when I need it worse than you. Does that make sense?"

"You mean until I learn which way is up?" I laughed to keep from crying.

"I mean, yeah, until you find your way. It brought me through a lot of hard times after Stan died. Just thinking about him and what he would have wanted for me."

"But right now, you're not lost," I said. "You need to be free of the weight of it for awhile." It wasn't a question. He nodded.

He stood up and pulled me to my feet. "We can't miss your plane!" I bent to unzip my pack and folded the bear and compass together into a bandanna.

"Hey, I just realized," he said. "You've got something borrowed and something blue there." Carey pointed to the compass and the fetish. "All you need is something old and something new."

"Always a bride. Never a bridesmaid," I said. We both laughed until we could pretend our tears were from the hilarity.

"My boots are old now," I said. "After eight thousand miles plus." Below my hiking shorts the boots were raggedy, dusty. "I guess they could walk me back to Tennessee if they had to."

"No chance. You're getting on this plane."

"What's new, then? The bear fetish is new," I said.

"No doubling up," he said. "But, I mean, just look around. Everything is new. Today is new. You're new."

Carey was smiling when we got to the gate, but a forced smile. His eyes glittered and spilled over when he glanced down to set the duffel bag by my feet.

"Don't," I said. I dropped my pack and threw my arms around him. "Don't." We rocked back and forth. The most unlikely, likeliest couple. We'd stayed together, just like our high school class had predicted.

I dried his eyes with the cuff of my chambray shirt. "This should be easy," he said. "I mean, we're totally sick of each other, right?" We laughed. He hugged me close and started crying harder. His voice was warm in my hair. "This is one of those awful times when what I need is the person who's leaving, but my heart is breaking because the person I need is leaving me!" He laughed.

"Stop, Carey." I pulled back and then we were apart as I stepped into line, toward the attendant. I picked up my bag. "Don't ever say I'm leaving you. I won't ever, ever leave you."

The first few moments of flying through the morning dark, I couldn't name any direction but down. Gravity focused in my limbs. The balloon lift in the pit of my stomach sank when the plane turned as if it might fall out of the sky. My chest and heart squeezed with the pull and shift, and I couldn't breathe deeply enough to slow my racing pulse. There was nothing between me and upside-down oblivion besides the moan of wing flaps and sheet metal and rivets, glass, plastic, bolts. To the rest of the world, I amounted to nothing more than blinking lights in the dawn. Higher and higher I would become that silver needle drawn through the sunrise. The jet shuddered through low clouds as we went through turbulence Carey had described to me.

My ears popped like they do climbing mountain roads. I held on so tight my hands hurt. This time I was climbing nothing but air. Outside air, inside air, everybody in the plane breathing in and out, air and flesh and loss and the memory of good-byes they'd just said, all trapped inside the bodies inside the surging body of the plane. The charcoal dark pinked out the window as we climbed and listed and leveled again. The red seatbelt light dinged off, and then I wasn't leaving anymore. I was coming home.

I raised up, stretching myself above the heads of the woman and her baby sharing the window seat beside me. The faces around me brightened in the increasing natural light—flight attendants, couples, fat-cat men in suits reading newspapers, businesswomen in pumps that had to hurt, a grandmother I'd watched at the airport hugging her family good-bye. So many dressed up people on the plane, but lots of regular people like me, in my shorts and boots. The mother beside me with baby spit-up souring on her shoulder was wearing jeans and a sweatshirt. All of us together just this one time, which could be just a blip of an hour in a lifetime. Passing through. Landing and taking off or landing and staying put. Wheels down. Feet on solid ground.

Adrenaline and peace are twin reactions. After the tense takeoff the mother and baby reclined against their seat. She couldn't have been more than twenty, her young skin the model of her little boy's cheeks. Their mouths pursed the same, the silhouette of their full lower lips against the brightening window, her hair the same as his silk chestnut. She brushed his forehead with her palm, ran it over his curls, absently down his bibbed torso. He barely opened his eyes when she wiped the silver thread of drool that ran from his mouth. He fell asleep in minutes. His mouth twitched and sucked. His fists opened and closed like a kitten kneading. Translucent eyelids and dark lashes flinched on his eyes roving back and forth in dreams.

The burden of fear that had fitted around me like a corset loosened into a different ache to watch the boy sleeping in his mother's arms. He must have been around a year old, maybe less, in his beautiful round babyness. I wondered if it grieved her to see him change every day, to think he wouldn't even remember the details of their first years together. In the bright dawn on the plane, I prepared to face down my usual crave and envy for a baby. But there was something changed. The only hurt was my private grief. He was someone else's real son, flesh and blood. He was not a possession to covet.

You're something new, I thought. He was. And I was, too. The plane pitched and rocked through another jolt of turbulence. The mother must have dozed off, too, because the motion made her gasp and flail like a fish coming onto dry land. The boy started crying before his eyes rolled open.

"Here I was praying he'd sleep the whole way, and then I go and wake him up." She tried a little apologetic smile but focused on the rise of his keening squall. People around us shifted and craned for a look. "I think he can feel how scared I am," she spoke louder above him.

"I thought it was just me. You're nervous, too?" I said.

She nodded. "My husband's in the Air Force, but I hate to fly. He tells me it's safe, but I still don't want to go through it."

From behind us the stewardess pushed a cart of drinks and coffee. The mother clapped her hand over her mouth. "That smell—" She seized up, clenching the baby with one hand and the back of the seat in front of her with the other. The baby cried harder. Her eyes were wide in her blanched face. "Let me out," she said.

Heads in the rows in front of us loomed around seat backs. The baby's face was purpling in his silence, and then what I could see coming. As Mama would say, he screamed like a banshee.

"I think she's sick," I shouted above his fury to the attendant as the mother shoved across me, her baby struggling. The attendant backed the cart out of the way, but the mother couldn't get around her to the bathroom.

I pushed myself up to stand behind her. "Here, give me the baby. Let me hold him." She hesitated. "I'm not going anywhere." I reached for him as she lunged past the cart in one clumsy squeeze. And there I stood, holding the gyrating, kicking baby, his spine wiggling against my breasts, heels kicking my pelvis, fists pulling his hair and clawing backward for mine as we faced a plane of angry faces.

"Ma ma ma ma ma!" He blubbered until he had to come up for air. I tried to turn him to face me. He doubled up silent and infuriated, bolstering another oncoming wail.

I couldn't keep from laughing at him, and I got him turned around to look at me as I sank into my seat. He shoved his feet into my crotch and stamped, and then he collapsed in a heap, little tears rolling down his face.

The woman across the aisle shot me a look. "These kids," she said. "She can't be more than eighteen, do you think? And another one on the way."

"Oh. You think so?" I realized how obvious it was. She had morning sickness.

"That's ridiculous to ask you to hold him. That's how they are, just dumping their burdens."

"You think so?" I repeated my stupid question, and then I felt defensive. That anyone would think of holding a baby as a burden. "She didn't ask. I offered," I said, rocking the boy on my lap as he quieted a little.

He twisted to try and turn around to see where his mother had gone, but I stuck my tongue out at him and started blinking and talking, just mumbling to him about the lights and his shirt and the buttons on my shirt. He looked at me with a sad, swollen face, but he stopped crying, and his eyes focused on mine as he listened.

"What in the world do you think Tobey thought of Kevin the first time they came face to face?" I asked him, as if it were a fun riddle. "What do you think he'll think of me?"

The mother was gone for quite a while, and when the baby started getting restless again, I moved over to her seat and dug into the diaper bag she had stuck underneath the seat in front of her. I kept talking to soothe him. He struggled nearly out of my arms as I felt with one hand around disposable diapers, a box of baby wipes, and things my fingers didn't recognize.

"Aha! There it is. There. Look here! Here's a juice bottle, ready to go." I held him tightly toward me, trying to resettle him on my lap, but he twisted forward again, screaming until he strangled. He reached toward the seat in front of us. His ears turned red, and his fat little neck. He smacked my hand and the bottle away, and began to lose his breath, pushing his feet against the seat back. The man sitting there shifted angrily. But there was nothing to do but laugh at him, and everybody glaring at me, thinking he was my responsibility. Which he was. He cried, furious, and it got even funnier.

"I don't blame you one bit," I said. I tossed the bottle onto my empty seat and got a better hold just as he nearly slipped out of my grasp. His strength surprised me. I tried and tried to get him to face me so I could calm him down. "I don't blame you. Where'd your mommy go, anyway? I wonder where'd she go?" He turned to look in the direction she'd gone, behind us, pulling his little claws at my fingers holding tight around his middle. He grunted and turned around to face me, intently watching then for her to reappear, successfully distracted.

"Yes, if I were you, I'd wonder where she went, too," I said softly. "She's been gone a long time. But look. She'll be back. You just watch out the window. Look." I pointed. "Where's she going to run away to? See, baby boy, where we're going? Way up in the middle of the air, and you don't even know how amazing that is."

He shuddered and stilled and sniffled as I talked low to him and cleaned his face with my sleeve. I rubbed the hair on his forehead the way his mother had, and in a moment, he sighed and leaned toward his juice bottle. I picked it up and he grabbed it out of my hand.

"How's he doing?" A flight attendant appeared, whispering down on my head. I turned to see that she'd helped the mother back to our seats. Her lips were pale. "She's had it pretty rough. Are you a friend of hers?" Yes, was the only answer.

"I'm so sorry." The girl nearly whimpered. Her face was sallow, and her eyes ringed black, as if someone had beaten her. She fairly well fell into the aisle seat I'd left empty. Her son barely raised one hand to reach for her, then when his bottle slipped and whistled with an intake of air, he latched both hands onto it, and slumped in my lap. The gray window filled up with dawn-splattered fields, bronze and radiant, fog below lifting like blue smoke from patches of woods. I touched around my gut for the terror I'd felt before, but there wasn't a single scared cell in my body. Holding the boy, keeping him from being afraid, had made me strong.

"See, look there." I pointed with the baby's closed fist in my own hand, touching it lightly to the cold glass. He pressed his face to mine, then lurched across me, a sidewise grin around the bottle hanging loose in his mouth. He wanted to show the view to his mother.

She shook her head against the pillow the attendant had given her, holding a paper bag on her lap. She closed her eyes and grimaced. "Are you sure you're okay with him? I don't know what I'd have done."

"Are you kidding? He's great. The flight attendants are jealous you gave him over to me. He's fine, aren't you, baby boy? He's a heartbreaker. What's his name?"

"Shane," she said. It made me laugh, to think of the old western, one of Daddy's favorites, but she was probably too young to know the reference.

"Shane," I whispered a cry. "Shane!" He looked at my foolish watery eyes with his big eyes while I talked, grinning when I opened my eyes wide or held my mouth at an angle. Eventually he turned around again, both of us facing forward. He slumped into me, his body sweating into mine as I watched woods eclipse fields, fields rising into banked ridges, water glinting like shot silver through the blueness of the world below.

"We are just about home, baby boy," I whispered. "I can tell." The jitters that rose up then weren't about flying or landing, but about being in the place I used to call home. How could I ever stand it, every place saturated with memory, good and bad and awful and wonderful? I kept thinking when I got to the trailer, Daddy would be there. Grieving for him would change, just like my grief for the baby would change the moment I told Kevin. Grief for missing Carey, for the journey that was over. Grief like invisible filaments breaking and healing and breaking and healing.

There were those days when Daddy was alive and we were happy. Weren't there? I would remember those at some point. I didn't have to dread him any longer. I could aim to remember the rare times. Days we could see through to the shining core when he levitated the whole house. The house on Genesis Road.

How could I learn to bear that he would never grow old enough to see himself through my new sight. There were mornings I was a girl and thought, *I can do anything. I could maybe fly. Because he's my flesh and blood, charming the sun right up over the hills.*

I patted the baby's back when he turned around and nuzzled his sleepy face into my neck, trusting that what I gave was pure. Comforted to hold and be held, I watched the morning world lit to green fire with the boy warm and heavy and real against my body, our breaths marking the window where other breaths had been. I handed him back to his mother only after she asked for him a second time.

And then all I had was lightness. Beneath my heartbeat a quickening to think about seeing Kevin. He was surely already waiting for me at the airport. He was pacing probably, with those lanky arms folded, or hands in his pockets, or tugging his beard.

I pushed ahead in my wish for what would happen, past the first hello, the first awkward hesitation of words and looks and the way we might avoid looking. The gestures that stop just shy of putting too much faith in the future or too much blame on the past. I felt lost then, trying to prepare myself, rehearsing how I should present myself to him, what to say, how I ought to act. But it made me queasy. *Should* was a lost cause.

What mattered was only the road home. It came to me then, the only plan I needed, the opposite of straight-edge jet travel and the direct, controlled fall from the sky. We'd take the crookedest, narrowest way home. The route came clear in my head. We wouldn't take the interstate, a brief hour between the airport and Mama's. Instead, I'd ask Kevin to please take the long road home, the scenic, beautiful route from the airport through Maryville and Townsend to Little River Road through the Smokies, the mountains my ancestors had settled and given up and lost and grieved. The mountains I was bound to love, even though I had been in exile, too.

We'd lean against tight curves inside the boundary of the national park, past creeks, overlooking rapids that ran downhill from the peaks. Late morning would color to a deeper blue above the long tunnel of woods, sunlight spinning through the limbs. The laurel and rhododendron would be in bloom, and that thought actually made my heart beat faster, to picture the faded magenta, blood pink. If we wanted, we could stop at the creek, watch the water striders and let the roar of waterfalls eclipse what we weren't quite ready to put words to anyway.

Then highway 321, winding from the throttle of Gatlinburg, past Pittman Center, unrolling down a gauntlet of high-shouldered knobs of Greenbrier, to the sunlit Cosby Valley, where my family first cradled itself long ago, rimmed by English Mountain, the blue solid wave of snub-nosed ridge just five miles from the final end of my journey, five miles from Mama's trailer door.

Or was that the end? I couldn't pass by English Mountain without showing Kevin the past. And my future. Genesis Road. The twelve acres that had fallen to me. A detour from the long way home would come to this: Our two voices under trees, the call of birds, the burr of early noon, the shadows harboring us, the secrets we needed to tell. And in the telling we'd close the distance between us.

I would tell him about the boy on the plane, the sweet baby boy, and that would get me to the threshold for the words I needed to say most. To tell Kevin about our baby would alter all the mourning I had gone through, and it would begin his mourning. I would have to be strong. And even if that common loss was all that lasted between us, then that loss would be a haven, a sacred space only the two of us would ever understand, a hard gift I had come the longest way round to share.

Two voices under trees that weren't even standing years ago when my family abandoned our ruined farm. I would move my arms, my whole body, my face and eyes, telling Kevin in every way possible, *you're the first and only person to come here with me.* He would be the first to see me standing on ground where I began, where my memory starts, on land as old as any on the planet, at the edge of the most ancient mountains.

I'd explain to him in words he would understand, confess to him that whether in love or regret, in grief or joy, through peace or suffering or bliss, those tangled woods—gone wild and loved beyond repair—those twelve acres are mine.

I would tell him, "This place belongs to me."

ACKNOWLEDGEMENTS

I can't be grateful without acknowledging regret and even sorrow.

I'm sorry my mother—in the latter stages of dementia—is no longer able to read. Being unable to share this novel with her is a loss among many losses. She taught me to read. In distant memory, if I'm on her lap, she's reading a book to me.

My mother also told me women's secrets. During a time no one talked about miscarriages, I held those stories of loss as sacred. Though I didn't suffer a pregnancy loss, I have borne witness with women and families who hold sorrow for what might have been. Thank you and continued healing to my cousin Sara and her husband Sean, parents of Gavin, whose absence I dwelled on as I wrote this novel.

Thank you to my students, who have enlarged my life beyond what I deserve. My creative writing students are my greatest accomplishment and among my best teachers, whom I also thank—especially Fred Chappell, who continues to teach me how to be a good literary citizen. Thank you to the writing community in Appalachia and beyond, especially Linda Parsons, who herded this novel toward its home. Thanks to the Madville family and Kim Davis, who is a wonder! And Mike Hilbig, whom I have never met but who is a gift in my life.

Perhaps my most earnest appreciation goes to my colleagues during my thirty-four years in the classroom. I watch them work miracles of intellect and grace daily. Thanks to Shawn O'Hare for suggesting several years ago that I take Fridays to write. Thanks to Jennifer Hall, Mary Baldridge, and Maria Clark for their kind confidence in my writing life. The Tennessee Arts Commission provided a grant during the early drafting of this novel, and our college allowed a sabbatical leave. A brief portion of the novel appeared in a much earlier incarnation in an anthology edited by Ernest Lee.

Many people in my family and my husband's family have been steadfast supporters, especially my dad, who is a better storyteller than I'll ever be. Thanks to many lifelong friends: To Davena for inspiring my stories. And to Bill Houston and Krista Reese, who time and again tugged me from the tedium of revising to feed my appetite and my spirit.

Dave, just as we vowed, you have always devoted yourself to our creative life together. You're the best travel partner I could ask for. You're my map and my compass, my Polaris, and my heart's GPS. Where to next?

About the Author

Susan O'Dell Underwood grew up in Bristol, Tennessee, the daughter and granddaughter of public school teachers who also farmed. She earned an MFA in Creative Writing from the University of North Carolina at Greensboro and holds a PhD in English from Florida State University. She directs the creative writing program at Carson-Newman University, where her husband, artist David Underwood, also teaches. Besides two chapbooks, she has one full-length collection of poetry, *The Book of Awe* (Iris Press), and her poems, nonfiction, and stories are published in many journals and anthologies, including *Oxford American*, *Ecotone*, *Bellevue Literary Review*, *Still: The Journal*, and *A Literary Field Guide to Southern Appalachia*. Her new poetry collection, *Splinter*, is forthcoming (Madville 2023).

9 781948 692847